LANN DÀN –
BLADES OF DESTINY

Revised Edition III

Lann Dàn – Blades of Destiny

DÀN CYCLE ONE

Revised Edition III

JAMES RAQUEPAU

BOOK COVER ART © 2024 BY NADIIA KOLPAK & JAMES RAQUEPAU

ILLUSTRATIONS © 2024 BY JAMES RAQUEPAU

LYRICS © 2024 CLAIRE ODLUM, MUSE CILLA, & JAMES RAQUEPAU

EDITED BY HOLLY ATKINSON (EVIL EYE EDITING)

ISBN

979-8-9896602-4-7   *IngramSpark Paperback*

979-8-9896602-1-6   *IngramSpark eBook*

979-8-3473136-4-8   *AudioBook*

Brought to you by:

Destiny Cycle Publishers

Gaels Rule!

www.destinycycle.com

Lann Dàn – Blades of Destiny

Dedication & Author's Note

For my family – Cynthia, Jereme, and Gwyn
Thanks for supporting this dream!

Dear Reader – Please note that I occasionally use some Gaelic. If
you would like to learn more about this language, I have included
a section in the back matter titled *Guide to Gaelic Language.*

There are also sections in the back matter that list *Central Characters
& Places & Terms* (with pronunciations), provide a summary of
Mythology & Legends, and offer an overview of *Gael Druids & Sigils.*

I point these sections out, as some readers suggested they would
have used this information had they been aware of it.

TABLE OF CONTENTS

MAP OF EASTERN ERIN

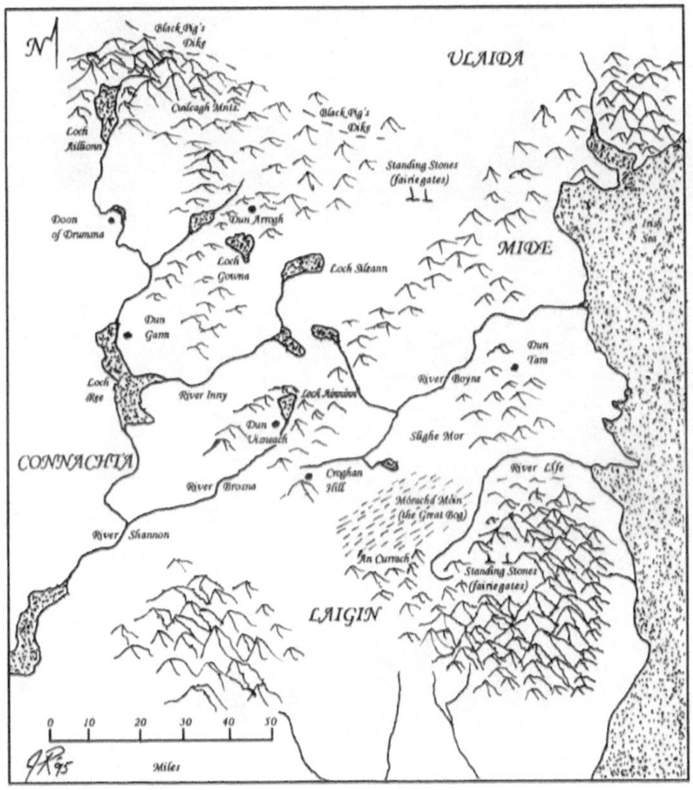

Blood Bonds

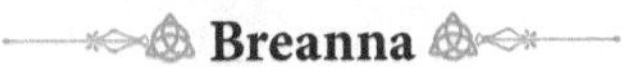

Breanna

Breanna Ban Morna rolled to her left to evade her opponent's sword stroke, the soft green grass of the glen briefly cradling her shoulders. Calm filled her despite her vulnerability. Breanna had successfully seized the *void*, feeling the exact moment she managed to touch that place between the material world and the Tuatha realm, what the *Aos Dána* called *urghabháil an neamhní*, and her opponent could not. In battle, she could see her rival's countermove in her mind before he even started his arm in motion.

Prepared, she was on one knee, the sinews of her arm and shoulder muscles snapping tight like drawn bowstrings, bracing her frame for his next strike. With her left arm raised over her head, the hand holding her weapon nearly where the iron joined the wood, Breanna caught her adversary's blade on her crossguard and drove in with her other blade.

As quickly as he had been within range, he managed to leap clear of her thrust. His fierce expression made it clear he wanted to crush her in their blades dance; the slight upturn at the corners of his mouth added a taunting touch. But his confidence would not be enough today. Being one with her blades, one with the ground at her feet, and even inside her opponent's mind—seizing the *void*, now *that* could bring victory.

Fortunately, this time, her mind managed to hold onto the *void*, where she was just an extension of her surroundings. Spinning as she rose, Breanna blocked his roundhouse slash with the weapon in her slightly weaker right hand. His strength and height proved an advantage when their blades locked, and he pushed her over backward. Breanna let the motion flow over her as she twisted aside before rolling to the ground like water poured from a bucket, her white-haired ponytail flowing after her motion. Her challenger followed his last move with an overhead swing.

Breanna anticipated his reaction again, and, to her opponent's surprise, she came up with her long blades crossed. She caught his heavy two-handed sword on the axis of her blades and swept the other's blade down and away. As her attacker lost balance, Breanna promptly brought around the black oak haft of the long blade in her left hand and struck him in the side of the head. Then, she sprang clear of any possible retaliation. Her blade would have sliced through his throat if he had been a genuine opponent.

The young man with whom she was sparring went down, sprawling ungracefully as his sword slipped from his hand, clearly knocked out. Confidently and with some bravado, Breanna whirled both long blades a few times before letting the smooth wooden hafts slap against the boiled leather vambraces strapped on her forearms. Then, finally, she released the *void*, as there would be no response from Fergal Mac Conall today.

"*Cum air do làimh*!" one of those watching cried.

Breanna stood down as commanded, letting the tension pour out as she calmed her pounding heart and heaving chest, hardly having even noticed the effort she had worked up during their duel. She wondered if maybe the *void* had shielded her from feeling her body's strains as she drove her blades into the grass.

Breanna glanced down, taking in her light green tunic and darker green leggings, neither of which were the right green to hide the grass stains. She was pleased to see that there was not even a scratch on her body and wiped the sweat from her brow. Then she rolled her shoulders, turning to her Chief with the smallest of smiles touching her lips, one born of ultimate satisfaction.

She assumed the Champion title with her victory over Eoin's cousin, Fergal, who had goaded her into making the challenge. As Eoin's Champion, it was now her role to fight for him in any duel—a Chief was not allowed to take on a single combat challenge directly, especially when he was a Prince of the Blood.

Breanna heard their band of young men and women whisper in awe, and they softly thumped their spears against their shields in approval. Few had bested Fergal Mac Conall, certainly never with long blades against a heavy two-handed sword. He was their best warrior, having earned his gold Gaelic Knot armring before most had even gained a silver, and Breanna had only taken a moment to put him on the ground.

One of their warriors said, "I would have gladly cut off my braids to move with such speed and grace, with such intuition."

Another lad claimed, "That duel had to rival any show of blade work that Connachta's Maeve could put on!"

Another argued, "But Maeve didn't defeat Ulaida's greatest warrior and guardian of the great Dun Emain Macha."

Her cousin, Toal, nodded in agreement. "You're right. A better choice would be Macha Mong Ruad, the first female warlord of Ulaida and *Ard-Banríona* of Erin."

Breanna watched them, somehow seeing that, at that moment, they believed their new Champion was someone from a Bard's tale, with the sun bursting through the morning mist. As she pulled her beaded green Connemara marble-laced thong free, she caught the glare of sunlight in the shimmering white hair falling about her shoulders.

Breanna sighed explosively, breaking the spell her fellow warriors had been weaving over her victory. Her impressions of the match were different, her aching muscles and sweat-covered body telling her that their *comórtas* had taken much longer. Certainly not something for the Bards to spin a tale over. Her ability to seize the *void* was not that solid. She still had much to learn. Today, though, she was driven by Fergal's infuriating challenge, which had worked in her favor. Still, she held her head high, ensuring her shoulders were straight.

Despite how she may have looked, she could see that those around her did not think of her as haughty. Breanna knew they all had been in the shadow of her Chief's cousin when it came to battle. As her blue-eyed gaze swept over their band of young warriors, Breanna's finely arched, pale eyebrows and sharply lined face expressed defiance; she hoped their band would take it as a challenge to practice harder under Eoin and his cousin's keen eyes. She wrapped her grandmother's beaded hair tie—she did not like her hair braided as many of her fellow warriors did—around her neck and released the tension in her body.

Knowing none of them had expected her to beat Eoin's cousin, Breanna pointed to the warrior she had knocked out lying on the ground. "Help him. Fergal and I might not agree often, but he at least deserves to have his head examined. Go fetch one of the *Aos Dána* apprentices."

Toal was the first to move to Fergal's side. The young red-headed lad had always admired the older warrior, following him like a hound's whelp, so the frown that fell over his boyish face surprised no one as they watched him survey the damage. Another lad took off at a run for their dun as commanded.

As Breanna turned away, their appointed Chief Eoin said, "Well, Bre, you've proven you're the best and bravest of us, and it was clear you seized the *void* where Fergal could not. You're now my Champion, our Red Branch Champion."

Lifting his chin proudly, he added, "I think it's time you help Fergal and me train these children who would be warriors of our dun."

Breanna did not respond as she wiped the sweat from her brow again, still flushed from her efforts. Instead, she watched two other boys several years younger than herself step forward to help Toal get the barely conscious Fergal into a sitting position. Fergal groaned when they lifted his shoulders off the ground. Then he hissed at Toal as the lad pushed aside the muddy red hair that covered the large bump on his temple to inspect it. He slumped back to the ground, holding his head.

Breanna sighed, relieved she had accomplished her goal without seriously injuring Eoin's cousin, fool that he was to challenge her. They couldn't afford to lose him. That much was clear, though she doubted Fergal thought likewise of her. She turned slowly to her Chief as she plucked her long blades from the ground, her eyes narrowed. "Eoin, not this again. My skills with the *void* are—unstable."

"Are you questioning me? Your unstable control is mastery compared to mine," he countered and stepped toward her, cocking his head defiantly. His newly braided bright red beard and plaited hair made him a fierce-looking warrior, and his muscular frame was as imposing as ever, though he was only two years older than her. While Breanna was tall for a young woman, he was a bit more than a head taller than her. When she did not answer, Eoin added, "If so, I will challenge you myself. You'll have to accept the role of Red Branch Chief if you best me in combat. That will leave you with no other choice."

Breanna's eyes flew wide. Eoin appeared to cringe when the nostrils of her thin nose flared, and she exclaimed hotly, "No! As I have said before, it's not my place to teach, and I don't take kindly to your attempts to force me. Creating another Red Branch was your idea! Forming a *fian* might have been more appropriate for our dun, with you as our *Ceann-buidhne*. That would have allowed you to join the High King's army and request protection."

Eoin sputtered and took a step forward. "*Fians* are for Fir Bolg clans—not true Gaelic warriors! No warrior with noble Ulaidan blood would swear as a *Ceann-buidhne* to the *Ard-Rí*, that useless arse of a Connachta-spawned king!"

Unfazed, Breanna continued, "Since you did not, Eoin Mac Cairbre, this is yours and your cousin's responsibility. But know that I'll do what I must when I have to. I'll be your Champion, but no more. I have another charge that I have always focused on, and you know it."

Her Chief recovered his wits, saying tightly, "Come, girl, you've seen seventeen summers! Any warrior here would give a finger for the honor of leading our Red Branch."

Breanna snorted derisively. "Well, that shows you I'm not just any warrior, nor just any *woman*, you oaf!"

Then she buried her long blades in the earth—an intended *miss* just inches from his toes. She hesitated, letting her jaw jut out slightly, then turned on her heels and stomped away.

Eoin watched her as her streaming, stark-white hair contrasted sharply with the surrounding green of the forest she was marching toward. Silence settled over the glen, except for the song of a few yellowhammers. He peered around at the others in his band, yet none were willing to step into the hornet's nest he had bashed open.

"The Red Branch needs you to be strong," he called after Breanna. When she kept walking and did not reply, he turned to face those watching the exchange and barked, "Dawdlin' about isn't going to stop Hakon's Dreadriders. Go find something to do!"

"Like what?" one of the younger lads rejoined. "Challenge one of them to a duel like I'm Breanna? If she can kick Fergal's arse like that, then a Dreadrider would kill me in a heartbeat."

Despite having earned the gold Gaelic Knot tier of their warrior class, which should have commanded their loyalty, Eoin knew his grip on this band of young fighters was tenuous, for he was only a few years older than they were. Even though many considered him Dun Arrogh's Chief, their *Ceann-cinnidh*, he was, at times, yet another boy with whom they had shared their childhoods. He had to be strong for them to accept his leadership—something they had seen little of from the elders of their fort since the Dreadlord had killed their former *Ceann-cinnidh* and begun his rule.

Eoin took a threatening step toward the boy, and then he remembered that one of the *Aos Dána* had once said words could be as powerful as blades. Perhaps using a Druidic wisdom approach was the best approach here. Instead of striking the lad as he had intended, he said, "The old Red Branch warriors of the Clan Ulaid were never foolish. They attacked when the odds were in their favor and showed bravery when the odds were against them. We will challenge the Dreadriders in our own time. Until then, we have weapons to make and food to harvest and gather.

"At the very least, you can gather rushes and peat for the dun or fetch water. Set yourselves about helping with those tasks. Remember, the Dreadlord benefits when we bicker and appear divided, allowing that *dubhchaile* to continue his ungodly rule. When we follow that path, it weakens our gods and strengthens his gods."

With that, Eoin pulled Breanna's long blades from the earth, turning after his new Champion with a dramatic swirl of his multicolored cloak. Yet he knew his followers would say no more, as they knew all too well the truth of his words. The Dreadlord had kept them divided, kept them weak. Many of their fathers and older brothers had either died at the Dreadriders' hands or were now hostages—sometimes called *daor aicme*, even though they might once have been freeborn—to the white-haired invader.

Hakon Skadi had come to their land like a thief in the night, stealing what had been theirs before they knew it. His ways had been different, catching them off guard. What cost them most in battle was that they had used chariots and footmen, while Hakon's Dreadriders had attacked riding upon giant steeds. While Dun Arrogh's warriors occasionally rode their hill-bred horses, especially when pulling chariots, they were no match for warhorses. Even outnumbered, the Dreadlord's warriors had carried the day with that one advantage.

Because their small dun lay between the major Ulaida, Laigin, and Connachta clans, no one came to their aid to keep them free and *saor aicme*. The provincial kings—and even the *Ard-Rì* in Mide—viewed the Dreadlord of Garm as a small buffer between rival clans. In the eighteen years since usurping control of their land, the Dreadlord was always careful not to engage those powerful clans in outright battle, especially those most in the

High King's favor in Mide. He never posed a significant threat to other clans, instead focusing on small cattle raids. Those living within the narrow strip of the territory claimed by Hakon Skadi were the ones to suffer.

And so the Clan Mórdha's Red Branch warriors had begun to slip away to do as their Chief bade them: do what they could to stop Hakon Skadi, the Dreadlord of Garm. Eoin could only wish that the elders of Dun Arrogh would stand with him and proclaim him as their new *Ceann-cinnidh*. Yet that was a wish for the future.

He found his new Champion sitting on a fallen log inside the tree line of the woods. She had finished unlacing the vambraces from her arms and set them aside. She crossed her arms tightly over her chest to emphasize she was still mad at him. He stuck her blades in the ground at her leather-thonged feet, missing her toes as she had just done with his. Sitting beside her, he said softly, "You forgot these."

Breanna only nodded and continued staring at the small, now sun-filled meadow dotted with buttercups, with Fergal still lying in the middle of it, holding his head. They had taken to calling it their Grove of Instruction, just like Ulaida's old warriors of the original Red Branch used to do at Emain Macha many hundreds of years before. It was where their heroes taught their children the art of war. Save for Eoin, Fergal was considered the best warrior in their offshoot Red Branch band. Because Eoin was their Chief and was forbidden to fight in single combat, Fergal Mac Conall had been their Champion for the last two years.

Now, Breanna Ban Morna was their Red Branch Champion. And unlike others who sought to use swords like those wielded by the Dreadlord, she had chosen long blades. They were traditional in her clan, though many had given over to short swords, and some even to long ones, over the past few decades. As ancient weapons, long blades typically had tapered bronze or iron blades, the length of a man's forearm, and ash or oak hafts roughly two inches in diameter and as long as a short man's leg. Short crossguards were set where the metal blades and handle joined to protect the wielder's hands.

Eoin knew her clan well, and that Breanna had the fortune of possessing iron-wrought long blades, a set that had once belonged to her father. Before that, her grandmother, Cahira, had used them in battle; they had passed to her father, Nevan, as his mate Morna chose not to take the warrior's path as Cahira had. Given that many generations of Clan Dálaigh warriors had grasped the old blades, the black oak hafts had worn smooth. He knew she treasured her blades, for her father and grandmother had wielded them, both blooded Gaelic warriors who had earned their gold Celtic Knot armrings, as she had recently done.

Unable to take the silence, Eoin heaved a breath forcefully as he absently tugged on one of his plaits. "Bre, I'm sorry. I shouldn't have pushed so hard back there, especially in front of the others. It's just that you fought so brilliantly. You were like a warrior touched by the gods. And Fergal and I could use an extra hand."

"Few want to train with the long blades," Breanna countered dryly, though she looked pleased by the compliment.

Eoin countered, "While true, it seems that lately you fight with a confidence few can match, and your ability to anticipate an opponent's moves in battle when you seize the *void* is growing sharper daily."

At those words, Breanna leaned forward to retighten the leather straps, which she wound in a crisscross pattern from her feet to her knees. "You know I won't bother with other weapons. Especially swords like the one wielded by the Dreadlord."

"His Dreadriders make effective use of such blades, just like the Red Branch once did."

Breanna shrugged. "Long blades are lithe and quick and suit my fighting style. A longsword would be too heavy for me. With four edges, I can dance and dazzle in motion, allowing me to strike and kill. Fortunately, I only knocked out Fergal. Yet, he did not pull any strikes. If the *void* failed me, as it has before, it would be me on the ground and not him, and I'd likely be bleeding out."

Eoin winced at the thought but had nothing to add to that. Instead, he let the Grove's peacefulness settle over them. Continuing to push at Breanna now would only make things worse.

Next to Eoin, Breanna chuckled. "He's going to have a sore head. Given that either of us could have drawn blood, we should have had a Healer on hand for this challenge."

"Aye, foolish of us," Eoin agreed.

Breanna

Breanna noted only Fergal and Toal remained in the empty clearing, their fellow members of the Red Branch having slipped away into the woods.

She knew spears, arrows, and bows were always in demand. Breanna's uncle, the smith in their small dun, often let her young warrior friends help make spears and arrowheads from the bits of molten bronze, copper, or iron left over from his sword-making efforts for the invaders who ruled them. But, unfortunately, it seemed as if they all tarried in some way or another for the brooding Dreadlord of Garm. Breanna assured herself that it was something she would change, though she was unsure how to rid their land of the Dreadlord's stench.

Eoin distracted her, saying, "Only a few days until Samhain. There won't be many more warm days like this until spring—nothing to look forward to except rain, sleet, and wind. Listening to Cahir prattle about what it means for a Gael to wear the warrior's armring is not how I want to spend the winter. Yet, I suppose our younger ones need such guidance. Perhaps we can help them improve their *ability to seize voids*. That's something even Fergal and I need help with."

"Aye, seizing the *void* is hard," was all Breanna offered.

"Yet you could help with that, as you're our best at it."

"Och, maybe, yet it doesn't feel so. Today, it answered me, but I'm inconsistent. I'm missing something and don't know what it is."

"Maybe we can make a trip to Dun Uisneach to see if their Druids could be of help?"

That suggestion finally got Breanna's attention as she turned her eye to his and let a quirk of a grin creep to her lips. Then, she reasoned aloud, "Traveling to Dun Uisneach at this time of the year would not be easy, and we would have to head east before going south to skirt the Dreadlord's territory. Not to mention that we have much to do to prepare for winter."

Eoin shrugged. "Aye, we do. Maybe next spring. It's too close to Samhain anyway, and few want to cross the land now."

Samhain, time of the spirits, Breanna thought. With that, she wondered what her father had been like, wondered where his essence—his *anam*—wandered. Breanna had never known him, something the Dreadlord had made sure of before she was born. Her uncle was the only clan member who had tried to provide a semblance of a father figure for her, and at that, Kyras always had his own family and had worked hard to tend to it as the Dun's smith, leaving little time for her.

Ulicia, their Druid Healer, appeared on the far side of the meadow, wearing a green robe and red tunic. Around her pranced her apprentice, a young lady dressed in a simple brown shift, a few years younger than Breanna. The older woman hobbled on her walking stick, occasionally shooing the youngster away. She took a long while to cross even half of the small glen with such a short gait. When she reached the center, the Ollamh paused to examine Fergal and apparently demanded to know what had happened.

Still helping their former Champion, Toal motioned and pointed in Breanna's direction. The well-aged woman's chortle carried across the space between them, likely an insult of some kind. Then she reached into a pouch at her belt and gave him a herb before moving on, leaving her young assistant to help the warrior wash it down. Even from a distance, Breanna could see the fire rising in Fergal's face, but she knew he would not say anything; one did not insult an Ollamh.

"Wonder what brings Ulicia out here?" Eoin commented. "The Druids usually only send an apprentice when no blood has been drawn."

"Again, foolish of us to assume so, as even a head injury could be serious," Breanna suggested, leaping to her feet. She grabbed her long blades and slipped them into the harness on her back, then slid her leather vambraces over them before marching across the meadow toward their Healer. "Anyway, let's find out."

She was starting to wonder if it was a good thing to be Eoin's Champion. If not for Fergal's arrogance, he would not have goaded her into challenging him as Champion and becoming his replacement. Yet Eoin's cousin constantly tested her, somehow suspicious of something, but of what she did not know.

Ulicia

Ulicia greeted Breanna and Eoin in the warmth of the sun-filled meadow where they usually trained. The latter asked quickly, "What brings you so far from Dun Arrogh?"

"Someone had to see to Fergal," she answered, then eyed Breanna. "I assume you had that duel everyone was talking about? Eoin should have had at least my apprentice here to attend to any wounds."

"Aye and aye," Eoin confirmed. "Fergal goaded Bre into challenging him. She was masterfully able to use her *void*-seizing abilities, so much so that Fergal didn't stand a chance. She is even better than I am at seizing the *void*, leveraging it repeatedly. I certainly can't slip in and out of it at will as I saw her do during Fergal's challenge. It should have been a close match, but it was not. She fought as if the gods touched her."

Ulicia took in his words, turning back to stare at Breanna. While not a Seeress, she could command the *Aos Dána* vision state, and the *sight* took her. After a glimpse of Breanna's destiny, she shook her head and said, "Then that makes you Eoin's Champion. Poor timing, this."

"That may be," Breanna countered. "Fergal still needs to learn to seize the *void* to become the warrior we need him to be. Yet, that is another matter. The *Aos Dána* would not send a full Ollamh to check on a slightly cracked head when, you said, your apprentice could have handled it."

With a frown on her weathered face, the Ollamh replied, "Bad tidings about your mother, Bre. Morna's taken a turn for the worse. I doubt she'll last the night."

"No—" Breanna whispered, her knees sagging. Then Ulicia saw the young warrior's spine stiffen as Breanna added more firmly, "I should be at her side."

Ulicia nodded to her, narrowing her eyes as she assessed the young warrior's mettle further. Then Breanna turned away and raced toward their dun at a run, her long legs flying across the terrain. Ulicia turned to catch Eoin's eyes, and the concern revealed in that glance made her wonder how Breanna would handle the otherworld pulling her mother back into the *Cycle of Time.*

She knew Eoin Mac Cairbre was as close as anyone to the odd girl. That Breanna had always been different was not something anyone ever dared mention. Intense, distant, as if she were a stranger in their dun that all knew of but trod carefully around.

Few said anything about such traits as her white hair and bright blue eyes with their striking red flecks, for they knew if Morna caught wind of such talk, even the stoutest of men would pale under the tongue-lashing she would mete out.

When, long ago, some of the older warriors had questioned her daughter's use of the Clan Dálaigh's name, Morna Ban Cahira had nearly ripped off their heads. She'd marched up to them with her mate's long blades crossed before her, claiming insult to her dead companion's memory and ready to challenge them. Breanna was of their blood, and that was that.

To say Morna was a formidable woman was an understatement, and such words were seldom uttered again and never to her face.

Eoin fell in at Ulicia's side as they walked from the glen. When he offered an arm, she snorted at him and hobbled along with her walking stick. Breanna surged ahead, making for home. Ulicia noted Eoin had watched his new Champion's firmly muscled yet sleek figure as she quickly faded from their sight. Then, silence settled between them. Ulicia noticed he let her uneven gait set the pace, and she picked their path through the sharply rolling hills surrounding Dun Arrogh.

Their fort lay nestled between two small lochs. Save for the highest elevations, the land was covered by a forest of black oaks, leaving a dusky light beneath the tree canopy. It provided enough cover for the moss-covered rocks, ferns, and ivy to grow in the shadows, even though the sun was still shining.

After the forest had enveloped them and the murky light made it seem that the sun was setting, Eoin asked, "Is there nothing you can do?"

"Morna's lost the will to live," Ulicia replied. "Even the greatest Ollamh has no magic to counter such power when that happens. Erin's *Cycle of Time* seeks to respin her soul. I'm more concerned about Breanna. She's likely to take her mother's passing hard."

"At least she still has her sisters," Eoin offered.

"You know as well as I that they have never taken to Breanna," the Druid said with a scowl. "Even her uncle keeps his distance, always letting her go her own way. Maybe it's because Bre's mother loved her so much, and Kyras hated to do anything that would have caused strife for Morna after the Dreadlord killed his older brother."

Eoin thought for a moment and then nodded. "Given such an inflexible man raised her, Bre has always been able to do as she pleased, hasn't she? While Toal bows to his father, Kyras only allows the boy to be in my Red Branch because it gives him a reason to learn better smithing. If that man knew how much Toal wanted to be a warrior, he'd not be pleased."

"So you see, Bre would surely not be a warrior if it had been up to her uncle. Nor would his mate, Lissa."

"Aye," Eoin concurred. "Even with her mother's blood-right to the warrior class, it's doubtful Kyras would have allowed one of his daughters to pursue such an art. And Morna's oldest daughters, like their mother, did not choose the warrior's path. Only Breanna followed Nevan's footsteps; never once did Morna try to discourage her. Don't get me wrong—I'm glad she didn't."

Ulicia agreed. "Her grandmother had a similar drive."

Eoin shrugged. "I didn't know Cahira very well, as I was young when her grandmother passed. Yet, Bre's the best warrior I've ever seen wield the long blades, and lately, she always seems to be able to anticipate her opponent's next move—not just one of them, but all of them. As I said, she has a command of the *void* in duels that is nearly masterful. Our Red Branch would be nothing more than a band of boys without her. Besides myself, the only warrior we have who could stand against one of Hakon's Dreadriders is Fergal."

"Only you three can defend us; that will not be enough."

"I only hope Morna doesn't try to change Bre's mind about being part of our Red Branch. But, unfortunately, deathbed requests can hold much sway over those left behind. And we need Bre. That much is certain."

"You worry about what cannot be," Ulicia confidently informed him as they caught another glimpse of Breanna's lithe form flying up a steeper, rocky slope that was mainly devoid of trees, her white hair streaming in her wake. The Healer was glad they would not be taking that path. "It is Bre's destiny to be a warrior. Even one without the *sight* can see that."

Eoin conceded, "You're right, and Breanna's iron-willed nature leaves little room for any doubt about that."

They watched the forest swallow her a moment later as she ascended directly toward their fort. They had been circling that same hill to take a more indirect route to their home, as the Ollamh was too old for such climbing.

It was well past midday when Eoin and Ulicia arrived at Dun Arrogh, following the well-worn trail around the rise. She knew they had taken the long way back and were at least a half-span behind Breanna.

As they passed between the gates, Ulicia took in the small hut that Breanna shared with her mother. "I am concerned about how she'll get on without Morna to shelter her."

"As her sisters are married, she has rights to her mother's hut and belongings," Eoin countered stiffly. "We should give Breanna the afternoon with Morna and her sisters."

"Aye, that we should."

Morna

Morna and Breanna's hut might have been little, but it was drafty. Breanna huddled around her mother's bed with her two older sisters, who had traveled to be at her side once news reached them that their mother was ill. As she eyed each of them, Morna sighed, her body tired and old, a used-up shell. Unlike Breanna, Orla and Ronat possessed their mother's soft, oval face, though not her wavy red hair. Their raven locks were straight, and their figures were short and stocky like their father's. Were the pair boys, they would have followed their uncle's smithing trade or taken their father's or grandmother's warrior path.

Yet girls they were, and with Nevan's death, both had handfasted young: Ronat to a merchant trader, Orla to a cattle raiser. Both always sought to be elsewhere. The former lived a day's ride northwest on the loose border between Connachta and Ulaida, and the latter's mate managed a steading located in Mide, about a two-span horse ride to the east of Dun Arrogh, with a fair number of cattle. At least their mates kept them out of the Dreadlord's reach. Yet, they were not for sure out of harm's way, as they lived in a barely civilized land.

In contrast, much to Morna's concern, her youngest had remained single, showing little interest in men. All had thought Breanna would handfast with Eoin Mac Cairbre, but she kept him at a distance. She insisted he was a friend and no more, claiming she had to focus on ending the reign of terror the Dreadlord had brought upon them.

Yet, Morna had commanded a Druid to cast an ugly destiny upon her daughter. For that, the *Cycle of Time* would shape her fate when her *anam* was released. She hoped to find Nevan again but knew she did not deserve him. Not with the fate she had cast upon her unborn daughter, one that stained Morna's very soul.

When Ulicia and Eoin stopped by to see Morna much later in the afternoon, the Healer brushed everyone aside to check on her patient. Morna said sourly, "By the Gods, Ulicia, I'm dying. Let me go in peace."

Ulicia glowered at Morna but said nothing. Instead, she pulled her herb pouch from her belt and began rummaging inside it. Finally, she held a tiny pinch of some unnamed herb from a small sack within the larger one. She commanded, "Orla, hand me that cup of water."

Morna groaned. "Not another of your foul-tasting concoctions."

Depositing the herb in the water, Ulicia replied, "Something to help you with the pain and to sleep."

Morna groaned again but drank the potion and grimaced. "There, are you happy?"

"*Taingeil*," Ulicia growled. Then she knelt by her patient, placing one hand on her forehead and the other on the packed earth floor to call on her Druidic Earth Elemental power, feeding it to Morna. "There, you can thank me later."

Morna sighed at the infusion of energy and then insisted, "I have something to discuss with my youngest daughter. Please, give us some room. Then I'll get the sleep you think I need. Orla, Ronat, you too."

"But Mother—"

"Ronat," Morna said tightly, "would you bring dishonor to your mother on her deathbed?"

Ronat shook her head and turned away. She and Orla could barely stifle their sobs as they slipped through the door with the Ollamh. Morna grinned at the thought of her elder daughters. The two of them had always been so like one another. It was a comfort that they had good mates.

The smile faded as she focused on Breanna and Eoin. If only the same were true for them, but her youngest daughter's destiny lay on a different path.

Eoin put a hand on his Champion's shoulder, the two warriors' eyes meeting and holding for a brief moment before he said, "I'll see you later."

Morna saw more in that glance than Breanna had. Although her daughter was now supposed to be the one to protect him, to be his Champion, Morna knew Eoin would die to keep Breanna from harm. It was good that she had such an ally, as what was to come would require all the help she could get.

Alone with Breanna at last, Morna said weakly, "My daughter, my love, you know all I have left will be yours when I pass on. You must also know something else before I die, something you may not want to accept. When I was young, a Druid once told me that the hard truth is better than an easy lie. I've lived the latter ever since Nevan was taken from us by the Dreadlord."

"What is it, Mother?" Breanna asked. "It is something about my father?"

"Yes," Morna said as she squeezed her eyes shut. A tear ran down her cheek and into her graying red hair. "Have you ever wondered what your father—what Nevan, looked like?"

Then, opening her eyes, she saw Breanna had taken a step forward and sank to her knees beside her. "Father? No, I don't suppose I did. I assumed he had fair—"

"He had long black hair, much like Orla and Ronat's—the mark of Fir Bolg lineage—much like his brother Kyras and his son Toal," Morna confirmed, closing her eyes, hoping to see a memory of his face. Then, a moment later, she glanced up and added, "Few in the land of Erin have your white hair and blue eyes. Red hair and blue eyes, yes, but not white."

"What are you trying to say?"

Morna hesitated. "That Nevan was not your father."

"Was not my father?" Breanna said, echoing her words in confusion. Perplexed, she took her mother's hands and asked, "If he wasn't my father, who is?"

"He lives south of here, in Garm," her mother answered.

"In Garm?

Closing her eyes again, Morna said tightly, "Yes, your father is Hakon Skadi."

"What? He is who?" Breanna demanded, and Morna forced herself to gaze up at her wide-eyed daughter.

"When the Dreadlord first came to our land, he raided our dun," Morna began, this time more slowly. "After killing your father, he raped me. Only Ulicia knew what had happened when you were born, but I did not tell her who had done the deed. Yet I think she knew. Then, when Hakon returned that following spring for his tribute, I discovered it had been the Dreadlord himself who was your father. I've told no one else about it to this day."

"Some in our clan must suspect that I'm a half-breed!"

"I castigated anyone who dared to suggest you weren't truly of our clan, as we Gaels trace our lineage through our mothers."

"Curse him!" Breanna seethed.

"Speaking of that, you also should know I had our Fáidh place a *geas* upon him and you, even before you were born. Our Druid Seeress, Beatha, cast it so that the *geas* would lie coiled like a snake until I died, and then the seed sown by his lust and murder would rise against him and be the source of his destruction.

You are that seed. How you'll accomplish this feat, I cannot say, but your *geas* compels you to destroy him."

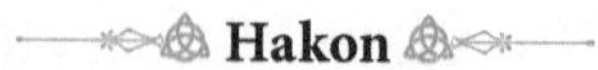 **Hakon**

Earlier that same day, Hakon Skadi strode through the yard of Dun Garm, contemplating the rumors about neighboring Ulaida and Mide readying themselves for a new round of raids on each other when the seasons cycled into spring. His position on the northeastern side of Loch Ree had always been a sore point with the local clans on this side of the River Shannon. Since he'd created a small buffer with Connachta, they had tolerated him, especially given that the High King was a Uí Néill clansman descended from that northwestern kingdom. With Niall's first mate being of traditional Ulaidan lineage in the northeast, Hakon had to tread carefully there, so he mainly kept his raids to the southwest.

Given Dun Garm's growing control in his region, though, Hakon's need to spread out was becoming evident to more than those who had joined him in exile. He just had to keep the various clans warring amongst themselves for a while longer. Especially when the *Ard-Rì* was off warring with anyone and everyone across the sea—he'd be too strong to displace from his foothold. If he made peace with his brothers back home, they could send him enough warriors to expand his territory in this land.

Thinking about how he could foment more vicious raids among the Gael clans, he stepped into the small round hut. He demanded of his Seeress, his völva, "I need my prophet to tell what the spring will bring."

"Then I must cast my Blood Runes."

Hakon stepped up behind her, peering over her shoulder, to watch her perform her magic in the dim light of her small, windowless hut. Runa turned her intact eye, the chill expression on her wrinkled face making it clear she wanted more room to work, but Hakon ignored her. He needed to know what threats might arise to undermine his plans for domination.

After an awkward moment, Runa growled at Hakon, who ignored her dark gaze. Finally, she shrugged and turned back to her altar. He could barely see her, save for her gray hair, as she had dressed in a simple wrap of deep blue wool over the same colored linen shift. The lone candle she used for light flickered out as she plucked a crow from a nearby cage, and Runa waved a hand to relight it.

With the bird trying in vain to bite her, Runa muttered a curse and added some ancient Norvegr spell words Hakon understood to be an invocation of a god, and another candle burst to life. Then, using her other hand, she snatched up the small jewel-handled knife that hung with other Norvegr glass and amber bead swags from a round silver brooch pinned above her breasts. In a smooth, swift motion, she sliced off one of the bird's legs and let the blood from its severed claw drip onto her altar of white marble.

The crow loosed a strident squawk, valiantly trying to bite at the hand that held it, but the old hag gripped it firmly so its beak could not inflict any damage. Then Runa quickly jammed barley flour into its tiny stump to stem the blood flow, then tossed it back into its cage. It cawed in protest as she cackled, "My crow still has one more leg to give me."

The völva turned back to her altar and cried, *"Urd! Verthandi! Skuld!"* Then she cast her Blood Runes onto the large flat stone.

The black rectangles of stone clattered, some turning up arcane white marks, some covered in blood, some neither. Impressed as always, Hakon watched Runa analyze the symbols.

As she paused over each rune stone, the völva hemmed and hawed over every detail.

"*Ihwar* bare of blood: change comes.

"*Tyr* in blood: a band who plots against your rule.

"*Uruz* in blood: ill fortune in the future.

"*Perdhro* bare of blood: an action with negative results.

"*Naudhiz* in blood: something from your past returns.

"*Gyfu* in blood: the power of gods in play."

Then she shook her head, adding, "Bad stones in such a combination, but what do they mean? What are my little black beauties trying to say?"

Runa stopped murmuring, letting silence fall over the room as the *sight* took her to that space between the Earthly realm and that of her distant Asgardian Gods.

And with that, Hakon Skadi, warlord and son of a Norvegr Jarl, was swept up by her magic, and the dark room faded away.

Pulled back in time to when he had initially led his fellow warriors up the River Shannon in his first few months here, Hakon ripped his sword across his newest attacker's gut. A moment later, the startled Gaelic warrior was collapsing, sword slipping from his fingers, body crumpling to the ground.

With no other opponent ready to challenge him, the Norvegr warlord grinned as his warriors dispatched the remaining Gaelic fighters facing them. He took a particular delight in watching those warriors who had joined him in his exile, knowing they would be stalwarts in his goal to dominate a section of his newly adopted homeland. Covered in blood, his warriors taunted the locals as they cut down the Gaels they faced.

Hakon and his warriors had ripped through the local Gael defenses at their latest stop while traveling upriver, using their greater steeds to their advantage. He had insisted his warriors leave enough of their rivals alive to tell the story of each assault on the Gaelic Clans of Erin. Enough to let the belief spread that a new warlord had come to this green land, sending the cream of their warrior class to the otherworld, and would not be easily displaced. Let them throw their lives away.

He had searched for a spot to establish a fort for months. Still, the lowlands on the ribbon of water he learned was named the River Shannon had not yet revealed a suitable place to establish his presence as a new overlord. Finally, however, he had heard that there was a place upriver, at the intersection of three powerful kingdoms, where he might be able to settle.

Lost in his thoughts, Hakon nearly failed to notice a Gaelic warrior who had broken through the lines and charged him with his sword ready. Hakon spun left, letting his blade lash out as the Gael overreached his mark. With exquisite timing, he sliced through the back of the wild warrior's neck as he passed. Blood sprayed as the Gael tumbled dead to the ground, his head nearly severed.

Hakon snapped back to the present as he swayed, dizzy from the strange shift in time. What did it mean? How had he been back in time, reexperiencing his campaign along the River Shannon? It had never happened before. To cover his lapse, Hakon demanded, "What do you see, old woman? Will Ulaida and Mide clash in the spring?"

"Patience. The Goddess Gullveig demands patience above all else," she crooned as she stirred the rectangular Runes through the blood with one long fingernail, peering closely at the symbols on the small stones. Silence commanded the room, and it seemed like time had stopped, if only for a heartbeat. Then the völva jerked into motion. "Ah, yes, I see. Even from distant Asgard, you guide your *seið-kona's* eye well, Gullveig. Very well, indeed."

"What have you seen? Has your goddess spoken to you?"

Using ancient Novergr words, where Hakon again only understood enough to know his völva had thanked the one she worshipped, she turned her withered face to him. Her useless right eye rolled up as if briefly in a trance before she said, "Gullveig showed me there are three potential warriors the Tuatha gods have set in your path—one in the south, one in the east, and one in the north.

"One of them will come to challenge you. Each young warrior has the potential to blossom into something greater. Through their Druids, the gods of this land cast a *geas* on each of them, an invocation that binds a soul to a purpose. I can't see which true soul enjoins the required *geas*, yet one does, or maybe all of them. All who are a product of your seed."

"My sons will challenge me? Here, at Dun Garm?"

The hag shook her head, pausing to take in her stones again. "We do not know that yet. They were all babes you sired in your early days in this land but have now come of age. One who bears you great hate, one who seeks justice, and one driven to destroy you. A father killer for the father killer."

Hakon grimaced as Runa cackled at her choice of words. That he and his father had never seen eye to eye was still a sore point, but he did not regret the actions that had led him to this land. His father had been an old fool, though only Hakon had seen the truth of this in his family. His father had not been willing to risk expanding his realm, even when they would burst at the seams if he did not. His brothers, blinded by their passions, would have killed Hakon had he stayed in their homeland.

And by Thor's hammer, the whole village would have risen against him had he tried to assume the position of leadership held by his father. He was rash when he should have bided his time. Their clan's völva had pronounced that the punishment for such a heinous manslaying was lifelong banishment from their homeland, and should Hakon attempt to remain, he would bring doom upon them all. The word of Runa's sister carried much weight back home, and Hakon had known he had no choice except to flee. Now, he could never return.

Pushing his idle thoughts aside, he asked, "How will I know this Destroyer?"

Runa glanced at him slyly, and Hakon wondered if she could read his mind. Then, with a slight grin, she gazed at her Blood Runes one last time and said distantly, "Hard to say. Look for one each from your territory's northern, eastern, and southern edges. They will all bear your brand. Mirror images of yourself, like sharply edged blades."

"Well done, Runa, well done. I shall reward you for this."

The hag only nodded and collected her stones from her altar, wiping the bird's blood off with an old, rough-spun cloth. Hakon had used her many times to keep the native Gaelic population in check, spy out opportunities for conquest, and help them stay ahead of the surrounding clans. She seemed more adept at wielding magic than her local counterparts, which was a source of pride for Hakon.

Knowing what dangers lurked in the darkness of the future was a definite advantage. And Runa had not failed him in the roughly eighteen years since his flight from the mainland and arrival here. Why she had joined him had always been a mystery.

Maybe it was because she could not hope to displace her sister as the head völva of their clan back home in Alfheim.

Hakon left Runa's conical hut behind—she preferred to be away from those who made Dun Garm their home, so he'd built her a little hovel at the southeastern end of the fort, yet close to his tower—and made his way toward the main hall. The air was cool and refreshing, and he shielded his eyes from the bright sunlight after being in the near darkness his völva preferred.

His concerns about possible future raids shifted to those of this unknown Destroyer. He thought of what duns lay north, east, and south of Garm but still within his territory. While not within his reach, Dun Uisneach came to mind southeast of his fort. He'd raided their borders and raped women in surrounding lesser settlements, so there were possibilities. Yet the clans with solid ties to the *Ard-Rì* had pitched Dun Uisneach along the High King's Road. Their Chieftain, Faolán, a cousin of King Niall's, had always been adversarial and never engaged in any trade. While no significant duns lay east of Dun Garm, he could have sired a child at one of the settlements around Loch Síleann. It was the same for a dun to the north near Ulaidan territory, where he remembered that his Dreadriders had heard of some young Gaelic warriors trying to band together.

Runa had sussed out some of the island's legends and myths, so he knew there was an original Red Branch, an ancient clan of fierce warriors founded by Rory the Red. Hakon had encountered Ulaidan descendants only a few times when attempting a cattle raid too far north. While their power had diminished in recent years, he respected the abilities of those warriors. Their hopes for glory had been kept alive by King Niall Noígiallach's first mate, Inne, who was born into an Ulaidan clan, and then his second mate, Rignach, was a mix of northeast and southeastern clans.

It made Hakon wonder if the unknown warrior he had named the Destroyer was among this ancillary band. If his son led Gaels anything like those of the old Ulaidans, Hakon could have a real battle on his hands. That Runa had foreseen the rise of this Destroyer with at least some detail was a boon. One who would come to challenge him, one of his very own seed. He smiled at the thought of killing a bastard son, a young cretin impudent enough to raise a hand against his father.

That he had been too lusty with the unwilling women of his newly conquered lands in those first years was a mistake, and he certainly had left behind more than his share of bastards. Keeping encounters with women limited to those who had joined him from his homeland or those who came to live in Dun Garm might have been wiser. He had never considered choosing a mate, as there had been too much to work on over the years. Yet he did need a son to follow in his footsteps—something to consider as he cleaned up his current mess with this Destroyer.

Hakon passed his tower as he made his way to the north side of the main hall. As the center of his fort, the spire was the only multi-tiered stone living quarters he had yet to see in Erin's heartland. However, he had seen others like it in the rocky southwest of Mummu and the northwest of Connachta when they had traveled up the River Shannon upon arriving on the Emerald Isle. The High King of Erin, the *Ard-Rì*, was said to have the largest fort in the land, called Dun Tara, that lay to his east. The sprawling Dun Uisneach to his southeast was a bit grander than Dun Garm and commanded as many warriors as he did.

Still, his tower was something of which he was most proud. It had a private upper level for his needs, while the lower level housed his servants. When he had first settled in the area and built Dun Garm, he'd taken hostages from the surrounding regions and found the local smiths produced inferior weapons just as their builders constructed shoddy huts, halls, and forts. Yet he had his artisans work with them to enhance their skills. The efforts refined and improved their construction and smithing.

Hakon had built his fort on the highest hill in the area, and the added height provided a good view of the surrounding plains. After raiding several duns his first summer in Erin, he had decided that having such a stone dwelling built within his fort would deter the locals from attacking.

He'd added extra feet to the ramparts to be more like those of Dun Uisneach than the smaller Gaelic forts nearby, serving as the fort's main line of defense. Sharp pickets topped off the stone and earthen fortifications, and he had constructed his gates at the north end of the fortress with stout timbers. Those details were something rival duns had failed to pay adequate attention to. Thus, Hakon's aggressive battle tactics quickly winnowed his opponents' offensive capabilities without concern for retaliation.

The main hall loomed before Hakon. As he stepped through the door and down a short ramp, he noted fresh rushes had been gathered from Loch Ree and spread on the floor. It was good to see his hostages keeping up with their duties, though he had overstepped the Gaelic tradition of the practice by many years. Overhead, the large, inverted, boat-shaped expanse had a newly thatched roof for the winter. The upper half of the timber-framed walls had been covered with wattle and daub, while the lower half was packed earth covered with a vertical row of timbers to hold it in place.

A raised space between the wicker walls and the main floor provided a communal sleeping area for guests and some servants. A hearth and a cooking pit were at the room's far end. It was nearing the midday meal, and the smell of baking bread filled the air.

Unlike the Gaels, Hakon did not keep a separate table as the Jarl of Garm. Instead, his Dreadriders and the lesser warriors had gathered at two rows of oaken tables that stretched the length of the hall. All were restless and ready to eat. Rude comments wafted about, most aimed at the cook and his assistants.

Off to the sides sat Norvegr women and children who had come to this land or been born here. They waited for their turn at the tables, passing the time by working at looms, spinning wool, or doing needlework. He wished for more warrior women, but that had not happened yet. More women in his homeland took the warrior's path, while only a handful did so here.

Hakon approached two of his more seasoned Dreadriders, Donalt and Royd. The latter knew the northern reaches of his lands better than he did, for it was the warrior's task to collect the tribute from the duns in that area. He stated, "There's a rumor that a splinter group of Gaels are working to create a new rebel band near the northern border of Ulaida and Mide. Any thoughts?"

Royd responded, "From our last pass through there, when the duns had all paid their full tribute the previous fall, there was no sign of any real warriors. It seems to be only talk. I can investigate the matter when we collect this year's tribute in the next fortnight. I'm more concerned about the real Ulaidans."

Hakon nodded and turned to Donalt, commanding, "Find Alrik for me—I have a mission for the two of you."

Moving on, Hakon decided not to send Royd on the mission he had in mind for the north. Maybe the old warrior was getting lax, which meant he could miss something important. Besides, he did not want to wait for the tribute collection to arrive.

Farther down the table sat another pair of Dreadriders he trusted with his life. They were twin brothers who had been born eighteen years earlier while at sea on their voyage to Erin. Lunt and Lang had lost their mother during the crossing, and when her mate had tried to save her, he'd also been lost. Thus,

Hakon had taken them in. Now, at almost eighteen, they had matured into burly warriors with bulging, well-tanned muscles, each always ready to battle for him, preferably back to back.

Unlike the natives, who preferred braids, they wore beards and had shoulder-length blond hair free of ties. While this could hinder them in battle, they believed courage overcame all. They also wore sleeveless wool tunics, allowing their massive arms to be unencumbered. It pleased Hakon that most of his Dreadriders had kept to the ways of their homeland. So he asked the two brothers, "May I join you for this midday meal?"

"We would be honored, my Jarl," the twins replied simultaneously, as they were prone to do. Lunt added, "We have been training hard this morning, working on developing the skills of some of the younger whelps."

"Well done, we need that," Hakon commented. Then he demanded that a nearby indentured Gaelic servant who worked in the kitchens and main hall bring ale. When the man had brought three tankards filled to the brim, they raised their cups to thank the gods of Asgard. Lunt and Lang nearly drained theirs in the first gulp, though Hakon was more reserved.

The cook came by with a pot of fish stew, stopping first at the Dreadlord's table. As Hakon's warriors assailed Dun Garm's cook with complaints that he was taunting them by not serving the red meat first, he said with a sigh, "Such carnivores! The roast boar will be ready shortly."

"No doubt, Jarlson, no doubt. Thanks for your efforts."

The dun's cook nodded and walked around the other tables as his staff helped him. Hakon watched his fellow warriors quickly slurp the stew.

Then, Jarlson's servers brought out the platters. There had been a successful boar hunt yesterday, and the long, slow cook over an oak fire filled the hall with savory scents. Of course,

Jarlson came to Hakon's table first to offer him the best cuts from his oversized platter.

The cook began to dole out the finest joints of the boar, but, given he was not overly hungry, Hakon commanded, "Let these two have the choice pieces. They've earned it."

Lunt said, "A boon, my Jarl. We thank you for this Champion's portion."

Lang only grunted his appreciation as he tore into his joint. Grease ran down his lips and into his pale, young beard; that he nearly inhaled the meat was not something anyone bothered to point out. The bread on his plate was also untouched. On the other hand, Lunt ripped a large piece of meat from his joint and wrapped it with a hunk of rich, dark bread.

Hakon let them eat, watching with pleasure as his two favorite warriors satisfied themselves. He only picked at the soup in his bowl, his thoughts elsewhere. Finally, as they had nearly finished, he said quietly, "I have a task for both of you."

"Hmmm," Lunt said as he swallowed. "As always, we are yours to command."

Hakon smiled, but then the thought of his völva's words and visions of his potential Destroyer crept to mind. "Runa has foreseen that there are three young warriors who will potentially rise against me, all spawned by my loins in our early days here, days when you were but babes. They could be to our south, east, or north. You two will take the north. You will know him by my brand; he bears my eyes and hair color, and you will see me in their facial features. Find him and bring him to me. You can kill him if he resists, but I'd rather you subdue him."

Lang said, "Hmm, so north, that is a wide range."

"It is—I don't have any more information than that, and neither does Runa," Hakon said with a grimace as he rose—he hated not knowing more about his bastard sons. "You two will search to the north, where I used to raid when we first came to this land. I'll send Alrik to the east, and Donalt will take the south. They know those areas better than you two.

"Talk with the older warriors who collect tributes there before you leave, as they can help you with their memories of the north. Runa could only give those three directions. And ask if there is any truth to the rumors that a band of Gael warriors might work against us there to pull in support from Ulaida."

"We'll set off as soon as we finish our meal, review what our senior warriors know, and gather supplies from Jarlson," Lang said to his Jarl. "We will ride soon, my Jarl."

"I know it's close to Ancestor Night, their Samhain, but do not let that concern you," Hakon replied. "May the gods of Asgard guide your steps. Runa will cast ahead for your safety. Do not be overzealous. I prefer no battles, so tread carefully around the Gaels. I look forward to what you have to report."

——— ⚜ Breanna ⚜ ———

Breanna, stunned by the news, rose slowly to her feet. *The Dreadlord's daughter!* A moment later, she asked, "Is that why you let me train with Eoin and his Red Branch? So I could fulfill your *geas*? So I could be your Destroyer?"

"I'm sorry, my love," her mother said, pulling her daughter back to her side. "I shouldn't have done it. I had thought I would hate his child. Then you came along, all sweetness and light, and doused my thirst for revenge. You were just so easy to love."

With her eyes downcast, Breanna whispered, "How could I not see this?"

Morna could only shrug. "At first, when you said you hated the Dreadlord and would one day kill him, I would laugh with everyone else. How would my little girl defeat Hakon Skadi and his Dreadriders?

"While you have the right to the warrior class by your grandmother Cahira's blood, fewer women now aspire to such a life. Fewer still earn the gold Celtic Knot as Cahira did. But after you chose the warrior's path like your father and grandmother, you showed such promise, even at an age you should not have been able to. When you followed that up by earning a silver armring at thirteen and began to use the *void*, I believed your destiny was true, and it was my *geas* at work."

"Yet you still could not tell me?"

Morna shook her head, tears in her eyes. "Then you earned your grandmother's gold armring last summer at Dun Uisneach. Our *Aos Dána* informed me you could seize the *void* and use it to create a blade dance like no other. When I heard that, I knew my actions before you were born were more than just a hateful wish.

"I would have to tell you about the *geas* one day—only I could never utter the words. How does a mother tell her child that her father is a monster everyone hates?"

"Oh, Mother," Breanna said as they wrapped their arms around each other.

Morna sighed. "I hope you will forgive me, my daughter."

Breanna stumbled from their shared hut, tears on her cheeks. Who was she? A true warrior, or just one driven by a magical *geas* born of hate and revenge? Feeling her notorious iron will start to crumble, she sagged to her knees. Why couldn't her mother have kept such awful knowledge to herself? Why couldn't she have taken it to her grave?

Breanna was nothing more than a bastard daughter of Haken Skadi, a *diolain*!

---⊹✦⊹ **Eoin** ⊹✦⊹---

In the dusky evening light, Eoin strode across the yard toward the main hall. There was a chill in the air, especially now that the sun had slipped beyond the horizon, and he huddled in his checkered wool cloak to keep out the cold. Eoin briefly wondered what Breanna's mother had to tell only her, but his growling stomach quickly won out over his concerns.

The challenge for Champion today was one of the few days he had not sparred with his band of warriors, so he decided he could skip a stop at the communal bathhouse. As he approached the main hall, Eoin observed that many of the huts required repairs. With winter expected to set in shortly after Samhain, he knew there'd barely be enough time to patch the thatching and wattle walls. It was something he'd have to talk to the elders about.

Since the Dreadlord had killed their *Ceann-cinnidh*, Eoin's father, eighteen summers before, few true warriors remained at Dun Arrogh. Indeed, none had the spine to stand up and take the mantle of Dun Chief. All feared the Dreadlord and his Dreadriders would not look favorably on one with such aspirations.

Eoin had commanded his mother, Aife, to make him a cloak with five colors, which had raised more than a few eyebrows. Yet his clan traced its roots to Conal Cearnach and the Ulaidan Clans, and such was his birthright. With such a lineage, he could wear garments fit for a Royal Prince of the Blood. Once their Brehon had confirmed his request, Aife and Lissa, their Master Weaver and Dyer, had set out to make such a cloak. They used alder bark to dye half of the wool squares black, allowing them to sew a checkerboard pattern with white for the main body. Then, madder for a red collar, and woad for blue stripes down the front opening, plus weld and gorse to make a light green hem.

Eoin chuckled now at how he had strutted about in it. Then he remembered being forced to keep his cloak hidden when a Dreadrider had come to the dun seeking their tribute. It was something he'd vowed not to repeat. The odious Dreadlord's attempt to rule them made him see red for a brief moment. Then, regaining control, he thought about what they had done to outsmart Norvegr Jarl and his men, such as building hidden root cellars in the surrounding woods to ensure they always had enough food for the winter. The crops had been productive, and soon, the Dreadriders would make their rounds to collect Hakon's share.

Eoin put aside his thoughts of the Dreadlord as he entered their central hall. It, too, was a bit run down, with old thatching on the roof and dirty rushes on the floor. Here and there, he spotted small holes in the wattle and daub walls. To create distinct spaces within the large hall, movable cedar screens were set up, allowing the women to work on weaving or needlework near the front while meals were prepared and served at the back. The hearth at the room's far end held a pot of boiling stew, the smoke from the peat and oak fire escaping through a small hole in the roof above.

The high table sat empty because they still had no *Ceann-cin-nidh*, something Eoin planned to correct soon. Dun Arrogh needed a Chief. Men, women, and children sat at the lower tables, and each was lost in their bowl of stew. A few warriors who had already finished eating were in the corner playing *dìsnean*, a game of chance using marked stones. From the groans he heard as he passed, Eoin knew Breanna's Uncle Kyras was winning again. Their smith was always one for that game.

Seeing Fergal eating by himself, Eoin made for his former Champion. He asked, "How's the fare, cousin? Calla's efforts as good as ever?"

"Kerill brought down a nice fat doe this afternoon," Fergal said between mouthfuls. "It didn't take much for her to improve nature's doings. Go get some for yourself."

Eoin nodded and made his way to the kettle. Calla, a short, portly woman with dark hair and features that marked her as of Fir Bolg lineage, doled out a portion and handed it to him.

"Where are the joints?" he demanded of her. "Venison stew on the day Kerill brought the beast down?"

"Meat's already in the smokehouse," Calla said, her exasperated tone making it clear this was not the first time she had heard the complaint. "Winter's on the way, ya know."

"A warrior shouldn't have to live on this," Eoin grumbled.

"You should thank the gods you're alive to enjoy it!" the cook countered. "Maybe get your arse in the kitchen and help!"

Eoin only scowled at Calla, but the stew was better than berries, nuts, or cooked roots. After pouring a cup of ale, he drained half off in one gulp, refilled it, and then took his bowl and a hunk of dark bread back to the battered oak table where Fergal was finishing his meal. Before taking his first bite, Eoin asked, "How's your head?"

Fergal just grunted as if to say it was nothing. Eoin didn't press the point and began to devour his stew. A moment later, he commented, "Well, let's not talk about the fact that she knocked you out. Bre's mother will probably not see it through to sunrise."

"Aye, so I've heard," Fergal said flatly. "May Lugh watch over her *anam*."

There was more silence between them as others from the dun swallowed the last of their meals and began cleaning up. Eoin noted the dull buzz of activity in the hall. The Bard of Dun Arrogh was getting ready to spin his evening tale, and some women were already working quietly at the looms or spinning wool. Two lads, one with a fiddle and one with a lute, were finishing a mournful tune. Though a few men remained huddled in the corner playing *disnean*, most now sat with their ale cups, talking about the coming winter between songs.

When the lads put their instruments aside so their Bard could start, Eoin turned his gaze to the table where the elders sat and thought about prodding them into getting repairs underway before the first snow, but that could wait after Samhain.

Then he took another gulp of ale and noticed the sizable red welt on Fergal's temple when his cousin brushed his hair back. The sight made him consider Breanna again. Ah, that girl was indeed a challenge. He had always felt there was more between them than she would admit—or allow. Leaning back in his chair with a sigh, he asked his friend, "Do you think losing Morna will interfere with Bre being my Champion?"

The question brought a little color to Fergal's face. "I doubt you'll be facing any challenges before spring. Hakon's warriors are too busy collecting the tribute and preparing for winter. Besides, I doubt her accomplishment will stand until then."

Eoin bristled at Fergal's bravado and rejoined with disdain, "It was enough to beat you. Her ability to seize the *void* today was impressive, something you'd best figure out. It's like you're averse to the magic of our land."

Fergal growled, "But we've yet to see how she does with a Dreadrider staring her down."

"Nor have you or I faced one of Hakon's lead dogs," Eoin countered. "Only the two of us have ever taken trophies, and those were not Dreadriders."

"That's my point," Fergal said tightly. "The Red Branch doesn't need women as warriors!"

"We need all the warriors we can get," was Eoin's chill response. He was surprised by his cousin's display of gender prejudice and added, "Would you tell all women they can't be part of our Red

Branch, even if they can claim warrior class blood rights and have earned a gold Celtic Knot armring, one her grandmother earned and passed on to her? One who can seize the *void* as Breanna does?"

"Well, they shouldn't be allowed to *comórtas* for the Championship."

Eoin opened his mouth, a stinging retort at the ready that it was his fault for pushing her, and then paused. He knew Fergal's comments about the role of women in their Red Branch were just a way to cover what was bothering him: losing his *comórtas* with Breanna. A moment later, he observed quietly, "If you hadn't continually goaded Bre's use of long blades, she would have never exploded and demanded a challenge match to see which of you was indeed the best warrior. And you'd still be my Champion."

"You can't tell me you're not pleased with the outcome," Fergal accused Eoin as he rose from his chair. "You've always been soft on that girl. Now you have to count on her for your life."

"That I will and that I do," Eoin concurred darkly. "And I know she'll not let me down, especially not with her command of *urghabháil an neamhní* in battle. Something you'd do well to learn. Yet that will only happen when you stop being averse to the magic our land has gifted us, that the Tuatha Gods have granted us."

Fergal started to let the barb on his tongue slip. But their Bard cleared his throat and blew a few notes on his flute to signal he was ready to begin his traditional narrative. First, he would recount part of their Celtic history and his interpretation of the tale's meaning in relation to their daily life.

Fergal muttered, shook his head as he picked up his wooden bowl and cup from the table, and said, "I've had enough for one day."

Eoin rose with him. He was the taller of the two by nearly a full head and stepped next to him to make it clear he was in charge. Both knew that Eoin had obtained his features from Clan Ulaid's famed warrior Conal Cearnach, and the latter carried Fir Bolg blood through his mother. It was a difference that gave Eoin the right to wear the cloak of a prince.

Eoin commanded, "I will not waste this fair weather, cousin. Pass the word, we meet in the Grove at sunrise."

"Aye," Fergal managed to say as he turned away.

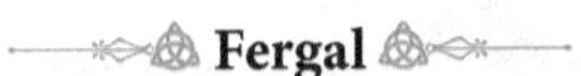

Fergal

Fergal thought trying his hand at a game of *dìsnean* would get his mind off the disaster of a day he'd had. At least in that, he would have a fair chance at winning. However, when he saw that Kyras was still tossing the stones, he couldn't suppress a grimace. A fair bet, indeed!

But as he approached, the burly smith rose with a groan, saying, "My knees need rest. The stones are all yours, Fergal. I've had enough winning for one day."

Fergal took the stones, smiling at those around him for the first time that night. He thought that maybe his luck was changing, but as Kyras walked away and Fergal made his first toss, the mark of the crow turned up on all three stones. He could do little more than groan to himself. Always a loser.

Hakon

Hakon walked around the circular room at the top of his stone tower, gazing out the south window first, then crossing to the east window, and finally to the north window. While they were only small slits, they gave a view around his dun while keeping out most of the wind. As he sat near the north window, a lone candle burned on a table near his bed, and the evening was losing its twilight quickly. His two giant wolfhounds, Hati and Skoll, were already asleep on the floor beside it.

Hakon wondered about the ones who sought to destroy him, the father killer for a father killer, as Runa had named him. What was driving his sons? What were they doing at that moment? Where were they, the spawn of his loins, lurking in the dark? Maybe he should have done more than send his Dreadriders out to search. Instead, he pondered if he should march a circuit around his territory with his host of Dreadriders and warriors to raze the land.

It would certainly instill fear in the hearts of those who would support this possible Destroyer. But, then again, such a show of force might also raise alarms among the Gaels. If the warriors at Dun Uisneach, ruled by Royal Mide itself and located to his east, got wind of such a march, High King Niall Noígiallach would have to respond.

Then there were always those at the ever-watchful Doon of Drumsna, a river fort manned by Connachta's best, which lay along the River Shannon to his northwest. He did not need another skirmish with the clans from that area. In his travels up the River Shannon eighteen years ago, he'd had enough of the Connachta and Mummu clans to the west, constantly harassing and skirmishing.

Only Ulaida seemed preoccupied enough to leave him alone this fall—mainly because their king had just died, and a new one was still trying to establish himself. Yet, chancing an engagement with either the Ulaidan clans or those of Royal Mide made the Dreadlord think twice about gathering a force to root out his true Destroyer. Had it not been for the *Ard-Rì* of Erin's desire to pursue raids abroad, Hakon knew he would not have survived his earlier years when he was establishing himself.

He continued to regard his decision to settle on the loose border of three of the five major kingdoms of Erin as sound, for the other clans still seemed more interested in making war with each other than dealing with him. It had allowed him to act with moderate impunity. That would change once they saw his growing presence. Those in his dun had been patient but would only remain so for a few more summers.

There were already some who had settled outside the protection of his fort. With Garm straining at its seams, more would soon follow, which could start them fighting amongst themselves for the choicest locations. He needed more land, and to hold it, he needed more warriors. That made him think of his brothers, Gefion and Tyrin. Maybe, in the spring, he would send two of his longboats back with a proposal to trade some of his land for muscle and steel. Hopefully, time will have smoothed the waters with them.

A knock at his door startled him out of his contemplations, unsure how long he had been musing. His two dogs were already on their feet, alert for signs of danger. Yet it was now dark, with a waxing moon hanging high above and countless stars dotting the sky. The harshness of his voice was more than evident as he commanded, "Come."

It was Runa, though he did not have to look, as the jingle of her bead swags that hung from the brooches over her chest was well known to him. She said nothing as she stepped into his chambers and waited. If not for the late span, his manservant, Sveinn, one of his retired warriors, would have asked before letting her come to his door, and Hakon would have said no in his current mood. The völva's unexpected arrival certainly did not settle well; lately, she rarely had good news.

Without turning his gaze away from the black night, he asked darkly, "What brings you here, old crone?"

"My poor little crow has given me its other leg," Runa replied, easily matching his caustic tone. "You should know what my Blood Runes revealed about the father killer."

"I believe you meant to name them Destroyers?"

Runa quickly amended, "Yes, my Jarl, Destroyers."

"I've sent Lunt and Lang north to seek that one out," Hakon said firmly as he finally rose and shuttered his windows for the night, his dark mood passing so suddenly he could have been another person. "I have also sent Alrik to the east and Donalt to the south. If anyone can find them, it will be those four. When they do, they will bring him here or kill him if he resists."

"I believe you're mistaken," the crone corrected as she smoothly crossed the floor to where he stood. "They may find him all right, but they'll not bring him to you. They will fail because your potential Destroyer is a mighty warrior. And that doesn't even consider that he is protected and aided by the gods of this land. Through my Blood Runes, I have foreseen that the Destroyer will soon be traveling, seeking a piece of forgotten Tuatha magic before coming to try and kill you. I cannot say how to find this old magical weapon, but the gods of the *Tuatha Dé Danann* will ensure that it finds its way into his hands."

"Then summon the gods of Asgard to aid us!" Hakon demanded, but he saw doubt in her eyes.

Runa shook her head. "If only it were that easy. But, unfortunately, our gods are far away, tied to our homeland and people. They can reach me through my link to them, but they can neither directly wield their power here nor in any part of this land."

"Then may Thor's hammer protect us," Hakon intoned as he sat again and let his gaze wander back to the night. If the Tuatha gods were aiding his Destroyer, he would face more challenges than he had thought.

"Neither Thor nor his hammer can help us," the völva informed him. "But there are many gods in this land, some of whom may aid you. Long ago, near the time the gods of the *Tuatha Dé Danann* came to power, another people known as the Fomorians had settled in this land. They and their gods lost Erin to the Tuatha—ever since then, those gods have been at odds with one another. The Fomors hate the Tuatha and their gods, which might be enough to enlist their support."

"Are there any other options?" Hakon questioned. "What about this One God? Some at Tara now worship him, it's said, and if Niall Noígiallach tolerates such nonsense, maybe there's something to such a god. Can we call on him?"

"The One God who would chase away the many gods of Erin, and Asgard for that matter," Runa snorted as she raised a hand, warding off the very idea. "They believe in no other gods. And because we do, their god would not heed our request for help. Thus, this One God is not for us. Besides, I doubt he would have much power here in Erin. Aside from those in Tara, few have heard of him, and even fewer offer him worship. A god's power comes from those who worship him, so we should not bother with that one."

"Very well," Hakon said as he faced her. "Then it's the Fomorian gods we seek. However, I'm concerned about whether they have the power to assist us. Are they strong enough to face the gods that the Druids follow?"

"Only one of the gods, once worshipped by the Fomorians, is a threat to those who aid your Destroyer," Runa replied. "When the Tuatha and their gods first defeated the Fomorians, these fallen gods attracted another following. If it were not for the Fir Bolg, a wave of settlers who had arrived before the Tuatha, the Fomorian gods would be gone altogether. Still, with few clans paying tribute to them, their powers are weak, only a shadow of their former selves. It's the most powerful of these Fomorian gods whom we seek. His name is Tethra, and he commands a host of sea demons. With rivers crossing this land like so many ribbons, his minions should be able to go nearly anywhere."

"Can you do it? Can you call on this god named Tethra?"

Runa shrugged. "For eighteen years, I have been laboring quietly, learning all I can about this land's magic. The Druids keep their secrets well hidden, and I am an outsider—they still call me a *baobh*, a Fury, a dark völva. Nonetheless, I have persevered, so there is a slim chance. It's near the time when the spirits of this land are closest to the world of the flesh. The veil is thinning. If we wait until Ancestor Night, I might be able to do it."

"Will this Tethra do as you bid?"

"Not my bidding, but maybe yours," Runa corrected. "You must be the one to convince him to aid your Dreadriders in locating the father killer—ah, I mean Destroyer. Remember, Tethra and his demons despise the *Tuatha Dé Danann*. So if gods like Lugh and Danu are aiding your bastard Destroyer, this otherworld god of the Fomorians might be more inclined to help."

"Tonight, I must know tonight," Hakon demanded, taking a step toward her.

Runa's tone was firm. "We have no choice except to wait for Ancestor Night—the Feast of the Dead is the only time I dare work such magic. The Fomorians are tied to this land and have an overlapping Samhain festival. I have learned that angering a god is not something to do lightly. And to call them when the veil is not thin enough for them to cross from their world to ours would not be in our interest. Besides, a day won't matter."

"Then prepare yourself for the Feast of the Dead," Hakon commanded. "You summon him, and I'll convince him to support our cause."

SEEKING THE DESTROYER

Lunt and Lang had visited five small duns and settlements along the outer reaches of their Jarl's territory the afternoon they set out, and they had then worked their way north along the River Shannon. Now north of Loch Ree, their big mounts could take the softly rolling, grassy terrain at a gallop as they followed the riverbank. Unfortunately, searching for the potential Destroyer had yielded no results, but the weather remained good, and the cowering locals had been hospitable enough.

Lunt knew his brother would have preferred ending their quest for Hakon's bastard sooner rather than later, as Jarlson's ale and cooking were better. The two Dreadriders spent their first night beneath the stars, which bothered Lang more than Lunt. It was close to Ancestor Night, the Feast of the Dead, when spirits walked the land between sunset and sunrise. With Lang jumping at every sound, his skittishness showed he had not slept well.

Early the following day, the warriors reached the outer edges of their Jarl's territory. The River Shannon took a northwesterly track, and if they pursued its course, it would lead them to a fort that the Connachta called the Doon of Drumsna. Wanting to stay clear of those clans as they took affront to any challenge, they headed northeast, following a tributary that forked into the Shannon.

Barely a span later, they encountered a small dun eking out life along the estuary. There were only a few huts inside the ringfort, most of which were in desperate need of repair, with the thatching on all except the main hall having holes in various spots. The wattle-and-daub walls were not in much better shape. The dun's earthen ramparts had eroded over the years and were now useless, with no one to maintain them. Mainly, older adults populated the hovel. Neither Lunt nor Lang knew the name of the dun, and it didn't look promising. Still, they stopped, hoping to glean some information from someone.

When he saw how much work the huts needed to make them livable, Lunt said to his brother, "Better to sleep beneath the stars than here."

"Maybe last night," Lang countered. "But tonight is Ancestor Night, and I will not sleep beneath the stars on the Feast of the Dead. Instead, we'll find someplace with a roof. You can count on it."

Lunt just laughed, letting the subject drop. An older man dressed in rags approached with his head bowed low. Others from the dun stayed within the doors of their huts. The warriors dismounted, stretching their stiff ground-slept bodies as they did so. Lunt noticed that a few red-headed lassies going about their chores had stopped to admire their muscles that rippled across their massive frames. They were a fierce-looking pair with swords strapped over their shoulders and their white hair flying in the breeze, each a replica of the other. Iron-studded leather belts encircled their waists, and their wrists were the only accouterments to their attire of white woolen tunics and cloaks, along with knee-high deer-skin boots.

The older man stopped before them. "What can I do for such mighty warriors?"

"We are searching for a warrior much like ourselves," replied Lunt.

Lang added, "Yes, one with our white hair and blue eyes, but not as large as us because he'd be a half-breed."

"You'll not find any warriors here, with white hair or not," the old man informed them.

The statement surprised neither Lunt nor Lang. The latter turned to remount his horse. Lunt, however, probed with, "What about any Ulaidan descendants forming a new band of warriors? Heard of anyone like that?"

The older man glanced up as if surprised. He answered carefully, "Who hasn't heard of the fierce Ulaidans that spawned such greats as Rory the Red, the Hound of Ulaida, and Conal Cearnach? One of the great tales spun by our Bards."

"Not historical ones," Lunt corrected. "A new band, one led by a young upstart."

"Here, in Mide, under Tara's gaze? The *Ard-Rì* would surely frown on that."

"These are Hakon Skadi's lands, not Niall Noígiallach's," Lang informed the old man stiffly.

"Whatever you say," was the reply, a smile briefly touching his aged lips. "Niall of the Nine Hostages may tolerate the Dreadlord, but I doubt his son would."

"Well, have you heard of any new bands forming?" Lunt pressed.

"No, but it would have to be led by someone who could trace back their lineage to the original Ulaidans," the old man advised as he looked away to the northeast, where the original Red Branch had once roamed. "Someone with that lineage. There's an arm of the Clan Mórhda at Dun Arrogh. They draw their roots from Conal Cearnach. You might try there."

Lunt and Lang glanced at each other, their eyebrows arching in unison; it was their first lead since leaving. Then Lang said, "How far is it to this Dun Arrogh?"

The older man rubbed his jaw. "You'll easily reach it by nightfall on those beasts. Just follow the river, then go east at the split."

Lunt flipped the old man a silver coin, saying, "Hand that to the next Dreadrider who comes to collect my Jarl's yearly tribute. By our decree, given your openness, he will take only half of what's due."

With that, the pair mounted up and slowly rode out of the dilapidated dun, saying little as they left the older man behind.

Donalt

Donalt and Alrik rode out through the gates of Dun Garm, each charged with a mission to seek out their Jarl's Destroyer, with Alrik having the longer route to the east to search. Before Hakon had staked his claim, that border would have been the River Shannon, but it was now west of Loch Síleann and north of the River Inny.

The two older warriors had agreed with their Jarl that each would take the area they knew best. For Donalt, it was west to Loch Ree and south to the High King's Road, also known as *Slighe Mor*. Hakon had declared that matches for his potential bastards should come back with him to Dun Garm, and it appeared that such an effort would require more resources than what Hakon sent him with.

Donalt's task was to search the territory south of Dun Garm so that he could follow the shoreline of Loch Ree down to *Slighe Mor*, the High King's Road. Then, if he discovered nothing about the bastard, he would follow the road toward Dun Uisneach, as there were settlements around the fort Hakon had raided during his early days in Erin.

To help Alrik skirt the hills directly east of Dun Garm, the warriors rode together on the way south for a short time. Then, looking toward the east, Alrik said, "This is where we part ways. It's poor luck with you drawing the more difficult path, as Dun Uisneach is not our friend."

"Aye, they are not, and, yes, it is time we part," Donalt replied. "Our journeys should take about the same time, my friend. I expect to see you back in Dun Garm in two nights. It should get us back to Dun Garm on the eve of Ancestor Night. Worst case, the day after. Good hunting."

"Agreed, and you as well," Alrik answered. "I want to make it to one of the Loch Síleanne settlements before nightfall. As you said, it is the season's end and the start of the dark time. Hopefully, the settlers might reveal something about our quarry." He pulled his reins to the left and pushed his heels into his horse's flanks. As he headed northeast, the beast surged into a gallop.

Donalt did the same, letting his horse have its head, knowing there was a friendly settlement at the south end of Loch Ree where he could ask around and spend the night. The next day would see him reach the High King's Road and another small dun at the road's intersection with the River Shannon. He suspected the settlements near Dun Uisneach would bear more fruit, but it was best to be thorough. That said, he knew he had to tread carefully around the clans of Mide, as they would certainly like to catch an outlander alone in their territory. Moreover, he would have to move swiftly from settlement to settlement or dun to dun in his search for Hakon's bastard, as word would travel about a Dreadrider seeking a young white-haired warrior.

His ride was uneventful, and within about two whole spans, he was fording the River Inny. Later in the day, as evening drew near, Donalt came upon the settlement he had been seeking at the south end of the loch. It was nestled where the larger body of water flowed into the River Shannon, yet had no fortifications. Since he often patrolled the territory south of Dun Garm, he knew the folks here and had always treated them respectfully. Nevertheless, the first few years had been tense as the Gaels got used to the Norvegr presence just to their north.

As he pulled his mount to a halt and slipped from his saddle, one of the stable boys ran up to help. "Donalt, what brings you here?"

"Searching the southern area down to the High King's Road and east for a young warrior," was Donalt's answer as he strode away. "I need to speak with your father. Take my horse to the stable and fetch him for me. I'll meet him in the hall."

A short while later, he took a cup of ale and watched the cook cut him a hunk from a freshly baked loaf of bread, one of many that would be part of the evening meal. Then, as Donalt bit into his piece, he turned to see the stablemaster enter the central hall of the settlement. Swallowing, he said, "Aodhán, it is good to see you."

"Aye, the same for you, Donalt," Aodhán agreed. "The lads have a fresh catch of trout that Aoife will be cooking up shortly. I assume you are staying the night in my stable."

Given that it was not a question, he gulped ale to wash down the bread before responding. "Indeed, your boy is already looking after my horse. I appreciate your offer of a place at the community tables and a spot to sleep in your loft. Yet before we get to enjoy the evening, I have a question central to why my Jarl sent me south."

"Of course," Aodhán said with a hint of curiosity. "How may I help you?"

Donalt paused to take another gulp of ale, then said, "As I'm sure you recall, we outlanders were somewhat overzealous in our desire to control this area when we arrived here. As such, my Jarl took some liberties, leaving behind offspring. Only a few, but they are of age now. He is interested in seeing if they want to learn about their Norvegr heritage. Do you know of any lads in the area with white hair like ours, ones seeking the warrior's plaid? Anywhere between here and the High King's Road, likely as far east as Dun Uisneach?"

Aodhán scratched his beard. "Well, lads here, who usually *comórtas* for their bronze, silver, and gold armrings in the summer, mentioned three white-haired warriors had competed and added they were curious about that because of you, making them wonder if those Gaels might not be purebloods."

"A *comórtas* is a fight, já? How do they work?"

Aodhán answered, "While in open battle, Gaels warriors aim to kill and claim the head of any foe as a trophy—Chiefs usually put those cloven heads on pikes before their gates to show the prowess of their warriors—a *comórtas* is a challenge between two warriors until one of them yields or the judges declare a victor. No killing allowed. Once a year, those challenges determine the granting of warrior armrings."

"I see. Would your lads know which settlement these white-haired warriors hail from?"

"One was from a settlement closer to Dun Uisneach, though I doubt they knew which. The others were east and north."

"Excellent news," Donalt said. "That makes my evening lighter. So let's enjoy it!"

Alrik

Alrik followed his planned course east, staying below the hilly terrain to the north, and let his mount take them around those hills and up the valley that led to Loch Síleann. The riding was easy, and he made good time, stopping only briefly to water his horse at a crossing stream. He pulled a travel ration from his pack during the pause, then was off again. Keeping with his plan to go to the northernmost settlements of the loch first, he pressed on until the light was getting dim.

Then, he spotted a small but familiar settlement where he had collected tributes over the years. It was close to Loch Síleann, so fishing was one of its primary sources of food and trade. Alrik noted a few wattle-and-daub huts built next to each other, but there were no earthen ramparts or gates to protect them. There was also no central hall. Instead, they had a large, round, open-air structure with a thatched roof where they gathered for meals. The cook had placed his stone oven and fire pit in the center of the area.

Several burly Gaels emerged from the abodes as he rode into the main yard, looking warily at the Dreadrider. Alrik slung his leg over his mount and slid to the ground. "Good evening, good folk. I seek guest rights for this night. I will provide a silver for your inconvenience and the opportunity to share your meal. Perhaps, exchange tales since I see you have no Bard for this night."

One of the stocky Gaels, clearly a farmer, strode toward him with his field scythe. "I recognize you. You're one of those outlanders who demand we make a tribute to your overlord. Yet you take and only bring ill winds in your wake."

Alrik sighed. "I am not here for tribute this time. Just information, a meal, and a place by your fire while I eat. It is why I made a generous offer of one silver for your hospitality."

The Gael farmer shrugged. "We don't appreciate your sort, but we can share our food and fire for a silver piece this night. And tolerate you."

"Outstanding," Alrik replied. Seeing where they tied off their diminutive hill-bred horses, he led his horse to a picket just a bit away from them. Next, he unsaddled his mount and pulled a brush from a pouch to groom his beast. Then, after fetching a bucket of water and some feed for him, Alrik returned to the central covered firepit with its combined stone oven. While he had tended to his horse, others had queued up for a turn at the pot bubbling over the fire pit and the pail of ale.

"We will need a few extra coppers for the horse feed and the information you seek," the Gael added.

Alrik chuckled and handed the man the silver and a few coppers. "Good bargaining. I like you, Gael. My name is Alrik."

"I am Seoras," the shorter man said. Taking a bowl, he stepped in between two of his fellow settlers, begging their pardon, and scooped a ladle full of fish stew into it before handing it to the Norvegr and then passing him a cup of ale. Alrik nodded his appreciation. Finally, sitting by the fire, Seoras asked, "What information do you seek?"

Alrik took a moment to answer. He scooped some of the stew into his mouth with his fingers and then washed it down with ale. "Compliments to your cook. As for the information I seek, I know this is a sensitive subject, but our Jarl is concerned he may have been overzealous in his early days when we first came here. He most certainly left behind offspring and now wants to make sure they have the opportunity to grow into the fine warriors they could be. Removing their burden from your clans."

Seoras nodded. "Hmmm, maybe your lord would like to add more warriors to your cause."

"Aye, it would seem that way," Alrik agreed, chewing slowly on the fresh bread. Then, after swallowing, he added, "Yet it would not be enough to change the balance of power either way. Our Jarl is only looking for those he sired, a number that should be no more than three within his territory. We believe one could be in this area. He would have white hair and blue eyes."

The Gael nodded and gulped his ale. "You are correct. Someone like that could be in this area. So now we bargain some more. Two more silvers for what you want to know."

Alrik peered shrewdly at the farmer, then nodded.

"There is only one such young man around Loch Síleann, now with seventeen summers under his belt, that fits your description. He wields a sword reasonably well in our seasonal games around this region. Ride to the south end of the loch, and you will find him in a settlement there."

As if sensing he would get no more out of Seoras, Alrik held out his cup for more ale. "Very well, I'll bid you goodnight. When I leave in the morning, you'll have two additional silver pieces."

They nodded their agreement. Seoras dipped the cup into the ale bucket while Alirk rose to accept it. Then he turned to fetch his bedroll from his mount. Alrik decided to settle near the picket line that held his horse, preferring to be slightly apart from the settlement folk. He was pleased to see that the area was relatively dry, so he spread his oiled bedroll tarp next to his saddle and then placed his softer bedroll over it.

Scanning the dark sky, he considered Seoras's tale, wondering whether the young white-haired warrior to the south could be his Jarl's Destroyer. Then, with a shrug, he laid down and ducked beneath the bedroll, throwing his waterproof cloak over himself.

Finally, he tucked his sword at his side and rested his head on his saddle to seek a good night's sleep.

The morning light woke Alrik. He found all as it had been the night before, and the settlement was stirring to life around him. As expected, a few women were gathered around the covered fire pit and stone oven, pulling the first-morning bread from the latter. His horse stood nearby, looking down at him as if to suggest it was time they moved on.

Alrik grunted as he stood, stretching to work out some muscle kinks. It had been a while since he'd slept on the ground instead of a pallet. He moved off to a side creek to relieve himself, then washed his face, neck, and arms to clean off the previous day's grime. Seoras stood by the main oven and returned, ready to hand him a bowl of cooked oats with his breakfast.

With the bowl passed between their hands, Seoras turned to snatch up a mug for the massive warrior, filling it with a warm tea that was in the ale bucket, saying, "I will ask no more for providing your breakfast. It is only civilized. Yet, before you leave, I believe you have something for me."

Alrik nodded and accepted his mug of tea. He sat by the oven and used his fingers to scoop his meal into his mouth. When finished, he rose to gulp down the tea. "As we agreed, my friend."

Seoras replied, "No, not a friend. I'm not stupid enough to insult you, knowing the skill you possess with your blade. Yet, as a farmer, I know how to use the land to feed our mutual people, so I know you see value in my continued existence."

"Well said," Alrik responded with a nod as he reached into his pouch and handed the Gael two coins. "Here are your promised pieces. Given Samhain is upon us, may your settlement thrive."

With that, Alrik mounted his horse and rode south, leaving the settlement behind. The ride along Loch Síleann was easy in the calm morning, with a mist drifting over the water. Even though the rising sun was cloud-covered, the fog along the Loch Síleann shoreline eventually burned off as Alrik rode on.

The morning passed without happenstance, and the terrain was easygoing. A considerable settlement appeared as the end of Loch Síleann drew close to where the River Inny began. It was a bit larger than the one he had left that morning. Having collected many fall tributes over the years, he knew this settlement was centered on farming and fishing, as well as raising cattle and goats, and breeding and training horses—one of the main villages that supplied the people of this land with its bounty.

Alrik rode to the suitably sized stable before dismounting. A boy ran up to the Dreadrider, saying, "Great warrior of the outlanders, let me take care of your mount."

"Já, boy," Alrik answered, letting his reins drop. "Who is your Horsemaster?"

"That would be Epona," the boy answered, turning to lead his horse away. "Follow me. She is in the training yard working with a mare."

Alrik followed the boy to a large square structure, with the front half covered and enclosed, providing two rows of stalls, and the back half was just covered, each area having a thatched roof. The stable and a loft that kept hay dry sat off to the left. As they entered the training yard, a sturdy yet shapely woman turned from her efforts that were focused on a medium-sized mount. Her flaming red hair was plaited into braids, revealing her bare arms and shoulders, which showed off her toned muscles. She quieted her horse by pulling its head down; it was not as small as the hill ponies raised in the north, yet not anything like the size of his mount. However, if she let his horse crowd her, the beast could intimidate her mare. Deftly, the Horsemaster circled her away from the sizable stallion that was his.

Epona flashed her gaze to the warrior, then back to his steed. "A great beast, outlander. I have an eye for a horse's capabilities and potential matches. Maybe we can exchange something to breed your stallion?"

"Maybe," Alrik said to the horsewoman. "Yet I seek something else."

Epona nodded. "Boy, take his mount to water and feed. I don't need him sniffing at my mare here. Make sure you keep him a stall or two away from our mounts. And you, what brings you to our humble settlement?"

Alrik smiled as the boy did as commanded. "I am Alrik, Dreadrider of Garm. My Jarl is seeking young warriors whom he might have sired when we first came here. What, now, seventeen years back? Only three of them have developed some prowess, with one excelling in this area. He has white hair, blue eyes, and sharp features like his sire's. This lad is said to have participated in last summer's competition for his Celtic armring. Point me in the right direction, and you can breed a mare with my stallion without bartering."

Epona smirked. "That sounds like bartering."

"Then it is," he answered. "What can you tell me?"

"Two."

Alrik nodded. "I grant you two mares to be bred with by my mount."

"Damn, too easy! I should have asked for three," the Horsemaster muttered.

Alrik smiled. "I could sweeten the deal, but only for you."

"You mean with me!" Epona nearly exploded. "I think not!"

"It would get you three mares bred by my stallion," Alrik said with a wink.

Epona shook her head. "No! I don't want to see more of your kind spring forth between the legs of our women nor from my own."

Alrik shrugged. "Your loss, then. Now tell me where the young warrior is?"

"His name is Braoin," she answered, her eyes still narrowed. "The lads are always working in the fields or hunting or fishing for tonight's and the next day's meals for the settlement. They will be back before the sun sets."

Alrik nodded. "All right, then. I'll have an ale or two in the main hall while I wait. Let me know if you need anything, such as a third mare you'd like to have bred. Should you accept the challenge, such a *mare* must be a very sturdy match, understood? As to the first two mares, I'll be here until midday tomorrow. So use my stallion wisely before I leave."

With that, he turned his attention to the main hall.

Alrik observed the clan members as they filtered into the central hall, scanning for the lad Epona had called Braoin. Roughly twenty men, with a range of old to young, found seats at the long tables. One remained standing, taking in the Dreadrider. Alrik held the other's gaze, seeing a younger version of his Jarl before the lad sat on the bench with his fellows. He noted Braoin's eyes straying to him occasionally as if wondering why he was in their hall.

Servers had set cups beside the ale buckets as they made their way around the tables, each scoping out a share. Alrik, interested in how the settlement operated, saw that the cook had bowls of fish stew and bread baskets delivered to the tables first. Then, he sent out platters of baked trout and bowls of roasted root vegetables. Finally, the musicians started to tune up their fiddles while the kitchen staff cleared away bowls and plates and refilled the ale buckets.

With that, Alrik stood and strode to the lad's table. "I understand you are Braoin."

He sensed wariness in the young man's eyes, knowing he cut an imposing figure, but the Gael firmly answered as he rose, "Yes, I am Braoin."

"I see you wear a silver armring."

The lad lifted an eyebrow, answering, "Aye, earned it at Dun Uisneach during the regional Gaelic *comórtas* this past summer."

"I would have words with you, preferably outside."

"As you will."

Alrik nodded and turned to lead the way out of the main hall, noting that the young warrior trailed behind him reluctantly. More than a few eyes followed them as they went out the door. As they stepped outside, Alrik took in the chilly evening air, his gaze traveling up and down the young warrior's solidly built frame. Contemplating the silver armring that Braoin wore just above his left bicep again, he found it was unlikely this one was Hakon's Destroyer. He asked, "You know where I'm from?"

Braoin nodded. "Dun Garm."

"My Jarl—Chief as you would call him—asked me to seek you out, as you're likely his offspring," Alrik stated. "He would like to meet you. Is that something you would do?"

Braoin's eyes narrowed. "To what end?"

"That is to be determined," he responded evasively. "You sleep on it. Maybe we can spar in the morning to gauge your skills. Then, if you're capable, you can ride back with me to Dun Garm so the Dreadlord can assess your mettle."

"And if the Dreadlord finds me less than desirable, what then?"

"You'll return here," was the answer. "Continue your life as before."

"What's in it for me?" Braoin asked. "My people need me."

"No worries—Hakon, my Jarl, will compensate you and them appropriately," Alrik responded as he jingled his purse. "Skip going to the fields or hunting in the morning, and we'll spar for a few rounds."

Braoin nodded and headed back into the hall. Alrik took a moment to gauge the lad as he stood in the doorway, curious whether he could be good enough to cause Runa to think of him as the possible Destroyer. It seemed unlikely, but best to know.

As he was about to head back to his bench for another ale, Epona strode from her stable and hailed him with, "Alrik! Good news. Per our barter, I had two of my mares in heat who found your stallion worthy of them. So let's have a meal and some ale to toast my luck that both mares will have fruitful encounters!"

"Hmmm," Alrik responded. Then, he added with a wink, "I think better luck would be that you have three chances for foals, maybe have a stallion all your own."

Epona took the warrior's arm, pulled the door to the hall closed behind them, and responded with a grin. "While that sounds interesting, I think not. As I said, I'm against seeing your kind spring as babies from between our women's legs, especially mine. While Braoin's a good lad, I'm not interested in seeing more like him around here."

Alrik shrugged with, "Your loss."

Epona smiled darkly. "Don't be so sure. Had I accepted, you might, at best, have awakened without your manly parts intact. At worst, I'd have cut your throat.

"Anyway, it was a good bargain otherwise. Hopefully, I will end up with two stallions bred from your superior Norvegr horseflesh that I can sell to Chief Faolán at Dun Uisneach. It would be good to see two Gael warriors riding against your kind, each mounted on horses we provided them with."

She rose, tossed back her cup of ale, and added, "I think I'll eat with my kind tonight."

Alrik sighed, wondering if his bargain might not have been as good an idea as he first thought. She had what she wanted, and he did not. Hopefully, his negotiations with Braoin would end on a better note.

After spending a restless and wary night in a hayloft above Epona's room, he checked his private parts when he rose the next day. After all these years, the Gaels hated them still. Then, shaking off his thoughts, he walked through the mists swirling off Loch Síleann and into the settlement.

He entered the main hall to see Hakon's bastard sitting at one of the tables with an older man. He strode toward them, took up a bowl, and poured cooked oats into it. "Good morning, Braoin."

"Alrik," came the flat response. "This is my uncle, Garyth, my mother's brother. He now looks after me, as my father passed when the Dreadlord *visited* this settlement before I was born. I thought it best for him to hear your proposal."

Alrik nodded to the man, then dug into his bowl for a while, ignoring the world. "Well met, Garyth. As I told your nephew, my Jarl—"

"The Dreadlord, who raped my sister, killed her mate, left her bereft, all to slake his desire to assert his authority over us?"

"Ahh, yes, that would be him," Alrik answered nonchalantly. "But that was many years ago. Now that the lad has grown, he must know his true father. Before taking that step, it would be good to have a no-blood duel to assess his skill level."

Garyth's eyebrows drew together as he demanded, "And if he says—"

"Uncle," Braoin injected, "I already accepted his challenge. I'll go to see what this is about. There's more here than what we see. And I'll get compensated for my time, which could benefit our settlement."

"Good lad," Alrik said with a nod. Then, after they finished breaking their fast, he added, "Come, we should retire to the yard and check your skills with a blade."

Braoin

As Braoin rose to follow the Dreadrider, Garyth held him back, saying, "Remember, your mother had our Fáidh cast a *geas* to ensure that you bring justice to her and the one who your father should have been. So may your path be true."

Braoin bowed. "I remember, uncle. I feel the weight of my *geas* every day."

Alrik

By noon, after Alrik had tested the lad and found he had reasonable blade skills—he used two medium-sized swords over one larger two-handed single broadsword—that he thought could be enhanced with more training, he decided they should return to Dun Garm together. His Jarl and Runa would determine if Braoin was who they sought, and fortunately, the lad was willing. So, as the young warrior packed, Alrik went to the stables to get the lad a mount and find his own. They'd both had a busy time at this settlement.

Seeing Epona, he said, "Horsemaster, I need to borrow a mount for the lad so we can return swiftly to Dun Garm."

"I figured as much," she answered with a dark smile. "I have a mare ready for Braoin. Needing to assure her return, I took the liberty of mating your stallion to a third mare just now. He rode her well, and the mare is pleased with herself."

"You took liberties I did not bargain for with my stallion, woman!"

Epona laughed and then, with a wink, replied, "I did, but you need my mare, do you not?"

Alrik shook his head, knowing he had negotiated poorly with this shrewd woman.

When he sighed in resignation, she advised, "I suspect you haven't bargained with a Gael woman before. You might want to think twice about that next time."

Donalt

Donalt broke his morning fast with those who rose early in the main hall. Then, he rode south, leaving the settlement at the intersection of the River Shannon and Loch Ree behind. The easiest path to the Dun Uisneach area was to follow a narrow trail south along the river so he could pick up the High King's Road to ride east and north. It took several spans for Donalt to reach *Slighe Mor*, where it intersected with the River Shannon.

As expected, he soon arrived at a small settlement he had briefly stopped at during a previous ride in this area to see if they should challenge Dun Uisneach for control of the villagers. Built along the road's north side, it was mostly a fishing village that bartered its catch to travelers on the High King's Road. They also managed the river crossing on behalf of the High King.

He pulled to a halt and dismounted since he needed to water his horse. He led the beast to a watering trough that the settlement kept filled for travelers. Then, seeing a sword that stood against its side, he glanced around and caught sight of a sturdy young man. With a smile, he reached into his pack for a few travel rations and strode toward him.

The ferry was the only way across River Shannon, regardless of the time of the year, as the flow was almost constant because of the size of Loch Ree—a massive body of water. At the moment, the lad carried no more than his spear and fishing net, as there was no demand for his muscles to pull the ferry across using the guide rope. A good-sized bucket half-filled with fish sat on the riverbank.

"Good day," Donalt called with a smile. "It looks like the fishing is going well!"

The bulky lad turned, giving the outlander a wary glance. Donalt understood his concern, especially given that he bore a great sword, whereas the lad only had a spear. The young man glanced at his blade in the distance by the watering trough, his muscles tense as if needing to be ready for action.

The Gael fisherman answered cautiously, "Aye, it is."

"I wish you good luck with your efforts, especially given your Samhain festival is near," Donalt continued, deciding to use a carrot instead of a stick to beat the Gael. "Care to share my travel rations? I've some jerked boar our cook smoked up."

The lad seemed to relax. "That would be a welcome change to a heavy fish diet. My name is Crogher. What brings you to the High King's Road?"

Donalt raised his hand and offered a hunk of boar to the lad. "I'm just passing through to the east—name's Donalt. Last night, I stopped at a settlement north of here, where the River Shannon flows out of Loch Ree. My friend, Aodhán, the stableman there, mentioned something I'd like to ask you about."

"I've met Aodhán. A man who is good with horses."

"Indeed, he is," Donalt agreed. "My stallion has bred with some of his mares. As I see you have a sword and wear a silver armring, I thought I'd ask if you were at the summer trials."

"Aye, of course," the lad answered. "I plan on winning my gold ring next year."

"Best of luck with that," Donalt offered. "Would you know of a lad in the area with white hair like ours, one who sought his warrior's plaid and armring last summer? Aodhán mentioned his lads had competed with one, but they did not know his name or which dun or settlement he hails from."

"That would be Bradaigh," Crogher answered with certainty. "I understand he is from a settlement east of here, on the north side of the road, but I don't recall him mentioning its name. He said he spends as much time as possible working at and around Dun Uisneach because they let him train their blooded warriors. He beat me in our match and won his gold. Why the interest?"

Donalt smiled at how informative and open Crogher was and answered with a shrug. "Well, you noticed he has white hair and blue eyes like ours, right? So we expect he is partly Norvegr and would like him to know he's welcome to visit our dun."

"Hmm," said Crogher, "I hope he gets to know his kin. Now, I should be fishing. Everyone expects a feast for the next two nights of our Samhain festival. With others hunting or gathering roots and vegetables in the fields, I must supply the fish!"

Donalt slipped a hand into his belt pouch and pulled out a silver piece. "Here, Crogher, you've been a great help in my task. Buy something for yourself or a lassie."

"Appreciated!" Crogher took the coin as they clasped hands in a warrior-to-warrior armlock. "I've not met many of your kind unless it was in defending what's ours. I did not expect our encounter to be so hospitable."

As they parted, Donalt mused about how easy it was to get answers with honey rather than arrogance. He wished their younger warriors, like Lunt and Lang, would learn this sooner rather than later. But, unfortunately, even Hakon was too ill-tempered at times. Shaking his head, he mounted his horse and turned for the road.

Donalt could not believe his luck in discovering so much about Hakon's bastard. That this Bradaigh had earned his gold armring meant he could be the one his Jarl sought, but he was unsure how to convince the lad to go to Dun Garm with him. He kicked his mount into a canter, expecting to reach the settlements between him and Dun Uisneach by mid-afternoon, especially given the going was more manageable on the broad, clear road. Yet, he knew he should not be overly optimistic about finding his quarry this day, as Crogher had not recalled the name of the settlement Hakon's bastard hailed from.

After two spans of riding and one unsuccessful inquiry at a small settlement, Donalt came upon a dun with ramparts topped with a wooden picket. The barrier ran parallel to the road, and two guards stood before the dun's gates bearing long pikes.

Donalt slowed his horse and jerked him to a standstill. He took in their stance and how they reacted to his arrival. Then, observing they were tense, he said, "Hail, my fellow warriors. Peace be with you."

"You're not welcome here," one of the guards stated dourly. "Why do you stop at our gates, outlander?"

"I am seeking one of us who might live among you," he answered. "A half-breed."

The guards eyed each other briefly before the same guard replied, "We do not care who or what you seek. We will have no business with you. Unless you have a writ of travel, move on."

Donalt sighed. "No, I do not have a writ. His name is Bradaigh. Have you heard of him?"

"No writ," one said, shaking his head. "A piece of advice, Norvegr. If one of Chief Fáolan's *fians* catches you without one, they will take you hostage until you can pay for passage on the High King's Road."

The other guard said nothing, just stared. Then both leaned their pikes his way as if daring him to dismount. Donalt bristled but knew he would not engage any Gaels in battle on his mission. Hakon did not need these clans launching any late-season campaign to ensure they reined him in. In a head-to-head battle, the Norvegrs often prevailed, but now was not the time to test their mettle. As further discussion was pointless, he returned his horse to the road and headed east.

Again, after another span of riding, he came upon a similar dun with similar guards. Their stance indicated any interaction would lead to the same result he'd just had at the last one. Given this, he kept his horse moving along the road. Then, knowing he was getting close to Dun Uisneach, he decided not to press his luck with no writ and headed north at the next opportunity the terrain allowed, as it was time to return to Dun Garm.

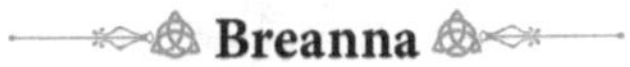

Breanna

Overwhelmed by the weight of the words, *your father is Hakon Skadi*, Breanna stumbled out the door of her mother's hut, soon to be her hut, and sagged against the steeply sloped thatch roof. She doubled over and retched, but nothing came from her empty stomach. With her dry heaves barely under her control, she shakily tried to rise as her uncle, Kyras, appeared at her side, extending a hand, offering to help her to her feet.

"Bre, are you all right?"

In the light of the firebrand he was carrying, she managed a nod, keeping her eyes downcast, unable to look up at him, fearing her shame would expose her. She wondered if he knew—if he could see she was Hakon's spawn. Ignoring his offered hand, she sputtered, "I—I'll be fine. My mother is passing."

"She is," Kyras agreed. "We will miss her."

Breanna just nodded. Yet, he must know she was a *dìolain*. A bastard!

Kyras said with concern and some sorrow, "Breanna, while your mother is passing, know we will be your family now."

"How could you?" Breanna demanded, waving him away.

Kyras appeared confused momentarily, then said, "Because, no matter what others say, you are of our clan. Never forget that."

Then he pulled her to her feet, adding, before turning away, "Your clan needs you to be strong."

"Be strong?" she whispered shakily to herself.

Despite the long day and little food, Breanna wasn't hungry. And even though her skin was grimy with sweat and dirt from her battle with Fergal earlier in the day, she could not bring herself to seek out the communal bathhouse, for this was when many washed. So, not wanting to encounter anyone else, she made for the gates of the dun. The wind had picked up, and the cold made her draw her mantle close about her neck. Few dared to travel at night, especially this close to Samhain, for one never knew what the spirits would do with those caught alone in the dark.

Breanna was too numb to be concerned about tales of ghosts and fairies. Learning that her mother would probably be dead by morning was bad enough. Yet the revelation that hers was not pure Clan Dálaigh blood, that something else flowed through her veins, had dazed her beyond feeling.

As a child, Breanna had hated Hakon Skadi and had not known why, but then, as she grew up, she'd been given a good reason due to how Hakon treated her people. All Gaels in Dun Arrogh despised the Dreadlord for his iron-fisted rule. Now she knew better, knew that a Druidic *geas* was driving her urge to destroy him. Every fiber of her brain, heart, muscle, and bone had been committed to seeing Hakon dead by Beatha's magic before she was born.

In her dreams, the man who was suddenly her father had twisted on her blades countless times, writhing in agony as she split him from chin to groin. Now, no matter what happened to the Dreadlord, whose face mirrored her own, she had to accept that.

Heading south from the dun, Breanna walked in the darkness, following a path leading into the forest that circled west and north. While the large oak trees cut the cold wind, the thought of her father's Norvegr blood running through her veins made her shiver as if she stood naked in a sleet storm.

There was little moon or starlight in the dense woods, and she ran afoul of many bushes and tree limbs. The path became very narrow as Breanna moved deeper into the woods, with vines and brush catching at her feet.

She wasn't sure how far she had gone when she stumbled and fell. A sob escaped her lips, and she began to cry. Cry because she was tainted and had been spawned by such dreadful darkness. Would she come to be like her father, cruel and hated? Would those of Dun Arrogh shun her, cast her out? Was that her destiny? The weight of her newfound lineage was an overwhelming pressure, dragging on her shoulders like a boulder. Alone and afraid, she could not hide her tears as she lay on the damp forest floor.

When she heard her cries echo back, Breanna willed herself under control. The forest around her also grew quiet, but the mimicking sound continued. It made her skin crawl, and she wondered what haunted her. The eerie cries began again, this time sounding closer and with a slightly different tone. It was a moan that grew into a steady wail, rising in pitch until it turned into an ungodly scream, filling the night air like nothing she had ever heard. As the remnants of the shrill faded, Breanna did not dare rise. Whatever had caused such a commotion was in the trees above her. Any attempt to run would be pure folly.

A chill ran down her spine as she realized it came from something outside her world, something otherworldly. She had heard stories of fairies, those called *Bean-Sidhe* and whose voices could enchant. You're the here were also *Sìthiche*, fairies who were mischievous and could be both benevolent and malevolent. Once people were under their spell, the fairies would take the poor souls off to one of the *Sidhe's* underground villages; few escaped their grasp once taken to such a place.

Breanna let a hand drift over her shoulder to the haft just below the crossguard of one of her long blades. She lay nearly motionless, hoping whatever it was would pass on.

It was not to be. A wraith wrapped in a blue-white glow appeared over Breanna, floating gently in the air, yet she did not know if she was a *Bean-Sidhe* or a *Sìthiche*. The fairie was a stunningly beautiful young woman. She had long, golden hair and sharp, elfin features, and wore a nearly transparent white gown. Surprised by the elegance of the Tuatha fairie, Breanna asked hesitantly, "What do you want?"

"*Bean-Sidhe* seek those who cry in the dark of night, especially at this time of Samhain," came the melodic reply. "Do you also cry for the dead?"

"No," Breanna said cautiously. "Is that whom you cry for?"

"Yes, I cry for the dead, our warriors, the lost souls of the *Tuatha Dé Danann*. While our battles with the Fomorians and Fir Bolg are over, those who once fought for us are those whom we must remember. Among all fairies, only the *Bean-Sidhe* can remember our dead with honor. So why do you cry if you don't cry for the dead?"

Breanna stiffened, unwilling to share her newly discovered lineage. Angry and frustrated, she spat, "Maybe I do cry for the dead. My mother is dying this very night."

Floating closer, the *Bean-Sidhe* gave her a hard, steely-eyed look. "You lie. You cry for yourself."

"How can you know that?"

"I understand crying deeply," the *Bean-Sidhe* said indignantly, floating away. "Every *Bean-Sidhe* does. We've had eons of experience and know when someone is crying because of a true loss—like when a Fomorian cuts down a brave Tuatha warrior before their time—or when it's just someone taking pity on themselves."

"I was not crying for myself," Breanna countered, her anger bringing her to her feet. Her long blades were in her hands so quickly that she hadn't realized she was drawing them. Her voice was hot as she exclaimed, "My mother is dying this night, but not before she told me my father was not who I thought he was—that he is the Dreadlord of Garm!

"You would cry if you discovered your father was an evil man—maybe a Fomorian. Someone who everybody hated, a man you hated with every muscle you possess because your mother used an *Aos Dána* to lay a *geas* of hate, of destruction, on you before you were born. It is a hatred so deep that you can feel it coursing through your veins every moment of every day. A man you wanted to kill more than anything, even if it cost you your own life!"

The *Bean-Sidhe* backed away another few yards, more from the vicious sound of Breanna's voice than because of the blades, stating, "There is something about the fury within you. You have a *geas* in you that is far more profound than what typical Gaelic Druids usually cast. Yours is the work of the Tuatha gods."

The fairie gave Breanna another long, searching look. "Yes, I see the Dreadlord in your face. He's an enemy, an enemy who deals with other gods, gods not of this land. Gods which the Tuatha consider rivals."

"You know of him?"

"The *Bean-Sidhe* know many things about the world of man," the fairie flatly stated as she drifted closer, her eyes capturing Breanna's gaze more deeply. Then, after a moment, she nodded as if having made a decision. "You will be destined to seek what our gods lay before you, something greater than just a Druid's *geas*. As you described, I feel that otherworld *touch* flowing through your veins, not just your father's. Because of this, there is something more to you, something fated that I must not interfere with. I will not, cannot, enchant you and take you under my mound. Instead, I will guide you to a Grove where others of my kind dare not go. You will find one of your magic workers who can help you fulfill your *geas* there."

"Somewhere safe?"

"Yes, it is a Druid's place," the fairie informed her with a sigh as if the whole conversation had put her out. "But you must not cry again. The time of Samhain brings many of my kind into the woods. Other *Sidhe* might not be as taken with you as I am, may not see our Tuatha gods touch upon you."

Breanna could only nod warily, wondering why she had left the safety of Dun Arrogh. Sheathing her blades, she followed the *Bean-Sidhe* through the forest with some hesitation, its glowing form drawing her through the darkness. The trail's overgrowth made any progress an effort, as it was little more than a deer run, and Breanna soon doubted the *Bean-Sidhe* had spoken honestly. Maybe she had been enchanted and was being led to an underground *Bean-Sidhe* mound. At that thought, she stumbled as she struggled through the woods. Frustration flared within, and she nearly broke down and cried out, *enough!* Then her pride asserted itself, and she surged onward.

The fairie seemed slightly annoyed that her agreement to help was costing her so much time. Breanna considered using her long blades to cut a path, but thought better of it. Her *Bean-Sidhe* guide might not approve of a stranger going about hacking up a sacred *Sidhe* forest.

Breanna lost sight of her fairie guide, and as she pushed through some thick brush to follow, she stumbled into a small clearing. At the center stood a massive oak with a trunk wider than Breanna's height. The boughs were thick enough to be trees, their considerable lengths forming a complete canopy over the bare earth where the forest did not infringe on the Druid's place of magic.

A stone-ringed fire burned before the ancient oak, and seated beside it was an old Druid dressed in a tattered blue and red mantle. The colors signified she held the title of Fáidh, the Seer branch of the *Aos Dána*. Though the blaze momentarily blinded her, Breanna could make out few details beyond what she knew from their Bard's teachings.

"Welcome to my *fidh*," said the Druid without turning her gaze away from her stone-ringed fire, gesturing broadly around her. "This is a sacred grove not found by many."

"Forgive my intrusion, ancient one," Breanna said as she started to back away, now able to see more clearly. "A *Bean-Sidhe* led me here, saying it would be safe. I had been wandering, and then—"

"One of the *Bean-Sidhe* had you in her grasp and let you go?" the Druid questioned sharply, turning a blind, withered eye toward Breanna. "Well, well, a *Sidhe* enchanted by a Gael warrior. Or her story. No one ever knew that to happen with a fairie."

"It was more likely my story. The *Bean-Sidhe* said I was fated and she should not interfere."

As the Fáidh locked a one-eyed gaze on her, Breanna noted a milky film covering the Druid's other iris, and she knew the *sight* had taken hold of her. Then the old crone cackled and surprised her by commenting, "You are Morna's daughter, Breanna, of the Clan Dálaigh. And now, I understand, Eoin Mac Cairbre's Red Branch Champion. Come, sit beside me, share my fire. There are matters we must discuss. The *Bean-Sidhe* was correct in her assessment of you."

Breanna's legs obeyed even though her mind said to run.

"I am Beatha," the Druid said softly. "One-time Fáidh of your dun."

"You!" Breanna spat and started to rise. "The one who cast this *geas* on me!"

"Sit," Beatha commanded softly, her gravelly voice as imposing as the ancient oak tree behind her. "Your mother cast your destiny, and the gods likely had a hand in it, too. I was just an instrument."

Breanna sagged back to the ground. "So you say."

"Aye, that I do."

"The others speak of you as the hermit," Breanna said. Then, warming herself by the fire—she hadn't realized how cold she was—she added almost absently, "Since Aodhfin is still just an apprentice Seer, we have no real Fáidh in the dun now. Few think much of his abilities."

A smile came to Beatha's weathered face, but it was gone as quickly as it had come. Silence, save for the crackling fire, fell over them for a time. Breanna dared not disturb the Druid, noting that the *sight* had taken hold of her. Then Beatha said quietly, "May Lugh watch over your mother tonight. As for you, a new life starts when the sun rises."

"That I know all too well," Breanna grumbled. "As do you, as you cast the *geas*."

Beatha studied her visitor, her chalky iris rolling up with the *sight* again. "You have no idea how difficult the task ahead will be. Not yet, anyway."

"The task ahead. And what is this task?"

"Have you ever heard of the Book of Danu, the *Leabhar Námhaid Steach*?" the Druid asked, ignoring Breanna's question, her voice now more than a whisper. Then, when there was no response, Beatha drew her rag of a shawl back over her shoulders and said, "I suspected not—few outside our kind have. It's also been called the Book of Invasions. Some say it was written by the Mother Goddess Danu and gifted to her *Tuatha Dé Danann* upon their arrival in Erin.

"Others say it is a Fomorian thing. Either way, few know of the many treasures which the Tuatha possessed. Long ago, an ancient Druid discovered a *Sidhe* path to one of their sacred islands, Falias, where he laid eyes on the *Leabhar Námhaid Steach*. Someday, we will write down the words Amergin passed on to us from the great tome. It will ensure that no more historical details will fade through the generations."

Breanna sucked in a breath of amazement. "He found the seat of the Tuatha gods?"

"Some call it that," the *Aos Dána* confirmed. "As I said, Amergin discovered the Book of Invasions in their halls. Being a fairie place, he could read the strange writing despite only knowing the Druid language of Ogham. The book not only recounts the history of the *Tuatha Dé Danann* and their conquests over the Fomorians and the Fir Bolg but also the future. And because their shadowlands mirror our own, that includes our future. Through his quick wit, Amergin escaped from Falias—the fairie folk rarely let those of our world leave once we've found one of their places of magic. Nonetheless, Amergin was able to pass his knowledge on to his followers. Since then, pieces of the book, *Leabhar Námhaid Steach*, have been handed down from Fáidh to Fáidh."

"And what does this book tell us will happen?" Breanna questioned, her interest stirring.

"Much, and not all of it good," Beatha replied as she poked at her fire to get it blazing again. "About the coming of the Dreadlord, those with the *sight* have known of this for some time. He is one of many to come from beyond the Ninth Wave and invade the land of Erin."

"You all knew this would happen?" Breanna asked incredulously.

"Yes, but not when, who, or how," she answered. Then, after a pause, she added, "*Leabhar Námhaid Steach* foretells that Erin's Hero will rise again and again if we remain strong in our worship of the Tuatha gods. Is that clear?"

Breanna nodded, saying nothing.

"Good," Beatha continued as if talking to a child. "Ćroí Dàn chooses Erin's Hero. I believe you already know she is also called the Heart of Destiny. Each such hero will lead us to face that given wave of invaders. You are one of those of whom I speak."

"Me? A hero?" Breanna protested and shook her head. "Erin's Hero? I can hardly believe that."

"It does not matter what you believe," Beatha said dryly. "The gods have willed this. It is your destiny to end the Dreadlord's reign of terror. The *geas* your mother laid upon you before your birth will blossom tomorrow. It's up to you what that flower produces."

"You don't understand," Breanna protested as she rose again. "He's my father!"

"I know this," the Druid said quietly. Then she demanded, "Sit! There is more to my story and your story."

Feeling small, Breanna did as Beatha ordered, a colossal sigh exploding from her lungs as the weight of what Beatha had said dawned on her. First, according to her mother, the Dreadlord was her father. Next, the Druid had called her a hero. Not just any hero. Erin's Hero! If you counted Lugh, only five were claimed by the Heart of Destiny.

"Please, I don't want to hear it," Breanna begged. "How can you ask me to kill my father? I hate him, I surely do, and I want to see him dead. Yesterday, I would have gladly stuck my blades through his belly. Yet, I don't know if I can be the one."

"Be quiet and listen," Beatha commanded. "All I know is that the gods have made it your destiny to stop him, though no one can say how you will accomplish it. Ending the Dreadlord's reign will pose one of the greatest challenges, for he is a mighty opponent. Left unchecked, he would one day rule a greater part of this land and do so with the iron fist we know all too well at the intersection of these three provinces. When others in his homeland follow him to our land, we will be worse off, likely ruled by the Norvegrs. Still, there may be some tools that will help you in this task."

"Tools to help me kill my father," Breanna mumbled woodenly.

"Yes, Bre, if you insist, tools to help you kill your father," Beatha said in a tone that showed how thin her patience was becoming. "There is more to Amergin's story. He found other treasures in Falias, such as Nuada's magic hand and a sword now wielded by the Sea God called Answerer. Then, there was Lugh's great spear and sword. He even peered into the Stone of Destiny, *Lia Dàn*, and beheld our emerald isle from coast to coast."

"You mean he went to *Tír na nÓg*? The place where Niamh lured Oisín into the fairie lands?"

Beatha said, "That is a fairie tale our Filídh Bards spin to keep the curious from being where they shouldn't be. Yet, our Bards do tell true stories about the wonders Amergin beheld.

"They say or sing nothing of another wonder, one which we Fáidh have kept silent about, have kept to ourselves. For with its magic, one might be able to rule our land."

"With fairie magic?" Breanna asked doubtfully.

"No, with the magic of the Tuatha gods," the Druid corrected. "The tale we've passed down amongst our kind since Amergin's death speaks of a set of long blades made of oak and diamonds called *Lann Dàn*, the Blades of Destiny. While shaped much like your own long blades, these are magic-wrought weapons said to enable a warrior to conquer enemies who wield magic against them.

"Legend has it that the Dark Goddess traveled to the Ice Island north and west of Erin, summoning two massive, elongated diamonds from deep in the heart of a volcano's caldera on its southern coast. Badb Catha and the smith god, Goibhniu, worked together to craft the large gems into magic-bearing long blades."

The notion of possessing an all-powerful weapon held a certain allure that the warrior part of Breanna could not resist, especially since they were long blades like her own. She asked excitedly, "Did Amergin say how these long blades worked their magic?"

Beatha shrugged. "We don't know how they aid their wielder. The story is fading, but it's certainly related to magic. Nonetheless, Amergin managed to take these long blades with him when he escaped the grasp of the *Tuatha Dé Danann*. He quickly hid them, thinking our gods would pursue him to reclaim their treasure. He left vague directions to his apprentice, indicating their location, and commanded that we should seek out *Lann Dàn* and call on their mighty magic if the need arose one day.

Unfortunately, Amergin died at the hands of the Tuatha without revealing his hiding place."

"And you want me to find them and use their magic to kill my father," Breanna whispered.

"Yes," confirmed the Druid, her one-eyed gaze holding Breanna's lock to her own. "Now listen closely. Amergin's directions have not survived in full. We know it is a place that lies both north and south of Black Pig's Dike, where the sun shines only after reaching its zenith. From this place flows a river that feeds the land. Within this place, one can find *Lann Dàn*. Look closely, for many rocks hide the fairie's treasure."

Intrigued, Breanna asked, "And do you know this place?"

"Some of us have tried to solve the mystery," Beatha replied. "None have succeeded. We believe Amergin hid the blades in a cave on the west side of Cuilcagh Mountain. Rivulets from the cave feed the Shannon, and the river feeds this land. Lean forward so I can make sure you can recall the words as I have given them."

Breanna nodded, trying to remember the area, as she slipped from the log and onto one knee. Beatha stood and moved to place a hand on her forehead. When they were younger, Breanna, Eoin, and Fergal had tried to follow the Shannon to its source. They had only reached Loch Aillionn, but the Cuilcagh Mountains, the source of the Shannon, had not been much farther beyond the lake. She had seen the tallest mountain, Cuilcagh itself, in the distance. And now the Druid was saying she must seek its heights.

Beatha closed her eyes and murmured a chant, and then Breanna jerked her head back as if a tiny bolt of lightning had struck her. The Druid said, "I have sent your request."

As she rose face to face with the Seer, Breanna demanded, "So, it's up to me?"

"Yes," the old Druid replied. "It's up to you. Samhain will be upon us at sunset tomorrow. That is the time to ask for help. If it is the gods' will, *Lann Dàn* shall be yours."

"And how do I get the gods to answer my call?"

Beatha looked perplexed momentarily, saying, "The gods always answer my call, in one way or another, whenever I seek it. Sometimes, they only speak to me through their *sight*. Yet, tonight, they are speaking loudly and clearly. No one knows how they hear, but they do. You know how to seize the *void*, yes?"

"Not reliably," Breanna answered sourly. "The *urghabháil an neamhní* can be elusive."

Beatha nodded. "I sensed that you have it in you, more strongly than you know. It takes practice. You should seize it in calm moments, not just when you're in a battle. Let it guide your mind, not just your weapons. Our Lawgivers, Seers, Bards, and Healers have individual uses for the *void* or the *sight*. To the *Aos Dána*, the *urghabháil an neamhní* and the Elements are our power source. Yet, we are not teaching our warriors how to seize the *void* as we have in the past. Your grandmother could command it better than most. It can also be your source of power, help you survive your *geas*, one that will lead you to end the Dreadlord."

"I will need the *void* to call the gods, yes?" Breanna asked.

"Certainly. It would be good to practice tomorrow before the sun sets. But, as a test, try it now to ensure you can find the directions I implanted in your mind."

Breanna closed her eyes and tried to still her thoughts. At first, it was a challenge with the chaotic images from the past day's events swirling through her, but then she felt a tingling on her forehead where Beatha had touched her, and the words sprang forth in her mind. She repeated them to the Fáidh and then added in wonder, "I did it. I heard the directions in my head, which were in your voice."

Beatha nodded with a smile. "You did. Now, be here when the moon is high tomorrow night and call upon our gods to aid you in your quest. I'll be here and light a fire so you can find this Druid's Grove."

Dawn's first light was touching the horizon when Breanna Ban Morna returned to Dun Arrogh. The sky had a dark purple hue, something Breanna thought fitting, as it matched her somber mood. She knew her mother had passed on, and she should be helping her sisters prepare her body for the passage rite this evening. While she tried to connect with her siblings, they had always kept a distance, not just because they were a few years older. Yet, Breanna did not want to dwell on that now. Their gods had cast her into her new destiny. It seemed fitting that her mother had died on the eve of Samhain, and Breanna hoped her spirit—her *anam*—now wandered with her father's.

Breanna quickly corrected that thought, knowing her mother would find Nevan, not the one who had spawned her. Maybe the pair could once more find life together when the *Cycle of Time* turned somewhere not plagued by the Dreadlord, her birth father. She did not want to think about being commanded by the Fáidh and, ultimately, Danu to kill Hakon Skadi. Yet, in her heart, she knew she would defend her family, her dun, and her clans if her father attacked. Seeking him out to destroy him was something she had not yet come to accept.

Vowing not to tell anyone about her newly discovered lineage, Breanna entered Dun Arrogh with some trepidation. She hoped few were about to test her resolve. Unfortunately, even though she was starving, it was too early for the morning meal—Calla was just now stoking up the hearth, getting the peat burning once more in the dun's main stone oven to cook breakfast. So Breanna went to the bathhouse since there was little to be done about it until Calla had something to feed her. One thing she didn't need was for her sisters to ride her about showing up to help prepare their mother's body for burial in such a dirty and smelly state.

Breanna sighed with relief that the communal bathing and clothing-wash hut was still empty. She was pleased that whoever had the morning bathhouse preparation duties had already set buckets of clean water near the peat fire that burned in the hearth at the back corner of the room. Breanna set her long blades aside against the wall with a groan over her sore muscles. Then, she stripped off her harness, cloak, tunic, and boots. Next came the belt holding her dagger sheath, then leggings. Finally, she approached a large bathing tub and placed an empty warming bucket under a drain at the bottom edge to draw out any settled dirt and silt, followed by another one before she replaced the plug.

After pouring out the dirty water through a stone drain, she grabbed a bucket of warm water in each hand and brought them to the big tub to refill it. When she found the water was still cool from sitting overnight, she added both buckets of warm water. Refilling them, she set them by the fire and slipped into the still-chilly tub. She used a cleaning rag and soap to scrub herself. It took two dips to feel somewhat human again and then another two to wash her hair. After wringing it out, she brought her beaded thong from her neck and tied her wet hair into a ponytail.

The door opened, and her Aunt Lissa stepped into the bath hut. Each was equally surprised to see the other.

Lissa said, "Oh, my dear, I'm sorry your mother has passed. You will always be one of ours. You're clan to us."

Breanna nodded but said nothing as Lissa prepared a tub for herself. Lissa eventually settled into the water and scrubbed herself down. Breanna was unsure what to say to her aunt. She no longer felt like one of their clan and was more self-conscious of her outlander appearance than ever before.

Lissa said, "Toal cannot say enough good things about you, you know?"

Breanna knew she had to answer, saying, "He's a good lad."

"I am relieved he has you to protect him," Lissa continued.

"I will always do my best," was the response as Breanna climbed from her tub and took the time to scrub her tunic and leggings. Once she had wrung them out, she threw on her cloak and pulled on her soft leather thongs, wrapping their leather straps up to her knees.

Breanna knew Lissa was watching her as she soaped herself and rinsed several times. Her aunt, who was Dun Arrogh's Master Weaver and Dyer, said when she emerged, "I know Kyras didn't have much time for you while you grew up, but he does love you in his gruff way. As do I. Hmmm—poorly said, for I'm anything but gruff."

"I understand, Auntie," Breanna said, taking up her wet clothes and weapons as she turned uncomfortably toward the door, not wanting to let anyone get close to her lest they discover her real father's name. "I must help my sisters prepare for my mother's ceremony tonight."

"Of course, as a young lady should."

Yet Breanna could not help but wonder what her aunt and uncle honestly thought of her as she marched to her hut. How could they not know?

She found Ronat and Orla already tending to her mother's body, readying it for burial. Both were teary-eyed, and Breanna said little to them as she put on clean clothes and hung the wet ones to dry. Despite the cold reception her sisters gave her, she spent a few moments in silence with them. To Breanna's relief, neither asked about their mother's last words. Still, she wondered if they were being short with her because Morna had delivered no final message for them.

Only then did she realize she had always held a special place in her mother's heart, more so than Ronat and Orla. Her mother's protective shield had kept the talk between her sisters suppressed all these years.

Orla broke the silence first, declaring, "We need to decide what things our mother would want to carry her *anam* into the afterlife, hopefully, to find *our* father."

Breanna felt the dig but did not respond, suggesting, "The ivory sewing needle he gave her, for sure."

Ronat added, "Of course, she sewed *our* father's garments and skin with it after he battled. Something she couldn't do with his head once Hakon relieved him of it."

Breanna's jaw dropped as Orla piled on, "Her silver comb would be good. She always had such fine Gaelic red hair."

"Unlike Father's and ours," Ronat said icily.

Breanna knew they suspected what Morna would not confirm, but neither would have dared to hint at it in such an awful way when their mother was alive. If they had muttered those thoughts to each other, others in the dun must have done the same.

Breanna's brave front faltered momentarily, making her wonder what the elders would say if they discovered the truth. She would probably be turned out of the dun once word got out she was Hakon's *dìolain*. She would be an outcast!

Only her outrage at her naivety, outrage over being so blind as not to see where the rumors were leading, kept her emotions from breaking through. She was a warrior, Dun Arrogh's Red Branch Champion, and would not let any allegations break her. One day, she would prove them all wrong, and that day would be when she killed her father—killed the Dreadlord!

Breanna seethed, "On this day, you would dig so deep, both of whom left your mother and me to our plight and escaped the horrors of the Dreadlord, leaving us behind to be safe with your mates."

Before the silence between the sisters became even more uncomfortable, Ulicia came by their hut to assist in adorning Morna's corpse with herbs that would aid her passing to the spirit world. The Druid eyed Breanna critically for a moment, and from that look, Breanna thought Ulicia would ask about her lineage, but then the older woman moved on to tend to Morna's body. Their uncle and aunt also came by to offer their help, with Lissa carrying a tray of honey cakes. As they all sat in the tight quarters of the small hut, hungry beyond belief, Breanna devoured the cakes all by herself, leaving none for her hateful sisters.

Seeing the women still tending to their duties, the burly smith excused himself and went off to make sure the mound was ready for the burial of his brother's mate while Lissa helped the Druid dress the corpse. Morna had asked to be placed next to her mate's body in their Grove of Remembrance, something they all had expected, especially given she had never really gotten over losing Nevan. Within a span of time, her daughters had gathered the personal belongings they knew their mother would have wanted at her side in her burial mound. It was mostly small things Nevan had given her when they had first married.

"There," Orla said as she pinned a silver brooch on her mother's chest.

"Yes, I think the gods are ready to receive her," Lissa confirmed. "You did her up proudly."

Ronat started to cry. It was a performative moment Breanna had witnessed before; her sister had always been soft. Breanna turned away, saying, "Then we've nothing more to do than wait for sunset. I need to get something to eat and ask Eoin to join us tonight."

Eoin had never been close to anyone in her family except her mother and herself, so she hesitated to see if they would protest. But Orla just nodded as she moved to comfort Ronat. Surprised, Breanna could only shrug before stepping from the hut. She had been hoping to get into an argument, which would have helped her vent some anger.

Finding herself thwarted, Breanna understood it would not be the last time that she wished her mother had taken the awful knowledge about who her birth father was to her grave, and since she had not seen it coming, she was again furious with herself.

Despite consuming her aunt's honey cakes, Breanna knew she had to eat something more substantial. She met a few cousins in the main hall, and they paused long enough to wish her mother's *anam* a good journey. But Breanna had little to say in acknowledging the condolences, just giving them a nod of thanks.

After filling her stomach with some of Calla's deer stew and bread from the morning's bake, drowsiness swept over her. Given she had not slept at all last night, she trudged back to what was now her hut. Her sisters had left, probably to seek out the baths and breakfast as she had. Breanna sank onto her bed. Her gaze found her mother's still form, and her strength failed her as she rolled into a ball and drifted off to sleep.

Breanna stirred from her slumber a few spans later as Orla and Ronat returned to their mother's side. She rubbed her bleary eyes and sat up with a heavy sigh. It was time to get moving. After lacing on her vambraces, she grabbed her long blades, telling her sisters, "I need to find Eoin to let him know he's welcome tonight."

Breanna found none of her fellow warriors at the dun, so she went to her uncle Kyras. It turned out that Eoin and Fergal had gone to train with the others, hoping to take advantage of the good weather before it turned. Breanna, unsure of how long she'd slept, wondered if their band might have already finished their workout. If so, she might have to rely on working through her blade forms by herself instead of sparring with someone.

Breanna quickly marched forward to work off some anger. As she crossed the central yard of the dun, several more cousins stopped her so they could express their sorrow that one of their own had passed. Breanna managed to nod at each of them and kept walking, wondering what they honestly thought of her as she set out for the Red Branch's Grove of Instruction.

Then, she was away from those she knew as fellow clan for a moment and was relieved to be alone. A blustery wind buffeted her as she walked, and she felt thankful not to be on edge about letting her mother's secret—which was now hers—slip, leaving behind cousins and clan asking how she was coping. Coping! She was doing anything but that! She was a bastard, and positive they had all whispered the same thing Orla and Ronat had recently insinuated to her face! Her sisters ensured she would now be self-conscious about her appearance when she faced those who lived within Dun Arrogh.

Breanna's expression was grim as she tried to act as if nothing had changed, as if her blood was rooted in the lineage of the Clan Dálaigh as she had always thought. But how she would be able to face Eoin was another matter. Could she keep her secret from him, or would he be able to read it on her face? And what would he think about her being the Dreadlord's daughter? Would he understand? After all, Eoin was her closest companion, and she knew he loved her. Her *geas* had always made her keep him at a distance, but she knew they could share more without that barrier. Then she wondered how that could be, especially when he was a Prince of the Blood, and she a tainted half-breed.

Yet, that thought buoyed her confidence; he would understand, as he always had. Maybe even become an ally in her quest. Then she wondered whether he might no longer trust her or want her to be his Champion. After all, she was tainted with Hakon Skadi's hateful blood. His cousin Fergal would hold it against her, using her tainted lineage to sow seeds of distrust.

"If so, my quest is just something I'll have to do alone," she muttered aloud. A moment later, she met Toal and the others. As Eoin and Fergal were absent from the band, she demanded sharply, "My Chief, where is he?"

"He and Fergal decided to clean up in the stream instead of using the bathhouse," Toal answered. He hesitated before adding, "Sorry about your mother's passing, Bre. Our family will miss her. If I can do anything for you, you will let me know, right?"

Others nodded in agreement and offered their condolences. Then, given that Toal needed some acknowledgment from his iron-willed cousin, Breanna pulled him into a hug, something she rarely did. He stiffened for a moment and then hugged her back. Breanna said, "I will. You've always been my favorite of our clan. Thanks for those words."

Untangling herself from her cousin, she added, "I need to let Eoin know he's welcome at the burial tonight. I'll see you back at the fort."

As her band moved on, heading for Dun Arrogh, Breanna altered her course slightly, angling somewhat on a path where she knew Eoin and Fergal would be. They often used that stream to clean up in its chilly waters. A little less on edge due to her cousin's heartfelt offer, Breanna crossed the south end of their Grove of Instruction and started up the last significant hill before she could see the narrow creek. Yet when she crested the top, what she saw stopped her dead still.

In the vale below, two of the most sizable white-haired Dreadriders Breanna had ever seen were locked in combat with two Gael warriors. One thing was clear—they were defensive against her father's Dreadriders. And they could be none other than Eoin and Fergal!

Lunt

It was well after the sun passed its zenith in a sky partly filled with fast-moving fluffy clouds when Lunt commanded they stop for their midday meal despite Lang's urge to push on. His brother had demanded they find a dun before nightfall and was ready to eat on horseback to accomplish his quest. Lunt laughed, scolding him for his fear of the Gaelic fairies, and picked a small valley with a stream feeding the Shannon estuary they had followed earlier.

Lunt had not traveled so far north and east for several years—mainly because Hakon usually sent older Dreadriders to collect his annual tribute—so it was hard to remember all of the settlements in the area. The dun that the old man had referred to was not one they remembered clearly, given the years since they'd been in this area. It was mainly because of the older man's directions that Lunt knew they didn't have to push themselves.

Their cook had put together some travel rations of smoked salmon and salted boar for when they couldn't find a dun to sate their stomachs. They could have hunted for their meals when they had such leisure, but neither wanted to spend the time, as the faster their search was over, the sooner they could head back to Dun Garm. Someone was always there to fill their ale skins.

The pair tied their reins to a birch tree and sat quietly in the lush grass, enjoying the rare sunshine while they ate and drank the cool water. Afterward, they returned to the nearby stream to wash up and water their warhorses.

It was there they spied two Gael warriors a few hundred yards downstream. The Dreadrider brothers mounted quickly and were pounding through the shallow water at a full charge before their targets even looked up. By the time they had closed on them, both had their cloaks thrown back, and they'd drawn their swords. Lunt and Lang reined in their mounts a few yards short of the two redheaded warriors, with Lunt stating, "I would have words with you instead of battling."

"We have no words for Hakon's Dreadriders," the taller Gael warrior replied.

Lunt dismounted with a swagger. He was confident they would be victorious in any fight with such locals and motioned for Lang to follow suit. "Making words is easier than fighting. We're interested in talking with a young warrior of the bloodline of Conal Cearnach, who was said to be collecting warriors for his cause. Someone about your age, I suspect. Someone with the gold Celtic Knot armrings—blooded warriors. I understand there is an arm of that clan at Dun Arrogh, along with, maybe, a fair-haired warrior?"

The two Gaels glanced at each other, their expressions nearly revealing their surprise. Then, finally, the shorter of the two shook his head. "Like my cousin told you, we have nothing to share with the Dreadlord's dogs."

Lang launched himself at the one who had insulted them, and a battle erupted.

Breanna

Breanna bolted toward the fighters, pulling her long blades from the sheaths over her shoulders. She saw one of the Red

Branch warriors start to go down, a sword stroke passing just over his head, but the move turned into a shoulder roll, and he was suddenly out of range. Recognizing the maneuver, Breanna knew that it was Fergal Mac Conall. Shifting her focus to the other, she saw Eoin Mac Cairbre's checkered black and white cloak now clearly visible. By the stars! Her Chief was engaged in single combat without his Champion!

Iron clashing rang through the vale as the four warriors danced among each other's blades. Eoin got a slice in on his opponent's leg, but it cost him a glancing gash on the head as they separated.

Breanna pushed herself to run faster. As she surged forward, her legs flying over the terrain, Fergal barely blocked a sword stroke that nicked his upper left arm. The Dreadrider slipped under his defense and opened a wound below his hip when the Norvegr deflected his counter. As Fergal staggered back, Hakon's dog followed with a thrust that caught the Red Branch warrior high in the right shoulder. With his sword arm now useless and unable to dance clear of his attacker, Fergal stood defiantly as his opponent swept his sword back as if prepared to take the Gael's head off with one blow.

Breanna needed a spear to span the distance between her and the Dreadrider to save Fergal, yet she did not have that option. She did what an old warrior from Ulaida had once told her was the worst maneuver one could make when fighting with her favorite weapons—she decided to use one of her blades as a spear. Unfortunately, not only were they poorly balanced for throwing, but Breanna would be nearly defenseless if her aim was off, especially with only a single long blade to counter a Dreadrider's sword.

She gave herself a fraction of a moment to reach for the *void*. Then, feeling time slow, her eyes sharpened with focus as she saw the trajectory, and she let the power from the Tuatha realm flow into her veins, infusing her muscles. The weapon sailed clear of her hand and toward its target. When, in what should have been an improbable fling at best, her long blade found its mark, the white-haired warrior threatening Fergal went down screaming in pain, the blade buried high in his right thigh.

Breanna was on him a moment later, jerking her blade free before he knew she was there. As the Dreadrider barely managed to choke back a second scream and groaned loudly between clenched teeth, he scrambled up on his good leg.

Breanna grinned at his stunned expression. She took advantage of that moment, and it almost cost him his life as she lashed a blade across his left shoulder. Still, the wound did not affect his sword arm, and he countered with a powerful overhand strike. It was Breanna's turn to grunt as his sword met her crossed blades, her muscles tightening to hold off the blow.

Unable to withstand his strength, she swept the other's blade away from her and came around with her hafts to crack him in the ribs, using the same move that had taken down Fergal during their challenge. The Dreadrider gave a deep grunt as he took a stumbling step away, then turned to face her again, standing between her and Eoin. Although he had a limp, the Dreadrider was still free to attack Eoin as he raised his sword to the guard position.

Her Chief, the man she had sworn to protect, was also limping badly, and a scarlet stream was flowing from a gash over his left eye. She could see that the blood was impairing his vision, and Eoin was on the defensive. His attacker was pressing in for the kill. Seeing the Dreadrider's next strike in her mind, she leaped over his downward-slicing blade, even as he started the motion. The ground rushed up to meet her as she flowed into a somersault. It brought her up behind her opponent; she swept his legs from beneath him with a backswing of her hafts. He went down with a thud, and Breanna laughed triumphantly as the air exploded from his lungs. As he lay there gasping for breath, Breanna sprang toward the other Norvegr.

"Lunt, behind you!" the downed warrior managed to gasp.

The other Dreadrider, who had backed Eoin into the stream, was forced to turn away before he could try to strike again. Growling at the annoyance, he attempted to brush Breanna aside with a wide slice of his sword. It was a significant miscalculation. She dropped below the flashing piece of steel, raking his hip just beneath his leather belt with one of her blades as she passed to get in front of Eoin. When Lunt turned to face her, she used her other blade to jab his thigh just beneath a wound Eoin had made previously.

Lunt cursed as he let his sword sweep back, but the move was clumsy, and Breanna was too quick for him, dancing clear by jumping into the stream. He planted his feet firmly and took a big overhand stroke. Still holding the *void*, Breanna foresaw his thought and feinted with a crossed-knife block. Yet before their iron blades clashed, she spun to her left, letting the powerful motion of his muscles carry the Dreadrider into the stream. He nearly stumbled and fell as she climbed from the water, drawing him after her.

Enraged, Lunt stormed out of the stream, letting his blade swing straight for her neck. Having anticipated him again, Breanna laughed and ducked to the left. Returning to a solid stance, she drove one of her blades into his groin. As Lunt doubled over, she drew her other blade across the hand holding his sword. He dropped the weapon as if it were a red-hot brand and instinctively put his good hand on her shoulder to steady himself.

Lunt examined Breanna's eyes and hissed, "Destroyer. My Jarl sent us for you. There is no mistaking he spawned you, given the death you hold in your eyes—his eyes."

Breanna gave him a cold and calm gaze.

"If you wore armor and helm," he said, "I would say you are one of Odin's Valkyries, death-maidens who ride winged horses and choose which warriors live or die in battle. Is that you? Will you carry me to the halls of Valhalla when you take my life?"

"No, Dreadrider," Breanna sneered. "I'll ensure one of the Mórrigan's crows eats your eyes out before you die."

Lunt whispered, "Then you're just Hakon's bastard Destroyer, just a woman and barely at that?"

"Never been called a *Sgriosadair* before," Breanna darkly replied as she jerked her blade free, causing him to hiss in pain. "Being a girl, I am no less capable and have bested you both!"

"Bre, behind you," Eoin warned Breanna as he limped from the stream and tried to wipe the blood from his eyes again. She let Lunt sink to his knees and spun to face the other Dreaderrider again. He was nearly upon her.

She went for his other shoulder this time, sensing the man's ego in the *void* would not let him think the opening she presented was a trap. Breanna spun to her left at the last moment and ducked enough for his outstretched blade to cut the air just above her head. As his sword arm carried itself over her by his inertia, she laughed again and rammed one of her blades into his armpit.

The white-haired man screamed and pulled himself free, dropping his sword and staggering in a circle, trying to keep his feet under him. With a grunt, he bent to grab his sword with his other hand and backed away from his nimble opponent.

Breanna circled him as he stumbled toward his horse and clutched the reins, her blades twirling as a threat. Lunt, leaning on his sword, managed to half-crawl, half-drag himself out of the lurching blade reach of Eoin Mac Cairbre and to his brother's side, who struggled to stand. She also took in her Chief as he sank to his knees, bleeding before her. Fergal crawled to his side.

"Bre, kill them!"

Breanna moved to stand between Hakon's dogs and her charges, breathing steadily, eyes narrowed as she stared them down. She had a decision to make. Fight the Norvegrs, kill them, or save her Chief by ensuring he doesn't bleed out.

Lunt croaked, "Lang, get me on my horse before she decides to kill us."

Lang, who still had one good leg, managed to get his brother mounted despite his nearly useless arms before throwing himself on his warhorse, knowing the white-haired warrior woman was at his back. Breanna stood motionless, save for continuing to rotate her blades with meaning as she let the *void* dissolve. Then, giving them a dark smile, she watched them flee.

Eoin got a knee beneath himself and cried, "Bre, stop them!"

She made no move to follow the command and merely watched the pair ride off, both barely able to stay on their mounts. Then she turned to check on Eoin, saying confidently, "I am your Champion. You take priority, and I cannot risk you bleeding out. They won't be back."

"They may not, but Hakon will," Eoin said stiffly. "They came seeking a young warrior from Clan Mórhda. Someone about my age."

"How did they know part of your clan was in this area?" Breanna demanded.

Eoin countered, "A more important question is *why* were they searching for one of the Clan Mórhda?"

"The Red Branch?"

"I think so," Eoin agreed, nodding as Breanna tore two strips from her linen undertunic, the smaller one to bind up the gash on his head and the larger for the nasty slice on his left thigh. Her Chief added, "That means the Dreadlord himself might know about us. And if he doesn't, he soon will."

"I need to patch up Fergal as well," Breanna said urgently. "Then we need to get you two to Dun Arrogh."

Moving to Eoin's cousin, she tore strips from his tunic to tie off his wounds. She ignored Fergal's grimace as she bound up the various slices the Dreadriders had inflicted and got him to his feet.

Fergal told Breanna, "Nice move back there when you went low and took that Dreadrider in the groin. Wish I had thought of it."

Breanna pretended to ignore the compliment. "Can you walk?"

"It's not that bad," Fergal replied, but he groaned with each step.

Lunt

The brothers didn't remain mounted farther than the next valley before stopping to tend to their wounds. Lunt quickly checked his private parts, for that was where Hakon's bastard warrior had injured him most gravely. He half-expected to see his manhood split in two or have his jewels spill into his hands. That he might bleed to death was of little concern by comparison.

An explosive sigh of relief washed over him when he saw that he was whole where it counted; the blade had entered at an angle, just missing anything vital, and dug into the flesh toward his left hip. Blood ran from the gash, but not as freely as he had anticipated. Still, wrapping the area proved a challenge. After that, he set to binding up his other wounds. Once finished, he turned to find his brother struggling to stem the blood flow from the wound beneath his right armpit. With Lang's injuries making his arms useless, Lunt had to help him.

As he worked, Lunt asked, "Did you see her eyes?"

"Yes, as well as her face," Lang answered.

Lunt grimaced, saying, "She fights like one of Odin's Valkyries. She always seemed to know what move or counter I would make before I knew it. So when she stood over me, I thought I was bound for Valhalla."

Lang nodded. "I expect Hakon himself could find her skills challenging."

"A woman, who would have thought it?" Lunt tore off another strip of cloth using his teeth and one good hand. "And did you hear her laugh at us as she fought?"

"Never felt so humiliated," Lang spat, hissing as his brother tied off the wound on his left shoulder. Lunt did the same for the deep puncture in Lang's thigh, where the Gael had flung her knife in what should have been an impossible throw. "I had no idea she was coming or where she came from, nor how she could have thrown one of her long blades at such a distance so accurately. I thought it was a spear!"

From the bloodstain spreading over his brother's side, Lang said, "That gash under your arm won't be easily staunched. Let's hope we can slow blood loss until we find a Healer. There's no mistaking she came from Hakon's loins, though. I'll cut off my beard if she's not his daughter, his bastard."

Lunt nodded in agreement. Then he thought again and countered, "But is she our Jarl's Destroyer? Remember, Hakon spawned a few children in those early years, especially in raids to the north. After all, he mentioned he sent Alrik to the east and Donalt to the south. So they could be the ones to find his Destroyer."

Lang smiled grimly. "You're saying there's no telling if she's the one? After all, Hakon never said to look for a woman, and I don't think his völva is certain."

"Runa would know if she saw her," Lunt commented. "I'd be willing to wager on that. And I'd wager that we met the Destroyer in her vision."

"A wager? How much?"

Lunt jerked on either end of the strip of cloth he was using on the wound beneath his brother's arm, causing the other to groan as he commanded, "Be serious! I am talking about telling Hakon we let a woman beat the two of us."

"Escaping with just our lives, barely, is not something to be proud of, is it?"

Lunt finished tending to Lang's wounds and stood with a grunt. "Not exactly."

"Maybe we don't tell Hakon the warrior he thinks is a son but is, in fact, a daughter?"

"And how could we leave out a major detail like that?"

Lang shrugged. "Tell Hakon the Destroyer attacked us at night."

"How would we have known it was his bastard?" Lunt asked.

"We saw his white hair in the firelight."

He shook his head. "I don't know. Let's get help and talk about it later."

"Good idea," Lang agreed. "It is Ancestor Night—I don't want to sleep under the stars."

Lunt growled, "If we don't find help, you won't be sleeping anywhere—you'll be dead."

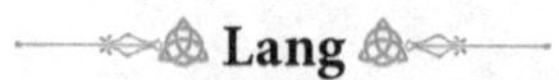

Lang

That evening, the pair rode into a small dun southwest of Dun Arrogh and dropped hard from their mounts. Lunt had lost the most blood, mainly because he could not stem the rivulets that coursed down his leg, so it was left to Lang to stagger toward the tattered main hall. There were no Samhain celebrations in the central yard, and Lang wondered whether they had no Druids to perform their sacred rituals; that did not bode well, for it might mean they had no Healer. Save for the Dreadrider, nothing stirred. Even the animals were in for the night.

When Lang finally stumbled through the hall door, all eyes came around to stare at the white-haired warrior. He said, "I am a Dreadrider in need of a Healer. Any man who helps my brother and me will have the gratitude of my Jarl. And Hakon Skadi can be most generous to those who help him and his."

The people in the room turned their heads back to their tankards and conversations, ignoring him.

"I said my Jarl would be most generous," Lang repeated.

A gray-haired man said rudely, "The Dreadlord has never been generous to anyone. At least not to anyone outside of Dun Garm."

"Then I claim Guestright!" Lang demanded.

No one else in the shabby hall had any words for him. Near the hearth at the room's far end, a short, reedy man was the only one still staring at Lang. A woman with a kettle full of water groused at him for gawking and commanded his help. He jumped to take the heavy iron pot from her and scurried out a small door near the hearth. Silence settled over the room.

Lang spat a curse and limped from the hall. Returning to his brother, he muttered sourly, "No help here. They wouldn't even grant us Guestright."

"By Thor's hammer, we'll be dead by morning if they don't help us," Lunt moaned.

"Lead your mounts over here." The short, wiry man Lang had seen in the hall crept from the shadows. "I've sent for help," he said. "Our Ollamh apprentice will help you. She's not a full Druid but has been keeping us alive when there's a need."

Eoin and Fergal limped into Dun Arrogh with Breanna's help. When she left the pair just inside the gates to fetch their Druid Healer, Eoin said, "That was a closely fought battle until Breanna arrived. Once more, she controlled the *void* as if it were an extension of herself. We need to get better at doing the same."

Fergal just grunted as the smith turned away to his work.

Ulicia arrived, and with help from Toal and Kyras, they moved the pair onto pallets outside her hut. His mother, Aife, arrived shortly thereafter, gasping at the blood-covered pair.

Aife growled, "Damn those Norvegrs. I lost my mate to them, and now they nearly took my son, too!"

She said nothing while Eoin hissed and grimaced as the Healer and her apprentice sewed him up and then did the same with Fergal. It took several spans in the late afternoon before they finished.

As the Healer finally finished wrapping each of their wounds with bandages, Eoin sighed, "Thank you. Those two Dreadriders posed more of a challenge than we expected."

Ulicia nodded tightly. "A near thing. Either of you could be lying next to Morna this evening and joining her *anam* in passing to the otherworld! If not for Breanna, that is."

Eoin raised an eyebrow, asking, "What did she say?"

"Nothing. Your Champion didn't need to, given she was covered with blood yet bore no scratch when she found me."

Eoin shrugged. "True enough. She was, indeed, brilliant."

As the scowling old Healer motioned for her apprentice to pack her bag, she added, "Try not to do that again. Toal, please help me get them both lying flat on the ground. They each need a gift from the Mother Goddess, or those wounds could fester." Then, Ulicia drew on her Earth Elemental power to aid their healing.

Toal soon brought buckets from the bathhouse and helped to get them washed up, and eventually, the two young men rested comfortably in Clan Mórhda's roundhouse. As Fergal dozed off, Eoin heard Ulicia command Aife that they be left alone, something he didn't mind, given that he was dead tired.

Eoin sighed, "Luckily, I'm not truly dead! Thanks to Bre."

Breanna

The younger warriors in their little band crowded around Breanna, asking how she had accomplished such a feat as beating two Dreadriders. Still, her mood didn't match the exuberance displayed by her fellow warriors. Putting them off with a short comment that the Dreadriders had underestimated her, likely because they thought women couldn't fight as well as men, Breanna grabbed a fresh change of clothes and left the band behind. She had a mother to see buried; now was not the time for celebrating. Heading to the bathhouse, Breanna was determined to clean up so she could see her mother off to the *Cycle of Time* as a daughter should. Yet, being covered in blood while standing next to her half-sisters might be fitting.

Later, Kyras had helped place Morna's body next to that of her long-dead mate's burial mound, and the Druids chanted her mother's soul on its journey to be with Nevan. Afterward, Breanna left her clan to check on Eoin. She wanted to tell him about her visit with the Druid Beatha and the quest the Druid had charged her with, though for now, the part about her new-found lineage would remain her secret.

Fortunately, Breanna entered the large Clan Mórdha hut while Aife and Eoin's younger sister, Eithne, sat in the main hall having their evening meal. Only Eoin and Fergal remained, and both were asleep.

Breanna knelt beside her Chief's bed and touched his shoulder. Eoin opened his eyes slowly. "Sorry that I couldn't join you for your mother's burial," he said. "I know it was hard when I lost my father, and now you've lost both your parents. "

"Don't worry about it," Breanna assured him softly, yet her expression was tight as she turned her eyes away. "It was fine, save for my sisters being churlish."

Eoin asked, "Over what?"

Breanna rose and walked to a table where jugs of ale and mead sat. She poured herself a cup of honey wine and asked a bit too lightly, "Ale?"

"No, not tonight. Ulicia's draughts are hard enough to stomach, and adding ale might stir the pot too much. Yet, I do sense something happened between you and your sisters. Bre, please, talk to me."

Breanna shrugged without letting their eyes meet. "It's a private matter between sisters, Eoin. Best to leave it at that."

She brought him a cup of water, which he gulped down before adding. "Aye, I'll leave it for now, but not for long."

Breanna winced at that declaration, yet she had enough mind to seize control of the conversation, stating, "I have a more portentous tale."

"More important than your mother's funeral?"

Knowing she'd have to let part of her story slip but not trusting herself to keep the pieces she wanted hidden from her Chief, she rose again and turned away to ensure he could not see any emotion flicker on her face. Then, looking out the door, she said hurriedly, "I took a walk in the woods last night and met our old Fáidh, Beatha, the one our *Aos Dána* call the hermit. She told me about a set of long blades of fairie origin called *Lann Dàn*. The blades are said to be able to conquer even the mightiest magical warriors, and that means I should be able to kill the Dreadlord with them when he comes searching for you."

"Fairie long blades?" Eoin questioned. "Bre, what are you talking about?"

"The Fáidh told me to seek out the magic weapons in a cave on the west side of Cuilcagh Mountain," Breanna said excitedly as she faced him again. With the challenge of her quest foremost in her mind, she added, "If the gods are willing, I'll find them and defend Dun Arrogh against Hakon's scourge. Beatha told me to go to her Grove tonight and call on our gods to guide me in finding *Lann Dàn*."

"That old lady is crazy," Eoin exploded as he tried to sit up. Then, gasping in pain, he slouched back with a grimace. "No one in their right mind would go to a Druid's sacred grove, especially on Samhain's night."

"Leave that to me. Should the gods heed my call, will you help me find *Lann Dàn*?"

"I'd follow you anywhere, Breanna, you know that. Still, these wounds will not heal overnight. It will take a few weeks before I can endure such a trek, and I doubt you'll wait that long if the gods do indeed speak to you."

Breanna blushed over her Chief's words, wondering which of them was whose Champion. He was always so committed to her, and it was apparent to more than a few, including Breanna, that he loved her. She had known it for years, but the *geas* burning in her did not allow room for such emotions. Knowing her father's identity made it even more challenging to acknowledge their bond. She found the silence uneasy and bit her lower lip, uncertain how to respond. Then, getting her wits about her, she turned and sat next to him, asking, "Who do you think I should take with me then?"

He sighed. "Well, Fergal is worse off than I, so he's out. It has to be Toal. He's the only one of our Red Branch brave enough to go on such a quest, and he's not a bad shot with his bow. Since he's kin—he'll not cut and run if this fairie place is more dangerous than you expect."

Breanna winced over Eoin calling out her cousin's bond, yet agreed, saying, "Yes, Toal's a good choice, even if a bit young."

"His father won't like the idea—his mother even less so."

"I'll tell Kyras that the Goddess commanded his son to join me," she countered. "He respects the Fáidh and their visions too much, especially that one, to risk angering them. If I say the gods will protect us, he'll not say a word."

"Be careful out there tonight."

"Always," she responded, her hand brushing lightly over his as she rose, her eyes locking intently on his, looking for any hint that he knew her secret. The spark that had always been between them seemed unchanged for a brief moment, and then Breanna was gone.

Eoin

"Lugh, watch over my Champion," Eoin whispered to the Sun God. But no one was there to hear him as the rough-hewn door closed solidly behind Breanna as if cutting her off from him. Instead, the darkness of night swallowed her—the darkness of Samhain's night.

The thought of being out on such an evening made Eoin shudder. It was a chill that could not be warmed by a fire or huddling in his bed. Yet he still pulled his woolen blanket around his shoulders. He muttered a Druid's charm to ward off the feeling of foreboding and hoped Breanna knew what she was doing.

Unable to sleep, he picked up a book that his mother had given him years ago. It was written in Latin by a poet, and Aife had used it to teach him how to read. When he had mastered it well enough to read on his own, he'd started to tutor Breanna.

As he leafed through the book, he fondly remembered how they spent many long winter evenings reading strange stories from a different land together. That made him sigh as it brought his love to his mind once more, something he was doing often of late.

And now she was off to seek out their Tuatha Gods over a crazy tale by Dun Arrogh's one-time seeress. Her quest would surely spin a tale stranger than any of those in his book.

QUEST FOR LANN DÀN

Donalt

Donalt rode into Dun Garm on the eve of Ancestor Night. He was frustrated that he had not found out more about Hakon's bastard than his name. He handed his reins to a stable-hand, asking, "Has Alrik returned?"

"Nei, great rider," the boy answered.

Donalt headed for the main hall, which he found full of the dun's warriors and artisans—unsurprising because it was a festival night. He spotted Hakon making his way among the tables, his manner easy and rather pleasant. With the ale flowing, all seemed to be having an enjoyable evening. Donalt strode to the Dreadriders' table and filled his cup.

"Donalt!" Royd exclaimed. "You're back!"

"Clearly," he replied as he took his cup and drained off half of it in two gulps. "A frustrating quest, that's for sure."

Hakon glanced up as Donalt entered the hall. The Dreadrider saw his Jarl excuse himself from the table he had been sitting at. Then, as they met at the Dreadriders' table, he asked, "Donalt, what news have you?"

Donalt heaved a sigh. "I found what might be one of your bastards, but those around Dun Uisneach kept me from laying eyes on him. His name is Bradaigh, and he earned his golden armring at their *comórtas* this past summer."

Hakon said, "Tell me more."

Donalt answered, "While he was not born in the hillfort, it seems like he spends a fair amount of time there training with Dun Uisneach's warriors. Unfortunately, I did not get any response when I asked if he had hailed from one of several settlements along the High King's Road, and they commanded me to move along, saying our kind was not welcome. They even warned me that I needed a writ of travel to use the High King's Road. We are certainly not appreciated in that area."

Hakon gave Donalt a sharp look as if to say his warrior should have pressed harder in his mission.

Donalt could concede he could have, especially since the discovered bastard wore a golden armring and was potentially the Destroyer Runa had foreseen. His tone was measured as he said, "Well, we have at least a potential lead. Alrik, Lunt, and Lang should return in a day or two. Let's see what they've found."

Breanna

Breanna Ban Morna left the Clan Mórdha hut behind, charging into Samhain's night with a fire in her belly. The idea of killing Hakon Skadi was getting easier to live with, for she knew he cared nothing about her except how to use her. Still, going through with it might be more of a challenge than Breanna wanted to admit. Despite her years of training as a warrior and earning a gold arm ring, she had never taken a trophy. Breanna always seemed to end up sparing her opponents after soundly defeating them. And, now, she had even let Dreadriders live when she could have easily killed them.

Putting such errant thoughts from her mind, Breanna walked past the main hall, where most of the dun had gathered for the evening's Samhain celebration. After slipping in the kitchen door to grab food to sustain her travel for the night, she headed to the dun gates. She nodded to the Druids gathered in the courtyard for their Samhain rituals. Their fires burned bright, and chants filled the air as if they expected the otherworld to provide a sign that all would be set right in their corner of the world. The more prominent forts of the Gaels usually sent their Master Druids to Tara for the Samhain Fires and Great Invocation. However, tonight, Breanna did not need their kind to talk to their gods—she would do what few of them had ever dared: ask them directly for their aid.

With her long blades strapped to her back, she charged into the ancient black oak forest, confident she could find Beatha's Grove without a *Bean-Sidhe* to guide her this time. The night swallowed her, and Breanna strode confidently through the dark woods. She followed the same narrow path as the night before. The moon rose above the treeline, darting out from behind passing clouds. Maybe it was because she walked with such purpose that she was sure a *Bean-Sidhe* would not challenge her this evening, or perhaps the *Bean-Sidhe* she had previously encountered had been told by their *Sidhe* masters to leave her be. In either case, Breanna was pleased to be undisturbed as she marched along the pathway in the gloomy forest.

Like a moth drawn to a flame, Breanna found the Grove faster than expected, as she did not have to deal with tangled brush and vines this time. The moon had not reached its zenith when she made it to the Druid's empty grove—empty save for the giant oak tree and the stone fire ring to contain the embers beneath its boughs. Beatha had started a small fire for her as promised, yet Breanna had no idea where the old Druid was on this most magical night of the year. Certainly not at Dun Arrogh, as she no longer called that place her home.

Breanna made for the fire, her heart suddenly pounding at the thought of what she was about to do. She sat heavily beside the ring of stones on the same log she had used the previous night. Behind her, the sacred oak tree of the Grove rose like a father wrapping his arms around his daughter. She could feel its roots reaching deep into the ground, feel them seeking back to a time when heroes walked the land, wielding might and magic.

Beatha had said it was her turn to be a hero, Erin's Hero. The thought brought goosebumps to Breanna's arms, and she was thankful for the fire set by the Druid. Even if the evening had not been chilly, she was unsure the fire would warm her as she faced a new fate this evening.

As she gazed into the flames, Breanna realized she had no idea how to call on their gods as Beatha had commanded. Seizing the *void* seemed easy when she faced a battle. Yet, there was no battle now, and Breanna needed to reach for the fairie realm to call their gods. She did not yet know how to seize the *void* when not in motion. Did she think of one or another of the Tuatha legends? Or call out their names into the night? And which name should she call? Lugh? Badb? Danu? Dagda? Was there a chant that would bring them into her world? If so, she had no idea what it could be.

Breanna calmed her racing thoughts, took a few deep breaths, and tried to find her center. Yet the *void* did not come, would not come. With her eyes closed, she touched her forehead as a test to see if she could recall the directions on how to find *Lann Dàn* provided by the Fáidh called Beatha.

After a moment, the words cascaded through her mind. That brought a smile to her lips. At least that part was still in her. She recalled her battle with the two Dreadriders, where the *void* had felt closer, and sought the moment when the Tuatha magic sang through her veins—trying to find her center and sink deeper into herself. As someone approached from the north, a staff thumping the ground, Breanna pulled herself out of her attempt to find that magical place between the realms.

When the Druid Beatha hobbled into the small grove and sat before the fire, Breanna said quietly, "I have no idea how to seize the *void* without a battle around me. I thought I had it last night when you passed the words into me, but now, it's gone. Earlier today, I came upon two Dreadriders in combat at midday with my Chief and his former Red Branch Champion, the one I replaced two days ago. I drove them off using the *void*, hurting them badly.

"Yet I am now my Chief's Champion, and I had to attend to Eoin and Fergal to keep them from bleeding out. But because I let them go, Hakon will likely learn of me and attack our dun."

Beatha shrugged. "It's all right, child. I had not expected you would be able to divide your warrior-self so easily. It's good that you can do this in battle. I have personally seen the Dreadriders at work, and they are fearsome."

Breanna said, with some disdain, "They could not touch me with their heavy blades. With the *void* guiding me, I foresaw every move that flashed into their minds. It was intense, for certain. Yet, I've never felt closer to my true self than at that moment."

"You truly have a warrior's heart, Breanna," Beatha said proudly. "I suspect that has to do with the *geas*, but you must also think about the greater world. Warriors do not just battle in the narrow half-seconds between a slash of a blade, nor when you have engaged just foe to foe. The great ones use strategy, like our Sun God, Lugh. While he won the final battle against his grandfather by drawing a rainbow into the facets of a stone and then casting it with his sling, he kept his head about him during the times in between battles."

Beatha favored her with a searching gaze before adding, "You need to think about your next move or strike ahead of the current action before taking the first one. It is a lot to ask, as you're a young soul destined to be Erin's Hero. It will be a hard road, and you'll make many mistakes that cost you dear lives."

Breanna followed her gaze overhead to see that the moon was now at its zenith.

Beatha continued, "You will grow into your role as our hero. It will challenge you, yet you'll be up to the task. Tuatha Gods do not choose poorly. The time for doubt is over. I have a chant to open a pathway to the Tuatha realm, but then I must leave. It is up to you to ask the Tuatha gods for help, not me."

"I understand and will make it so," Breanna confirmed.

Beatha remained motionless for a time, her eyes closed, her breathing steady. Then she murmured ancient words of another language before she said aloud, "Great Mother, guardian of your children, we require your protection. There are those arrayed against us by thought, word, and deed. We need their efforts to fail. Let their evil return to the lower darkness. Please give us your protection, Great Mother!

"Wolf and stag, old signs of might. Lend me your strength this night. Courage we need and the power of steel—energy, willpower, and defense to feel. Hark, great powers all, join us in our quest to end the reign of those who stand against our land. Aid us in our quest to end the reign of Hakon Skadi, the Dreadlord of Garm. So mote it be!"

With that, the Druid rose, and so did the fire. Breanna had to squint at the flare, and Beatha disappeared into the flames. When the fire returned to what it was, she saw nothing except the night. Breanna knew that Druids could be Elementals, but not that Beatha could command Fire. Yet, she had left her to whatever god would answer the call for help. Breanna could do no more than stare into the fire and listen to the noise of the surrounding forest.

It seemed quieter than before. It was as if the Fáidh's chant had drawn the very breath from the woods. The silence was suddenly absolute. Even the fire burned without making a sound. With her heartbeat the only thing she could hear, Breanna pondered if Eoin had been right. Maybe Beatha was *craiceáilte*. Perhaps this idea of a quest for magic weapons to save her kin and herself from the Dreadlord was nonsense.

Breanna jerked her eyes up suddenly, startled by the appearance of a massive silver wolf that had bounded into the Druid's Grove. The beast looked around the clearing briefly before trotting over to the fire and sitting directly opposite her. Its eyes were glowing a yellowish gold, flecked with firelight.

Breana resisted the urge to bolt, somehow knowing the monstrous creature would be able to catch her in a few strides. That thought kept her seated on her log as she held the wolf's gaze. There was an intelligence behind those intense golden eyes, making her question if this was a messenger of the gods.

Remembering to breathe, finally, Breanna asked, "Well, my friend, have the gods sent you?"

The wolf raised its head and let loose a blood-curdling howl. Breanna cringed; perhaps that had been the wrong question to ask. A moment later, the wolf shimmered and transformed into a tall woman with a silver breastplate that nearly covered her torso, yet left her shoulders bare. At her waist was a white kilt, and the silver shield strapped to her right arm was polished so that even the reflecting firelight was bright enough to dazzle the eyes.

Breanna, stunned at the sight of her goddess, jaw dropping open wordlessly. Every Gael knew of the Silver Huntress, the primary Triple Goddess of Mother, Earth, and Moon. She now ruled the land hand in hand with the Sun God Lugh, the Dark Goddess, and the All-Father—the four of them wielded magical abilities that made the *Tuatha Dé Danann* immortal.

Danu's form was muscled yet sleek, with powerful legs wrapped in white leather boots that reached her knees. Just above her breastplate was a sizeable heart-shaped ruby that Breanna knew from Druid's tales to be the Heart of Destiny, called *Ćroí Dàn* by some, held there by a golden chain. The Bards of *Aos Dána* taught their people tales and legends about the *Triple Dáns*, of which the magical ruby was the last one.

Their Druids explained that Badb Catha had carved the large gem, and she had influenced its creation, insisting the Heart needed sentience so she could freely choose Erin's Hero. Yet it was, ultimately, the Mother Goddess who conceived and bore *Ćroí Dàn* into their world, enabling her to develop intelligence and assess and select its Hero, making her a new goddess housed within her ruby body.

Breanna rose to step around the fire and knelt on one knee before her goddess. "My Lady, I had no idea my quest would involve you."

In Danu's left hand was her glowing sword of magic, and on the hilt, attached to the end, was a crescent-shaped moon that enclosed a small crystal orb swirling with what seemed to be clouds trapped inside it. Breanna had heard their Bard describe it as a legendary blade with powers only the Mother and Moon Goddess could wield. Their Druid's tales of the *Tuatha Dé Danann* claimed her short sword was also a sentient being, much like the magic that made *Ćroí Dàn*. The sword endowed Danu with preternatural speed and power. She had a sleek, small bow carved from white ash slung across her back, yet she needed no quiver as she could manifest arrows on command.

"Few who've earned the gold armring of the Celtic Knot ever think beyond the next battle," Danu said scornfully—her expression was dour at best—as she sheathed her sword at her hip. Then, the Mother Goddess grasped the heart-shaped ruby necklace hanging just above her breastplate. "Yet, I sense there is more to you than what I find in the Gael warriors of today. Something, something..."

In mind-speak, the Sword of Danu said, "*Its strength, courage, and determination are needed to counter her hate, rage, and drive, to balance her geas. She is one of those you foresaw.*"

When Breanna heard the sword in her mind, she was dumb-founded and thought, "*Who are you?*"

"*I am Cosantóir, Protector of our Mother Goddess.*"

Then Danu's eyes glazed over, and Breanna knew the *sight* had taken hold of her. It was surprising to see it happen to one of their gods, thinking only the *Aos Dána* worked such magic, and then it was only to talk with the gods. Breanna felt someone like Danu would know everything, yet she used the *sight* here. With whom was she communicating?

"Aye, one of the three, the lass," the Mother Goddess said aloud. Then the world lurched to a stop, and Breanna realized she was witnessing more than simple magic at work. It was something akin to the *void*, yet much more profound and powerful. For a long moment, she doubted Danu would ever let it go.

In that heartbeat, Breanna and her goddess shared that same *sight*. Time became meaningless as she watched the Fomorians and their gods throw themselves at the Tuatha and her gods. Muscle and magic were the tools of their battles, though it was more of the latter. The Fomorians lost because their gods lacked the cunning and power of the *Tuatha Dé Danann*. Their magicians could not command the magic wielded by the Goddess of War and the All-Father, and the Fomorian generals were no match for the might and wit of Lugh, their Sun God.

When the fierce Gaels had come to what they named the Isle of Erin, the *Tuatha Dé Danann* no longer had the numbers to withstand another invasion. So when Breanna saw her land overrun by white-haired Norvegrs, she knew that Beatha was right. The Gaels had to stand united, and stopping the Dreadlord had to be their top priority before he brought another invasion to Erin.

Then, all appeared normal as Breanna swayed under the earth's motion, turning beneath her bowed knee again. The Mother Goddess, Danu, stared at Breanna, an expression of revelation settling over her face. Breanna could only speculate what the *Cycle of Time* could have told one of such power to cause surprise. It had shown Breanna that she must accept her *geas* or all of Erin would be lost, and the *Tuatha Dé Danann*, the gods they worshipped, would wither and die. She shivered under the weight of that responsibility.

She thought, *"Me! Why did it have to be me? Why couldn't someone else be the hero?"*

She had to hug herself to quell her urge to rise and run. But it worked; save for one hand nervously tracing the ornately worked pattern on her Celtic Knot armring, she was mostly in control of herself once more. With that, Breanna lifted her eyes to look into her Mother Goddess's, showing the strength she felt filling her and the power to be what her land needed.

Danu released the ruby pendant, her expression curious, as she asked, "Are you a hero who can defeat the Dreadlord?"

The gem resting on her goddess's chest repeatedly pulsed bright red, and then *Cróí Dàn* was crying inside Breanna's head, *"Mine! Mine! Mine!"*

"Please, calm down, Daughter!" Danu admonished.

Breanna stated to them in mind-speak, *"I hear you both."*

Danu muttered, "I wish I had never let Badb Catha talk me into making another sentient piece of magic; between an edgy sword who assumes to advise me on how and when she should protect a demanding child goddess and me, I get no respect!"

Taking control of her interaction with *Cróí Dàn*, the Goddess informed her Heart, *"I will bring your desired hero into our fold. Watch and learn."*

If a gem could mutter, *Cróí Dàn* did, adding, *"You better. She is mine!"*

"*Cróí Dàn* has chosen you as one who has the blood of your land and the Norvegr outlanders," Danu said with a grimace. "Why have you called on me?"

"Beatha, our Fáidh, commanded that I summon one of our gods to aid me in my quest for *Lann Dàn*," Breanna replied hesitantly. "I did not know it would be you who answered that call."

"And what do you know of *Lann Dàn*?" the Mother Goddess questioned suspiciously.

"They are magic long blades that could help me defeat the Dreadlord of Garm."

"So Beatha's been talking," Danu sourly mused, and she took several steps forward. Then, standing over Breanna like a tower, she added, "Like all Fáidh, the Druid knows Amergin's story. Search where she commanded."

"She said others have tried and failed," Breanna ventured. "Could I be given some magic to aid in finding *Lann Dàn*? Something to use in my quest to destroy the Dreadlord?"

Danu pursed her lips, seemingly displeased with the request. Then, she crossed behind Breanna to touch the old oak tree. As Breanna's eyes followed her Mother Goddess, she noted that another expression of surprise settled over her face, similar to when the *sight* had released her earlier when touching the *Cycle of Time*.

After a moment, Danu shook her head and, glancing at a crystal ring on her hand, said, "This tree tells me you are at the center of the *Cycle's* pattern, a pattern I put into motion before you were born. So, while I had not expected the chosen one to be a young woman or that *Ćroí Dàn* would select you as her Hero, your request is a considerable matter."

Cosantóir chimed in, *"I agree with Ćroí. She's the one!"*

Breanna smiled at the interjection as Danu just rolled her eyes at her sword's opinion, saying, "These damned sentient magical constructs are more opinionated than Gaels!"

Then, Danu informed Breanna, "Because the Heart of Destiny has made it clear the world is taking shape around you, I offer this charm created by the Dark Goddess of Knowledge." She proffered a clear, glowing crystal ring. "She named it *Maorgairme*, the Summoner. Fire comes to life when near other Tuatha magic or when foul Fomorian magic is present. It will show you when you are near the Sun God's long blades."

Breanna reached for the ring; its smooth surface reflected the firelight brilliantly. She slipped it on her left forefinger, surprised it fit like someone had made it for her. "And for the help with facing the Dreadlord?"

Danu hesitated again, her gaze nearly a glare, then shook her head. "*Maorgairme* is a thing with its own life, not sentient but close. It responds differently to each person and listens to some better than others. You will need to learn when and how to use it—talk to it with your mind or voice—and then you will see the results. Like many of Badb Catha's works, I find it a fickle piece of magic. Much like her crow animal form of the Mórrigan, her ring can be capricious. Anyway, you'll never know when or how her ring, *Maorgairme*, will decide to help you."

"But how can it help? What do I ask of it?"

The frown on Danu's face nearly made Breanna cringe. The Mother Goddess said briskly, "Anything, everything, or nothing—use your imagination. Yet, never ask for help in battle. *Maorgairme* will expect you to carry your weight there, just as my Dark Sister, the Goddess of War, would demand. If your father uses magic that your skill with the long blades cannot counter, it will most assuredly come to your aid. And if you are ever desperate, the ring can summon one of the Tuatha Gods to your side. Just call my name three times. It is magic to use wisely—after the third time you call on us to help you, *Maorgairme* will vanish from your hand and return to me."

"Thank you, Mother Goddess," Breanna humbly offered as she examined the crystal ring. With *Maorgairme* and *Lann Dàn*, she could stop the Dreadlord of Garm. She could fulfill her destiny. Maybe it was the Heart of Destiny influencing her? Yet she felt more sure of herself.

"One more thing," the goddess commanded, startling Breanna from her introspection. "After you've used my charm to find Badb's *Lann Dàn*, take the Tuatha weapons to the Mountain Mother, the Goddess of Knowledge and War. Seek out the *Well of Segias*, where the headwaters of the Boyne are born, but be careful while near the great bog—many dark things are drawn there by my triple-faced sister.

"On the night of each new moon, you'll find Badb Catha, the Mórrigan, at the northern end of the *Móin Mórachd*, just east of Croghan Hill. Use the ring to guide you. My dark sister can tell you how to use her magical long blades to accomplish your desire to remove your father from our land. Tell her I commanded that you drink from her Cauldron of Knowledge. Only then can you face the Dreadlord and have a chance to save your land. Our fate is in your hands."

With that, Breanna watched the Goddess Danu, dressed as the Silver Huntress, shimmer back into her great wolf form. Then the beast trotted from the Grove on four massive paws, fading into nothingness.

Breanna seemed to sense that both *Ćroí Dàn* and *Cosantóir* were smugly pleased with themselves. Then she heard the howl of a wolf, and her pack answered in unison. It was time to find her way back to Dun Arrogh.

Runa

Hakon Skadi's völva, Runa, stood with her back toward him, the one who had led her to this land. Her chamber was dark, save for one candle burning on her white marble altar. A yard-wide band of flat, jet-black stone had been laid into the floor, forming a circle around her, the black contrasting with the pale limestone surrounding it. As usual, the völva was wearing her darkly dyed robes. Only her white hair stood out against the murky backdrop.

As she spread her arms in supplication before her altar, Runa announced, "I am ready—step within the ring. Once I cast the Cone of Power and call on the Fomorian God Tethra, do not cross outside this line until he has departed and I have nullified the spell. Obey this command, no matter what he does or says or what you see or think you see. If you ignore my warning, I cannot be responsible for what happens."

"And what could happen?" Hakon demanded.

"Tethra could decide to take your life instead of agreeing to take your bastard's life," Runa said coldly. "Perhaps draw you into his realm and use your soul as your wolfhounds gnaw on their bones."

Chilled, Hakon stepped forward and could only say, "Then cast your spell."

The völva momentarily eyed her Jarl intently as if sensing his apprehension. Then she cackled, "You need to embrace our gods—they are as real as the Tuatha Gods that the Gaels worship."

Hakon growled but said nothing.

Runa turned away and lifted a short, jewel-encrusted sword that hung between her small breasts in one hand and four candles in the other as she stepped in front of her altar. She went about setting each candle at a cardinal point and then returned to the northernmost one on the jet circle. After a moment, Runa intoned, "In a place that is not a place, in a time that is not a time, on a day that is not a day, I stand at the threshold between this world before the gates of Asgard. By Nordhri's name, I call on the Ice Ruler to grant us shelter where there is none."

Letting her little sword tip drop, she snapped her fingers together to make the first candle flare to life and then set it on the band of inlaid jet and rose. After precisely placing the tip of her short sword on the northern point of the black stone circle, Runa dragged it along the floor to the easternmost point. She caught Hakon rubbing his bare arms at the grating sound of her blade. It was the first time she had let him watch her work her magic in such detail. Normally, she would do no more than cast the Blood Runes in his presence.

Runa continued, "By Austri's name, I call on the Air Ruler to grant us breath where there is none." Another candle came to life, and the sword scraped on the floor to the southern point of the black circle. Again, Runa summoned her gods. "By Sudhri's name, I call on the Fire Ruler to grant us warmth where there is none."

Hakon watched, entranced.

After the third candle erupted, she moved to the western point of the circle. "By Vestri's name, I call on the Water Ruler to grant us the drink of life where there is none."

Once Runa's magic brought the last candle to flame, she returned to the northern point and said, "By Norori's name, I call on the Earth Ruler to grant us the grain of life where there is none.

"As Odin's four Dwarves who hold up the sky, I command protection within this Cone of Power. May the Ancient Ones help and protect us this night!"

At those words, she struck the tip of her sword on the circle of jet stone. A spark flashed, and a silver-blue flame leaped to life, racing around her and Hakon.

"The Cone of Power is complete," she informed him. "While we stand within this circle, nothing we call from beyond the gates of our world can harm us."

Hakon nodded as his gaze followed the ring of silver-blue fire around him. Runa gave him no time to think about it and moved to her altar. "On this Ancestor Night, the Feast of the Dead, the night for contact with the shadowlands, the night to call on those who now dwell over Bifrost, the Rainbow Bridge to Asgard. Lift the veil so that I may call on the power of our gods to aid us. With that power, we call on the ancestors of the Fomorians to aid in the summons of the great God Tethra!"

The völva swung her short sword in an arc to strike her altar. Once more, sparks flew, and once more, her silver-blue otherworld flame leaped to life. This time, it engulfed the white marble stone circle. Runa dropped to her knees, arms resting on the crossguard of her short sword, its tip now on the floor.

Hakon

Runa then began to chant something from a language Hakon had never heard, a tongue so alien he wondered if she were babbling. Time stretched on as a chill fell over the small hut. Then the air erupted in a fiery red orb before her altar, just outside the Cone of Power, and Hakon nearly wet himself.

Waves of heat rolled from the strange ball of fire, and the roar from the *void* linking their realm to the Fomorian's realm was deafening. The flames grew and elongated into the rough shape of a human. Within the inferno, a face formed, its features pinched and pained, creating sharp lines on a grotesquely enlarged head. The God Tethra looked like something that had been worked over with a branding iron. Perhaps, Hakon wondered, if the Tuatha had only maimed the old god.

As he explored Tethra's fiery eyes, Hakon felt the world lurch to a stop. He could not break the gaze as visions swept over him. He saw the land of Erin as it had been before the Tuatha engaged in battle with the Fomorians and the Fir Bolg. Then, the two forces clashed, throwing their respective might against each other and using incredible feats of magic to conquer their sworn enemy.

Hakon stood on low rolling hills that led down to the sea, and around him, chaos raged. Tuatha legions followed their Sun God in what appeared to be a final charge into the Fomorian lines of misshapen demons. As the sun broke through the cloud, it created a rainbow, and Lugh drew the multi-colored light into glittering stone, one he set flying into Balor's malevolent eye. With that, Hakon knew the Tuatha had sundered the Fomorians—King Balor of the Baleful Eye was dead—and Tethra fled to the islands off the northwest coast of Erin. As he took in the vision, Hakon noted thousands died that day, some falling to the blades of their opponents, others to the mystical powers wielded by the gods and their followers. Both sides suffered significant losses, but the Fomorians sustained greater casualties.

The scene shifted to another time, where, despite his weakened powers, Tethra returned to help the Fir Bolg, as the fight was not over for the Fomorian god. However, when the *Tuatha Dé Danann*, specifically the God of Healing, Dian Cécht, along with his daughter Airmid, began using their healing springs to revive the dead, Hakon watched Tethra turn and flee, as he could do little more than escape with a few followers to sustain him. Most of those had to worship him in secret to avoid the Tuatha discovering them.

Then the world was in motion again for Hakon, with the heat from the link between the realms subsiding to at least a somewhat tolerable level, and it seemed a curtain fell over the *void* to shut off the tremendous noise. He had to shake his head. If what he had just lived through were accurate moments in the past, no warlord in Erin could hope to stand against the magic wielded by these gods. But perhaps their powers had waned over the years.

An angry rumble from the old god brought his attention to why he had called this god from his slumber. Tethra raised an arm, pointed at Runa, and said, oozing malice, "How dare you, a mere mortal, summon me to this world?"

When Runa glanced down at the floor and said nothing, Hakon knew it was his turn to speak. Swallowing, he stepped forward next to his völva. "I, Hakon Skadi, the Dreadlord of

Garm, have summoned the great god Tethra, summoned him to request his aid in one more battle with his fiercest enemies, the gods of the *Tuatha Dé Danann*."

"And what do you know of those blasted gods?" Tethra growled.

"That you hate them," Hakon replied evenly as his confidence swelled. When he walked to the front of the altar, Runa hissed at him to stop, freezing him in his tracks. His feet were inches from the band of jet stone holding Runa's otherworld fire. The heat rolling off the image of Tethra was intense, and he had to wipe his brow to keep the sweat from his eyes now that he had closed the gap. Hakon continued more cautiously, "I know you once ruled this land with other Fomorian and Fir Bolg gods, but now your powers are waning."

"Yes, gods need people to worship them, lest their powers wither and die."

Hakon nodded. "But your power remains strong, so I have summoned you on this darkest of nights to lay a challenge at your feet. My Seeress has foreseen that the gods of the *Tuatha Dé Danann* will aid one who seeks to destroy me. Therefore, I require your power to counter theirs."

"And why should I help you?"

"Because if you oppose my Destroyer, you oppose the Tuatha and their gods."

Tethra muttered, "Gods like Dagda, Danu, Lugh, and the Mórrigan are mighty."

"You need not face them directly," Hakon suggested. "Just seek out the one who uses their magic. He will be traveling the land soon, seeking shelter."

"My demons can only work on or near water, and they do not like the fresh water of the Shannon," Tethra countered, though this time, his voice held a seed of acquiescence and interest.

"Do they not hate the *Tuatha Dé Danann* more?"

"True, the Tuatha are our most hated enemy," the god agreed.

"Aid me, and you hinder them."

"Yes, but there must be a price. Would your people worship a god such as me?"

"That I cannot promise," Hakon informed him. "My people come from another land. They know the gods of Asgard and frown on placing others above those they have worshiped their entire lives. But I can promise my people will fight the gods of the *Tuatha Dé Danann*."

"I will aid you," the God of the Fomorians decided. "Though given your location, I will have to press my people to join in this conflict, for there is much fresh water near the head of the River Shannon where you have drawn me to. But I cannot move until the *Tuatha Dé Danann* show their hand and openly aid your Destroyer. And only when he is near water."

"I ask for no more."

"Then set yourself about tracking down this Destroyer of yours," Tethra commanded. "If the *Tuatha Dé Danann* gods have marked him, I'll set my demons on the task of seeing that those gods do not come to his aid. And if your Destroyer uses Tuatha magic, we will be drawn to him like flies to a new cairn."

"And how will we know if you have taken him before us?"

"I will speak to your völva through her Blood Runes."

Hakon smiled at that. "Many thanks to the great god, Tethra."

Tethra's expression did not change, though he nodded slightly to acknowledge the tribute. Then his form started to dissolve, the fiery orb that preceded his appearance coalescing. The heat was intense again, and Hakon had to turn away to keep from being burned as the hole between the two realms opened again. The roaring sound of a gale returned with a rush, and then Tethra pulled his raging fire into the *void*. As if the god had never appeared, Runa's hut was quiet and dark, save for one candle that still burned.

Hakon turned to his völva. "By the Four Dwarves of Asgard, if I never see that god again, it will be too soon!"

Runa cackled and went to light her other candles and clean up the remnants of her ritual.

Alrik

Later that same afternoon, with the sun low on a horizon of broken clouds, Alrik cantered through the gates of Dun Garm on his stallion, with Braoin riding beside him on the mare Epona had assigned him. Alrik watched the young Gael's expression for signs of being impressed by their fort but saw none. Instead, the warrior cast his gaze around the dun, his eyes critical. Seeing the hostage huts by the ramparts near the gate, Braoin frowned. "I see my father keeps *daor aicme*. Does he hold to the law and free them when they've served their hostage time?"

As the stable boy rushed to help Alrik, he swung himself out of his saddle, demanding, "Get these mounts tended to. We have business with the Dreadlord."

The half-blooded warrior followed suit, taking up after Alrik as the burly outlander made his way to the Dreadlord's tower. Braoin asked, "Do I get an answer?"

"Like other Chiefs, sometimes."

The stone tower was impressive as they approached, and two guards stood tall as each pulled open one of the double doors to let them enter. Coming to a halt before a tall, sandy-haired older man who sat at a desk off to one side, Alrik said, "Sveinn, summon our Jarl."

"Of course, Dreadrider," he answered formally and rose to lead them farther through the main floor entrance hall to a large table. The manservant ascended the stairs to fetch the Dreadlord.

In the meantime, Braoin glanced around the tower's main floor as if surveying its construction quality and stated, "Good craftsmanship here. Like the dun's ramparts and gates. My kind could learn a thing or two here to improve our building skills."

"Já, we've learned a few things from the Romans," Alrik agreed, "and we've been building long ships for centuries."

A moment later, Hakon descended the circular stairs to the lower floor of his tower, his wolfhounds flanking him. He said, "Alrik, Sveinn informed me that you were successful in your mission."

"Indeed, my Jarl," he responded. "I would like to introduce you to Braoin, who hails from a settlement at the south end of Loch Síleann. He agreed to visit Dun Garm to meet you, as I believe he is one of the warriors you seek."

As Hakon reached the last step before the table, he said, "Braoin, well met."

"Indeed," the young Gael answered. "Alrik mentioned you were seeking, how shall I say it, offspring you sired from your early days in our land. I'm sure I wasn't the only one, and now you're searching for us. All of us, I assume. What happened to the man who should have been my father and the woman who is still my mother? I can say the former you killed and the latter you raped—which makes me your *diolain*.

"After all these years, what is your interest in bringing me into your fold and discovering who I am? Or, more correctly, who are we? That's my take on this sudden turnabout."

When Hakon paused, Alric eyed his leader's astute and clever spawn, stating, "So my Jarl here is not just interested in learning more about his offspring?"

"Aye, sure he is," Braoin nodded. "But not for any concern of us. It's an interest in us, maybe the threat we pose. It's just a thought I had, and, thus, why I accepted your suggestion to come to Dun Garm and meet with my father."

Hakon

"Hmm," Hakon murmured to buy some time as he thought about how best to deal with the truculent lad. He was distinctly, yet accurately, a suspicious Gael. Were the lad's Tuatha gods in play here? He offered, "You're astute, yet be careful about being insolent."

Braoin shrugged.

Hakon decided to change his tactics on how best to determine if Braoin was his Destroyer, offering, "You seem to have thoroughly considered our meeting on your ride here to Dun Garm. But let's gather in the main hall for the evening meal so we can explore your questions about your Norvegr half."

Hakon turned to Sveinn. "Fetch Runa for me. I'd like her to join us in the main hall for our meal."

"As you wish, my Jarl," Sveinn answered with a slight bow and departed.

Hakon strode through the doors of his tower behind his manservant and turned left toward the main hall while Sveinn headed right to seek out the magic woman. Alrik and the white-haired lad tailed closely behind his Jarl, following him into the capsized boat-shaped building and down a ramp to its packed earth floor.

Braoin whistled. "While your stone tower is impressive, this hall is even more so. You must be able to seat a hundred men in here!"

Alrik shrugged without comment as Hakon saw Donalt sitting at the table usually commandeered by the Dreadriders and approached him. The older warrior exclaimed, "Alrik, I see you had more success than I!"

"Já," the other answered. "I found this lad who seemed like a match."

Hakon instructed, "Have a seat, Braoin. Jarlson, our cook, will soon bring out the platters. In the meantime, let me introduce you to Donalt, another of my Dreadriders. Donalt, I believe ale is in order."

The older Dreadrider reached for three more cups and dipped them in a bucket on the table. A few moments later, Hakon's völva entered the hall. She tottered over to Hakon. "You summoned me?"

"Indeed, Runa," Hakon answered. "I did, as I'd like you to meet this lad, Braoin, who lives east of here in a settlement near Loch Síleann. Alrik discovered he was one of the warriors you suggested we seek out."

Runa turned her one-eyed gaze on the young man and said nothing, sitting across from him. After a moment, she nodded. "He is one of yours whom the Druids have singled out. I feel Tuatha magic lying heavy upon him."

Hakon gazed narrowly at the Gael. "So, you're the one?"

"The one what?" Braoin asked, clearly confused.

Runa interjected, "My Jarl, while the Tuatha gods have influenced the Gaels, it does not mean he's the one. They could all have the traits we seek to confuse us. You must continue the search."

Alrik met Donalt's eyes, noting rising tensions, decided a subject change was in order, and said, "So, Braoin, tell Donalt about how you won your silver arm ring. Was it this past summer when Dun Uisneach held their *comórtas*, já?"

"Aye," the lad said as his eyes shifted to the older Dreadrider. "I fought Bradaigh, but he won the duel and earned his gold."

"Congratulations!" Donalt said. "I heard it was a challenging event. The other day, I talked about those games with a lad living near the King's Road crossing of the River Shannon. While contesting for his gold, he also won a silver arm ring but lost to that same white-haired lad. He hails from a settlement near Dun Uisneach. Anything special about him?"

"Special?" Braoin questioned.

Alrik put in, "It must have been a grand battle. When we sparred in your settlement's yard, you showed a good balance with your blade."

Donalt asked, "Were there other white-haired lads like yourself competing? Besides Bradaigh?"

Braoin paused, and his left eye twitched. Then, shaking his head, he answered, "No other white-haired lads like me were competing for gold at those games."

Hakon and Runa exchanged glances as his völva signaled her belief in the truth of his statement, the former rising to say, "We have a mystery. Let us retire and see what tomorrow brings. Hopefully, Lunt and Lang will be back by then."

Lang

Lying on a bed of straw, Lang stared into the darkness, listening to his brother's labored breathing. He wondered if the Druid who had come to their aid had secretly poisoned them. Maybe it was all a ruse to lull them to sleep just to kill them. Then again, with the shape they were in last night, it wouldn't have taken much to put a knife through their bellies at any point.

Lang decided that the young apprentice Healer had used her skills to the best of her ability. She had said his wounds weren't severe—easy for her to say—but he had lost a considerable amount of blood, which would keep him weak for several days.

On the other hand, Lunt had taken a deep wound near the groin and would need a few more days to recover. He sounded worse than he had just after Hakon's Valkyrie had descended upon them. Even now, Lang could hardly believe a woman—and a young one—had done such damage. He and his brother were among the Dreadlord's fiercest warriors, and he convinced himself it must have been because she had surprised them with her silent attack and then shocked them by being female. If they were to meet again, Lang planned for the outcome of their battle to be vastly different.

Lang struggled to sit up and groaned as he did so. He finally got his legs under him, standing shakily, and took a step. After the next one, he leaned heavily on the door jamb. Making it outside, he followed the wall of the hut around to the back so he could relieve himself. With that, he limped to the doorway and was surprised to find his brother was awake. Sitting up with a groan, Lunt asked, "Should I be standing vigil while you rest in case one of the locals decides they don't like having Dreadriders in their dun?"

"You're a mess," Lang said dryly, but he was pleased to see his brother had awoken. Well, for a moment, anyway. Lunt slumped back to his bed of straw, and it was clear a dark and deep sleep took him under within a moment of their exchange. Lang did the same for a time and was unsure how much time had passed when he finally stirred to life again.

He would have rather slept longer, but something was biting his neck. Sunlight filtered through the cracks in the shed walls as he opened his eyes and found a pike at his throat, its sharp point digging into his skin. He took in the dull gray eyes of an old Gael warrior, who held his gaze steadily; Lunt decided the man's expression was icy.

Noting his broadsword was out of reach—not that he could have used it with his wounded arms—Lang grated, "Kill me or put up your pike, I don't care which."

When the shabbily dressed Gael shifted, Lang hoped it was because the warrior was thinking about his choices. Then, the older man shrugged and lifted the pike, grousing, "Och, canna' do it! Takin' your life when you have no weapon in your hand would not be honorable, no matter how deep my desire to drive this point through your throat. If you hadn't claimed Guestright, I'd never have let Crevan help you."

"Or maybe it's because you know my Jarl will reward you."

"I'd rather slit my belly before taking the Dreadlord's blood gifts."

"I have a knife on my belt if you'd like to use it."

With that, the old warrior grinned. "Brave lad, you are."

Using that small opening, Lang probed, "What is the name of this place?"

"Dun Moyne," the warrior said as he spat toward the left of the shed and muttered derisively about the vile warriors lying in his shed as he walked toward the yard.

Lang could only shake his head and roll to a sitting position – his arms were still useless, and he groaned in pain at the effort to see how his brother was faring. Lunt's breathing had settled, and he was still sleeping soundly. That was a good sign. Letting him rest, Lang struggled to his feet and stumbled to the door, leaning against its frame. The small shed they occupied stored the dun's vegetables and grains. Large buckets of beans, peas, and barley had been piled next to baskets of leeks, onions, and garlic. The aromas brought a grumble to Lang's belly; he was suddenly ravenous.

He didn't remember much of the dun from the evening before, save that it was little more than a small collection of rundown hovels southwest of Dun Arrogh. His dismal first impression didn't change as he scanned the buildings around him. Several huts had collapsed into jumbled piles of wickerwork, thatch, and wattle and daub, and the defensive ring, which had once protected against raiders, was of little use now.

Upon scanning the area for their horses, he found them still tethered outside the shed under a nearby lean-to. Lang was surprised to see the beasts, having thought one of the locals might have decided they would fetch more in trade than the Dreadlord would give for helping his warriors, as a single warhorse was worth five of the Gaels' smaller mounts. But Lang smiled and noted that their captors had also set aside their saddles, travel packs, and weapons. Maybe being a Dreadrider carried more weight than he thought. He rummaged in one of the packs with his better hand and pulled out a piece of salted boar meat.

As he chewed on the tough, dried jerky, he probed his wounds to see how much pain they would cause. Trying to raise his right arm made him grimace; it was clear he'd not be using his sword for a fortnight or more. While his right leg was stiff, his left arm didn't bother him as much as yesterday. If it were not for his excellent physical shape, he was sure his recovery would be considerably longer. Yet his movements caused significant pain, something he could not ignore. Thinking back on how quickly Hakon's bastard had taken them down, he cursed and limped back to their shed.

His brother was stirring, so Lang moved to his side to give him something to drink. Lunt accepted the battered wooden cup, slurping greedily at the water. Then, finally, he croaked, "Where are we?"

"It's called Dun Moyne," Lang answered. "We are a full day's ride to Dun Garm, I'd guess."

"Might as well be a fortnight," Lunt groaned as he tried to sit up; Lang had to help. "I certainly won't be able to ride much before then. Damn that Valkyrie of Hakon's, anyway."

"I've thought the same thing several times," Lang said as he rose stiffly. "But then, it could have been worse. She could have cut off your jewels."

"I'd have come back from the depths of Asgard to rip her heart out if she had."

Lang laughed. "How do we tell Hakon that his bastard is a woman? That is my question."

"Or you could ask, how do we tell him we let a girl kick us around like dogs?"

"That says it another way, a more blunt way, maybe," Lang countered dourly before taking a drink himself. "The other warriors at Dun Garm will think we're fools and weak for letting a mere girl beat us so badly. And we didn't even let one of our blades lick her!"

"Já," Lunt muttered, holding his hand out for the water again. "I think we should omit the part about Hakon's bastard being a woman. Your idea about him attacking at night might work, especially if we say *he* was joined by those other two. But how *he* knew where to attack us and why might pose some questions."

"We went to Dun Arrogh asking questions," Lang continued. "They must have followed us, and the ambush was unexpected."

"Do we say anything about the Red Branch?" Lunt asked. "We still don't know if Clan Mórhda is involved. Hakon should go check it out."

"Yes, that way, he can find out for himself that his bastard is a devilish bitch."

Lunt grunted. "Help me up—I need to piss, and neither you nor I don't want me to do it in here."

Breanna

After returning to Dun Arrogh from meeting with their Mother Goddess, Breanna Ban Morna slept in her mother's hut, now hers, with strange dreams of gods, goddesses, and the great magics they wrought. It was still well before dawn when she bolted upright, suddenly wide awake, as if the images in her dreams of dark demons attacking were real. She had never had one like it before and hugged herself to stop the trembling, hoping the demons that she battled in her nightmare would not find their way into her quest for the Blades of Destiny.

She rubbed her eyes and glanced about, still not used to the idea that this hut was now hers to do with as her whims took her. Kyras had suggested she might want to move in with their clan branch, but Breanna had declined. It was easier to be by herself, easier not to be concerned with letting her secret slip.

Lying on her cot, she watched the fire she had set the night before, the cut peat and oak still crackling in the center of the room, the smoke escaping through a vent in the ceiling above it. Across the room sat her mother's bed, far more comfortable than hers. Still, she could not bring herself to sleep in it, especially not with the image of her dead mother lying in it so fresh in her mind. She muttered, "Maybe I should just burn it."

The previous night's events with Beatha and Danu had her mind churning. Breanna would have hardly believed it had happened if it were not for the ring on her finger. But the goddess had chosen her, chosen her to fulfill a destiny laid upon her before she was born. Her confidence wavered as she thought about what lay ahead.

How could she ever hope to stop the Dreadlord of Garm? A fortress backed him with nearly a hundred warriors!

Breanna whispered Danu's name as if it would strengthen her resolve. The ring on her finger pulsed to life with a pale silver glow. Surprised, she covered it with her other hand, vowing not to play with the magic unless she genuinely needed it.

Breanna finally slept again; it was late morning when she rose and dressed. Stepping outside, she noted the weather had finally turned. It was a gray sky with a nip in the air, something she should have expected at this time of year. Her first stop was the baths, and once clean, her second was to see Eoin and Fergal at the Clan Mórhda's hut.

All except for the two warriors had already left to focus on their daily chores. It allowed Breanna to recount her tale about the night before. They naturally did not believe her when she mentioned meeting the Mother Goddess. At least not until she held up the crystal ring Danu had given her in the middle of the night.

She told them it was named *Maorgairme*, and it gave off a silver glow at the mention of its name.

Being his Champion, Breanna felt obligated to ask for Eoin's leave to go on the quest. He agreed readily, letting her know something more significant was happening to them than pulling together a motley band of warriors. Breanna smiled when he proclaimed the gods had chosen wisely to entrust such a quest to her. Then, given his approval, she turned and charged Fergal Mac Conall with the safety of their Red Branch Chief.

Fergal bristled as if wanting to say something he knew he shouldn't. Instead, he just nodded. As Breanna turned, Fergal muttered something about her chasing fairies and gods, proving that women shouldn't be leading their Red Branch. Before the door closed, she heard Eoin command his cousin to shut up;

that brought a smug grin to Breanna's lips. Relieved and with her first task accomplished, it was time to convince Kyras to let Toal join her on her quest for *Lann Dàn*.

Breanna crossed the central yard of Dun Arrogh, leaving the Clan Mórhda's hut behind and making for her uncle's forge. She had to dance through a knot of children playing at being warriors, their black oak sticks shaped into swords, smacking against each other. They clamored for her to join them, but she deftly declined because they had no long wooden blades for her to spar with them safely.

When their woodwright's youngest son proclaimed himself the dun Chief as he raced by on a miniature chariot drawn by a massive hound, the children's attention turned away from Breanna. She marveled at how the boy had pieced together the creaking cart, its small wooden wheels bouncing over the rutted ground, and then heartily laughed when she had to dart out of his path as he returned.

When she reached the forge, she found Kyras pounding out the shape of a sword from a long bar of red-hot iron and knew she would have to wait to be acknowledged. Waves of heat rolled from the stone forge behind him, but his face was redder from the effort of raising his hammer. Sparks flew as he struck his blows on the sword, and slag fell away from the blade.

Sweat covered the rippling muscles of his stocky frame, his shirt long ago thrown aside despite the crisp air. Breanna remembered many times when she and Toal had mixed the clay and hay with their feet, pumped the bellows, fed air into the clay-smelting furnaces, and chopped wood for the charring pit. It was brutal work.

Finally, after a moment of pounding, the iron had cooled enough to be no longer malleable. Then, Kyras turned from his anvil to jam the blade back into the fire and saw her.

"Well, girl, what can I do for you?" he asked as he worked the bellows before his finishing forge. When Breanna didn't answer, he eyed her briefly. She squirmed under his gaze and briefly wondered if he saw Hakon's face in hers. The gentleness of his expression told her he saw Morna's daughter.

She began hesitantly, "The Druid Beatha charged me with a quest."

Her uncle frowned and momentarily stopped stoking his forge. Then, the bellows were in motion again as if the lapse had not occurred. "She's nothing but trouble."

"Trouble or no, she's a Fáidh, one I know you respect, and the gods have spoken to her," Breanna countered. She took a step toward him, her confidence swelling. "She's charged me with finding a magic weapon left behind by the *Tuatha Dé Danann*."

"Tuatha magic is for Druids," Kyras advised, shaking his head. "Leave them to it, as they should be talking to our gods, not you."

Breanna sighed at his negative comment. "If only it were that easy. After Beatha charged me with this quest, the Mother Goddess appeared and gave me a Tuatha charm she called *Maorgairme*. It's for protection." Breanna held her hand out to show him the glowing crystal ring on her finger. "The goddess said that only by finding these magic weapons, called *Lann Dàn*, can we hope to remove the Dreadlord from our land."

Kyras frowned again, his arms hesitating at their work. A low whistle rolled from his mouth, and he looked at the ring glowing with its magic. "The Goddess Danu?"

"Aye," Breanna confirmed. "I could hardly believe it myself."

"These are strange times, but the magic of the *Triple Dáns* is powerfully prophetic in our Bard's tales," Kyras put in as he started working the bellows of his forge again. "But why do you tell me this? It's a matter for the Druids."

"The quest is mine, not our Druids', and Danu charged me to find someone to aid me in it," Breanna answered. Then, deciding to stretch the truth, she added, "Danu knew Eoin and Fergal were in no shape for such a quest after their battle with the Dreadriders, and she commanded that my aide be someone of my blood. That someone is Toal."

"My son? Involved with fairie magic?" Kyras fumed as he let his arms come to rest once more. "I don't think—"

"It is the goddess's will," Breanna reminded him.

Kyras let his jaw work like his bellows, but no words emerged from his mouth. Then he managed, "To where does this quest lead?"

"The Cuilcagh Mountains—it's not far from Loch Aillionn, where Eoin, Fergal, and I ran off that time to find the source of the Shannon," Breanna answered.

Kyras scowled. "I know where Cuilcagh is, girl. When do you leave?"

"In the morning."

Kyras appeared to mull it over, then nodded. "While I believe Druids best handle this, I suppose it's not too far. Lissa won't like it—she still thinks of Toal as her little laddie. Even if his voice cracks most of the time, she doesn't hear that it sounds more like a man's voice than a boy's each day. And I certainly would not want to second-guess the Mother Goddess in this, even though I can't see how a boy his age could help."

Breanna said, "He is thirteen, soon to be fourteen, after all, and handles his bow very well."

"Aye, that he is and that he does, and you will be there to look after him, to make sure he doesn't get into trouble." Kyras's tone said she better not let Toal get so much as a scratch on him.

Breanna smiled despite her uncle's stern expression. "Can we keep this quiet—the part about the goddess and the quest for the Tuatha magic—until Toal and I leave?"

"Don't want everyone thinking you've gone *craiceáilte*?" Kyras asked, tapping a finger on his forehead.

Breanna nodded; having the dun think she was crazy wouldn't help when they found out who her birth father was.

Her acknowledgment of his question made her uncle smile, and he added, "You understand it is a fanciful story."

"I do. Believe me, I do."

He briefly eyed her before returning to his bellows, saying gruffly, "Now, be off with you. I've work to do."

Breanna turned from the forge and went to find her younger cousin.

Later that day, the pair started gathering supplies for their journey. Toal had been thrilled by the news. His father's approval had stunned him into silence more than Breanna's tale of the Druid Beatha, the Goddess Danu, being loaned a magical ring named *Maorgairme*, and her quest for *Lann Dàn*. Even Eoin and Fergal were impressed that Breanna had persuaded Kyras to agree.

Cilla, Calla's daughter, filled their ration sacks with dried deer meat, nuts, fresh fruit, hunks of dark bread, and a few onions. Breanna had said they needed enough food to last them six days, and they would have to hunt for extra meat if they took longer than that. Breanna had Toal pack a change of clothes, but other than that, they would be traveling lightly.

Breanna sat with Kyras, Lissa, and their children at the evening meal in the main hall. There was idle talk about the day, but no one raised the subject of the quest. Lissa was not pleased about her mate's decision to let her son go. Yet, she knew better than to bring it up during their meal.

After dinner, Breanna sent her young cousin to bed and left her clan to tell Eoin's mother, Aife, that she would bring her son and his cousin something to eat and see how they were faring. Aife, a Princess of the Blood from Dál n Araidi, thanked her for her concern with a warm smile.

Recruiting Cilla's help, they brought the convalescing warriors a skin of ale, trenchers of food, and a small jug of mead for herself. She sat by the fire, silently watching them as they slurped up Calla's fish stew, bread, and cheese. For the first time, she realized that warrior-to-warrior, she was their equal in every way. Still, she was more conscious than ever of how different she looked and felt like a stranger in her land now that she knew about her father.

Determined to keep the dreadful knowledge of her lineage locked deep inside her, she found it easier to say nothing and let the crackling fire in the center of the conical roundhouse speak to her friends while she contemplated the strange ring.

Eoin pushed his trencher away on the table and rose from his stool in apparent pain. He had a bad limp as he made his way to Breanna's side with a cup of ale for himself and the jug of mead to refill her cup. She came to her feet as he approached, wanting to ensure there were deerskins laid out over a fresh straw bed. It would provide him with a comfortable place to lounge by the fire, and its warmth would ease his aches.

Fergal didn't take long to join them, a silver-banded ale cup in hand. He was in a surly mood, with little to say about the quest but much to grumble about the state of life. When his derisive comments finally wandered to Breanna's recent adventure, neither she nor Eoin responded, and silence settled over the room. Little more was said as they stared into the flames. Before they knew it, Fergal was asleep, snoring a gentle rumble that was easy to ignore.

Eoin turned to Breanna. "It's been a rough couple of days."

All she managed was a simple nod. Her Chief's eyes caught hers, and the tender look Eoin gave her was unsettling. He moved closer, adding, "I never did thank you for saving my life."

Breanna shrugged. "I am your Champion—you don't need to thank me."

"I wasn't thanking you as my Champion but as my friend and best companion."

With that, Eoin leaned forward and kissed her softly, his lips pausing over hers. For a brief moment, Breanna drank in the essence of him, his breath, and the saltiness he left behind. As his kiss lingered on her lips, she wanted to reach out and pull him to her, let passion engulf her. If only things were different, letting go would be so easy.

Then it struck her that the Dreadlord's blood ran in her veins, and destiny was taking her down another path. Nothing could become a barrier to her quest—her need—to kill her father.

She turned away abruptly to watch the fire, saying more roughly than intended, "It was my duty."

Eoin

Breanna didn't see the hurt expression on Eoin's face as he closed his eyes. He wondered what he needed to do to get her to drop the iron wall she kept locked around her heart. He had felt a spark between them, felt there was more to their companionship than duty, but now it was gone. After a heavy sigh, Eoin looked at the fire. He wondered how many times he could take such rejection.

Thinking back, he realized it had been four years since his first attempt to court Breanna, and she had never acknowledged his feelings, or her own, for that matter. Had it not been for the occasional ember of passion between them, he wanted to believe he would not have remained committed to her for so long. The thought nearly made him laugh, though bitterly. But, whether she ever admitted what he knew they both felt, he knew he would always love her—there was something about her that left him no choice.

After sleeping most of the day, Eoin was not even a little tired. He would settle for having her as his Champion if he could not have her as more than a companion. Unable to think of anything to say, he asked, "So, Bre, what did your mother have to tell you before her passing?"

Breanna stiffened as if struck by lightning. Then, she stammered a bit, yet nothing intelligible came out of her mouth. She turned away and stood, finally saying, "Just woman things."

"Like what?" Eoin probed as he struggled to get to his feet.

"No, don't get up," Breanna commanded as she effortlessly pushed him back onto the deerskins. "Now, I've got a long day ahead of me tomorrow. It's time I found my bed."

With that, she bid Eoin good night, leaving him with his mouth hanging open.

Something inside said she had misdirected him. But why? And what had Morna told her?

Lang

Lang struggled to ready his mount while Lunt watched. The latter was still recovering from the wounds inflicted by Hakon's bastard, and while he could walk haltingly, he certainly couldn't ride without tearing open the deep slice next to his groin. Nevertheless, a little color had returned to Lunt's face. At least they'd found a place to spend Ancestor Night under a roof instead of beneath the night sky.

Lang was recovering well, but his sword arm was still useless, making saddling his horse and getting the bridle challenging. There were no words between the two Dreadriders except his grunts and groans. They had decided to tell Hakon what had happened, even if they omitted a few key details. Waiting for Lunt to heal could give Hakon's potential Destroyer time to escape.

It was raining, and it looked to be a nasty, dreary day. Water ran down Lang's face from his long white hair, blurring his vision enough to make him stop tightening the straps on his riding gear. Every time he tried to lift his right arm to clear the water away, he regretted it. Finally finished with his mount, he said, "I'll have them send a chariot to bring you home."

"See you soon, then," Lunt replied, his expression pained. The pair had rarely been apart for any significant period, and neither cared for the plan to keep them separated for at least several days. Still, there was no speeding his healing enough to get him on a mount soon, and they had to tend to their duty. "Take care, brother."

Lang flung himself into his saddle. "Keep safe, brother." With that, he turned his mount for the broken gates of Dun Moyne.

Riding was more challenging than expected as he headed south toward Dun Garm. The rain added more than its share to his discomfort, but he would not relent. He rode throughout the day, pushing himself longer than he should have and only letting his mount rest when the beast showed severe fatigue. His weariness was something he did not want to acknowledge. The Dreadlord had always told his Dreadriders that they would be superior only if they could master the weaknesses of the flesh, and at that moment, Lang determined he would be such a master.

As the spans wore on, the hills and valleys began to feel like home. The rain finally stopped in the afternoon, but the damp chill in his bones would not leave. When Dun Garm came into view, Lang sighed and hoped Hakon's völva would have something to soothe his aching body and feverish head.

After passing through the massive gates and dismounting, he noticed a red stain had spread down his side; the wound beneath his sword arm had opened again.

One of the stablehands rushed to take his mount. "Lang, you've been hurt. Wait here—I'll send for Runa at once."

"No time," Lang commanded, putting his hand on the lad's shoulder to steady himself. "Tell her I'll be with the Dreadlord. I must inform our Jarl that we likely found his Destroyer."

"But where's Lunt?"

"Alive, but not by much," he growled. "Now, be off with you."

A moment later, the wounded warrior staggered into the main hall. The Dreadlord rose as Lang limped across the floor, with the Dreadrider saying, "My Jarl, we might have found the Destroyer you sent us in search of."

"It looks more like my potential Destroyer found you, já?" Hakon said sourly.

Lang nodded and began to tell his tale, leaving out the details about his Jarl's bastard being a woman. He had never lied to Hakon before, so he wasn't sure how he managed to keep the guilt of the deed from his eyes. Lang knew he was fortunate the Dreadlord was concentrating more on his story than his face, and he knew his gods doubly favored him that Runa was not present as he spoke. Few details had ever escaped her attention.

As he finished the account of the attack, Hakon's völva ambled into the main hall. Lang could only sigh with relief when she started barking at those around her to fetch hot water and bandages so she could tend to his wounds. Any additional storytelling could come later, as getting some warriors together to fetch Lunt needed to be his next priority.

That same day, it was cold and gray in Dun Arrogh, with angry, low-hanging clouds threatening to make travelers miserable as Breanna and Toal emerged from the main hall, with Lissa and Kyras right behind them. Toal's unhappy mother had barely managed to hold her tongue but said nothing more.

Yet, outside and alone, she hissed, "Bre, I don't like this notion of my Toal joining you on your quest for Tuatha magic."

Breanna nodded. "I expected as much. Yet, I don't have the words to ease your concerns. Only that I will do my best to keep your son out of harm's way."

Kyras started to say something, but his mate said, "Shut it." Lissa pulled Toal into a hug and whispered, "Be safe, my son."

Breanna and Toal took their leave of the pair and headed out of the dun. Breanna occasionally cast a wary eye to the sky as she walked, but Toal seemed oblivious to anything that would ruin his first quest. Instead, with his sword strapped to his side, a spear in his hand, and his short bow and quiver slung over his shoulder, he proudly kept pace with his taller cousin.

Toal wore a linen undershirt, a short deerskin tunic and leggings, a full woolen tunic, and a long cloak made from squirrel pelts. Breanna had complained to her aunt that walking a span would cause him to overheat.

Lissa wouldn't budge, saying the weather looked nasty and the four layers stayed in place. In contrast to her cousin, Breanna had decided it wasn't far enough into the fall season to justify wool, opting instead for a deerskin tunic and leggings beneath her long otterskin cloak.

Dun Arrogh faded behind them as they made their way northwest. Their path led them through the lush, steeply rolling terrain between their home and the Grove of Instruction.

Beyond that, they swung southeast before heading west to avoid the steep climbs of the mountain they sought. The circuitous route was the easiest path to the Cuilcaghs.

When they passed the stream where Breanna had fought the Dreadriders, Toal was full of talk about how they might have to battle on their quest, and even though he had not yet earned his first warrior's armring, the lad didn't hesitate to say what he would have done had he been there. He drew his light, one-handed sword that his father had made, and danced around in mock battle, continuously chattering about how they would have tasted his blade. The young lad was even briefly critical of Eoin and Fergal—they should never have been on the defensive, let alone been wounded so badly. His bravado made Breanna smile, and she found the nonstop chatter oddly comforting as she walked.

At least with Toal, she did not have to be concerned about letting her secret slip; her cousin had wrapped himself up in visions. His mention of the two warriors made her think about being alone with Eoin while Fergal slept the night before. For one moment, she remembered a moment of bliss, feeling his lips on hers. Then, who she was and what the Mother Goddess had laid out about her fate had made it instantly uncomfortable. Though she could not deny the wonder she felt at the softness of Eoin's lips on hers, that was something she would not let happen again.

Her pace was comfortable, so even her shorter cousin could keep up. It was only a two- or three-day walk to the Cuilcagh Mountains from Dun Arrogh. Unfortunately, while it had been misty with drizzle earlier, it started raining steadily around midmorning. By the time they stopped to eat beneath a large black oak, Breanna was soaked, and even though her otterskin cloak blocked out most of the dampness, it did not keep her warm. Breanna groused when Toal announced his wool tunic was dry but would not admit that Lissa had been right about dressing in layers. That the bread in her sack was slightly soggy only added insult to injury.

Breanna relented once they finished their lunch. She slipped off her cloak, reached into her pack for her wool tunic, and put it on. Toal wisely said nothing as she pulled her otter skin cloak around her shoulders before setting out again.

The rain kept them moving, for it was too cold not to work their muscles hard. The dark clouds had lightened in the late afternoon, and the rain had returned to a fine mist. Breanna noted Toal was showing some wear from the day's effort, for the hilly forested land made for a slow, arduous pace. However, she pretended not to notice as she proclaimed they had traveled far enough when they found some flat ground.

Toal sighed in relief as the climbs were steep at times.

Breanna, seeing her cousin, reached down to put a hand on his shoulder. "Let's make a fire. I'll find us some kindling and dry wood. Get the pot out—be back soon."

A moment later, Breanna returned. "I found a small grove of oak trees where the ground beneath was barely damp. We'll camp there."

Seeing that Toal had recovered, she sent him to gather dry wood for a fire while she went off to see if she could spear some fish. Calla's rations were fine for normal traveling conditions, but something hot for supper would help take the chill from their bones. Breanna found some leeks at a nearby stream and took off her deerskin thongs and leggings to wade into the cold water with her small fishing net. It was a good time of year to catch trout running upstream, and the fish were plentiful.

Breanna caught a half-dozen on her second cast and a few more on her third throw. After that, she kept only two of the largest fish for dinner and two medium-sized ones for breakfast.

A short while later, she was on her way back to camp with chattering teeth and icy-blue toes and happy to find that Toal had not only already lit the fire but had also found some mushrooms to add to their evening meal.

Later, the sun faded below the horizon as they nibbled on the last roasted trout with the mushrooms and leeks. Toal muttered, "Being out on a night like this makes me shiver to the bones."

Breanna reassured him their gods had sanctioned their quest, so they had nothing to worry about. He wouldn't wake in the morning to find that the Sidhe had taken him under one of their mounds.

To get his mind off the tales spun by their Druids about fairies, she set him to work on scaling the fish. Not long after, they were roasting over their fire.

As they ate, Toal asked softly, "Bre, do you think we will find these magical long blades? Or are they just a story the hermit Beatha has heard?"

"Well, cousin, what do you think?" Breanna responded, finding his doubts humorous. She'd had some of the same concerns before Danu's appearance.

"The Mother Goddess did confirm the tale, right?" Toal put in seriously, at which she just smiled. "In that case, if anyone can find them, it's you and me."

"Good, let's get some sleep," Breanna said as she unrolled her oiled bed tarp, sleeping mat, and blanket. "An early start will get us to the top of the mountain much sooner."

Toal was snoring gently moments later, and Breanna wondered again if her quest was nothing more than a fool's dream. However, Eoin seemed convinced it was worth pursuing, especially with his belief in her visit with Danu. If he had been able, he indeed would have joined her.

Seeing Danu's ring on her finger in the fire's dying light made her sigh. When she whispered its name, *Maorgairme*, the charm came to life with a silver glow, sealing it for her. Maybe it wasn't a dream, and she hoped Beatha was right about *Lann Dàn* being able to defeat even the mightiest of warriors. Freeing her land of Hakon Skadi would surely be the challenge of her life. Perhaps she might find room for Eoin after that, but she didn't know what that could mean now. Her *geas* left her little room for such thoughts. Yet, knowing how it ruled her didn't make it any easier to suppress what she suspected her heart wanted.

Fortunately, the morning was dry, allowing Toal to cook up the other two trout. He added them to some trail bread for breakfast. Shortly thereafter, Breanna had Toal on the move again as dawn lit the sky, continuing to guide them on a north-westerly trek. The misty rain from the previous day returned and continued to fall until lunchtime, but by late afternoon, it had stopped, and the clouds began to break up. The Cuilcagh Mountains and the sister climbs of Slieve Anierin rose before them and to their north and west, growing as they drew near. Both warriors were sweating as they worked their way through steeper inclines. Soon, the sun was low in the western sky.

When they passed a small dun, Toal wanted to stop and claim Guestright so they could spend a warm night with the strangers. While Breanna didn't wish to have outsiders nosing into where they were heading, she shrugged, knowing it would save on their rations. The dark clouds hovered to the west again, indicating her decision should be to side with Toal. A night out of the rain would let them dry out.

As they strode toward the gates, a guard demanded, "Halt!"

"Peace with you," Breanna responded. "We are simple travelers who would claim Guestright. We have a matter elsewhere that we seek, but we do need shelter for tonight."

"From where do you hail?"

"Dun Arrogh."

"That's Dreadlord territory."

"Aye, it is, and we aim to more than poke a stick in his eye. But that's another matter."

"Then we have a mutual enemy, and your claim of Guestright to Dun Droma is honored. We have a small guest hut you can share. Yet to the main hall first!"

The guard escorted the pair through the yard, filled with sheep and goats, into a good-sized building in the center of the fort. They were each provided with a bowl of fish soup and a trencher featuring lamb, cheese, root vegetables, and bread. Since they had no mead, Breanna had to settle for ale.

A middle-aged lady dressed in Bardic robes stepped onto a riser sometime later. "I understand we have guests from Dun Arrogh this evening. Given their dark time with the outlanders, I have selected a long-forgotten song sung in dire times called A Bard's Plea."

Accompanied by three players, one on a flute, one on a fiddle, and one on a bodhran, the Bard pulled out a small travel harp. After a quick tuning of her instrument and playing some warm-up chords, she sang:

In times gone by, our clans did battle
To the sounds of fear and the drummers rattle
When Mystical Maeve, she fought Cú Chulainn
And Rory the Red, he reigned our land

Heroes they were and legends they made
But kings forget and legends fade
Our kingdoms bicker, our bright lights dim
Our people's fate is a fickle whim

Erin's Hero is needed once more
To rally her people
As in times before
To lead to victory
And see our land restored
To be the voice of those ignored

They rode horses through winds and hail
Crossed wide rivers where fairies wail
Some had pikes, swords, and spears
While others used their wits and jeers

Seeds were sown and stories told
Of spirits in forests and legends of old
Young blood runs deep and old hearts beat
Which one will win and take their seat

Erin's Hero is needed once more
For our Heart to choose as before
A hero born brave, unswayed by the waves
Fierce and bold, forever to hold

While those of Dun Droma cheered the Bard and her players by thumping hunting knife hilts on the tables before them,
Breanna turned her gaze from the *Filídh* to Toal and found him
staring at her. It was as if he knew why the Bard had chosen that
song. She just shook her head, indicating it was not something
they should discuss openly, and turned to seek out the guest
hut for the night.

The following morning, the pair rose and departed from Dun Droma; the song sung by the Bard stuck in Breanna's mind. Could it be possible that she was Erin's Hero, as Danu suggested? It seemed far-fetched, yet was it possible?

The ground was damp as they marched out of the dun and headed upward, making their way throughout the day and soon cresting one of the taller hills. Where the trees thinned, Breanna spotted the north end of shimmering Loch Aillionn to the west and knew they hadn't far to go. Thankfully.

When the sun was close to the horizon, they stopped at the foot of the Cuilcagh Mountains. It was too late to ascend into yet steeper climbs—the final slope of Cuilcagh would pose a severe challenge in the dark—so Breanna and her cousin made camp beside a tiny stream flowing down from the mountain above them.

Little light was left to bother with fishing or hunting for their evening meal, which set the pair to digging into the supplies Calla had packed. Since the evening was chilly, Breanna started a fire before they ate.

An old Gael approached as they labored over chewing on the dried venison—something considerably more challenging to eat than the juicy lamb they'd had at the dun the night before. Toal's hand went to the hilt of his short sword, but Breanna could see in the fading light of the day that the stranger held an open hand before him. It was a gesture that said he meant no harm. His other hand had a walking stick. It was hardly stout enough to be a weapon.

The man, dressed in drab gray robes under his cloak, asked in an aged and gravelly voice, "Can I share your fire?"

"Certainly," Breanna answered. "The Mother Goddess provided the wood, not I, and she commands that we share her bounty."

The man nodded as he sat, placing his staff across his lap. He stared briefly at Breanna's white hair before saying, "Most gracious of you. Name's Hgul."

"I am Breanna Ban Morna, Dun Arrogh's Red Branch Champion, and this is my apprentice, Toal," she said.

"Good to meet you both," the old man answered as he settled beside the fire. He fell silent, watching the flickering flames.

Breanna interrupted his thoughts, asking, "Have you eaten, Hgul?"

"Oh, aye," he said quickly. "Dun Droma keeps me fed."

Breanna surveyed the man, trying to assess if he was dangerous. His name was strange—indeed, not a Gael name, something which urged caution—and his clear green eyes revealed a hidden strength that contrasted sharply with his wrinkled face and stooped back. He had stringy, gray hair and clutched his tattered boar-skin cloak closely around him. The absence of a good cloak suited for the weather made it plain that Dun Droma provided him with nothing more than food scraps.

Breanna thought he had an otherworldly look like Beatha's and wondered if he might be a Fáidh. Yet he did not have the markings of a Druid—Healers wore green and red, Seers blue and red, Lawgivers white and purple, and Bards yellow and green. If a Druid failed in their duty, a dun could cast them out, but that was rare. They could transfer their sacred calling to another dun. Druid or not, she supposed, it did not matter, and asked, "We stopped at Dun Droma last night. Why did we not see you there?"

The man shrugged, rubbing his hands over the fire to warm them.

"Do they not let you sleep within its protection?" Toal asked.

"Ah, that." The older man sighed remorsefully. "It's a long and sad tale."

When he did not continue, Toal looked at Breanna and shrugged. Neither was sure what to make of him. So they both sat back to finish their meal. The silence was unsettling as they put away their supplies. Once they completed that task, Hgul asked, "And what brings you so far from your dun?"

Toal's eyes lit up, and his voice cracked as he began excitedly, "A quest to find—"

"Something left behind by my brother in a cave on Cuilcagh Mountain," Breanna interrupted, nudging her cousin to shut him up. "It's a family heirloom, similar to the long blades on my back. My father's and grandmother's."

Hgul looked doubtfully from Breanna to Toal and back again, commenting dryly, "Not wise to leave a thing of value lying about, especially for a warrior, and even more so for a Champion."

"True," Breanna agreed, taking note of his tone as she finished with her pack. Was he probing, or was he somehow attempting to be innocent?

"So, a warrior and her apprentice on a mission?" the old man asked. "I see you've earned your gold armband. Do you know the way of *urghabháil an neamhní*?"

"I can now seize the *void* when in battle—well, most of the time," she confirmed, rethinking her notion as to whether or not he was a Druid. Only one of the *Aos Dána* would know about the strange state she sought. How he knew about the *void* and the *sight* was an unsettling mystery.

While holding the *void*, Breanna's control had felt like little more than a warm-up battle during her duel with Fergal to become Eoin's Champion. Then, she'd manipulated the two Dreadriders with her access to that strange state. It had convinced her that she could, indeed, master the place in between her realm and the Tuatha realm. But, while access to the *void* seemed linked to her ability to fight, her shared moment of the *sight* with her Mother Goddess had told her it was something more.

Through Beatha, she knew that each branch of Druids, whether Ollamh, Fáidh, Breitheamh, Filidh, or the lost Laoch, each used the pattern of seizing the *void* or the *sight* to master their mystical arts. However, few knew or believed that the warrior class could do the same, even though the Druids had insisted the warrior class was no different and could master touching the Tuatha realm as they had.

"Ah, a hard thing to hold, let alone to wield in battle," murmured the old man, which snapped Breanna out of her musings, and she nodded. "There must be wise Druids at Dun Arrogh to have taught you that."

"Our apprentice Fáidh told the dun's warriors about it, but he couldn't teach us how to seize the *void* because he can barely manage to do so himself," she responded, maybe a little too sharply. "I had to find it on my own, alone, as our other Druids had little success passing the knowledge of the *urghabháil an neamhní* to us."

"Unfortunate, especially since our warriors will lose an advantage we worked so hard to instill," Hgul murmured.

Breanna narrowed her eyes. He had said *'we,' inferring that* he was a Druid. Or something else?

After another moment, the old man changed the subject, saying, "I know the mountain well. In which area is this cave where your brother lost your family heirloom?"

"The west side, in a low cave filled with boulders near the source of the Shannon," Breanna said with a scowl. She didn't like this stranger's probing questions.

Hgul scratched his head. "Might be the boulder choke called Pollahuna. The Shannon Pot is just below that spot."

Breanna perked up at the mention of the name. "You think you know it?"

"As I said, I know the area well," Hgul replied tightly, seemingly annoyed. "I can show you the way if you want?"

Breanna pursed her lips and eyed him critically, wishing Eoin were with her. He had a good sense of people, certainly better than her own. She and the stranger stared at each other briefly, and then Breanna nodded. "Why not? It would save us some time."

"Be back in the morning, then, and thank you for sharing your fire with me," Hgul said as he rose. Then, he departed without another word. As he slipped into the darkness, tapping his walking stick with each step, Breanna noted his gait was not like that of an older man, and he didn't seem to need his walking stick to make his way.

Toal looked across the fire to Breanna. "A strange man."

"Yes, but one who can help us, I think," she agreed, pulling her beaded hair thong free and wrapping it around her neck. "Still, be on your guard tomorrow."

Her cousin nodded as gravely as a thirteen-year-old could. Then he turned to unroll his oiled bed tarp, sleeping mat, and blanket as Breanna had done the night before.

A moment later, they were both asleep.

DEMONS OF THE DARK

Breanna

When Breanna and Toal woke the following morning, the sun barely cresting the horizon, the outcast from Dun Droma was sitting before their long-spent fire, gazing at the ashes as if they were still blazing. Breanna groused inwardly about his silent return as they broke camp, berating herself for not waking on his arrival. Yet, simultaneously, she wanted to rail at Hgul for the impertinence of his unannounced appearance. Something about the man did not sit well, and her intuition told her there was more to him than met the eye.

Irritated, Breanna didn't even give Toal a chance to finish his breakfast before she was on her feet and marching toward the mountain.

Hgul was already at her side, pointing out some feature or another of his mountains. From the valley they were in, the Cuilcagh Mountains towered over them like a dark, heavy cloud. Behind them, Slieve Anierin climbed into the sky, reaching nearly as high.

The moon faded as the sun rose, though it would be a while before it cleared the mountain peak. They stumbled and slid on the dewy grass and moss-covered rocks. The forest had given way to gorse and furze bushes, which dotted the hillside in large clumps, forcing them to change directions continually. Spans later, when the sun had reached its zenith, they came to the small pool called the Shannon Pot.

The little body had formed by water gathered from rivulets and underground springs and fed the narrow beginnings of the River Shannon. When Hgul informed them that the Pollahuna cave wasn't much farther, Toal sighed, and Breanna knew it was because they wouldn't have to hike to the top of the mountain.

They stopped beside the Shannon Pot for lunch, and Hgul accepted Breanna's offered food this time. Chewing quietly on some bread and pears Calla had packed for them, she eyed the older man, not understanding why he was helping them.

Toal's constant prattle helped distract him, with the boy spewing out questions about monsters in Loch Aillionn, how tall the mountains were, what it was like to live in their shadow, and what Dun Droma was like in the winter. The outcast responded distantly, his answers short and unrevealing. Yet, despite her wariness, Breanna could detect no sense of malice in Hgul.

Then she remembered that Beatha had told her to seize the *void* while not in battle to test her competence. Calmly, she reached for the space between her and the Tuatha realms. After a moment, feeling as if she were floating, she reached out to that place between the realms and claimed its essence. She was holding the *void*, not in motion, for once. It felt different than before, almost like it waited for a directive, an intent, a desire only she could fulfill, as she had been the one to seize it. Breanna opened her eyes and looked at Hgul, asking the *void*, "*Who are you?*"

Hgul smiled. "Interesting question. You will know soon."

Breanna narrowed her eyes. It was suspicious that he knew she had asked it inside her head while holding the *void* open. Maybe he was a Druid. "That is a dangerous response, Hgul. If that is your name."

The older man smiled and shrugged. "It is all I have for now. Let's find these left-behind blades you and your companion seek."

Breanna's eyes hardened even more. His return stare did not have an ounce of give in it. Relenting, she nodded toward Toal and signaled they should march on. A span later, the pair from Dun Arrogh stood with their guide before the mouth of the cave. Pollahuna was in a shallow, boulder-strewn ravine with a small stream bubbling through the jumble of gray rocks. The dark opening looked like a giant maw, ready to swallow anyone who entered.

Peering inside, Breanna said, "Looks like there's only room to crawl once you get more than a few feet inside. I hope our heirloom is not too far from the entrance."

"If this is the place," Hgul said.

Breanna shrugged and handed Toal her pack and long blades. Darkness enveloped her as she slipped into the cave and crawled inward. Behind her, she could see daylight streaming through the opening, but after a few moments, little of it reached her. The cavern was maybe five times as wide as it was tall, sloping down into the heart of the mountain like a door to the fairie places their Bards spoke of. She wished the boulder choke was tall enough to stand in, for the damp rocks she crawled over were biting into her knees. And despite scaring herself every time she bumped her head on the ceiling, she forced herself to delve deeper into the cave.

Water dripped from the ceiling, and a gurgle of a stream ran nearby in the darkness. As loose rocks fell each time she bumped left, right, or into the ceiling, she remembered that Danu's ring would tell her if she was near *Lann Dàn*. Looking down, Breanna saw *Maorgairme* glow faintly silver. Her throat tightened with excitement. She stopped and turned to sit, trying to see what she could in the shadowy dimness of the cave and get her bearings. Her eyes had adjusted to the lack of light, but it did little to alleviate the discomfort. *Lann Dàn* had to be there—*Maorgairme* confirmed it—but they most certainly would be very well hidden.

Breanna asked herself, "If I were a Druid, where would I hide such a treasure?"

Then, Beatha's words about Amergin's directions struck her. She was still for a moment and then touched her forehead. The words unfolded.

It is a place that lies both north and south of Black Pig's Dike, an area where the sun shines only after reaching its zenith. From this place flows a river that feeds the land. Within this place, one can find Lann Dàn. Look closely, for many rocks hide the fairie's treasure.

When she looked back toward the mouth of the cave, she saw two pillars of stone outlined in the dim light. Suspicious, Breanna used the ring on her finger as a guide and pointed her hand down into the heart of the mountain. The silver glow faded, then brightened again when she directed her hand toward the entrance. Breanna had crawled right past them. She scrambled toward the columns and cave opening, cursing as rocks beneath her bit into her as they did on the way in, and loosed a stream of vitriol when stones overhead tore at her scalp. By the stars, it was a tight fit!

Yet reaching them brought a smug smile to her mouth, and she began pulling stones from one of the pillars. That fool, Fergal, would envy her when she returned with *Lann Dàn*. The pillars had reached from the floor to the ceiling, more than was needed to cover the blades. Yet, while the mineral deposits on the stones made them appear part of the cave, they were not like the other rocks—someone had carried river stones into the cave and stacked them, packing clay between them to keep them in place.

Breanna had to give Amergin credit for hiding the treasure so well. Even the Tuatha had not found the magical weapons. Danu's ring was glowing fiercely now that it was so close to *Lann Dàn*, and Breanna was not sure how she could have missed it before.

Removing the first layer of stones revealed nothing except more stones. Disappointment started to set in. Then, a shaft of light pierced the cave as the sun set lower, and Breanna saw the glitter of a diamond blade from one shaft come to life. Her fingers hurt when she pulled the wet, crusty stones away to reveal one *Lann Dàn*. It was hard to make out much detail, but she saw it was wedged between the ceiling and the floor. Breanna closed a hand around the smooth shaft. It felt like metal but looked like wood. Then, she tried jerking it free; the handle moved maybe an inch, and stones rained down on her from the ceiling. If the blades held up the cave's roof, there'd be no freeing them without bringing down the cavern.

Cursing, she made for the cave opening. She emerged and said, "Toal, I need something to wedge the rocks. The blades are holding up the ceiling, and I'll bring the whole cave down if I don't put something in their place."

"You found them?" her cousin asked, his voice cracking on the last word.

"Aye, the ring confirmed it," Breanna answered. "Did you doubt I would?"

"No," Toal said with a shrug.

Hgul seemed amused. "Are your long blades the same size?"

Breanna understood his suggestion, though it brought a pained expression to her face—the weapons had been in her clan for generations, and parting with them was not what she had in mind—but she nodded. Hgul's odd smile bothered her. Yet she did not have time for his games and stretched her hand out to Toal for her long blades before she crawled back into the cave. Sitting beside the one *Lann Dàn* she had uncovered, Breanna hesitated, caressing the hafts of her blades. Then, nodding, she whispered, "Sorry, Nevan."

With that, she jammed a blade up into the ceiling. More stones came down, but they were mostly small. Breanna decided it would be wiser to uncover the other *Lann Dàn* next and place her clan's blade next to it before trying to jerk Badb Catha's otherworld weapons free of their interment. She moved to the second pillar to pull down more stones. After a moment, she called to her cousin, "Toal, I'm ready. You'll be digging me out if the cave comes down on my head."

"Be careful, Bre!" her cousin exclaimed.

"Right," she said sourly, putting her other blade in place to help hold up the ceiling, and moved between the magical blades. Grabbing the base of each haft with a hand, she planted her feet on some rocks. Then, wondering what Eoin would say when she returned with such magnificent weapons, she gave a heave.

As each *Lann Dàn* came free, Breanna rolled toward the mouth of the cave. A rock hit her head, but it didn't stop her outward motion. More rocks rained down, but her long blades, part of the Clan Dálaigh for generations, took hold.

Breanna hoped it had been a fair trade as blackness swept over her.

Hakon Skadi walked into the central yard of Dun Garm with a grim expression. He had selected his typical black tunic and leggings for his foray north, and the same-colored cloak hung over his shoulders. Only his silver helm and breastplate provided a break in his dark visage. At his heels strode his two massive gray wolfhounds. Unlike the previous few mornings, the sky was clear, and the air was not overly chill. A good day for riding, he decided as he mounted his black warhorse and surveyed the Dreadriders and lesser warriors assembled to join him. Of the former, Brede, Alrik, Donalt, Royd, and Thorvald were his most trusted and senior men.

He hailed his two oldest and most seasoned warriors, "How go the preparations?"

Alrik answered, "Almost ready. Our warriors are restless, and it will be good to stir up their blood one more time before winter."

Hakon nodded. The pair had joined him from the homeland because they wanted an adventure and were willing to follow an upstart Skadi, no matter what he had done to his father. Now, they lead the younger generation. "Anything I need to add to stir the pot?"

Donalt interjected, "Addressing the injustice inflicted on Lang and Lunt is enough."

Hakon rejoined, "I'd rather they join us, as they met my Destroyer. Yet there is nothing to be done about it now. They needed rest to recover fully. Runa assured me that they would."

His völva had told him an apprentice Healer from Dun Moyne had saved them. Whoever it was, they had tended to their wounds well enough for Runa to work her magic and restore them. Lang's drive to reach Dun Garm and tell his story had done a great deal to aggravate even his less severe injuries. Now, both brothers would have to wait a fortnight before mounting their horses to engage in battle again.

Hakon was undecided about what to do with Braoin and whether or not to pursue learning more about the warrior named Bradaigh. So he had Alrik ask the lad to wait until he returned from their search for his other bastard in the north, telling him that Braoin hoped he could introduce him to his other half-brother. In truth, Hakon wanted Runa to assess them together, as they still did not have complete confidence in which one was the Destroyer, backed by the *Tuatha Dé Danann*.

Since Alrik had managed to recruit Braoin, he'd sweetened the deal, informing the lad that there would be continued compensation of a silver coin a day while they searched for this mysterious warrior located north of Dun Garm. The Dreadrider had also assigned one of their more senior warriors to train with the half-breed, and Sveinn would ensure he had an escort and someone to teach him about the Norvegr way of life.

Hakon signaled he was ready, and the procession set off at a slow canter through the gates of Dun Garm. His two dogs stopped at the edge of the dun, knowing it was their place to guard their master's home. Dun Garm was well protected by them and those he had left behind.

As they rode, the older, battle-scarred Brede pulled up beside his Jarl, asking, "Do you remember anything about this Dun Arrogh?"

"It's been a long time," Hakon replied over the pounding of their horses. "We were raiding so much then that the memories are like looking through fog. Royd is the one I usually send to the northeast to collect my tribute there, and the place didn't impress him enough even last year to recall any details."

"Lunt or Lang have anything to add?"

"Nothing more than what Royd could remember," he replied.

"Then maybe this Red Branch isn't much to be concerned about," Brede commented.

Hakon looked at the old Dreadrider. "I've thrived in this land by not underestimating anyone. I don't intend to start now."

With that, he kicked his mount out in front of Brede's. Hakon had decided this campaign would allow his warriors to bond again, for he was sure they were getting too complacent. It could be why his Destroyer had bested Lunt and Lang. While they had said it was because they had been attacked at night and were caught off-guard, Hakon wondered if even the youngest of his Dreadriders had grown lazy. However, the reported attack had occurred during the darkest part of the day, and the odds were against them. Under such circumstances, the event might have challenged even him, especially if his Destroyer was the warrior Runa had foreseen.

They pushed on through midday, stopping only briefly for something to eat. Along with dried boar, Jarlson had packed fresh goat cheese and bread. The orchards had yielded some succulent plums, so he also included those.

The older warriors basked in the sun, letting its heat warm their bones; there would be few days like this until spring. The younger ones, those who had not yet attained the title of Dreadrider, were most eager to be on their way, all looking forward to finding the warrior of Dun Arrogh their Jarl sought. Few expected much of a fight, but they could always hope for a glorious battle.

Finally, later in the afternoon, when the sun was low, Hakon and his Dreadriders reached Dun Moyne.

As his band of warriors thundered through the broken gates, Hakon looked around in disdain. He had decided not to push on to Dun Arrogh due to the late start, and he wanted his warriors to be fresh and rested in case this Red Branch was more organized and well-trained than they assumed, but the state of this place was giving him second thoughts.

People scurried about as the Dreadlord and his five Dreadriders circled their horses around the inner yard. Then, finally, the outlanders stopped before the main hall of Dun Moyne with their procession of warriors. A cloud of dust would typically have followed them, but the rain from the day before had turned the yard into a muddy quagmire.

Hakon turned his horse around and frowned as he dismounted. He wondered if continuing to Dun Arrogh wasn't a better idea. When Hakon entered the hovel that served as the main hall, he could barely stomach the stench of the place. He commanded the Dun Moyne's head cook, "Clean this smelly pit and prepare a decent meal while I meet with the elders of your dun."

A few moments later, a tall, older man dressed in furs and a wide leather belt ambled out of a hut and approached the band of outlanders and his warriors with a short, reedy fellow dressed in a simple brown tunic held in place by a frayed rope around his waist.

The more prominent man, who had a long braided beard in the style of Gaelic warriors, said stiffly, "I am Lysagh, Elder of Dun Moyne, and this is Crevan. What can we do for you?"

"You recently helped two of my most valued warriors," Hakon informed them as he assessed the taller of the Gaels. Deciding the man had probably been a good warrior in his day, he added, "I wish to thank you for your aid. If your Healer had not tended to their wounds, they would have died. Few of those in my territory would have done what you have."

Lysagh looked to the shorter man at his side. "It was Crevan's idea. I wanted to let them die, but he advised against it because they had claimed Guestright."

Crevan shuffled about nervously, managed a nod, but said nothing.

"It was wise of them to make such a claim," Hakon commented. "That you honor your tradition, I will reward you with a wagonload of supplies for this uncommon act."

Crevan's eyes brightened, and he stammered, "Thank... th-thank... thank you?"

"I instructed your cook to clean your hall and prepare us supper," Hakon continued as he turned to the taller man. "See that she has some help while we tend to our mounts."

"Of course," Lysagh said tightly as he turned away.

Hakon smiled. He had not bothered to claim the Gael ritual of Guestright as his Dreadriders had; the elder's grumbling made it obvious he didn't appreciate his presence.

When the Norvegrs finished looking after their mounts and strode into the hall, they found it shabby but as clean as possible. The cook soon had a meal boiling in the big kettle and served ale and bread. Hakon and his Dreadriders took over a long, battered oak table in the center of the room. His other ten warriors were left to find whatever seats they could.

Hakon was given first honors at the pot when the main meal was ready. The rest followed, filling their bowls to the brim. It had been a long day of riding, and nearly anything would have tasted good. Others from Dun Moyne crowded around the room's edges, waiting at the pot for their turn of boar, onion, and pea stew.

As the six warriors at the main table ate, Hakon spoke with Brede, Donalt, and Alrik. "You two probably remember my brothers better than I do. How would they take a peace offering after all of these years?"

Brede hastily swallowed a mouthful of stew as he looked to Alrik—whose expression was doubtful—and said, "That depends. What did you have in mind?"

"Well, I've noted Dun Garm is getting—hmm, rather full," Hakon answered quietly, pushing away his bowl. He grimaced at the taste of the ale before adding, "Our sons will soon be looking to build duns for themselves, and I like the idea of a ring of settlements around Dun Garm as added protection. But for us to accomplish this expansion, we need more warriors. If the High King in Tara discovers we're doing more than acting as a buffer between the kingdoms of his land, he'll be on us like fleas to a dog."

"Expand, here in Erin? I had always thought we'd return home one day!" Brede exclaimed. The others looked down as their fellow warriors stuffed their mouths. Fortunately, his accent was heavy, and those of Dun Moyne couldn't understand him. However, it did get the attention of Donalt, Royd, Alrik, and Thorvald. The latter had the best relationship with his favorites, Lunt and Lang, among all of his Dreadriders; his quick wit was something Hakon wished more of his senior men had.

Thorvald leaned over and advised quietly, "Gaels have long ears, Brede. Any talk of plans should be among us and only us."

Hakon gave Brede a dark look to confirm Thorvald's warning. He continued in a hushed voice, "Alfheim was experiencing problems with overcrowding before we left. It couldn't have changed with the Gauls and Germans remaining as strong as ever to the south and west. That's why my father started sending out the longboat raiders—something to keep them occupied and away from home. But, as you know, I favored taking the lands they found instead of just raiding them. By the Well of Urd, they'd have to be busting at the seams by now."

It was Alrik's turn to argue—quietly. "Our sons might not like sharing this land with newcomers, even if they are ours."

Hakon countered, "Erin has more than enough space for both. We need to establish more holdings to keep the younger warriors happy. You know what happened when my father wouldn't deal with this problem, and I'll not have our sons turn on us for the same reason. To expand, I need more warriors. My plan would enable Gefion and Tyrin to send me some of their younger ones. If they fight for it, I'll assure them they can get a holding."

"Your brothers might just agree to that," Alrik commented as he finished his stew. "It's been eighteen years, after all. Certainly, it's been time enough for them to cool off. When did you have a mind to do this?"

"In the spring," Hakon informed them. "I thought we'd take the time this winter to get a pair of the longboats ready for the voyage. I want you and Donalt to carry my message back home. You can stay there or return with the new arrivals."

Donalt looked to Alrik, a bright twinkle in his eyes, and said, "It's been a while since I've been at sea. I think I like this idea."

Alrik nodded his agreement and drained his tankard.

"Good, then it's settled," Hakon put in. "This spring, we'll be expanding. Until then, we don't speak of it. If anyone asks, say we are retrofitting the longboats for sailing on Loch Ree. Is that understood?"

The five warriors nodded as they rose. It was time to look in on the mounts and determine where they would bed down in such a flea-infested hovel.

Breanna

"Bre! Bre! Bre, are you all right?"

It was Toal. Breanna could feel his presence over her. Pain shot through her head like an arrow as she cracked an eye open. Moaning, she put a hand to her head and felt something warm and wet. Blood, which was unsurprising, given how much her skull hurt. Feeling a haft of a *Lann Dàn* in her hand, she smiled weakly. "It was a fair trade, my old long blades for these."

"I can hardly believe it myself," her cousin proudly said as he helped her sit up. After ripping a strip of cloth from his bedroll, he pulled out his waterskin, wet it, and then washed the wound. He gently wrapped the fabric around her head.

Hgul loomed over them, peering at Breanna to see how she was. The older man's expression was briefly troubled, and then his eyes wandered to *Lann Dàn,* which lay tucked in next to her.

Breanna looked closely at the magical long blades for the first time herself. In the afternoon sun, the diamond blades glittered with a life all their own. And while the shafts appeared to be black oak, metallic flecks ran through the wood, giving them a smooth feel. Yet they did not possess the weight of such a crude ore.

"There," Toal said, interrupting her thoughts as he finished wrapping her head with another strip. "How's that feel?"

"I'll be fine," Breanna said with a pained expression.

Toal questioned, "Is that bravado?"

"Probably."

Toal informed her, "I can tell you the gash is no longer gaping open with the bandage in place. Try to keep it that way."

Hgul, still looking over Toal's shoulder, said longingly, "That's a mighty fine set of long blades. Not something one leaves lying about."

Breanna's grip tightened on *Lann Dàn* as if the stranger had threatened to take them from her. But nothing in his eyes suggested he would make any such attempt. Sighing, she agreed, "Aye, they certainly are fine. My brother never said they were something fit for a king. These hafts have a marvelous feel. It is like someone made them for me. While they may look like black oak, there's something more to them. And they're light."

"Even the High King in Tara is not fit for those blades," Hgul insisted.

"And why is that?" Breanna countered, not taking his bait to reveal more.

"Why—they're distinctly not Gaelic work," the old man countered.

Breanna asked innocently, "Really? Whose work is it?"

Hgul fumed momentarily, started to speak, and stormed down the mountainside. Then, over his shoulder, he yelled, "Only the *Tuatha Dé Danann* gods could work such magic. Now, let's get off this damned mountain before it gets dark."

Toal looked at his cousin. "He knows something."

"More than he's told us," Breanna agreed as she lifted a hand for Toal to help her up. She staggered to her feet, trying to regain her balance, and noticed her head was throbbing. It made her want to sit again, but Breanna looked at the westering sun and frowned, knowing they needed to get moving. Then, motioning for Toal to pick up her pack and bedroll, she added, "But he's right. We should get down to the Loch Aillionn before sundown."

Even though it took less time to scramble down Cuilcagh than to climb it, it was clear that dusk would be upon them before they reached the bottom. Nightfall would come even sooner, with the sky clouding as it was. They followed the bubbling stream of water that made up the beginnings of the River Shannon down to the Shannon Pot. Hgul kept his pace a few hundred yards ahead, leading them as before. Breanna's head continued to pound, and she knew she should stop and rest soon. Yet that would mean camping on the steep hillside.

She stumbled forward in the fading light, letting gravity pull her down the slope.

When she tripped, her cousin stayed at her side to help her along. Their guide seemed a bit impatient at the slow progress. When Hgul started to protest their pace, Toal glowered, demanding, "You know, you could be helping here!"

"How?" the old man asked.

"By the stars! Lend a hand," Toal grated out. "And, Bre, your bandage needs changing. At least take a knee for me, if only for a moment."

She did as he requested, and a moment later, he handed her the bloody cloth and ripped another strip from his bedroll. Seeing it, Breanna grumbled, "That doesn't look good."

"Aye," was all Toal said as he replaced the bandage.

While she knew she should rest, she rose and insisted they keep moving. As they traveled across the rough, grass-covered slopes, the ground became relatively level. It was more navigable than the steep descent from above as they endeavored to hold to the east side of the stream.

Over the next span, the tributary of the River Shannon widened and gathered strength from other rivulets. As it coursed through a series of ever-descending valleys, they found it too wide and deep to cross without swimming when they reached Loch Aillionn. Fortunately, they were on the east side of the loch and would have to do that.

Toal

With the sun below the horizon, Hgul halted their forced march down Cuilcagh Mountain. Breanna staggered to a stop, her knees buckling. Toal caught her and eased her to the ground.

He quickly removed her pack and bedroll, laying them out for her to rest.

Before he had accomplished that, Breanna had fallen asleep on the ground where she had collapsed. Toal was relieved that his voice didn't crack when he commanded Hgul, "Help me move her."

The older man grumbled about taking orders from a youngling, but he did as he was asked. Toal then tucked *Lann Dàn* beside her and quickly set about making a fire to keep her warm; the air was suddenly chill with the sun no longer present to heat it.

As Toal dug into their supplies for the evening meal, Hgul sat on a nearby rock and stared at Breanna. The young Gael held up the water skin and groused, "Could I get some help here?"

Hgul rose, strode to the boy's side, took the skin, and filled the two cups. When Toal had set out the bread, fruit, and dried meat, it became apparent that regularly feeding Hgul would quickly drain their supplies.

Not wanting to leave Bre alone, Toal asked Hgul to get them more water. His frown made it plain that a boy ordering him about was a source of annoyance. Yet, he said nothing and took the waterskins to the river. Once Hgul returned, the pair ate in silence. Although Toal was tired enough to fall asleep then and there, he began to pack up the supplies in case they needed to be on the move quickly. After that, he went to his cousin's side to change the bandage on her head.

Her blood had plastered the cloth wrapped around her head and dried into her white hair. Toal had to wet the dressing before he could peel the strands free, as he did not want to start her scalp wound bleeding again.

In the firelight, the gash still looked nasty, so he once again rewrapped her head with a clean cloth. Toal sighed with relief, hoping all that she needed was rest. Given they were far from their Ollamh, he wasn't sure where he would go for help.

Eying the glowing ring on her finger, Toal wondered what meeting the Goddess Danu had been like. With Tuatha magic before him and that which he had tucked safely beside her, he realized Erin's history was more than just fanciful tales spun by Bards. If only they could help heal Breanna now.

After stoking the fire, Toal spread his bedroll beside his cousin. Making sure his bow, arrows, and short sword were within reach, he nestled into his blanket and told Hgul he needed sleep. Their guide nodded and continued to stare into the fire.

It was still dark when strange wailing sounds roused Toal from somewhere in Loch Aillionn. As the otherworld moaning drew closer, he grew concerned. Their fire had died to embers. If Hgul was still there, Toal couldn't see him. Not wanting to wake Breanna, he rose and threw some dry branches on the fire. They quickly blazed to life, and he set a few logs on top as added fuel.

In the growing light, he could see Hgul sitting as he had before, only this time, he was staring out toward the water. As Toal followed his gaze, he saw in the faint light that the waters of Loch Aillionn were roiling. Sensing danger, he drew his short sword and moved to rouse Breanna. The surface of the Shannon churned and bubbled as if it had a life of its own. It seemed as if something was emerging from it. Unable to tear his eyes from the water, Toal shook his cousin to wake her, but she did not respond.

"Bre! Bre! Wake up!" he screamed as the rising mass of water started to take shape.

"Let me sleep," she mumbled.

Digging his toes into her side, Toal rose and said unsteadily, "May the gods protect us."

Breanna rolled over and climbed to her knees, grieving about his rude interruption of her sleep. Then, using *Lann Dàn* to help her stand, she looked around groggily. Her head felt like someone was pounding on it. By the time she had some semblance of wits about her, five forms had emerged from the river, their swirling, luminous shapes coalescing into hideously deformed humans. More were doing likewise from Loch Aillionn, each carrying a sword or spear.

Hgul was still sitting on his rock like a statue, holding his walking stick beside him. Breanna rubbed her eyes, unsure of what was happening. Then, finally, she asked, "What in Lugh's name is going on?"

"I—I doubt that even the Sun God knows," Toal said, shaking with fright.

"They are Tethra's demons," Hgul informed them without looking away. "Fomorians who gave up their souls to their god. The *Tuatha Dé Danann* defeated them long ago, driving them into the sea. Their powers were once nearly as great as the Tuatha. Some of the Fir Bolg still worship the god Tethra, giving him and his demons life. The water sustains them, and they can't stray too far from it. They usually stick to the coastlands but can frequent rivers like the Shannon if encouraged."

"What should we do?" Toal asked, his voice losing any hint of manhood. "Run?"

"You could not run fast enough," Hgul said coldly.

"I can run pretty fast with those things at my back," Toal countered.

Hgul shrugged, making Breanna demand, "You seem pretty calm about this. Care to shed some light on why they are here?"

His response was, "It's the magic of your blades. They are drawn to its Tuatha magic and will kill you to possess it."

"Are you saying we'll have to fight them?"

"If you want to live to see the sunrise."

"*Droch oidhche*," Breanna managed to swear at the night as she took up a fighting stance. Toal did likewise, but he did so a step behind her. The water demons grew silent, hovering just above the water. Their odd, darkly luminous forms stood out against the black backdrop of night, and it seemed as if they were communing.

When a giant demon rose from the loch's surface behind them, they all started to come ashore. Despite their eyes being empty black pits, they knew where Breanna and Toal stood, moving over the land straight toward them. Hgul had finally risen to stand behind the two Gael warriors, but Breanna knew his walking stick wouldn't help much. Likewise, Toal's lack of experience made her doubt whether he could handle himself. Still, she motioned for him to put an arrow through one of their hearts.

"No, through the eye," Toal corrected as he smoothly pulled an arrow from his quiver and licked the fletching. Putting it to his bowstring, his arrow flew straight and true, burying itself in a black, empty eye socket. The demon didn't even take notice of the shaft protruding from his head and just kept marching toward them.

"By the stars," Toal whispered. "What do we do now?"

"Toal, stand behind me," Breanna commanded. If his arrow did nothing, then his short sword would likely be as useless. She wondered, *"How am I going to protect us both?"*

There was no time for such thoughts as Breanna stepped forward to meet the first demon. She looked at *Lann Dàn* in each of her hands and noted they and *Maorgairme* held a fierce, white-hot glow as if they knew the creatures given up by the water were hated enemies.

The closest demon drove in with its strange, luminous black sword, something Breanna countered with a sweep of her left blade. Her other long blade slashed across the thing's neck, and *Lann Dàn* erupted in a gout of silver-white fire. The demon's head vaporized, its dark, lumpy mass of a body collapsing to the ground at her feet; its body no longer glowed with a strange purplish cast.

Then, more were upon them. Breanna blocked one thrust while seizing the *void* and spun to her right to help Toal. To keep her cousin out of harm's way, she sliced through the throat of an overzealous demon in range of her blades, and its head exploded as the previous demon's had. While Toal was swift, he was at a disadvantage due to his height. The young lad held his sword high as a demon towered over him, hammering away with its dark, otherworld blade, forcing him backward. Toal's steel blade held, but his muscles had not matured enough to withstand such an onslaught.

Before the next blow could fall, a howl erupted from the demon's deformed mouth as Breanna raked its back with a shining diamond blade. It whirled on Breanna and her magical blades, only to find she had already moved on to another water demon. Out of the corner of her eye, she saw Toal take the opportunity to drive his short sword deep into its back, but that action did not slow it down even a step.

He called, "Bre, behind you!"

Wrapped in the *void*, she had already felt the demon's presence. Breanna was in motion, spinning to lash out at the demon before her. It fell to one of her white flaming blades, and her momentum carried her other blade across another demon's chest behind her. Then, with a feint to her left, Breanna drove in with her other blade to finish it off. Once more, *Lann Dàn* erupted with its angry flare, and Toal's attacker went down, howling, before it exploded.

More of Tethra's followers were coming ashore, and not just by twos and threes. First, there were ten, then twenty, with the demons making the dark surface of Loch Aillionn look like it was boiling. Hundreds more waited farther from shore, their lust for revenge on the Tuatha drawing them toward *Lann Dàn* and Breanna, the hollow sockets that passed for their eyes riveted on her and her companions. In the heat of battle, Breanna's head had stopped throbbing, or at least she no longer noticed it wrapped in the *void* as tightly as she was. She wondered how long that fortune would carry her.

Breanna killed two more demons as they blocked her way, this time by rolling beneath the sweep of their strange, watery, flowing swords that were somehow solid. She rose behind them to rake their sides with her magical blades. Then, as the pair spun to face her, she removed one of their heads. The other demon got its blade inside her defenses and opened a gash below her breast. It didn't feel deep, but the stinging saltwater that clung to the demon made her hiss. Her response brought her around, allowing her to remove both of its legs in one motion.

Lann Dàn could cut through their otherworld flesh as if the demons were nothing more than air. Only the dark blades stood a chance, which Breanna ensured didn't often make contact. As she fought in the chaos, she held tightly onto the *void* to keep herself a move ahead of her foes. Yet, it was impossible to stop every thrust that came her way. She retreated as the demons inflicted minor wounds, keeping herself between them and Toal.

Then Breanna was at Toal's side, screaming, "There are too many of them!"

"My blade and arrows are useless against their magic," Toal informed her. "We must run!"

"Run, and you'll die," Hgul yelled.

Another swarm of demons surged into them, and while Breanna managed to clear her side with the Tuatha magic in *Lann Dàn*, they forced Toal back. He slipped and fell a step behind her. The demon he was struggling with erupted in victorious laughter, letting his dark blade streak downward. Breanna kicked aside her current opponent and dove for Toal's. As the Tuatha magic struck, the demon exploded in a shower of stinking black water. Five more replaced the one.

Whirling to face them, Breanna remembered her vow to Kyras and Lissa that she would protect their son no matter what. She let *Lann Dàn* strike again, its otherworld fire raging from the ends of the diamond blades as the demons fell or gave way. Breanna found hundreds waiting to take their place. With no way to even the numbers, she held her crystal ring aloft and cried, "Danu, Danu, Danu! Save us!"

A blinding flash came from where Hgul stood. Like the demons, with nearly all of them knocked back into the loch, Breanna and Toal were thrown to the ground. Their old guide, Hgul, was transformed in the next instant. Gone was the withered man with gray, stringy hair and a tattered boar skin tunic and robes, replaced by a tall, athletic, muscular young man with shining golden locks and a brilliant yellow cloak.

Toal exclaimed, "You summoned the Sun God?"

Breanna winced at the thought. Yet here he was, and his golden breastplate shone brightly, illuminating the area as if the sun were high overhead, and his magical sword, *Claimh Solais*, held a fierce gleam as if it knew it would soon be slaking its thirst for the demons' blood. Breanna drew a sharp breath when she realized his walking stick had transformed into the great golden spear *Gae Assal*, which their Druids spun legends about.

Lugh stepped forward, planting his sword in the earth, and extended his hand to help Breanna to her feet, saying, "Tethra's demons are like the stars—countless. If you want to live, you must join me in this battle. Only by fighting these demons together can we hold them until sunrise."

"What about Toal?"

"I expect they'll leave him be if he stays clear of you," the Tuatha God advised. Then, when Breanna looked doubtful, he added, "Tell *Maorgairme* to shield him from them. What they can't sense, they can't attack."

"The ring can do that?"

Lugh nodded and reclaimed his great Sword of Light. "Yes, but only for him. It is expecting you to do battle. So seize the *void*, let the *balefire* within *Lann Dàn* flow, and we all may live until morning!"

Stunned yet grimly resolved, Breanna nodded and turned to face her cousin. She said to the ring on her finger, *"Shield Toal!"*

A shimmering shield enveloped her startled cousin as she moved to face the demons and reached out to the *void*, her magical blades fiercely burning as they sliced into a dark mass looming over the two warriors.

Lugh strode before her, his spear and sword lashing demons with white Tuatha *balefire*. Where she killed one, he killed ten. The Sun God had no mercy for Tethra's spawn, sending them to their death at every turn as he slogged toward where the loch and the river joined. He cast *Gae Assal* to seek out demons as he swept *Claimh Solais* from side to side, unleashing its *balefire*. His spear took the hearts of many before slapping back into his hand.

Lugh called to Breanna, "Command the Blades of Destiny to flow! You don't have to touch the demons for the *balefire* to reach them! Project it!"

Then, he stepped onto the loch's surface as if it were solid ground, marching across the water as he dealt his deathly blows of *balefire* from both weapons. Around him, the usually clear water ran black with the unwholesome muck spilling from their sundered demon bodies. Breanna did what she could to stay next to the raging god, keeping his back guarded, but then the water was too deep for her to wield her blades.

Forced to retreat to the shore, she fought off yet another wave of the soulless demons emerging from the river. Breanna lost sight of the Sun God as she took a few more gashes from the countless blades flicking at her. Then, with her fury pouring into *Lann Dàn*, she shed their muck-born blood with its blazing *balefire* and burned a path toward the firmer ground behind her. She could now see that, far out on Loch Aillionn, Lugh had to be battling Tethra's demon leader, Balor of the Baleful Eye, one-time King of the Fomorians, and his grandsire. How the dark sorcerer he had once killed was back to fight him once more as a demon was a mystery to her.

Breanna remembered, when she was much younger, how their Bard had spun tales of Lugh and his victories. When the Tuatha and Fomorians had fought, anyone who gazed into Balor's tainted eye had died instantly. That was until Lugh used his sling to send his grandsire's dark eye into the back of his skull. That had been the beginning of the end for Tethra and his followers.

Yet now Lugh was battling with his grandsire again, carrying the fight to the demon leader, who countered him blow for blow, using a tremendous black blade against Lugh's mighty Sword of Light. Neither seemed able to gain the upper hand. The hateful vengeance of the Fomorian magic swallowed the flashes of the magical Tuatha *balefire*.

While the pair fought, Breanna once more had to hold her own, killing more water demons who dared venture near her, commanding the *balefire* to flow as she repeatedly swept her blades in arcs. Where before she killed one, now she killed ten to twenty at a time. It was glorious! After what seemed like spans, she finally sank to her knees when she could see the sun rising through the clouds that dotted the horizon. Its rays chased the otherworld creatures back into the water.

A moment later, the god Lugh stepped from the surface of Loch Aillionn with his great spear, its razor-sharp tip covered in the frothy, purplish blood of Tethra's demons, as was his blade, *Claimh Solais,* from clashes with the enemy's demon leader.

The Sun God's yellow cloak had been torn and tattered, and blood ran from several wounds. The gaunt look in his eyes told Breanna it had been a costly battle for him. Ignoring her wounds and weariness, she rose to help him. The god refused, holding his head high and surveying the black masses surrounding them. Under the power of the sun's light, the twisted bodies of the fallen demons were slowly dissolving.

Lugh advised, "My body will heal itself in Falias, but you should wash your wounds before they fester. Tethra's sea demons carry a dangerous taint, something the Shannon should be able to clean away."

Breanna frowned. "I want to know why they attacked us."

"As I said, the old Fomorian God Tethra leads this ilk," Lugh answered. "Only he could have driven so many sea demons into fresh water. If someone has made a pact with him, he could force his followers to seek you out. *Lann Dàn* must have drawn them to you."

"And if not for you, Toal and I would have died," Breanna proclaimed.

Lugh shrugged. "You summoned a Tuatha god with *Maorgairme*. I was closest."

"It seemed like you battled with more passion than Badb's ring could compel."

Lugh said wryly, "I may have had a bone to pick with them and him. Yet, you fought well, too, Breanna Ban Morna of Clan Dálaigh. The Blades of Destiny answered your call because of your ability to reach out to the *void*. You are more worthy of your grandmother's gold Celtic Knot armring than you realize."

In a nearby tree, a large crow, the color of night, cawed something that sounded as if it were echoing the Sun God's words. When Breanna gave a start, Lugh just smiled. A moment of silence passed between them and the bird, and then she got her wits about her to comment, "How could I not with such fine weapons?"

"Ah, *Lann Dàn*," Lugh said wistfully as the crow took flight and headed southeast. He watched it flap away, adding, "I'm glad they found a Gael warrior worthy of such fine Tuatha magic. It cost the Dark Goddess of Knowledge much effort to craft them. Danu commanded that you take *Lann Dàn* to Badb Catha, the Mórrigan. She will know you fought like one of the Tuatha themselves. You must drink from her Cauldron of Knowledge to know how to use those blades."

"If you knew where Amergin had hidden *Lann Dàn*, why did you not retrieve them long ago?"

Lugh's expression brightened. "They were a fancy for a time, something given to me by my parents after the Goddess of War had created them. My parents, Kian and Ethniu, thought I should try another of Badb Catha's weapons to be more diverse, but I preferred my sword, spear, and sling.

"Years later, when the Druid Amergin took them from Falias, I only halfheartedly tried to find them. And by then, the Fomorians and the Fir Bolg had been defeated, so I had little need for them. When Beatha set you on this quest, I became more interested in where they were. Danu told me the old hag gave you Amergin's directions, and thus, I made it convenient for me to tag along. When you have done what you must and defeated your Dreadlord, I will expect them back."

Breanna said firmly, "Only if you return my Clan's blades."

The Sun God's eyes narrowed briefly, and he guffawed. "You have spunk, girl! I like that. Very well, your blades for mine."

Breanna added wryly, "A suggestion for you. Next time you go incognito in our land, call yourself something other than your name spelled backward! You had us fooled, but our dun is out in the back hills. I expect those at Dun Tara or Uisneach would see through your guise."

Lugh chuckled, "Good point, and it's impressive that your mind puzzled it out.

"Now, I've tarried too long in your world. Remember, *Maorgairme* can only be called on twice more to summon one of us. And be sure to wash up well."

With that, the Sun God Lugh erupted into a ball of light and was gone. The fairie shield that protected Toal had faded with sunrise. When Lugh vanished, the lad whistled as he approached, saying to Breanna, "First Danu, then Lugh. And that crow could have been the Dark Goddess herself. What have you gotten yourself into?"

"I wish I knew," was her reply. "I truly wish I knew."

The Dreadlord and his Dreadriders set out at first light, all seeming pleased to be away from the flea-ridden Dun Moyne. The man who passed as the dun's chief told them that Dun Arrogh was just over a two-span ride to the north. The weather had turned cooler, and the sky was a patchwork of clouds.

Hakon Skadi led their party, scanning ahead for signs of trouble. No matter what Royd or Brede thought of the warriors of this area, he would not be taking chances. The Destroyer that his völva had foreseen—one that had nearly killed two of his best warriors—could be out there. Hakon would not be the next victim.

They came upon Dun Arrogh at full gallop up the hill, racing into it, and charged through the gates with their swords drawn. Some older women in the courtyard screamed and ran for cover, while the younger ones swept their children up and followed them. The dun appeared empty, save for the few men who stood with their work tools in hand. Hakon ordered his warriors to gather in a circle, each taking up a defensive position to cover a part of the ringfort. He had commanded that they would talk first as long as there was no trouble. Decimating the dun would not help with the year's tribute that was still due.

Hakon dismounted, signaling Brede and Alrik to join him. All three drew their swords. He went to the smith, who was working at his forge. "I seek a young warrior whom I fathered some time back. He would be about sixteen or seventeen now. You would know him by his white hair and blue eyes."

He barely kept the disdain from showing as he replied, "We've no boys here with white hair."

Hakon slapped the smith in the face with the flat of his blade. "You lie!" he spat. "He nearly killed two of my best Dreadriders. Now, where is the boy who did it?"

"As I said, Dreadlord, no boys in Dun Arrogh have white hair like yours."

Fury raged in Hakon as he reared back with his blade, ready to kill the smith. The smith held his gaze as Hakon let his arm slice downward. The sword stopped an inch away from the Gael's neck. He said darkly, "I hope you have not lied, for even one with your talents is not beyond my wrath."

The Gael said nothing in return.

Hakon turned and commanded his warriors, "Search this dun. If you find a white-haired boy or anyone who is wounded, bring them to me."

Hakon refocused on the burly smith, waiting for his men to fulfill his orders. Six warriors pushed two Gael warriors to the center of the yard a moment later. The pair looked ready to kill, but they were in no shape to raise a weapon that day. Each was limping, and one had his arm in a sling. They seemed to find the rough treatment an added insult. When the remaining Dreadriders and lesser warriors returned, they informed their Jarl that they had found no white-haired warrior.

Hakon Skadi left the smith behind without a thought, striding toward the two Gael warriors. He assessed them briefly, taking in their gold Celtic Knot armrings and the multicolored cloak one of them wore. Such a cloak signified the young warrior was a Gaelic Prince and might even think of himself as a Chief. Their armrings drew more of his attention, though, and he briefly wondered how good they had to be to earn the rank of gold. Like his other spawn, one with silver and one with gold.

Hakon commented dryly, "I see you have fresh battle wounds. The same thing recently happened to two of my best warriors, two of my most favored Dreadriders. They said three Gaels about your age attacked them at night. And if it were not for a white-haired warrior with them, my Dreadriders would have killed both. Does the story sound familiar?"

The pair did not reply, but they could not help looking at each other.

"I thought so," Hakon declared. "Now, I seek this white-haired lad who is said to have become a great warrior, and you will tell me where he is. I know he is my son—a son I sired when we first came here, making him sixteen, likely seventeen. I wish to welcome him to Dun Garm if it is true."

One finally said, "My name is Eoin Mac Cairbre, a Prince of the Blood from this area. As you can see from your search, we have no white-haired men, lads, or boys in our dun. As acting Chief here, I'd know that."

"And I suppose you did not battle my Dreadriders, either?"

Eoin just spread his hands innocently.

Hakon narrowed his eyes, ready to run the prince through. His anger subsided as he regained control, something he had had to work on continuously over the years; he knew that emotion could lead to rash decisions. Still, they needed to fear him, so he commanded his Dreadriders, "Burn a hut down! That small one there!"

Donalt, Royd, and Thorvald stepped forward, lighting brands from the forge. They strode toward the smaller hovel their Jarl pointed at and tossed their torches onto the thatch roof. Even the damp straw could not resist the flames for long, and soon the fire engulfed it. Fortunately, the wind was calm, and there was no danger of the fire spreading.

Hakon turned back to Eoin. He sensed that those who had fought with his Dreadriders knew more than they were offering and felt that the son he had named the Destroyer lived in Dun

Arrogh. So he asked darkly, "Do you still insist you do not know my white-haired warrior? Or shall I burn another hut?"

Eoin said stiffly, "You may burn the entire dun and still not find the lad you seek."

"Maybe you do not lie," Hakon offered. "But I still do not believe you are telling all you know. If this white-haired warrior came to your aid once, maybe he will do so again. Brede, I've wasted enough time. Have your men question everyone, including the women and children. Someone must know something of this white-haired warrior."

There was no response from the Gaels, so he turned to one of his men, saying, "Thorvald, find a spare horse and take Prince Eoin here to Dun Garm. I expect my son will want to see him freed. And to speed this lot along, select an item on this dun's tribute list to be doubled with each day that passes that he doesn't submit."

"Já, my Jarl. What about the other?"

"Leave him to tell my son that only by going to Dun Garm can he set his friend free."

With that, Hakon turned and mounted his horse, and the Dreadrider took hold of Eoin.

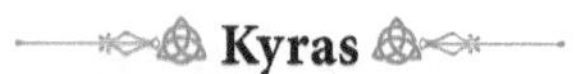

Kyras

Kyras bravely held the Dreadlord's gaze as he tried to puzzle out what the Norvegr wanted. A white-haired boy? Only Breanna had white hair in Dun Arrogh, and despite acting like one, she was unquestionably not a boy. Kyras wondered if she was the one Hakon sought.

Then Eoin and Fergal were dragged before the Dreadlord, and again, Hakon was probing to find what they knew about a white-haired lad. When that did not go well, he ordered his

Dreadrider to burn a hut. Kyras helplessly watched as they lit brands in his forge and set a small hut ablaze, noting it was where Breanna had grown up. He could only groan. First, she had lost her mother, and now it was her home. Had the Mother Goddess planned this for some reason that only she knew?

As Norvegrs led Eoin away, Kyras asked Fergal, "What was that all about?"

"Very strange. The Dreadriders we fought survived and returned to Dun Garm, but they lied to their Jarl about what happened in our battle."

"What are they hiding?" Kyras asked.

"That it was not a white-haired lad who beat them."

"It was my niece who shamed them?"

"She did," Fergal admitted.

Breanna

By the time Breanna had washed and bound the wounds on her arms, legs, and body in the icy-cold water of the River Shannon, the dead bodies of the demons had dissolved, leaving no more than dark mud stains on the rocky shoreline. The strange black swords had crumbled to dust. Fortunately for Breanna, none of the dark blades had inflicted any severe injuries, and the gash on her head she had received when pulling *Lann Dàn* free was not troubling her as much as she had expected it would.

Despite sore muscles, a cold wind kept her moving quickly, dressing faster than Toal could pull a change of clothes out of her travel sack. The previous set was stained and tattered, but she washed them anyway. Then, with no time to let them dry, she gathered her belongings, and they quickly put Loch Aillionn and the River Shannon behind them. The pair ate their breakfast on the move. It was hard not to glance over their shoulders to ensure the water demons were not coming to haunt them again.

Breanna kept them heading southeast once they were beyond Slieve Anierin, seeking valleys with easier terrain. Neither had much to say, for the previous night's battle had taken a heavy toll. She marched until midday before declaring she had to rest. It took Toal's urging for Breanna to move on a few spans later, but she didn't last long. They stopped in the afternoon, ensuring their campsite was well away from streams or lochs. Dead tired, Breanna didn't need another encounter with the god Tethra's merry followers. Yet, being away from any source of water did not help her confidence, for she did not know how far the demons' reach extended.

She dreaded nightfall, asking Toal to keep the campfire burning bright. To her relief, nothing bothered them, save for her nightmares. While Breanna's wounds were not festering, they were uncomfortable. Despite being exhausted, she did not sleep well. *Maorgairme* was still emitting a white glow on her forefinger, though not as fiercely as during the battle. Nearby, *Lann Dàn* held the same cool, otherworldly light.

As they ate the following morning, Toal commented, "You don't look so good."

Breanna scowled at her cousin; trying to stomach the dried deer meat she was gnawing on was hard enough without being reminded of how bad she felt. She asked wryly, "Has your father ever told you not to say such things to a woman? Next time, try something like, 'Cousin, you look ill.'"

Toal shrugged impishly, but the concerned expression returned quickly. "Bre, I'm just worried about you. You're very pale. Lugh said the demon swords were tainted. I hope I'm wrong. You've become my hero after watching you battle with those diamond blades. You saved my life. Anything I can do, I gladly will."

Thinking Lugh had done the life-saving, Breanna responded, "Not unless you have one of Ulicia's potions."

Toal just shook his head and handed her the waterskin. "If you can't go on, we could try to reach your sister's place."

"Ronat lives in the Doon of Drumsna's shadow," Bre countered as she peered about to get her bearings. "Besides, Arrogh isn't that much farther."

It was colder than the previous day, so the pair wasted no time setting out. If they pressed hard, they would make Dun Arrogh by nightfall. Breanna kept up the pace for the first few spans, but her aching muscles began to wear her down after that. By lunchtime, Toal was helping her along. Both knew they would sleep beneath the night sky again due to their lack of progress. Breanna didn't last more than two whole spans before her legs failed her.

Toal helped her to the ground and said, "I know I'm not supposed to tell you that you look bad, but you're deathly pale—like, parchment white pale, and extremely hot to the touch. One of your wounds must have festered, or the demons had some other poison on their blades. You and I know you're burning up and need an Ollamh soon."

Breanna nodded and pointed to the waterskin.

Handing it to her, Toal continued, "I'll start a fire and get you comfortable. Then I'll fetch Ulicia. The dun can't be too far."

Despite her fever, she didn't protest as he built a fire for her. A moment later, Toal was gone, and Breanna was dozing fitfully, her dreams filled with visions of demons, gods, fairies, and Dreadriders. Each struggled against the other to kill or save her.

Then, Hakon Skadi's face emerged from the shadows. He stood over her with his sword, ready to split her in half. Even in her fever-racked mind, she had the presence to point her magical blades at him and send him to his death. Only he didn't die. Each time *Lann Dàn* erupted and blasted him into oblivion, the Dreadlord returned, his laugh mocking her. It was as if they were locked in an endless struggle.

But why? Why was she so important? Was it because of the simple *geas* her mother had asked the Fáidh Beatha to cast on her before she was born? Her nightmares had no answers, only more of the same gruesome images.

Breanna stirred to life sometime later to find Ulicia kneeling over her as she lay on the ground. It was still dark, but a torch was sunk into the grass nearby, casting light to see by. The old Druid rubbed a nasty-smelling salve into her wounds. Once finished, the Healer kept one hand touching the earth as she chanted in a language known only to *Aos Dána* and then pressed her other hand to Breanna's forehead. Suddenly, she felt a little better.

Behind her stood Fergal, the firelight that flickered across his face showing an expression that held more concern than she would have expected. Maybe it was the brand he carried in his hand, a trick of the flames.

In a weak voice, she said, "We fought with some—"

"Hush," Ulicia commanded before she could finish. "Toal told us all about how you found *Lann Dàn* and the battle with the demons. You had quite a fight on your hands from the number of gashes I counted. It's too bad you missed cleaning that one beneath your breast. It was deeper than the rest, bringing on a fever when it finally festered. I've put something on it to draw out the sickness. Unfortunately, that nasty cut on your scalp will likely need stitches."

"You had us worried," Fergal informed her, though Breanna was not convinced of his sincerity, for his tone belied his words. As she wondered what had stuck in Fergal's craw, he added, "Toal came running into the dun all out of breath, squeaking out a demand that I bring a chariot out to get you. We could hardly understand him. When he said you were dying, that got us moving."

"I thought my side was going to burst by the time I got there," Toal said.

Breanna smiled, thankful for his devotion. Yet someone who should have been there wasn't. She demanded, "Where's Eoin?"

Fergal's expression turned hard as stone. "The Dreadlord has him."

"What!?" Breanna shouted and tried to sit up; the old Druid pushed her back down.

"I said hush," Ulicia barked at her. "Now, drink this, and we'll get you on the chariot. There'll be time enough for talk later."

The Druid handed her a cup of something, and Breanna grimaced at the taste. Then, as Toal and Fergal lifted her onto the creaking chariot, she said, "That's horrible! Uck! Though I guess it's better than dying."

After they helped her get situated, she added, "Toal, best you put your pack bedroll next to me so you can carry *Lann Dàn* for me. I trust you to look after them, cousin."

Toal nodded, taking the blades from her, and offered his arm to Ulicia to help her walk. Breanna turned to Fergal, asking, "How are your wounds?"

"Still bothering me more than I care for," he answered as he stuffed his brand into a stanchion on the side of the chariot and took the reins. "Let's keep it slow and steady. Our hill ponies know the way home in the dark better than I do."

At first, Ulicia and Toal tried to keep up, but the hobbled Healer eventually gave up and let the lad guide her as she held her torch to light the way.

Breanna managed to climb to her feet in the chariot and stood beside Fergal as they slowly wheeled through the night. She wanted to know more about Eoin, but between the concoction that Ulicia had given her and the gently rocking motion of the cart, she soon folded drowsily into Fergal's arms.

Startled by her collapse, she said, "Sorry, I need to sit."

"Certainly," he said coldly, easing her to the cart floor.

"So why did the Dreadlord take Eoin?" Breanna asked.

"Hakon came to the dun yesterday, searching for a son, a son he fathered some seventeen summers back," Fergal answered as he bent on one knee beside her so she could hear him over the jingle of the horses and creaking chariot.

His eyes searched her face in the torchlight as if he was looking for something he had not seen before, and his voice was no more than an icy whisper when he added, "The Dreadlord said that his son had become a great warrior and he had come to invite him to Dun Garm. When asked how he knew this son was at Dun Arrogh, Hakon told us that his son had recently fought against two of his fiercest warriors. He added that the Dreadriders were still recovering from their wounds."

"But why did he take Eoin?"

Fergal frowned. "Because you failed to kill his Dreadriders. They informed their Jarl that two other Gaels were involved, and both were wounded. Those two are Eoin and me. Why they lied, I do not know. When he could not find his *son*, Hakon took one of us. Eoin wore his cloak, which proclaimed him a prince, so he chose him. And he told us that when the Dreadlord's son returned to Garm, he would free Eoin."

"Why is he looking for a son?"

"He's not. He only thinks he is," was Fergal's answer. "All because his Dreadriders, the ones you did not kill, have lied to their Jarl."

"What are you saying?" Breanna asked, her mind still muddled, unsure of the implications.

Fergal's tone was dark when he said, "That you are the son, who is not a son, for whom Hakon Skadi is searching, Breanna Ban Morna."

Fine Line
of Truth

Breanna was shocked by Fergal's accusation. It hit her so hard that it was as if he had just thrust his sword through her heart. She thought to herself, *"How could he know the Dreadlord was her father? Him, of all people? And if he knew, then so did Eoin!"*

She was undone. They would surely not trust her, and she needed their help to kill her father. It was a disaster! The creaking chariot continued to wheel through the night, but Breanna barely noted the sounds of harnesses clinking and the muffled clop of horses.

She shifted her gaze from Fergal's eyes to his grim, twisted smile. That smile confirmed her worst fears—he thought she was tainted. When her eyes locked on his again, she saw distrust in their depths, suspicion of her outlander blood. How could she convince him she wanted to end the Dreadlord's reign as badly as he did?

Breanna could not hold up under Fergal's scrutiny as he knelt beside her. The silver glow from the crystal ring on her finger became the focus of her attention. Blackness swirled around the edges of her vision, and Breanna struggled to think, the toll of the previous few days and Ulicia's potion making her feel lost in a fog. Then, a thought pierced her mind like a beacon in the night, and she knew she had but one chance to protect her secret. She whispered silently to the magical ring encircling her finger, *"Maorgairme, he must forget. He must not know who my father is. No one can."*

As darkness threatened to swallow Breanna's consciousness, she heard a crow's mocking call. Fergal asked with a shiver, "Why is such a bird squawking in the middle of the night?"

Breanna was especially aware of this now that she knew the Mórrigan had watched her battle the demons. All Gaels knew the bird was an omen of the Dark Goddess of Knowledge. At that moment, the crystal amulet wrought by Badb Catha came to life with a flash that struck Fergal in the forehead.

Blinded by the silver flare, Fergal fell into the side of the chariot, his balance abandoning him, and he would have tumbled over the back had he not grabbed hold of the railing. Breanna, lying next to him, was lost on him for the moment. When he finally looked over and saw her, Fergal shook his head and muttered, "Bollocks! What were we talking about? *Tá olann ina hintinn agam!*"

Breanna heard Fergal say something about having wool for brains as he pounded a fist on the edge of the chariot, but her consciousness faded once more while they continued to roll on toward Dun Arrogh.

Kyras and Lissa waited with the dun's Bard and apprentice-Seer for Fergal to arrive with the chariot and Breanna. When Toal had run into their family hut, out of breath and rambling about Gods and battles with demons, they could hardly make sense of his story. Still, when he'd said Breanna had taken a fever and could die, it had been enough for them to wake Fergal and Ulicia and get them rolling out of the dun in their chariot.

Lissa admonished her mate, "Och, you said there'd be no danger. Just a hike to the mountains!"

Kyras shrugged but said nothing. Now, close to midnight, those at Dun Arrogh had lit torches to show them the way home and stood anxiously in the yard, wondering what had happened.

Cahir, their Bard, keeper of Gaelic histories and legends, asked, "What again did Toal say about a battle between one of our gods and demons? Surely, an adventurous yarn such as this has not been spun in ages."

Lissa scowled at the Bard. "Not enough to know more than that my niece was injured, and this adventure of hers likely put my son in danger!"

"But it could be a glorious tale to inspire our warriors to stand strong, one I could pass to my fellow Filidhs."

Aodhfin, their young Seer and Fáidh apprentice, concurred. "If the Tuatha gods have involved themselves with our kind once more, it could portend much, maybe that they plan to help us remove the Norvegrs."

Lissa spat, "Hakon isn't going anywhere until the High King decides he's a threat and not just a buffer from the other lower kings."

When the rickety chariot sent to get Breanna finally rolled into the yard, only Kyras, Lissa, Cahir, and Aodhfin remained.

The others who had joined to wait for them had slipped off to their huts and their sleep. As Fergal handed the reins over to Cahir and stepped onto ground that was not rocking, Kyras lifted their niece from the cart.

Lissa asked the warrior, "Is she hurt?"

Fergal grimaced and said through gritted teeth, "Not seriously. It seems a minor cut festered, and it brought on a fever. Ulicia has given her a potion to make her sleep."

"And what of my son and the Healer?" Kyras asked as he gathered Breanna in his massive arms.

"They're a short while behind me."

The portly Cahir said, "Ulicia certainly can't move as she used to."

Lissa just nodded, thinking the old Bard had little to talk about, and commanded her mate, "Put Breanna to bed on our spare pallet—Ulicia will demand she rests anyway. I'll wait for our son and the Healer."

While Kyras went to do as his mate bade, Fergal appeared to struggle with unhitching his horses from the chariot. Lissa demanded, "Aodhfin, assist Fergal—he is still recovering from his wounds."

The Seer asked, "Did Toal tell you anything else about their encounter with the gods?"

"No," Fergal muttered and turned away to lead the horses to their shed.

Then Lissa growled, "After her battle with those Dreadriders, I should not have let Toal join Breanna, and I certainly should not have listened to Kyras!"

Cahir countered, "At his age, had I had such a chance to become a man, I would have jumped at it. But it doesn't sound like he's any worse for wear."

Lissa turned a cold eye on the Bard, one that would have withered him if it had been a poisoned barb. "He's still a laddie, my laddie, and I don't think making light of this is any help!"

"I wasn't making light, woman," Cahir rejoined. "But saying he's a lad won't keep him that way. Face it: Toal's fast becoming a man. See, here he comes now, with Ulicia on his arm. The Ollamh would not let a mere boy support her."

"*O Shean Sgog*," Lissa called him and moved toward her son, with the Druids right behind her.

Aodhfin demanded, "Tell us what the gods—"

But Lissa cut him short. "My boy is tired and needs rest."

"Och, Mother, leave them be," Toal said, "They just want to know what happened, and I can certainly spare a few moments to tell them my story while it's still fresh in my mind. Could you help Ulicia to her hut and see if Father needs help with Breanna? Before I head to bed, I'll explain what happened to our Filidh and Fáidh."

"You are kind, Toal, to think of me," the Healer said wearily.

Lissa stared at her lad as if seeing him in a different light for the first time, seeing the man he was becoming, then nodded. She couldn't help glaring at Cahir as she led Ulicia away, but she knew the Bard was right; Toal was growing up. Still, her boy could have been killed or hurt by this dangerous adventure, and once she had pinned her mate with a few dirks, he would think twice before putting their son in such danger again!

Cahir

Cahir and Adohfin carefully listened as Toal retold their adventure, offering: "Well, it all began with Danu charging Breanna with a quest to find the hidden Blades of Destiny..."

Toal went on to detail the story—their trek up the slopes, stopping at a dun, meeting Hgul, finding the Blades of Destiny that were now in his hands, Breanna's head wound, retrieving them, the descent to the upper junction of Loch Aillionn and the River Shannon, the battle with the demons, Breanna summoning Lugh, and their battle ending as the sun rose. Toal added that Lugh commanded Breanna to seek out the Dark Goddess at the *Well of Segias* to learn how *Lann Dàn* could destroy the Dreadlord and save the Isle of Erin.

Cahir exhaled explosively. "If half of what you say happened, this will make a glorious tale. It weaves together a quest for lost Tuatha magic and a battle between demons and the great Sun God, Lugh. Leading to our gods re-engaging with their Gaels!"

Toal just nodded.

Cahir added, "This tale will be a challenge to spin."

The Bard hoped he was up to the task, for there had been few new yarns to excite their warriors while living under the Dreadlord's iron-fisted rule.

Aodhfin had kept close to Cahir's side as Toal spun his tale about Breanna's quest. He asked, "What of the gods?"

The Bard looked at the young, sour-faced apprentice and shook his head again. They had lowered their standards to accept the young and inexperienced into their ranks, thereby maintaining a reasonable number of Druids studying the arts.

Cahir was confident that he was a better Seer than Aodhfin in a pinch; it wasn't even a subject he had studied in much depth. Seizing the *void* to recall tales was easier than seizing it to pull the *sight* to himself, but he doubted the young Seer could manage even that.

As far as Cahir was concerned, the Seer took communing with the gods and watching for their signs too seriously. The young man would have to learn that one thing the gods didn't like was a Fáidh who thought more of himself than his dun.

One thing was clear: the apprentice certainly hadn't foreseen anything of Breanna's quest for the Tuatha magic nor any help rendered by the gods to ensure she kept it. If Cahir were the sort to gamble, he'd say that Beatha had her hand in the affair. Few saw the old hermit anymore, but she had foretold the Dreadlord's coming. Maybe he should seek her out and see if her *sight* had anything to tell them.

Either way, Cahir knew it had been centuries since new tales of Tuatha magic had taken place, and the Bard wondered if their people would scoff if he embellished that part too much. More and more, his fellow Gaels seemed to be falling away from the old ways of worship. Yet here, he had an opportunity.

Breanna

When Breanna awoke, it was dark. She had no idea how long she had slept or where she was. Nearby, someone was snoring softly. As she looked around and saw the dying embers in the hearth at the center of the room, she realized she was safe. Kyras and Lissa must have taken her in.

Then memories of creaking through the night with Fergal at her side returned to her in a rush. He had known her father was the Dreadlord and that she was tainted! She could only hope that *Maorgairme* had responded to her plea.

Deciding she would know soon enough, Breanna noted *Lann Dàn* tucked in at her side and let her hands caress the hafts. It gave her a boost of confidence, knowing they would be able to help in her final quest, and she silently thanked Toal for putting them within her reach.

Suddenly, sleep took her once more. Before, she had not dreamed, but this time, her dreams were about gods and fairie magic. She dreamed that with such powerful help, she could rid the land of her father's revolting stench. Then, as warmth filled her, she sensed their Healer nearby but slipped back into her dreams.

As she drifted in and out of sleep, she wondered how she had ever hesitated at the thought of removing Hakon from her land. It was something she could now understand, as it was clear to her that only by seeing his days at an end would their land once more shine with the power of their gods. Dreams of a land untouched by the Dreadlord's dark presence followed—dreams of a land where, just maybe, she would not be a *dìolain*. Then, what would she do? Right the wrongs where their matriarchal society had turned into a patriarchal one? Balance was needed.

Sunlight filtering through a crack in the door drew Breanna from her sleep, her dreams fading. Around her, she heard the hushed buzz of Kyras, Lissa, and Toal trying to dress quietly.

Then Ulicia was there, forcing another draught down her throat. Unable to stay awake, she drifted off again. When she came to once more, she lay still, trying to sort out her memories about her quest for the Blades of Destiny. Wondering who knew about her father, she would have to ask a few discreet questions to determine if the ring had worked magic for her.

Stirring to life, Breanna yawned, noting her aunt and uncle were back, probably to check on her. "Don't bother being quiet. I'm awake."

"Och, our nearly dead niece has finally arisen!" Kyras exclaimed. "Ulicia will be pleased, as she's been tending to you."

Breanna asked, "How long did I sleep?"

"Two days," Lissa informed her, which brought a grimace to her face. She was Eoin's Champion and needed to protect him—it seemed like a bad thing to sleep for two days, but she could not conceive why that would be. Finally, her aunt interrupted her thoughts, asking, "Hungry?"

"Hmmm, yes," Breanna answered as she stood and stretched. Given what she had been through, she felt surprisingly good, deciding Ulicia's potions and Elemental healing must have worked some potent magic on her to have left her with only a few stiff muscles from her battle with the demons. After two days of sleeping, few could rise without finding at least that. One thing she needed was a privy.

Then it struck her that Eoin was not here to protect—he was in the Dreadlord's hands—and she cursed the Ollamh for giving her such potions that knocked her out.

Lissa broke into her thoughts again. "I'll have Calla send one of her girls over with something."

With that, her aunt slipped through their clan's hut, leaving Kyras to tend to the fire pit. Breanna stretched again and turned to dress. Lissa had laid out some clothes for her, though they were nothing she would have selected. In reality, they looked more like they belonged to Toal. The two were nearly the same size, save for her longer legs, but that mattered little when wearing a kilt. Still, she wondered why her aunt had chosen such clothes from her cousin's hut. As she threw her nightshirt aside and struggled to pull on her cousin's slightly tight-fitting deerskin tunic, she asked, "Why did Lissa give me Toal's clothes?"

Kyras turned to her and said, "Ah, that. When the Dreadlord came, he burned a hut when we didn't tell him what he wanted to hear. I'm sorry to say it was yours."

"My hut is gone?" Breanna asked as if she had not heard correctly.

"And everything inside it," Kyras added hesitantly.

Breanna sank back down to her pallet and just shook her head, her voice holding only contempt when she said, "He's taken everything else. Why not this?"

Kyras sighed. "I know the Dreadlord has taken much. First, your father, and now your mother. Morna had not wanted to truly live since Nevan's death, save to see her youngest daughter fulfill her destiny. Yet, with your sisters on their way home to their mates and your hut burned, there is little left to keep you here, my girl. Given your skills as a warrior, any dun would be glad to have you."

"You think I should leave? I am Eoin's Champion! I made an oath to him when I accepted Fergal's challenge! I will not leave him in my—the Dreadlord's hands."

Kyras shook his head as he sat beside her. "No, Bre, that is not what I meant. If you must follow the Tuatha God's command of you, don't let ties to Dun Arrogh hold you back."

"What did Toal say?"

"He related the great tale of a battle that would have killed an average warrior, but we know you're certainly not that. It's a tale where you also somehow manage to keep him safe while a battle rages around you both. We should not forget the quest laid on you by our gods and those diamond blades, ones my son ensured stayed at your side. It can only mean that most of those details are accurate."

"Och, you're right," Breanna said wryly and looked at him, knowing he had diverted her, though she genuinely did not mind. "Even I can't believe most of it. Did Fergal have anything to say?"

Kyras shrugged. "Not that I know of, but the Druids say it's a sign from the gods of great trouble ahead."

Maybe the crystal ring had worked its magic, and she couldn't argue with the Druids about the coming troubles. "What do they say about my next quest?"

"You mean about your plans to kill the Dreadlord?" Kyras asked with a grimace. "That's always been your goal."

"I was asking about my quest to seek out Badb Catha."

Kyras continued quickly, "Well, you know as well as I there's not half of a Fáidh's ability between them since Beatha left us. They pass little more than wind about what the future will bring."

"They do not think I will succeed," Breanna stated flatly, her lips pursed in disapproval.

"What they think matters no more than a cow's droppings," Kyras fumed. "If Sun God commanded it, that's what matters."

Finally smiling, Breanna concurred, "That's true enough."

"I'm glad you agree," Kyras said as he rose. "Wouldn't want you to—"

A knock at the door interrupted them. Kyras waved a server in with a tray. It wasn't just any server—it was Cilla, one of Toal's archers and Calla's daughter. Seeing her brought a smile to Breanna's face.

Cilla shyly said, "I hope you're well now. Toal told me about how you and our Sun God battled against Formorian demons. It must have been glorious."

Breanna shrugged, "It was a trial by fire, lassie, but thanks."

Famished, she set it on her lap and dug into the cooked barley cereal and strips of seared boar meat while Cilla slipped out the door. The honeycakes went next, and Kyras smiled as he tidied up and watched her eat. After a moment, he asked, "So what's next?"

"Well, both Danu and Lugh commanded that I find the Dark Goddess near the headwaters of the River Boyne so she can tell me how to use *Lann Dàn* to stop the Dreadlord," she answered between mouthfuls of her breakfast.

"But you don't plan to heed that command?" Kyras finished for her.

Breanna hesitated, then swallowed her mouthful. "No, I set off for Dun Garm as soon as I've visited the bathhouse and gathered some supplies. I certainly cannot leave Eoin in the Dreadlord's hands a moment longer than I must. Only after that will I seek out Badb Catha."

"You present an iron façade to everyone, but I see you, Breanna Ban Morna," Kyras commented. "Much like your grandmother, yet she knew she had limits. Ulicia commanded that you rest. She will not be happy to learn you've departed without obtaining her leave."

Breanna countered, "There are many things in life Ulicia is not happy about."

"You know our Healer well," Kyras informed her with more amusement than the gruff smith usually showed. Breanna smiled at that, deciding her uncle had finally accepted her as an adult, not a child. Then, he added, "I'll get Calla moving on supplies while you finish eating. Is there anything else I can do for you?"

"Yes, tell Fergal he's in charge of our Red Branch band until I free Eoin," she commanded as she set her tray aside and turned to pack the clothes Lissa had laid out for her. Then, before Kyras turned through the door, Breanna said, "But wait until I'm gone first."

With a raised eyebrow, he said, "Fergal will not be pleased."

"Then Ulicia will not be alone with her ill temper."

Kyras winked. "You've become both a witty and fearsome warrior woman all at once!"

Eoin

Eoin stumbled and fell as the old Dreadrider, his escort from Dun Arrogh, pushed him into a small hut. The heavy oak door slammed shut. He heard two warriors take up their positions outside as his guards. Eoin groaned, thinking that even if he could escape on a horse, the forced march to Dun Garm had taken too much out of him to make such an attempt.

His throbbing leg felt as if their smith had taken his hammer to it, and as he lay on the cold ground, every ache and pain seemed magnified a thousandfold. It had taken nearly two days of being hounded by his captors to reach the Dreadlord's fort. Exhausted, he barely had the energy to look around in the fading light.

Much like any other storage shed at the harvest, Eoin's cell was stacked high with large buckets of peas, barley, and oats. Nearby were wicker baskets filled with onions, garlic, and various fruits. Despite his weariness, Eoin's stomach growled. He had been fed little on their journey, so he struggled to get to his feet and plucked an onion from one of the baskets. After peeling away the dry outer skin, he eagerly bit into the juicy, yellow center. Finishing off the bulb, he moved on to a head of garlic. Even uncooked, they tasted better than he thought possible. The fruit came last as he devoured several pears and plums.

Finally satiated, Eoin lay back on a sack of barley and stared at the thatch roof, trying to puzzle out what Hakon wanted. He hadn't had much time to think about it before that moment, what with his Dreadrider escort pushing him along or questioning him about their Jarl's Destroyer. Why they all felt the Dreadlord had spawned a son at Dun Arrogh was the confusing part.

Then he thought about how Morna had lashed out at anyone who had suggested Nevan was not Breanna's father; no one had wanted to press the point. And neither had he, as they had grown up together, with him only two years older. Yet, Breanna was the only person who looked like the Norvegr outlanders and was undoubtedly not a lad.

It was also clear that the pair of warriors they had fought with earlier had been lying when they had said they had been attacked at night by a white-haired lad. Eoin shook his head, muttering aloud, "But why? Why would they lie?"

Then it hit him, and he burst out laughing. "Couldn't admit a woman had beaten them!"

The notion left a smile on his face until he thought about the other events tied to their battle. Morna's secret last words to her youngest child, Breanna's strange behavior since that night, and Hakon's search for a son could only mean one thing—the young warrior sought by the Dreadlord was not a son, after all. It was, in reality, a daughter, a daughter whom he had come to love as they grew up together.

Stunned, Eoin wondered why he hadn't seen it before and had not connected her white hair with the outlanders. Maybe it was due to Eoin growing up with her, someone he'd always had as a friend and had hoped would have as a lover. What he couldn't understand was why Breanna had lied to him. They had always been able to talk, chatting for long spans into the night about how things would be different when they had rid themselves of the Dreadlord. It was a goal they had always shared. So why hadn't she trusted him now?

As his mind churned with the implications of his discovery, his tired and sore body drew him into a deep sleep that even dreams did not penetrate.

It was still dark when a sharp pain in his ribs woke him. One of Hakon's young warriors stood over him, barking something in a language he couldn't understand.

He realized he was supposed to get up and follow him from the gestures, but his body was painfully slow to respond. Then, the other guard was at his side, lifting him to his feet. Pushed through the door, Eoin could not keep his feet beneath him as the ground hurled up to meet him. Even though he was gasping for breath from the impact, the two warriors took hold of his arms and dragged him forward. He lifted his head and saw he was approaching a stone tower that could only be the residence of the Dreadlord of Garm.

By the time they reached the iron-bound oak door, Eoin was walking without help. Unfortunately, it wasn't for long as they flung him inside the tower, and his legs failed him again. He landed on a rush-covered floor with a thud, the river grass doing little to absorb the impact of the hard-packed earth. This time, the air left his lungs, and he could do little more than lie there gasping while trying to regain his breath.

Finally breathing again, he stared at a pair of black boots. When one of the rugged leather soles pressed itself to his face, he couldn't suppress the groan that passed his lips.

"Eoin Mac Cairbre, I understand you were born into the Clan Mórdha and are a descendant of Conal Cearnach. These facts make you a Prince of the Blood," said the owner of the black boots. Though Eoin couldn't see the face attached to the voice, he knew Hakon Skadi was standing over him. "I know little more than that, save that I understand you wear the cloak of a Gaelic prince, and I don't like knowing so little. Yet, sadly, few of your dun said anything more to expand my knowledge. So I will have to rely on you to tell me more."

As the Dreadlord lifted his boot, the guards pulled Eoin to a sitting position. Hakon, dressed in black, was hardly visible in the dim lighting of the stone tower. On each side of the Dreadlord sat a giant wolfhound, each with a hungry look in their eyes. Eoin glanced around and found two young warriors hovering over him like cats ready to pounce. He didn't recognize either of them, but behind them stood the two Dreadriders he and Fergal had battled with close to a fortnight ago.

Unable to remember their names, Eoin looked back at the Dreadlord and said grimly, "I have already told you I know nothing of a bastard son you may have spawned at Dun Arrogh."

A fist slammed into the side of his head and sent him sprawling.

Dazed, Eoin managed to climb back to his knees with help from the guards. Hakon said, "That was not what I wanted to hear. But let's try another approach and see where it takes us. I've heard rumors lately that some Gael warriors near your dun are plotting my demise. This band calls itself the Red Branch. That is a highly acclaimed name in the history of your land, one associated with many well-known heroes. You are a descendant of Ulaida's Red Branch, making you a Prince of the Blood. And, my Dreadriders tell me, you're a fair warrior. All of this could make one wonder if you are not a part of this new Red Branch. Maybe you're its leader?"

Still rubbing the side of his head, Eoin replied, "Any Gael worth his salt would want to see your rule over them ended. I am no different, Gaelic Prince or not."

Eoin saw Hakon nod this time before another fist connected with his head. The Dreadlord commanded darkly, "Do not dance around my questions! I asked about the Red Branch."

Eoin picked himself up off the floor before the guards got to him. Still, they were at his side quickly enough to ensure he did not rise above his knees. Instead, he glared at them before saying, "Despite my lineage, I know nothing of a new Red Branch. Gaels revere their heroes. It would be presumptuous to lay claim to such a name."

"Very well. Let's talk about my white-haired bastard. Lunt and Lang say that you and your friend would not be alive if not for my son. They say he is a formidable warrior, one who wields long blades. Do you still claim you know nothing of him?"

"I've said several times we have no white-haired men or lads at Dun Arrogh," Eoin maintained.

"Then who saved you that night?" Hakon demanded.

Eoin's mind raced for an answer. He dared not say the truth, yet he had to tell him something. He did not want to take a chance to gaze in the Dreadlord's direction when he said, "It wasn't at night, and he didn't have white hair."

"You lie," one of the Dreadriders barked as he stepped forward and drove his fist into the small of Eoin's back. He crumpled to the ground, groaning at the pain exploding from the area around his kidney. Then, gritting his teeth, he climbed back to his knees without even acknowledging the Dreadrider, one of the two he had battled with. He said nothing, leaving the next move up to the Dreadlord. The two warriors who had escorted him to the tower still hovered nearby, but the younger Dreadrider had retreated a few steps under his Jarl's disapproving gaze. The two wolfhounds had come to all fours and were growling lightly; they seemed to know their master's mood better than his Dreadrider.

Hakon said nothing for a while, then asked softly, "So you admit there was another warrior in the fight?"

"That I never denied," Eoin answered. "Mine and my cousin's wounds proved that."

"Nonetheless, you're not telling me everything," Hakon stated.

"I'm telling you they are liars," Eoin said and threw a long look of contempt at Lang and Lunt.

The Dreadrider stepped forward again, but his Jarl raised his hand and barked, "No, Lang, I will hear what he has to say."

Eoin looked back at the Dreadlord, his eyes catching the other's dark gaze. He looked away quickly, feeling he could not trust his voice. It would betray him for sure. Staring at the rushes on the floor, he wondered how to convey enough without revealing that Breanna was the daughter, not the son, that Hakon sought.

If he did, there would be no chance for her to fulfill her dream of seeing the Dreadlord dead.

That thought struck him hardest—how could she face herself, knowing who she was, knowing she wanted to kill her father? Breanna had always spoken passionately about the notion; he did not expect her discovery to change her view. Eoin doubted he could kill him had he been in her place, even if it was the Dreadlord. Then, knowing he couldn't lie under Hakon's intense gaze, he thought of a way that might help him avoid doing just that.

Choosing his words carefully, he lifted his eyes to Hakon's and began slowly. "My cousin and I were fording a stream just after midday when your Dreadriders rode in on us and started with their questions. We traded insults, and a fight ensued. Your warriors had us beat, but another Gael warrior came to our aid. With that help, we drove off your Dreadriders. The claim your hounds made about our battle happening at night was a lie, as was the fact that a man with white hair helped us."

There was a growl as Lang launched himself headfirst into Eoin's back. He tried to turn away, but the Dreadrider was on him too quickly. Then a fist slammed into his temple, and darkness swept over him. Eoin slumped into unconsciousness.

Hakon

Hakon spat, "By Thor's hammer, Lang, that did not help!"

"He lies," Lunt grunted from behind his brother as he helped him to his feet.

"He certainly knows more than he's telling," the Dreadlord said icily. "As do both of you. However, we'll address that later. First, tell Runa before you turn in for the night. I'll expect her to use her dark magic on him when the sun rises. And Brede, please drag our Gaelic Prince of the Blood into one of these tower rooms and ensure the door is locked."

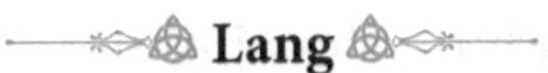

Lang

Lang filled two large silver-lined wooden cups with ale from a skin, handed one to his brother, and then proceeded to drain his own in just three swallows. He refilled it before sitting back against a pile of deerskins.

Neither said much as they stared at the fire burning brightly in their hut's center; words were unnecessary. Lang had left their Jarl's tower with his brother, wondering if lying had been the best idea. Now that the Gael prisoner had asserted their story of being attacked by a white-haired warrior at night was not true, Hakon would press them about why they would make such a claim.

Lunt groaned as he shifted his position, cursing, "Såret mitt gjør vondt!"

"At least you didn't lose your jewels to the bitch when she humiliated us," Lang countered. He asked in a hushed tone, "So, now what, brother?"

"It was your idea to lie about Hakon's Valkyrie."

"Yes, it is a problem, and our Gael friend is being cautious not to make an outright lie."

"Unlike ourselves," Lunt put in.

"This is true, but I say we stick to the story," Lang said as he swirled the ale in his cup. "The battle happened at night, and since we saw white hair, we assumed it was his Destroyer. But, unfortunately, we couldn't see that he was a she."

"While we don't want others to know a mere girl kicked both of our asses, what if she is caught and tells the Dreadlord the real story?"

"Then she must die before being taken prisoner," Lang said tightly.

"Já, before she can tell him anything."

Lang relaxed a little, thinking of the pleasure he would have in splitting her belly open. The way she'd laughed at them while they battled made him burn with anger again. She was not going to repeat it the next time they met. Yes, Hakon's Valkyrie would have to die.

When Lunt grimaced as he tried to find a more comfortable position, Lang rose to help him settle into the pile of deerskins beneath him. Lunt said, "Thanks for that. And seeing her dead would please me."

"Indeed," Lang concurred. "But we must be ready. So, despite Runa's orders to rest, we must start with light training tomorrow. It wouldn't be good for Hakon to order another search for his Destroyer and not have us ready to join the hunt."

"And if our Jarl questions us why the Gael made such a lie?"

"Stick to the story," Lang advised again. "The prisoner is lying to protect his white-haired friend."

Lunt nodded in agreement and held out his cup for a refill.

Breanna

After her bath, Breanna was soon on her way. She felt refreshed and ready to take on her next challenge. The day was chilly, and there was a threat of rain, but she had dressed for the weather this time. Lissa seemed to have a sense for such things; her aunt had advised her to wear four layers of clothes once more. Breanna had little choice in the selection since her father had destroyed her belongings. With thoughts of the man grating on her, she grumbled something about how surprised he would be when they met, especially with him looking down at her blades in his guts.

At least her secret was still safe, for she had circumspectly asked Toal about what Fergal had told him before leaving. Then, while fetching Eoin's sword, her cousin confirmed that *Maorgairme*'s magic had worked without knowing it.

The notion made Breanna smile as she shifted the weight of Eoin's sword from one shoulder to the other. She'd never understand how he lugged such a monstrously heavy thing like it around. Her old long blades were lighter by half, and *Lann Dàn* seemed like feathers in comparison. Still, she was pressing hard to make good time, and maybe it was that which made the weight of his blade seem heavier than it was. She wouldn't have noticed if only they had a few more riding horses like her father's fine steeds. And she'd make better time, too.

Breanna took a southerly track along the shoreline of Loch Gowna, letting the lake be her guide. The pure water shimmered even under a cloudy sky. She knew it was time to head slightly westward when the loch curled around to the east. Before leaving it behind, Breanna took a well-deserved rest. Without seeing the sun, she couldn't be sure how long the first part of the trek had taken, but given her pace, she decided it could not be past midday. She made her way to the water's edge, knelt as she made a cup of her hands, and dipped them beneath the surface. It was cold and refreshing, bringing a sigh from her lips.

As the ripples faded, Breanna caught her reflection in the stillness of the water only a foot away. The red flecks of her blue eyes were evident, as was her white hair. They were features bestowed upon her by her father; she did not want a reminder about them. Because of that taint, the Gods of Erin had given her a task to remove an even darker stain. She wondered if she would live up to the faith they had placed in her.

A curse had started to slip from her mouth for doubting herself when she thought she saw a different pair of eyes staring back from beneath the water. They were dark and menacing yet possessed no life, reminding her of Tethra's demons. There was a sinking feeling in her stomach that she had dallied too long at the water's edge, but before she could move, a black hand erupted from the lake's depths and locked a hold on her wrist.

Breanna screamed and tried to wrench herself free, but the grip was too firm, and she felt pulled toward the surface. There would be no hope for her if the demon took her into the loch. She would die, and the Dreadlord would reign over her land unchecked.

Regaining her wits, she commanded, "*Maorgairme*, be like the sun!"

The ring flared to life, and the dark hand of death that clutched at her exploded in a black, slimy water shower. Breanna tumbled back from the water's edge as the demon let loose a muffled scream of agony that rang over Loch Gowna. Nearly blinded by *Maorgairme*'s brilliant display, she came to her feet, ready for battle. She didn't remember drawing them, but *Lann Dàn* rested in each hand, the diamond blades burning as fiercely as her crystal ring.

She could hardly look at the Tuatha magic; it took several moments to see clearly. Breanna found all was as it had been, save for a grimy film floating on the water where she had sat. With a shiver, Breanna commanded the ring to be silent and sheathed her long knives. She gathered up her pack and hurried away, the loch slipping from view, her body trembling, and her heart pounding at what could have happened. She would have to be more careful!

It was late in the afternoon when the rain started to fall. The unexpectedly heavy downpour caught Breanna by surprise. Growling at the delay, she bolted for a nearby copse of trees and watched the water cascade from the sky. She had wanted to cover more ground, hoping to free her Chief sooner, but the weather was not cooperating.

If she couldn't walk, she might as well have dinner. Breanna dug through her supplies to see what Calla had packed for her. Earlier in the day, lunch had consisted of some trout left over from the night before; the cook had warmed the fish in the hearth and then wrapped it in green leaves and a small cloth to keep it warm. This time, she pulled out a few plums, strips of dried venison, a chunk of cheese, and some dark bread and began to eat. Not the best of fare, but if the rain let up, she wanted to be ready to move on.

Breanna tried to keep as dry as she could as she ate and watched the rain, hoping Eoin had healed enough to make good time once she arranged for his escape. How she was going to accomplish such a feat in the first place was something she had not yet puzzled out. However, one thing was clear—with her white hair, she'd be able to pass as one of the Norvegr's own once she got into Dun Garm.

Being tainted by his blood was something Breanna had tried to put from her mind. As if denying she had come from his seed would change it. But she couldn't deny it, not with her hair and eyes, and that fact rushed back with such force she felt more bitter than ever before.

"Drògaid bean-cinneadh," she muttered to the rain, knowing the Dreadlord's blood would forever contaminate her, that she could not be a true clanswoman to the Clan Dálaigh. He would always be a part of her, even if she fulfilled her mother's *geas*. At least she had that dark kismet to support her cause, and with the Gods on her side, she knew she'd see the end of the Dreadlord's days.

Nonetheless, the caustic truth of it ate at her. While her *geas* had given her little room for thought of Eoin, his kiss had stirred something inside her. Yet, how could she ever hope Eoin would love her once he knew what she was? And with him being a descendant of Conal Cearnach and Ulaida's Clan Mórdha—a Prince of the Blood through his mother—she doubted such a proud lot would ever accept children tainted by the outlander blood in her veins. If she and Eoin had children, his clan would shun them.

Choking back those emotions, she turned her thoughts to what mattered now. Whatever her fate, she had to free her Chief, and if it meant using her contaminated lineage, she would. Getting past the guards and into the dun might pose a problem, but she'd find a way. And if she ran into trouble, there was always *Maorgairme*. Thus far, the fairie ring helped when needed, and with the gods interested in seeing her succeed, it would do so again.

Thinking of the charm, she said to it, "*Maorgairme*, can you stop the rain?"

The ring pulsed to life at the mention of its name. Then the glow dimmed as if it had expended otherworld energy, and the rain suddenly abated. Startled, Breanna scrambled to her feet and snatched up her pack. She wasted no time questioning whether the magic of the gods had caused this boon or if it was just the luck of her timing before getting her feet moving. Around her, it seemed like the rain was still falling, but only a fine mist touched her shoulders. She walked on for a while, looking around in wonder. It was no coincidence, and she needed to call on it more often. Then she noticed the sky was darkening, and that picking a path through the forest was becoming increasingly challenging.

Had she been farther south, where the plains opened up, the tangled trees wouldn't have been a problem. She knew there was a dun nearby to the west, but getting there would be as hard as pushing on. Deciding she wouldn't waste the boon her ring had granted with the weather, she said to the charm, "*Maorgairme, can you show me the way?*"

The crystal ring flared, and a white glow suddenly enveloped her hand, illuminating the area around her feet. A surprised smile spread over Breanna's face, and she carried on with her march, confidently working her way over the uneven terrain.

Was there anything the Mother Goddess's magic wouldn't do for her? It was all such a wonder. Still, with each new work of the Tuathan charm, she couldn't help but be reminded that there was one matter she would have to deal with herself, which would be for her and her alone.

Danu had said that *Maorgairme* would not aid her in battle and that killing the Dreadlord would depend only on her warrior skills. No, it would have to be a fair fight. The ring was just an assurance that Hakon would adhere to those rules.

From the tales spun by their Bard, Breanna knew the Dark Goddess liked to see blood drawn in battle and that she had been one of the masters of magic in the war between the Tuatha and Fomorians. Those battles had been the bloodiest in Erin's history. Thinking of the war Goddess, Breanna wondered how *Lann Dàn* could help her and what magic they possessed. Or had she been given the strange blades to balance her father's magic worker? Maybe they would be no different from her blades in battle. But it didn't matter, for her father would die even if *Lann Dàn* were of no help.

She pushed on.

Breanna walked late into the night before stopping. She had covered more ground than she had hoped and would have gone on had her legs not been so sore and tired. While the rain had stopped, she was pleased to have found a dry spot under a massive oak to make her camp. Breanna made a fire before she rolled out her oiled bed tarp, sleeping mat, and blanket. After eating more jerky, cheese, and crusty bread, she commanded her ring to rest, and the baleful light within it faded.

Then she did the same herself, a huge yawn coming over her as she settled into her blanket for the rest of the night. Maybe Ulicia had been right that she needed more time to recover before venturing on this quest to free Eoin. Yet, Kyras had not gainsaid her.

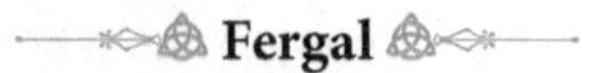

Fergal

"She told you what?" Fergal exploded, unsure if he was asking a question or making a statement.

Kyras shrugged and repeated, "Bre told me to let you know you were in charge of the Red Branch."

"By Nuada's hand, she had no right to go off alone like that," Fergal growled, fists clenched. His face felt hot.

Kyras frowned at him this time. "She's never been one to ask for permission to do anything, but given she is Eoin's Champion, I think that gives her the right to protect her Chief."

"That I know all too well," Fergal clipped out darkly. "When did she leave?"

"This morning," the smith said and turned away from the long table in the main hall.

"This morning!" Fergal shouted as he rose. All eyes turned on him. He knew he should have the sense to corral his tone, but her uncle challenged him in a way he could not abide. He strode to Kyras's side, and his following words had an edge as he demanded, "You could have offered up this hidden little jewel before now."

"Aye, but she requested that I wait," Kyras informed him casually as if Fergal had no merit. "In my clan, I abide by the wishes of my clanswoman, especially from a warrior such as Bre. Our gods are helping her. You think you can do more?"

Fergal fumed. Something was nagging at the back of his mind about Breanna and her quest for magic—something had happened, but he still could not ascertain what it was. Finally, frustrated, he quietly cursed the Gods with, *"Tá olann ina hintinn agam!"*

He stormed past Kyras, slamming the heavy oak door shut as he left. It was fully dark. He realized his jaw was clenched shut like a vise and forced himself to calm down. Whatever Breanna and Kyras had arranged, it was water under the bridge. Fergal took a deep breath and let the tension drain from his body. Overhead, no stars shone, blocked by cloud cover yet again, and the air was cool. It had rained while they were eating, and it felt like there was a threat of yet more.

Rain or no, he knew he had to go after Eoin's Champion, but the thought of walking to Dun Garm made him cringe. His leg, barely healed inside or out, ached, and Breanna already had a day's lead on him. It was the chariot or nothing, so he went to get it ready and gather some supplies. Passing the Clan Dálaigh's hut, Fergal called for Toal to help him. The boy darted to his side, asking what he could do.

"Breanna's run off on a fool's quest to free Eoin from the Dreadlord's hands," Fergal explained as he continued to make his way toward the small shed where his clan kept their horses and chariot.

"I know," Toal said excitedly, his voice sounding like a boy's. He forced a more manly tone, adding, "She told me this morning."

"Did everyone in the dun know this except me?" Fergal muttered.

"Bre said it was a secret," Toal said defensively. "And she let me fetch Eoin's sword."

Fergal couldn't help grousing, "And your mother didn't even think to tell me."

"She didn't know, either," Toal stated. "Well, Bre's gone now, so I assume you plan to catch her?"

"With my leg still not healed, I'll need a chariot," he answered. "If I set out at sunrise, I should be able to get to Dun Garm about the same time she does."

"And what good will that do if your leg is just as useless then as it is today?"

Fergal chuckled. "Are you volunteering to help? It's Dreadriders we'll be battling, lad!"

At that, Toal smiled wryly, saying, "I didn't say I'd be willing to do that. But my bow can be handy for fighting from a short distance, and a flaming arrow could wreak havoc on a thatched roof."

"That it might," Fergal agreed, feeling more at ease since he went out in the middle of the night to rescue Breanna. "Then we set out just before sunrise. And tell no one we are leaving."

Eoin

The door to the room that served as Eoin's cell swung open. The Dreadrider, whom he knew as Brede, entered, followed by Hakon Skadi, who towered over him. Eoin could see the red flecks in his blue eyes burning with anger, much like Breanna's did when she was furious.

The Dreadlord growled, "You're holding something back!"

Brede stood next to Hakon. His hands were clenched into fists as if he wanted a piece of him like the younger Dreadriders had had the night before.

Eoin lay on a pallet of rushes, rubbing his jaw, his eyes holding that icy gaze as he watched the Dreadlord and his lieutenant warily.

Hakon was flanked again by his trusted wolfhounds, massive animals who would kill for their master without hesitation.

"Brede, find a rag to clean up his face," Hakon commanded. "Runa will come to root out what he knows with her magic.'

The older Dreadrider nodded and left as his Jarl stood silently over their captive. With his arms crossed, the Dreadlord watched Eoin as if he were a falcon circling its prey. A while passed, and the old warrior still did not move, his constant gaze unnerving him.

Finally, Eoin could no longer hold the other's gaze and dropped his eyes to the floor. He knew he must protect his secret, even if it cost him his life, for Breanna would be lost if he gave in. However, keeping that knowledge in his mind might be challenging if this Runa the Dreadlord had possessed some magic. It was a thought that sent a shiver down his spine.

Then footsteps approached, and an old hag shuffled into the room. Strands of white hair escaped the woman's hooded black robes, and the only other notes of color on her were a bleached deerskin pouch at her side, a silver brooch pinned over the center of her chest, and her glass and stone bead swags. A short ceremonial knife hung on a chain from that brooch. Eoin could make out little else. He looked at her cautiously, knowing she had to be the Dreadlord's magic worker, the one referred to as Runa; she was here to discover what she could about Hakon's Destroyer.

He was uncomfortable being near the Druids when they worked their magic, and now, one much like them would inspect him. Under her steady gaze, he shivered again, bringing prickly bumps to his forearms. That shiver seemed to please her. Eoin could only mutter a curse at his display of weakness.

The old hag stated, "Lunt and Lang said you had a captive."

"I commanded that you use your magic on him at first light, Runa," Hakon snapped back.

Runa looked at her Jarl darkly as if ready to say more, but then shrugged. Her tone still held some acid when she said, "I needed to gather the correct herbs; otherwise, my potion would be useless."

The Dreadlord glared at her briefly before demanding, "Then work your magic, völva, and find out what he knows."

Runa commented derisively, "This Gael is injured. I need to check his wounds first."

The Dreadlord loomed over her. "I don't care about his wounds!"

"My magic will kill him if he's not healthy enough," Runa growled back. "Then you'd surely get nothing out of him. Leave this to me, and you'll know what he knows soon enough."

Brede returned with a damp cloth and handed it to Eoin, interrupting Hakon's ire. Then the Dreadlord commanded him, "Runa is going to check his wounds. You keep watch over him until she finishes. Then lock him back up. I'll let Sveinn know he has another *guest* to look after until we learn more."

Then he spun away and muttered something only Eoin couldn't understand as Hakon left for the main hall. His two wolfhounds were quickly on his heels; it seemed to Eoin that their master's anger had put them on edge.

"Be about it, Runa!" Brede commanded with a frown.

She cackled and turned to Eoin, saying, "Best not to tangle with Hakon, boy. Now, show me your wounds from your battle with Lunt and Lang."

"You mean with the Dreadriders who were searching for his son?" Eoin asked.

"Yes. Now strip and show me what Hakon's boys did to you."

Eoin rose from the rush-covered floor and hoisted his kilt to reveal the stitched-up slice on his left thigh. He knew she meant business and would try to extract the information her Jarl sought.

So, he decided it would be the Red Branch if he had to give up something. Maybe that would throw her off the trail.

Runa interrupted his thoughts. "Besides the cut over your eye, is that the only lick Lunt and Lang got in?"

Eoin nodded as she stepped forward and probed the leg wound with her fingers. She straightened and did the same with his forehead, then crooned, "Hmmm, good stitch work. It would have been worse if the Dreadlord's son had not shown up to save you. He must be a fiercer warrior than I thought to have taken on both Lunt and Lang. They are lucky he spared them."

Eoin was perplexed as he said, "Why is everyone so convinced the Dreadlord has a son in Dun Arrogh?"

"Because I say he does," the völva growled, reaching into a pouch at her side. When her hand emerged, she flung a handful of strange brown powder in his face.

Eoin flinched, choking on the dust. He looked up to find the room spinning as he sank back to the pallet. His heart was pounding as a numbness settled over him, and nothing could clear it. Finally, knowing his will was slipping, he conjured a vision of a redheaded Breanna as a young man. "Hakon does not have a white-haired son at Dun Arrogh."

Runa

Runa spent the next span asking Eoin questions, trying various tactics to get him to admit that Hakon had a son living among their clans. His potion-fogged mind fought her attempts to dig at the information she sought, but she kept attacking from one side and then the other, steadily wearing him down. Soon, he was answering her questions without resistance.

When the fact came out that he was indeed the leader of this new Red Branch, Runa laughed with triumph. Shortly after, she discovered that the band was mostly made up of lads and lassies, hardly something to be concerned about. If true, then the real threat was indeed her Jarl's Destroyer.

Since Eoin seemed entirely under the power of her magic, she demanded to know about the white-haired boy. She pressed him repeatedly, working on the story about his battle with Lunt and Lang. The Gael warrior continued to maintain that they had fought during the day and that it had not been a white-haired lad who had come to his aid.

When Eoin started to shake his head to emphasize his denial of her statements, she knew his animated behavior was a sign that her potion was wearing off. Runa turned away in disgust, and, despite the effort, she knew no more about the Destroyer than before she had used her potion on him.

Leaving Brede to deal with the now sleeping prisoner, Runa made her way out of the tower and across the muddy yard of Dun Garm, weaving a path through several wagons laden with the yearly tributes. They were the first to arrive, with more to follow daily for a fortnight. The storage sheds would soon be so full that even walking through them would be difficult. They would barter some tributes with other Gaelic Chiefs and traders for fine linens, jewelry, and other gold and silver wares.

Runa hardly noted the wagons, her mind churning to discover where she had gone wrong. Her visions had been clear. A seed sown by the Dreadlord would arise to destroy him. When Lunt and Lang said a white-haired warrior had attacked them, she was confident it was him, for she had also foreseen that. Had they just not found the Destroyer, was that it? Uncertain, she commanded her apprentice to catch another crow, and then she would make her Blood Runes speak to her again.

When she finally stood before her Jarl in the main hall, she was shaking her head, and her voice was tight as she said, "I tell you, he knows nothing of your son."

"How can that be?" the Dreadlord questioned, clearly disappointed. "He's hiding something—I can feel it."

"Já," Runa said with a chuckle. "He's hiding that he is the leader of this new Red Branch. But while he may be a Gaelic Prince, his followers are just a handful of warriors, mostly lads and lassies barely old enough to lift a sword."

"Then is our potential Destroyer, this Bradaigh from Dun Uisneach, that we seek?" Hakon asked. "Or maybe Braoin, whom we are both doubtful about. May be the one?"

"Hmmm, something tells me no to both. Yet, both may have roles to play in our coming battle."

"Then where is the Destroyer?" Hakon demanded. "Or is this just a dream of yours?"

"Was Tethra a dream?" Runa retorted scornfully.

"And what good has your Fomorian god done us?" Hakon snapped back.

Runa's tone softened. "My Blood Runes have told me Tethra's demons engaged your son a few nights back, and, as I suspected, the Tuatha gods came to his aid. From what I understand, it was a fierce battle that cost our ally dearly. But now that the Destroyer possesses some traceable Tuatha magic, Tethra should be able to find him again. It's just a matter of time before his minions fall on your son."

"And how do we know the Gaelic gods will not come to his rescue like before?"

"Because I believe Tethra himself will be involved," Runa informed her Jarl. "I doubt our Fomorian god took kindly to seeing the Tuatha Sun God aid your opponents' cause so openly, which bodes well for us. Still, if the Destroyer stays clear of water, it will be up to us to find him before he finds us."

Hakon was silent for a moment before he said, "I don't like leaving my fate in the hands of some ancient gods from a foreign land. Work your magic and find the Destroyer you have foreseen. And remember, your life hangs in the balance if it comes to pass that mine does."

Eoin

Eoin awoke to morning light filtering through the shuttered window above him, his mind groggy. Shaking his head, he scanned the room and found he was alone, still in the same room. He glanced at the massive stones that made up the outside wall—no way to get out that way.

Groaning, he rose, trying to remember what had last happened. Then, seeing the chamber pot, he relieved himself. While doing so, Eoin suddenly remembered Hakon's völva had used a potion on him. He had no idea what he said. That was a concern, but Eoin could do nothing about that. He had either spilled Breanna's secret or not.

He touched his jaw where Lang had slugged him and winced. That had been a mighty hit, and he was sure there was now a good-sized bruise on the right side of his face. Yet, it mattered not. He was hungry and strode to the door, pounding on it. A moment later, it opened, and Eoin growled, "About time. I was ready to piss on your door!"

The lanky man who held it open. "I am Sveinn, your keeper. Now shut your trap and follow me."

The old outlander led him to a large table at the center of the room and presented two plates of food already set out, each with various baked bread items, a lump of gruel, and some pieces of smoked boar.

A white-haired warrior was sitting before one of the plates, already eating. He paused and rose to acknowledge Eoin, giving him a slight bow. "Braoin Mac Lochlinn."

Before taking the seat before the other plate, he noted the warrior wore a silver Silver Knot armring, yet he carried Norvegr blood like his Champion. "Eoin Mac Cairbre, Clan Mórdha. I hail from Dun Arrogh, northeast of here."

"Well met," Braoin replied, slipping into a heavier brogue. "I am from a settlement at the southwest end of Loch Síleann. That's some bruise on your face."

Eoin replied, doing the same with his brogue, "I have had worse."

"Hmmm, indeed," Braoin commented. "There seems to be some interest in you."

"Aye," Eoin answered. "You're a half-breed, likely one of the Dreadlord's. Hakon thinks I know something about one of his sons who supposedly hails from my region."

"And you contend you do not?" Braoin asked.

Eoin nodded, answering, "I do not know of any more sons."

"I see," Braoin said. "I know of one other, who is called Bradaigh. We fought in the summer *comórtas*. He hails from one of the Dun Uisneach settlements. From what I understand, they are interested in him but have been unable to find his settlement. Yet, there is another they seek."

Eoin nodded. "Hmmm, indeed they do."

"I might have had a bout with such a *lad* last summer at the *comórtas*," Braoin added. "Fights like someone who is in your mind. Kicked my arse and earned a gold arm ring this past summer. Even with my two blades against *his*, I was no match."

Eoin smiled, saying, "I've heard of this warrior." Silence passed as Eoin tucked into the food. Finally having a moment to pause between swallows, he asked, "And you. How do you find your new father?"

Braoin's eyes narrowed, and he said quietly, "He killed who would have been my father and raped my mother. She then had our former Fáidh lay a *geas* of justice upon me. I hope that is clear enough."

"Aye, lad, aye," Eoin answered. "Again, sounds like someone I've heard of."

Breanna

Breanna rose with the sun, though she could not see it or feel its warmth as the heavy fog hung in the cool air. She gave herself time to limber up because she was stiff from sleeping on the ground. After working through her daily warrior forms, Breanna felt better and tucked into her travel rations for breakfast. Finished, she kept a swift pace and soon pushed on toward Dun Garm. By early morning, she was in the gently rolling plains of western Mide.

There was a heavy mist lying like a blanket over the land. Breanna only realized she was close to Dun Garm when the going became much more manageable. If it weren't for the hills to her right pushing her in a southwest direction, she was certain she would have lost her way.

Later that day, Breanna worked her way to the top of a hill and found that enough vapor had lifted to see the massive fort of Dun Garm atop yet another rise to her west.

Breanna knew the great Loch Ree and River Shannon lay just beyond the Dreadlord's den to the west, and the thought of being near that much water caused her to shudder, as Tethra's demons might be able to fall on her again. Steeling herself against such a possibility, she turned her attention to how she could free Eoin.

Unless she waited for nightfall, she sensed she was getting close to the dun. Doing so without being seen would be more than a challenge—it would be impossible, for there were cleared fields of oats and barley around it with Gael hostages bringing in the harvest.

With that thought, Breanna found a cluster of oaks and made camp even though the sun had not yet set. After drawing on her rations for her evening meal, she found it hard to resist the sleep that stole over her like a thief in the night, her weary mind and body succumbing to unaccustomed stresses.

Breanna's warrior sense brought her back to life, telling her it was near midnight and time to rise. This time, her legs protested even louder than before. Ignoring the pain, she moved on. The cover of darkness would be the only way to get close to Dun Garm. Low clouds blanketed the sky, threatening rain while they blocked out any star or moonlight, and there was still a mist in the air. She could easily get lost without the torches that lit her father's fort, but she knew the gods were smiling upon her, guiding her; she would have been led there by something else had the fires not burned.

Once through the grain and pasture fields, she circled the Dreadlord's hold, seeking a way inside. A narrow line of pickets topped the rampart, but she thought someone as thin as herself might be able to slip through. Breanna began climbing the earthen and stone wall as quietly as she could. The rocks and dirt were loose, and it was hard not to kick them down the steep bank. She finally reached the top and found wooden stakes tightly woven together; then she removed her pack and weapons and tried to slip between them anyway. A moment later, she was stuck. One of the pikes snapped as she attempted to push her way through.

The loud crack of the dry wood was enough to start the dogs in the yard barking.

When the noisy animals finally roused someone, the hounds were freed. Breanna tried to squirm her way out of the pickets but remained trapped. With a grunt, she heaved herself backward. Once more, one of the stakes gave, and another ripped her otter's skin cloak over her head. However, it wasn't a moment too soon, for the wolfhounds were scrambling up the inside of the ramparts of Dun Garm. The dogs, too big to squeeze through the pickets, stopped, but their barking had brought out some of the warriors.

Fortunately, most just yelled at the animals to quiet them and slammed the doors to their huts; the few that ventured out to investigate the commotion found nothing in the darkness. Breanna was quickly on her way down the other side, her weapons strapped to her back and Eoin's sword belted around her waist. She muttered a barely audible curse at having lost her cloak.

A few moments later, all was quiet, and Breanna glared at Dun Garm's walls from the outside. Knowing she couldn't remain near the fort, Breanna turned away and headed for the nearest copse of trees. She would have to understand the layout better if she hoped to free Eoin. Breanna's head hung low with her shoulders hunched as she dejectedly trudged away. Maybe she couldn't do anything more than get herself caught after all.

Then, both of them would be in the Dreadlord's grasp.

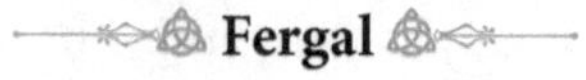

Fergal

Fergal handed Toal the reins to guide the horses more slowly along a bumpy, narrow deer path, saying, "I need to rest my leg."

"You're favoring it more than when we set out."

"Aye," was all Fergal said, giving him a nod and sinking to the rocking chariot's wet wooden floor. The action made him think of Breanna when they had been rolling through the black of night, and she had been too tired to stand any longer. Once more, he had a sense that he had forgotten something during that ride, something vital. The matter involved Breanna, Eoin, and the Dreadlord, but he couldn't remember it clearly. Frustrated, he grumbled a curse at the woman he was chasing.

Toal asked, "Is your leg still bothering you that much?"

"More than I care for," Fergal replied with a shrug. He had been pushing them hard throughout the misty day, and with no real track to follow, it had been a rough ride. With the light fading, he commanded, "Find us a place to camp for the night, Toal."

A short time later, the lad pulled the reins to stop their hill ponies under the canopy of a big black oak. "Will this do?"

"Aye," he agreed. "In another half-day, we'll be near Dun Garm. It is another story if we are in time to catch your hot-headed cousin."

With Breanna a full day ahead, Fergal had had no choice except to drive their chariot through the rain and fog like a madman. He had insisted on such a dash, saying it was the only way to catch their quarry, but even he wasn't sure. "What do you think? Have we gained any time on her?"

As Toal turned to assist Fergal from the chariot, helping settle him against the tree trunk, he answered, "It would only be a guess, but given how you lashed the ponies, probably. I need to rub them down and get these guys watered and fed if we hope to get anything out of them tomorrow. Hopefully, the weather will hold in our favor."

Once the lad had settled their horses, he used the reins to set up a picket for them before turning to make a fire between the chariot and the tree. Little was said as the pair ate their evening meal, and sleep stole over them a short time later.

Toal

At first light, Toal laid out breakfast: stale bread, dried plums, and jerky. Low clouds hung in the air, spreading a cold mist over everything, and he grumbled about the weather not holding as he had hoped. Then, he took the reins, saying Fergal should rest his leg. The two warriors pressed on, ignoring the damp discomfort; they were Gaels born and bred in a land that was often wet. They left the denser woods for open ground and soon were in the gently rolling plains of western Mide, lands the Dreadlord had claimed for his own.

By late afternoon, the clouds had fled, and Toal pointed out the stone tower of Dun Garm. Yet there was still no sign of his wayward cousin. Cattle dotted the land surrounding the vast fort, along with fields of oats and barley. Gaels who had become *daor aicme* to the Dreadlord of Garm were working to bring in the harvest, and a long line of laden wagons rolled toward the Dreadlord's hold. They had come in from the northwest, loaded with tributes collected from the settlements and duns along the River Shannon.

Toal and Fergal had been approaching from the northeast, and the younger lad pulled the horses to a halt behind a cluster of bushes, hoping they and their chariot remained unseen.

"Now what?" Toal asked.

"We wait," Fergal said as his gaze swept the land. "See how the cover on the grassy plain is sparse at best? Yet there's enough for one to hide behind a bale or stack. Your cousin is out there; that much I'm sure of."

Toal scanned the train of carts. His voice rose as he asked, "What about them? If one of the drivers saw us—"

"Then they saw us, and we'll know that soon enough," Fergal replied. "If not, we'll leave the chariot behind and try to get a closer look at the Dreadlord's dun."

"After sunset?"

"Aye," Fergal confirmed.

The last of the wagons for the day were now crossing the plain. Then, after a short time, a form flashed over the back of the trailing cart as it passed a pile of cut peat. "Did you see that?" Fergal asked. "Breanna?"

"It must be," Toal agreed, searching for more detail. "There's no doubt. But what is she planning to do?"

"That's Breanna's secret, but I'm sure we'll know soon enough."

"Then we'd better be ready to help her."

"Aye, that we must."

Rescue from Garm

Breanna

It was late in the day as Breanna watched wagon after wagon roll by, each overflowing with goods from various duns paying their annual tribute to the Dreadlord. Large buckets of barley, oats, peas, onions, and garlic were piled high in most carts that made their way through Hakon's cattle-grazing fields. Other wagons carried baskets of pears, plums, and apples, some stacked so high they wobbled perilously on the bumpy track. There was even an occasional cow tethered to one of the creaking rigs.

As the end of the train passed the pile of cut peat Breanna had taken refuge behind, she raced to jump onto the final rocking wagon, trying to flop softly over the gate using her battle training. The cart lurched over a rut, and her landing went unnoticed by her driver. As the sacks of barley shifted to cushion her, she exhaled in relief. The driver might have seen her if he had glanced over his shoulder to see what had caused the motion. Yet Breanna had already tucked herself behind a stack of fruit baskets, her weapons hidden beneath her. She knew the old Norvegr could see nothing directly behind him but felt him lean to the side as the cart briefly veered that way. Breanna commanded, *"Maorgairme, make him see a rut in the path!"*

Regardless of what he saw, the driver let the horses continue south, following the rig before him as they headed toward Dun Garm. Gazing at the fading blue sky, Breanna waited for the fort's gates to pass by as the cart creaked along the bumpy path. Now that she was on her way, she needed a plan. *Yet, what plan could I have? Other than sneaking in and freeing my Chief?*

Her rash notion still had a few details to work out, like how to get them out of Dun Garm. Or maybe she would face Hakon, and the matter would be moot, for one of them would be dead. If her father found blades in his belly, there would be little from which to flee, as she would rule Dun Garm and challenge every Novegr to ensure that.

Breanna was startled by the sound of horses pounding past her cart, heading away from Dun Garm with giant baying wolfhounds that followed. She didn't know what it meant. Yet, if Hakon's men had released the dogs, they were on a hunt for something or someone.

When the gates finally did pass overhead, the rig Breanna was in creaked to a stop. Breanna's attention turned to hiding safely inside the massive fort. She felt the driver climb down from his seat and heard people scurrying about everywhere. She watched them unload the harvest from various wagons, starting with the ones at the head of the line.

Sensing no one was nearby, she slipped over the back of the cart and rolled beneath it to get a better look at the layout of the dun. Through the wheel to her right, she saw several simple wattle and daub storage sheds along the western rampart, and ahead, she saw, between the horse's legs, the imposing boat-shaped hall. The boat-shaped expanse was four, maybe five, times the size of their hall at Dun Arrogh. The larger huts, which lay to the right of the main hall, were likely for the Dreadriders or groups of lesser warriors, and a stone tower rose to its left. She could see where he ruled his dun from the spire. Then there were cramped hovels near the gates for the *daor aicme*. While her observations were all suppositions, they all seemed to fit together. Other wagons and carts sat around the one she had hidden in, and the courtyard lay to her left.

As Breanna plotted her next move, she realized it would be hard to conceal her long blades without a cloak. She was still angry with herself for leaving the otterskin hanging on the pickets outside Dun Garm. Now, she had nothing with which to hide her weapons. Obtaining a cloak would be her first order of business. Breanna struggled into the harness that kept her long blades slung across her back. Then, creeping from beneath the cart, she pulled a sack of what turned out to be barley from a nearby pile and slung it over her shoulders, quickly heading for the nearest storage shed. No one said a word as she ducked inside.

Breanna tossed the sack aside, went to the back, and hid behind the bushels of fruit already stored away—which she snatched up and munched on. It was less than a span before sunset; moving around after dark would be much easier. Few would be inclined to stop her, what with her white hair and all, and to those who did, she decided she would tell them the truth—she was Hakon's daughter, come to see him from a nearby dun. The man hadn't raped only her mother but also had to have other children spread across his territory.

The workers unloaded the remaining tributes, and her shed slowly began to fill. It was growing dark when they finished, and Breanna relaxed as they shut the doors. There had been a few tense moments when one or two *daor aicme* would come near her to stack another basket of plums or pears. In the darkness of the shed, both *Lann Dàn* and *Maorgairme* held a fierce glow as if letting her know they were ready for battle.

Breanna admonished the ring, "*Maorgairme*, tell your friends to be quiet. And do the same yourself. That light of yours is going to give us away."

The ring flared brighter momentarily, as if indignant at being commanded to shut up, but then both *Maorgairme* and *Lann Dàn* faded to a dull glow that was hard to see. Still unsatisfied, Breanna tore open a sack of barley and threw the rough-spun cloth over her long blades—it would have to do for now—before she crept to the door. As she cracked it open, the warriors who had ridden out earlier came pounding back through the gates, and with them came four lathered wolfhounds. It wasn't quite dark, but torchlights flickered in the courtyard. Then, finally, there was enough light to show the warriors' faces. Breanna searched for the Dreadriders she had fought before. Unfortunately, she didn't recognize them, and the Dreadrider who led this party was certainly older than they had been.

One thing Breanna didn't need was to run into the two burly brothers before she could free Eoin. Only they knew who she was. And if she did encounter them, this time, she would make sure they were dead when the battle was over.

Hakon

Hakon Skadi stood in his tower chamber, watching a line of wagons roll through the cattle fields toward his fort. The tribute thus far had been bountiful, and his Dreadriders had encountered no trouble with the locals in getting them to deliver what they had committed. Bartering with other Chieftains and traders would keep most of his subjects in his fort appeased throughout the winter.

In years past, collecting his tribute was not as easy as it has been in recent years. Some northern duns had rebelled, and he had sent raiding parties to take what was rightfully his by force. He wished there were still a few holdout duns left, for it kept his men sharp. Now, he had to rely mostly on yard training and occasional skirmishes along his borders.

Hakon turned from his window. As he crossed the room, a knock fell on his door, and he commanded the person to enter. It was Brede, his senior Dreadrider.

"My Jarl, someone attempted to steal into Dun Garm last night. Late this afternoon, one of the guards found this ripped cloak tangled in the pickets. It's not one of ours."

Hakon examined the cloak and stated, "From its size, I'd say it belonged to a small lad. Not a muscled young man like Braoin."

"Já, I was thinking the same," Brede concurred. "Your Destroyer would have a build like the Gaelic Prince."

Hakon considered that as he turned the otter skin cloak over, contemplating who it might belong to. A few moments passed as the old Dreadrider shuffled uncomfortably from one foot to the other. He nodded in agreement. "Indeed, someone lithe."

Brede informed him, "I already sent Alrik out with a search party and had him take the dogs. They took the scent—we will see what they can find."

Hakon's voice held a note of enthusiasm when he said, "That's a sound plan. And Brede, check on our prisoner on your way out."

The Dreadrider thumped a fist on his chest and turned for the door. With that, Hakon was alone once more. He stepped back to the window that looked out to the north and hardly noticed the line of carts filled with his tributes rolling into Dun Garm. His thoughts centered on the Destroyer. The cloak in his hands could belong to anyone, maybe a local Gael trying to slip into his fort to steal supplies; it had happened before. Or maybe one of the hostages had tried to escape, but no one had reported a missing *daor aicme.*

No, his warrior sense told him there was more to it. His son was somewhere out there, lurking in the trees, studying the options. Hakon wondered what had driven the young man to become so vengeful, what had caused him to let the Gaelic gods rule his destiny. Had it truly been the *geas* that Runa discovered, which were cast by the Druids long ago? Had Hakon had the chance to raise his Destroyer, he could have made him a legend like the Hound of Ulaida. And together, they could have challenged the *Ard-Rì* in Tara for the heart of Erin, maybe even taken command of the entire island. Especially with Niall Noígiallach's attention directed toward raiding the mainland.

With such a legend at his side, the Dreadlord could embark on his planned massive expansion of his territory and bring in more warriors from his homeland with no concerns about where to get the homesteads they would demand. A warrior like Ulaida's Cú Chulainn at his beck and call would have been a great boon.

But such musings would not make it so. With or without such a son, Hakon was confident he would become a significant power in his adopted land, though his timetable might be limited. There was no room for thoughts about what could have been. If the Destroyer were as good as Runa had warned, Hakon would have to be careful. His son was dangerous. That much was certain.

Casting one last glance out the window, the Dreadlord left his private chambers behind. Maybe his prisoner had some insight into what the Destroyer would do next. After that, he would have to check on the tribute that had just arrived. Then, cursing about not having enough time, he turned toward the doors of his tower.

Toal

Toal watched the Norvegr warriors and their wolfhounds race by the train of wagons as they headed northwest, riding past their position. Then, the last cart in the supply train disappeared inside Dun Garm, and the gates closed behind it. To the west, the sun could be seen low on the horizon through a broken patchwork of clouds. The air was brisk despite a calm wind, and he shivered at the thought of spending another night beneath the stars. If the night before had been wet, tonight would surely be cold.

Toal said, "I'm not sure what that was about. Yet Breanna's inside, and we're out here."

"For now, I'm more concerned about that band of warriors and their dogs," Fergal mused. "They are on the hunt, and we are too exposed here. Let's go. We'll leave the chariot in those woods behind us and get closer after dark."

The pair scrambled onto the chariot, riding due north, and let the wood swallow them up. Then Fergal commanded, "Now, let's eat while we can. Once the sun is down, we can follow the edge of that line of trees to the west of us and then keep low along Loch Ree's reeds. It should get us close enough to dash across the fields and into the shadows of the dun's western ramparts."

Toal asked, "What then?"

"We wait for Breanna to make her move," Fergal replied. "If she needs us, we'll be ready."

"And if she can indeed get Eoin out of there?"

"We run as we've never run before," came the reply.

"Not much of a plan," Toal commented, his tone disapproving.

"You want to stay and fight the whole dun, Dreadriders and all?" Fergal rejoined.

Toal shook his head. "Of course not!"

Fergal winked. "Good! I didn't think Kyras had raised a fool for a son. Now, get your bow ready and keep your flint box handy. We may have to start a fire."

"Aye," Toal said, gathering his things as commanded while Fergal looked through their travel rations.

After they had eaten, Fergal asked, "Ready?"

Toal hoped Breanna had devised a plan to get Eoin out of Dun Garm. Otherwise, it would be a long night. As he looked toward the Dreadlord's fort one last time before the sun sank below the horizon, he finally understood the magnitude of the effort they faced.

Given the tales spun by their Bard about the old Red Branch of Ulaida, he had thought their band could muster enough muscle and wits to deal with Hakon Skadi. After all, the blood of the greatest warriors of their land was flowing through their veins. Now, he realized that any attempt at creating a band of fierce warriors like the Red Branch was just a dream. The odds were stacked against him. They would have to stop the Dreadlord another way. He had seen the magic in *Lann Dàn* that Breanna wielded against the demons, and he hoped she had found the right weapon to defeat the Dreadlord.

Cheered by that thought, he turned to Fergal and signaled he was ready.

Breanna

"Find anything?" Breanna heard someone bark at the Dreadrider who had led the party.

"No," was the reply. "Once our hounds lost the trail, they couldn't pick it up again. They had taken up the scent on that path leading to the northwest, but whoever wore this cloak must have used magic to cover his tracks. Even the Dreadlord's favored pair of trackers couldn't find a trace of him."

"Our Jarl won't be pleased, Alrik."

"Já, Brede," agreed the Dreadrider sourly as he dismounted.

The same man asked, "Should we leave the dogs out tonight?"

"Just let Hati and Skoll roam—the others are too jumpy and will bark at anything."

With that, Breanna watched the yard slowly clear as stable-hands came to take the horses. They muttered about the warriors heading for the main hall to get their supper before them. It took a span or so for the yard to clear enough for Breanna to creep from her hiding place. Keeping to the shadows, she began her search for Eoin by moving to the following storage shed. After checking to ensure Eoin was not inside it, she moved on.

There was a line of small huts filled with supplies and fodder. It appeared to be enough to support those living within Dun Garm's walls for nearly two seasons. It galled her to know they lived off the backs of others, allowing them to concentrate on honing their warrior skills and ignore the need to farm, raise cattle, or gather nuts and berries from the land. The only task his warriors carried out regularly was hunting for fresh meat, and Breanna was sure that if the action didn't help keep Hakon's Dreadriders in shape, they wouldn't have bothered with such a chore. When she finished her quest and her father was no longer among them, she would have to return these supplies.

The last of the storage sheds gave way to the main hall, bringing Breanna up short. It loomed before her like a giant boat that had flipped in a storm. With fog settling in over the fort, the hall looked like it was riding on a sea of mist. The strange sight was briefly entrancing, but then a burst of laughter from some warriors inside brought Breanna back to reality.

From the noise they were making, it was clear the evening meal was still in progress. Torchlights flickered brightly in the yard, making it impossible for her to cross from one structure to the other without revealing herself. Anyone walking from hut to hall or back would see her; many people were still coming and going.

As Breanna looked over her options, a chill settled over her, and she wished she had her cloak. She touched her Celtic Knot arm ring when she rubbed her arms to ward off the cold. It reminded her of who she was – a warrior, like her father and grandmother, which restored her confidence. The intricately worked gold symbolized her Gaelic blood, a sign that she was of the saor aicme, free warriors true to their clan. It did not matter that she carried Hakon's blood in her veins—the Gael part of her was more robust. And she needed that part to free her Chief.

Taking in the rest of the fort, she tried to assess where they held Eoin. More storage sheds were across the central yard, and she expected she would need to check them. The living quarters of the Dreadriders and their families were unlikely. Between the size of a storage hut and the larger huts for the warriors, one roundhouse stood by itself, and little torchlight reached it. That held possibilities, for why else would one put a building off on its own? Then, the Dreadlord's stone tower caught her eye—yet another option. Breanna could not decide which to check first.

Still left with the problem of crossing the yard, she returned to the main hall. Then, deciding to sneak along the rampart where the torchlight barely reached, she stepped toward the wall. A low growl stopped her, and she turned to find two massive wolfhounds staring her down. A curse slipped from her mouth, and she shivered as much from the cold as she did from seeing the finger-sized teeth bared and ready to rip her throat out. She wished she still had her cloak, for it was a frosty night with the clouds gone, and she knew her trembling could be mistaken as fear by the animals. Then she whispered, "*Maorgairme*, make friends with them."

Danu's ring flared, and the dogs whimpered. Surprised, Breanna held out her hand for them to sniff her, then patted each on the head. Then, an idea struck her that no one would bother challenging her if Hakon's guard dogs were escorting her. And if they did, she would first try to claim she was their Jarl's daughter who had come to visit from another dun to the south. Breanna thought with a smile that, should that fail, she could always command the wolfhounds to attack.

"I believe that Dreadrider called you Hati and Skoll," she said as she knelt beside the enormous hounds. Then, deciding to ensure her friendship, she reached into her pack and pulled a piece of dried venison out for each. Finally, she commanded them to sit and held out her treats, which the dogs eagerly chewed with their tails wagging.

Once finished, Breanna turned for the hut across the yard and boldly stepped into the flickering torchlights. A snap of her fingers brought the two hounds to her heels, and she moved confidently toward her target. Unfortunately, the yard was muddy, making for tenuous footing at best. Breanna could not cross it quietly as the mud pulled at her boots. Concerned that she would give herself away, she looked around in alarm, but those few warriors and their families out and about did not even acknowledge her as she passed. Breanna had to suppress the smile that wanted to creep at the corners of her mouth.

With the ground still relatively warm, the calm, cold air was drawing the fog she had seen earlier. As was often the case, the massive body of water that made up nearby Loch Ree would feed the thick blanket well into the night. Seeing it made Breanna want to shout a triumphant battle cry as her land protected her.

Ahead and to her right stood two guards at the door to her father's stone tower. They glanced in her direction, but the presence of the dogs quelled any interest. She crossed behind the three-story building and let the shadows engulf her, heaving a relieved sigh that she had made it this far without drawing her blades. Still tagging along like eager yearlings, the wolfhounds kept to her side, their tongues lolling out. Breanna commanded them to sit and stay when she reached the hut set apart from the others. Doubts about her choice of this hut began to creep into her mind as she slipped inside the dimly lit dwelling, for there were no guards.

She did not remember drawing *Lann Dàn*, but they were in her hands as she crossed the door's threshold. Seeing no one in the front room, she quickly checked the back half of the hut. It was unusual for a smaller dwelling to have two rooms, and when she passed through a door made of beads hung on strands of hemp, she knew why. From the magical trinkets before her, the hut could only belong to her father's völva.

The völva had become well known enough to the Druids within Hakon's territory for them to warn their fellow Gaels to stay clear. If Breanna remembered correctly, they called her Runa, referring to her as a *baobh*, a fury. When her father first came to Erin, Dun Arrogh's former Fáidh had speculated that Hakon's völva was adept at her work with magic because she could connect with one of the ancient Norvegr gods. After that, the Druids had given her the disparaging name. The notion of being near the foul magic maker's tools made Breanna shiver, and she spat a curse: "*Olc geasadair.*"

The heavy pall hanging over her in the völva's hut vanished as Breanna turned and went through the door. When she found the wolfhounds still waiting, she couldn't help but grin; having such obedient animals with her was good, and she had to pat each of their massive heads once more. Then, Breanna looked up and noted the fog was getting thicker. She threw her sack over *Lann Dàn* and tucked her blades to her side, deciding her Gods were undoubtedly smiling upon her.

Then, an old white-haired woman tottered out of the mist carrying a lamp, and Breanna's heart sank. It could be her father's völva, who had set Hakon searching for his Destroyer, searching for her! Breanna was sure that she would be her undoing. She just had to be.

Hakon

Hakon sat with his Dreadriders at one of the long oak tables in the main hall. With the answers—or lack thereof—from Eoin about his bastard son frustrating him, going over the tributes from the various duns with Brede was more than tedious. The harvest had been one of the best in years, and he frankly had more than he needed. That boded well for his spring plans to bring in warriors from Alfheim; starting a campaign on low rations would have caused concern in the dun. The thought of his storage huts stacked with supplies made him smile as he finished his supper.

The evening meal of fresh-roasted trout and garlic was quite tasty. Jarlson had outdone himself, quickly quelling even the most vocal complaints that there was no red meat. Given their unsuccessful hunt earlier in the day, it ended any grumbling when Hakon reminded his warriors that the kitchen scullions had provided an excellent meal with what his men had provided them.

Calling for another cup of ale, the Dreadlord relaxed as he sat among his fellow warriors, and thoughts of his Destroyer faded for the moment. He drained half of the brew in two swallows, complimented Jarlson on his latest efforts, and sat back to listen to the small talk in the room. Several men were playing a tactical board game called *hnefatafl*. One Dreadrider, a tall fellow named Thorvald, was particularly good at the game—as usual, there was just a hint of a smile on his lips as he moved his stone pieces during his turn.

A short while later, Hakon noted that Braoin, who was seated at the other end of the table, rose and took his leave. Then, as he pushed away his plate and finished his ale, his gaze fell on his völva. He heaved a sigh and rose from his bench, knowing he had to question his prisoner one more time.

As he turned to leave, Lunt and Lang entered the hall. Lunt was walking with a noticeable limp, and Lang had his arm in a sling once more. Both were flushed and breathing hard. With their big two-handed swords strapped to their backs, Hakon knew they had been testing their tender muscles in the exercise yard. They could not refute their lack of readiness for battle.

Lunt greeted Hakon, saying, "Evening, my Jarl. Did you leave us anything to eat?"

"Já, but from the looks of you two, it won't be of much help."

"We started training to get back in shape," Lang put in.

"I never thought it would be so hard," Lunt added.

"Did Runa approve this?" Hakon questioned them.

The pair looked guilty as they exchanged a glance. Then, finally, Lunt said, "No, but we couldn't just sit around and do nothing. With all this talk about the Destroyer coming to challenge your rule, we wanted to be ready in case you needed us."

"And you thought pushing yourselves before Runa confirmed you'd healed enough to train again would do that?"

Lunt and Lang looked like scolded puppies, and the latter said, "We failed you once before, and we didn't want to do it again. But with your Gael prisoner spreading lies about us, we had to prove ourselves somehow."

"Ah, so that's it," Hakon said, smiling. That they would be concerned about their perceived integrity made him doubt his prisoner's story. The Dreadlord turned to his völva, chiding her, saying, "Runa, your efforts to heal my Dreadriders are proceeding too slowly."

All heads turned toward the one-eyed hag. Runa ignored the stares as she pushed away her plate and rose with a groan. She muttered, "I'm getting too old for this nonsense." Then she straightened and made her way toward her Jarl. The others in the hall returned to their discussions when they saw the völva had no retort. Runa said quietly to her Jarl, "I've been working my magic to track your Destroyer. Just yesterday, Tethra turned my Blood Runes with claims that he nearly lost another demon to the Tuatha magic wielded by your spawn's hand. One thing is clear—our Fomorian god is not happy."

"Then he should work harder to see that the Destroyer claims no more of his demons," Hakon countered icily. "If that means involving himself, then so be it. As for you, make a draught that will heal my Dreadriders. Their skills are growing stale from disuse, and I've been without their aid for far too long. I want them healed."

"That will take considerable effort," Runa complained.

"Are you not up to the challenge?" Hakon questioned, his tone cutting. "If so, maybe I should have Brede bring back one of your sisters when he travels to Alfheim in the spring."

That brought Runa's good eye up to focus on her Jarl. They stared at one another for a long moment, Hakon's cold gaze not wavering. Then she nodded. "Very well, I'll make your healing draught, but ask nothing more of me for a fortnight. Then, Lunt, come to my hut after you've eaten. Lang, you wait until your brother returns. And both of you, only one ale each. I'll not have you spoiling my magic with drunkenness."

With that said, the völva picked up a lamp and hobbled into the night.

Hakon smiled and turned to his favored Dreadriders. "Do as she says. And don't make me regret pushing this point with her. If I need her magic and she's unable to respond, I may need your muscles to take her place."

"Já," Lunt said somberly. "As always, we are yours to command."

"And thank you, my Jarl," Lang finished as Hakon turned and stalked out the door.

Hakon caught a glimpse of Runa before she disappeared into the fog. He was pleased she had not put up too much of an argument over his request to heal Lunt and Lang, but those thoughts faded as he approached the guards at his tower's door. He asked, "Is all well with our prisoner?"

"He is resting, my Jarl," one of the guards said to him. "The other half-breed just returned to his room as well."

"Good," Hakon commented as he gazed around. Something didn't feel right—something about the fog, about the night—but he couldn't see anything out of place. The guards at the gates seemed attentive, and he had set his dogs to roam the grounds. Indeed, no one could slip into the dun with those measures in place. Someone who had already tried to help his Destroyer had failed once, and now that they were alerted to their presence, they would be more likely to catch him.

Still, he didn't like such a heavy mist in the air—it could hide his Destroyer. So he commanded gravely, "Even though Hati and Skoll are loose, keep your eyes open tonight. Runa says this warrior is one of whom we must be wary."

"Always, my Jarl," the second guard replied confidently.

Hakon nodded and entered his tower. He quickly shed his cloak, for it had become damp in the short time he had been outside. The lower level of his building had four rooms, one to either side of the stone staircase and the receiving hall in which he now stood. Overhead, massive timbers ran from one side to the other to support the second floor, and he had had a hearth built into the wall on the left. For security purposes and partly to keep out the wind, Hakon had only allowed small windows in his tower, each of which had shutters if needed.

One of the rooms housed his manservant and family. The other room was usually the Dreadlord's armory, but he'd moved the weapons to make it an acceptable cell for his Gaelic prisoner. Swords, knives, staffs, bows, and shields lay across the table or had been stacked along the wall. While each of his warriors was well armed, the Dreadlord believed in having a weapons stockpile for those who didn't usually join in the battle.

Hakon moved toward his armory and nodded an excellent evening to his manservant. "Sveinn, you and Idhunn get some supper. It's been a long day, and you two have worked hard cleaning out the armory."

Sveinn took a hesitant breath. "Are you sure, my Jarl?"

"Yes, our Gael friend isn't going anywhere," Hakon replied. "There are two warriors on guard outside. They can handle any trouble. Go eat something."

"As you command, my Jarl," the old gray-haired man said and went to get his mate from their room. The two were on their way to the main hall a moment later. His spouse nodded her thanks to Hakon as she passed.

Hakon watched them go, then snatched up the cloak they had found on the ramparts from the table and opened the door to his prisoner's cell. The stone room was bare save for a pile of rushes in the corner. Eoin had been asleep but sat up as the Dreadlord entered. The Red Branch Chief asked the Dreadlord of Garm sarcastically, "More questions about your son?"

"Maybe," Hakon said neutrally. "We found this on the dun's pickets. Recognize it?"

"Looks like a cloak," Eoin replied, his tone matching Hakon's.

"My men don't wear otterskin, so that makes it a Gael's cloak," Hakon informed him darkly. "And you still maintain that there's no white-haired boy in Dun Arrogh, maybe one who has come to try to rescue your miserable hide?"

Eoin smirked, saying, "It seems like you're baiting me. As I have told you, no white-haired boy is at my dun. If there was, given that your blood would be in his veins, I doubt his clan would have let him stay long enough to become a warrior."

Hakon mulled that thought momentarily. If his son felt like an outcast, he could turn that to his advantage. Maybe even enough to turn him away from the mission laid before him by the Gaelic gods. Finally, he stated, "So he would not be trusted by his clan. That could be unfortunate, for I might not trust him either. That would make him a good warrior without a home."

"A good warrior can be an asset," Eoin interjected. "Aye, they must be loyal and true, but acts and deeds over a lifetime prove their worth and a heart."

"So you think he's a good warrior?" Hakon asked.

"I wouldn't know, but you seem to think he is," was the Gael's wry answer.

A faint smile broke over the corners of Hakon's mouth, and he said, "So you maintain that I have no son in your dun?"

"Have I given you any reason to think otherwise?" Eoin rejoined.

"No, but maybe you've provided some insight into the position my son might find himself in. Being an outcast could open doors that I may pursue."

"Aye," Eoin confirmed warily. "It would seem tricky to win over one you sired, one you haven't bothered to find out about until now. Your steward allowed me to meet the lad next door, who looks like you. Braoin is his name, I believe. Is he the one you desire to convert?"

Hakon eyed Eoin narrowly. "You play a good game, Gael."

Eoin said thoughtfully, "I play no game, outlander, but I do take the interests of my land seriously as a Prince of the Blood, of Ulaidan blood. Blood of which my High Queen shares."

Hakon stood motionless, understanding the threat this Prince of the Blood had just thrown down. Kill him, and retribution would await one who issued such an order.

Since the Gael would not expand on his previous comment, it soon became apparent that Hakon had not earned enough trust from his prisoner to elicit more information. He knew Eoin was holding something back, but getting it out of him would now be impossible.

So, finally, he said, "Despite all of this conjecture on my part, you still maintain that no one could be my son at Dun Arrogh?"

Eoin countered, "If a boy with your Norvegr blood was in my dun, I think I'd know it. I am Dun Arrogh's acting Chief, after all."

"Já, that you are," Hakon agreed suspiciously. "And the cloak?"

"Clearly a Gael's," Eoin stated. "It may even belong to someone from Dun Arrogh."

"But not to a white-haired boy," Hakon finished for him; Eoin nodded, the same smile dancing at the corners of his mouth. Then, cursing, Hakon threw the cloak on the floor and stomped away, slamming the stout oak door behind him. He drove home the locking bolt before turning for his chambers on the upper level.

Something was being left unsaid; his prisoner's words were not a lie, but not the whole truth. He would ask Runa to talk with the Gael Prince again without using her magic. She had a way of seeing things not apparent to others. Perhaps his völva would even be able to devise a means to turn his son to his side.

Breanna

Panic gripped Breanna as the white-haired hag approached. She wanted to bolt, but fought the urge. There was no option except to face her. If it came to a battle and Hakon's völva tried to use her strange Norvegr magic, Breanna knew *Maorgairme* would come to her aid. And then there was always a chance her ruse would work.

The old woman said quickly, "The Dreadlord got you on patrol with his dogs, eh? That cloak they found on the pickets has him a little edgy. He thinks the Destroyer has come, as I foretold, and he's right. So keep an eye open."

"Aye," Breanna said, moving aside to the left to keep the Blades of Destiny and her magical Tuatha ring hidden at her side.

Runa stepped past her and then suddenly turned back to ask, "Have I met you?"

Keeping her left side in the dark, Breanna stammered, "No—no, I'm from the south. I recently came to Dun Garm to see my father. I drew guard duty to earn my keep."

Runa nodded cautiously, noting her accent was certainly not Norvegr. Most who had come with Hakon dropped the language of their homeland in favor of Gaelic to better blend in with the locals, but they still retained something of the Alfheim tongue. It seemed strange that this girl spoke as if she had never lived among Norvegr clan members.

Then again, few who had joined Hakon when they came to Erin had not settled in Dun Garm, and the girl said she had come from one of those steads. Thinking it was all very peculiar as she was about to turn away, Runa saw a slight glimmer coming from the dark side of the young woman's body and lunged for the arm closest to her, pulling the stranger off balance. The crystal ring on her finger glowed, and the same color flashed from beneath the sack that still covered *Lann Dàn*. With her useless right eye rolling in her head, Runa held up her lamp, demanding, "What's this? Tuatha magic? And those weapons under the sack, they're Tuatha, too!"

"Aye, they are," was her cold answer with a level look.

Seeing her red-flecked blue eyes, Runa hissed, "The Destroyer! So you're Hakon's bastard. A woman?"

"My mother also called me a Destroyer, but I believe *dìolain* is the Gaelic word that best describes a bastard!" the Destroyer said icily. Then she commanded, "*Maorgairme*, silence her."

Nothing happened.

Runa opened her mouth to call out a warning.

Before the völva could cry out, Breanna slammed her right fist into the older woman's stomach and followed it with a second blow to the side of her head, using the extra weight added by *Lann Dán* in her left hand to drive home the impact. As Runa crumpled to the ground unconscious, the two wolfhounds whimpered.

Knowing she didn't have much time, Breanna commanded the dogs to follow her as she made for the stone tower, muttering a curse about Badb's fickle ring. Yet, she knew what her gods said about *Maorgairme* – that the ring expected her to fight and battle. Though she had hoped to wait until the span had drawn closer to midnight, when most would be asleep, it was time to free her Chief from the Dreadlord's hands. At least the fog was still with her, which might be enough to prevent an alarm from being raised.

She crept around the back of her father's tower, hoping to find a way in without going through the front door, but discovered the windows on the first level were too high and narrow to fit through. With no back door, that left her only one option, and that was to eliminate the guards she had passed earlier.

Breanna readied her weapons, feeling a surge of energy rushing through her. *Lann Dàn* came to life in her hands, and she felt her battle sense take over. The wolfhounds continued to follow their new friend, though Breanna wasn't sure what they would do once she engaged the warriors.

Breanna seized the *void* and could already picture the two warriors' movements when she emerged from the foggy darkness. She was nearly on top of them before they noticed her. One startled warrior let his hand reach for his hilt while the other demanded, "Do we know you?"

"No," Breanna said as she whirled without hesitation, letting each *Lann Dán* lash out to catch the first and then the other in the throat. Their near cries of alarm died in gurgles of blood as the shining diamond blades wrought by the Dark Goddess sliced through their flesh. They slumped to the ground, their life draining out of them faster than Breanna thought possible. Aside from demons, these were her first kills. It was not unlike wounding the Dreadriders, save that these two couldn't raise their blades to threaten her again.

Her *geas* left her with no room for remorse. Her purpose was to destroy her father, and they had stood in her way. She could kill anyone who challenged that goal. For a moment, the thought made her shudder. Who was she to be so cold? Yet, when it came to her father, she was his Destroyer! Erin's Hero, if that was who she was born to be, there was no room for any Norvegrs who would claim her land!

With a nod of satisfaction that she had finally claimed her first warrior's life in battle, Breanna left the two wolfhounds sniffing the dead men and quickly slipped inside her father's tower. She saw a wide range of weapons scattered across the main table and noticed the stairway and three doors, one open and two closed. Breanna went for the last one on the left, near the stairs, because someone had locked it, and the other room was left unlocked.

When Breanna had quietly eased the bolt back and cracked open the iron-bound door, she couldn't help but grin as she caught sight of Eoin's startled expression. She hadn't been sure what she would do when this moment came, for he surely knew that she was the Dreadlord's daughter. Would he think her tainted and unfit to be his Champion? Would he no longer love her as she knew he did? But Breanna read nothing of that when their eyes locked for a brief, searching moment.

Before the urge to rush into his arms swept over her, Eoin started to ask, "Bre, how in the—"

She cut him off, whispering, "Hush, there's no time for questions. I brought your sword. We must get out of here, now."

As Eoin took his blade, he handed her a cloak. "A fair trade, I think. And I see you have a new set of long blades. So your quest for that fairie magic was successful."

Breanna took the ripped Otterskin garment in her hand, but she was more thankful that he had interrupted the outburst that had been building in her. With her iron will quickly back in control, she responded, "Aye, the quest was successful, and finding them was a minor challenge. However, what the blades drew to me on the first night after their discovery is a story for another time. If the Sun God hadn't come to our rescue, I can assure you that Toal and I would have lost the battle with Fomorian demons. Once we survived the night and the sun rose, Lugh commanded that I visit the Dark Goddess to learn how *Lann Dàn* can save us from the Dreadlord."

"But you had to stop off on the way," Eoin stated, smiling. "Before we go, I must introduce you to someone in the next room."

Breanna nodded as her Chief walked out of the room and turned left. Breanna followed him as he rapped quietly on the door. "Braoin, I have someone I know you'll want to meet."

Unlike Eoin's door, the unlocked one led to where the lad named Braoin was staying, and it cracked open in answer to the knock. A white-haired lad looked out, asking, "Eoin?"

He answered, "Aye, my Champion, Breanna Ban Morna, is here to rescue us. As I think you recall, she is someone you fought during the last *comórtas*. She is your half-sister. Breanna, meet Braoin."

The lad turned his gaze to Breanna. "Aye, well met, sister-mine."

Breanna inhaled sharply, saying to Eoin, "So you also know Hakon is my father?"

"Aye, Bre, I figured that out over the past few days," Eoin answered. "You could have told me, but I understand why you did not. But fear not, for you are my Champion and always will be, as I know our gods have chosen you."

Breanna choked back an exclamation. Yet before she could deny Eoin's accusation, Braoin asked, "The Tuatha gods have chosen her?"

"Aye, they have, lad," Eoin answered. "Look at the blades in her harness. They are the magical long blades known as *Lann Dàn*, the Blades of Destiny. Not just the iron blades that won her a gold armring at the contest, as I'm sure you remember from your duel."

"Braoin, good to meet you again," Breanna said, lifting her arm and offering a warrior-to-warrior arm clasp. "Brother-mine."

Braoin took her offer, grasping her forearm with his, answering, "Sister-mine. I had never believed it could be true. When we fought, you were brilliant, as if you were in my mind. Even though we both had two blades, your two were always faster. Then I watched you win gold, thinking we looked so much alike. You fought gracefully, like water flowing in a stream, and I only wished I could be as good."

Breanna smiled. "You will be that good if you join us in our quest to remove our father from our land. I shared a vision with Danu, who charged me with this quest. It is risky, to be sure. We could all die. Yet, only being brave will save us. So will you join me, Brother-mine?"

"Aye, Sister-mine!"

Eoin said, "Good! We're both now bonded to Breanna's cause. But, first, we need to escape from this fort."

With weapons drawn, they made for the main door of the Dreadlord's tower and into the foggy night. The wolfhounds still sat by the dead guards and wagged their tails when they saw Breanna again.

"Friends of yours?" Eoin asked.

"Sort of," she absently responded as she let her battle sense take over as it had before. "Now come, we must find a way out of this place before they discover you're not in your cell, and I've been roaming about, killing their guards."

Eoin said with a note of approval, "Good to see you've stopped sparing your opponents. Too bad you'll have to leave your first trophies behind."

Breanna shrugged, saying, "One day, but not this one. We must make haste." With that, she motioned for Eoin to follow, as there was no time to think about what she had done. Watching Eoin limp from his cell to the tower door made her more concerned that they would not escape quickly enough, as they could not run far. At least Braoin could support him.

A moment later, a warrior sauntered into the light cast by the torches on either side of Hakon's door, dashing her hopes. He jerked to a halt, seeing Eoin released and the slain guards. When he saw Breanna, he snarled, "You're the bitch who cut me up!"

Breanna recognized the Dreadrider, as did Eoin and Braoin. She reached out to seize the *void* and foresaw that Lunt would draw his sword and lunge. He quickly did what she expected and was faster than she expected, as if he were hoping to run her clean through. Yet her reflexes were better, with the *void* giving her a moment to react before his actions. Breanna flicked Lann Dàn over her shoulders and into her hands, then spun to her right, letting one of her luminous blades rake in to catch him along his ribs as he circled to keep his blade before him.

She heard Lunt hiss and knew she had scored a hit. He stumbled over the dead guards, bringing him within Eoin's range.

Eoin had already drawn his sword, and his arm moved in a downward slice. The Dreadrider turned just in time to lock blades with him. They momentarily struggled before Lunt pushed Eoin away and got his feet beneath him. He cried, "Guards! Sound the alarm! Invaders in the dun! We are under at—"

Breanna drove each of her glowing blades into Lunt's back, his words dying in a groan as the diamond tips emerged from his gut. She jerked *Lann Dàn* free, widening the slit in his bowels, and her enemy dropped to his knees, his blade falling to the ground. Instinctively, her opponent pressed his hands to his stomach to try to stop the crimson stain from spreading, and then, he looked over his shoulder into Breanna's eyes. All she let him see was her ice-cold hand of death as she circled to face him and spat, "Time to meet your gods!"

Lunt gasped, "Then say you are my Valkyrie, come to take me to Valhalla!"

"No, just a Gael warrior, come to take your head as a trophy," Breanna grated out as she let one of her blades lash across his neck. Lunt raised a hand from his stomach to his throat, but the blood gushing through his fingers was not stopping. He crumpled to the ground a moment later, the flickering torchlight dancing in his open eyes. Breanna thought he was still alive for a moment, staring at her. Could nothing kill a Dreadrider? Then she looked again and saw that he was dead—his *anam* had departed for their otherworld—for Valhalla, as the Norvegr believed. Or not, as she was not a Valkyrie!

His eyes no longer held any life, but Eoin bent to check the body lying in the mud anyway. Then, finally, the sound of guards crashing through the night brought Breanna back to the danger. She said, "The fog will help hide us, but if we get separated, we'll meet at the eastern pickets behind this tower."

"Sister-mine, that was impressive," Braoin said, a bit unnerved.

"A trophy like his is hard to leave behind," Eoin said as he turned away from Lunt and faced his Champion. "Carrying a

Dreadrider's head through Dun Arrogh would help rally our people, help rally our Red Branch."

"No," Breanna commanded. "There's no time. We must get out of here, now."

Eoin hesitated but then nodded as he and Braoin slipped into the fog. Breanna glanced back at Lunt and his head, wishing she had the time to take it. She knew her Chief was right about its potential to rally the clans from the various hillforts to stand against the Dreadlord.

Someone charged through the door and into her before Breanna could decide whether to take her trophy. A blade flashed by her head as they went down in a tangled heap. Mud sprayed as they hit the ground, and as they struggled, it covered their clothes. Breanna came up on top of the man, and for a brief moment, they just stared at one another. She recognized him at once, even though they had never met.

Hakon Skadi, her mother's rapist, her father's killer, the one her gods tasked her to kill. How could she not have known him? They were father and daughter, their faces mirrored by each other. Red-flecked blue eyes stared at red-flecked blue eyes.

Hakon exclaimed in confusion, "You're my bastard? The Destroyer Runa foretold would come?"

"That's not a nice name for your daughter," Breanna said darkly, "I prefer *dìolain!*"

Knowing she must not hesitate, she drove one of her blades toward her father's head.

Toal

Toal and Fergal sat crouched beneath the earthen and stone ramparts of Dun Garm, wondering what to do next. They had chosen the northern portion of the fort, so if the Norvegrs discovered them, Toal could still dash for their chariot.

Fergal had insisted, "My lousy leg would hold us both back. I will keep them busy to give you time to escape into the night."

If the worst happened, Toal must get word back to Dun Arrogh about losing its three best warriors. Though he had protested at first, Toal could find no fault in Fergal's logic. There was no use sacrificing both of them to the Dreadlord's blades, and Toal certainly wasn't skilled enough to face a Dreadrider.

Darkness had long since settled over the western edge of Mide, yet there was no word of Breanna, no cries of alarm. The pair was sure that some ruckus would start soon. It had to, for Breanna could only take so long to find and free Eoin or get killed herself. They could see thick fog settling in over the Dreadlord's dun from the guttering torches near the gates, which they each understood would bode well for Breanna.

As the night wore on, Toal and Fergal chewed on some more rations by the dun's ramparts, then dozed off in the long, quiet stretch. Toal had no idea what time it was when the first shouts of alarm came. It was clear from the guards atop the wall that they thought a full-scale attack was occurring.

Fergal turned to Toal. "Can you launch some fire arrows inside the dun?"

"I don't think they'll burn anything with this mist hanging about," the younger warrior advised the other.

"You just get ready while I start a fire," Fergal commanded, digging through his pack for dry tinder. Toal handed him his flint and striker and then turned to start wrapping arrows in strips of cloth he'd brought for just such an occasion.

Toal had taken an interest in the seldom-seen weapon a few years before when watching a traveler from Alba put on a show. The display of talent had made him want a bow of his own, and while it had taken several attempts to craft a good one, Toal had persisted.

After developing a reasonable skill by using local wild creatures as targets, he was now hunting men, and while his small ash bow was not made for distance, being so close to his target eliminated any concerns about range. Once he had several arrows wrapped, he pulled out a small pouch of tallow.

Fergal signaled he was ready, and Toal set an arrow to his string. After placing the wrapped head over the flame and letting the cloth catch fire, he turned and let it sail over the wall. While Fergal shielded the fire from the view of any guards atop their ramparts, Toal let three more arrows follow as he tried to refine his aim. Unfortunately, picking out a target in the dark and the fog was impossible. All he could hope for was to hit one roof or another amid the screams from the guards.

He heard his next shot hit stone and knew from his earlier view of Dun Garm that he had probably hit Hakon's tower. Adjusting his aim higher for a shorter flight and slightly to the east, he went for the roof of the large central hall.

After emptying his quiver, he turned to Fergal and said, "Now what?"

"We wait and see if your efforts bear some fruit," came Fergal's answer as he kicked out his fire. Then, it was only a moment later when someone screamed that there was a fire in the main hall, and chaos suddenly reigned over Dun Garm.

Toal smiled wickedly and snickered, "I did it!"

Fergal turned to the lad. "Aye, you did. Breanna now has the diversion she needs to get Eoin out of Dun Garm."

Eoin surged into the night with Braoin at his side. The lad had sheathed one of his swords so he could help Eoin limp along, letting the darkness and fog envelop them. While his wound still hampered his stride, his leg was not bothering him as much as he had thought it would. The previous few days of immobility had aided his healing and would help with their escape. Yet, he could hardly believe Breanna had managed to get into the fort even now. And now they had Braoin's aid.

Maybe the Tuatha gods had somehow helped, or perhaps it was her uncanny warrior skills. He didn't care; a little farther on, they could slip over Dun Garm's walls and into the safety of the night. As Eoin rounded the Dreadlord's tower and made for the eastern ramparts, he turned to look for Breanna. Swirling blackness filled his vision. There was a dim flicker of torchlight somewhere off to his right, but nothing more; his Champion was not at his side.

"Bre," he whispered urgently, but the only responses were shouts of alarm from the guards on the ramparts and muffled sounds of fighting. The warriors' voices seemed more frantic than before, as if they were under attack. But from whom? Had Breanna brought Fergal and a few of the Red Branch to help in the rescue? No, his Champion would not have asked for help.

"Will she be all right?" Braoin asked.

"Aye, lad, she is tough, can seize the *void* like no other, and is touched by the gods!"

Eoin led her half-brother on, thinking Fergal might have pursued his Champion on her mission, as he knew his cousin would not let Breanna outshine him. Then, something clattered against the stone over his head, startling him from his wandering thoughts and back to escaping the dun in one piece.

Breanna had said to meet on the dun's eastern ramparts behind Hakon's tower, but she'd never make it there if she were in trouble. Momentarily frozen with indecision, Eoin forced himself to leave the structure behind. Breanna was right; surely they couldn't hope to find each other by wandering in the misty darkness.

Eoin limped from Hakon's stone tower and scrambled up the rampart's rough wall with Braoin's help. Torchlights flickered at him through the fog as he reached the top, making him wonder how much time he had before the Dreadlord's sentries passed his way. Eoin would have the advantage in such a narrow space, but hoped it wouldn't come to that. All he could do was look back into the night and hope his Champion would soon follow.

Hakon

Hakon Skadi barely noted the strange glowing blade flashing toward his head, the face of his white-haired daughter filling his vision. His daughter! He tried to scream, but nothing came from his mouth. It was as if time had stopped, freezing his movements. Maybe this was what happened before death. Or perhaps it was some magic wielded by his offspring. How could she be his daughter?

One thing was clear—the Destroyer foreseen by his völva had indeed sought him out. Yet, his daughter had come in the visage of one of Odin's Valkyries, ready to send him to Valhalla.

Then the world lurched into motion, and Hakon threw himself to one side. He felt the edge of the strange, clear knife nick the skin on his neck. He twisted beneath his daughter, using the slippery mud to throw her off-balance, and with his next effort, pushed her aside.

They both got their feet beneath them and started circling in crouched stances as the fort came alive with shouts of alarm, the Dreadlord's warriors lighting every torch they could find. The defenders of Dun Garm were scrambling up the ramparts, straining to see through the fog, but their guttering brands did not reach far enough into the darkness to show anything except shadows. Soon, the dogs were barking, and it sounded like they were under siege. Even Hakon's hand-raised wolfhounds had run off into the misty darkness, chasing unknown creatures of the night.

Hakon quickly put thoughts of attack out of his mind, for he knew it would take all of the warriors from Mide's Dun Uisneach to breach his walls. Instead, he turned to assess his daughter, noting that she was not as tall as he was and had a lighter build. That meant he had strength in his favor, though she would most likely have speed in hers.

Yet, if Runa was right, she was a formidable warrior, and he'd have to be careful. His daughter lunged at him, forcing him to dance to his right before he could give his völva's words another thought. He kicked something, almost tripping, glanced down to see Lunt's lifeless eyes staring at him, and a curse slipped from his lips. Maybe she was a Valkyrie.

His Destroyer drove in on him again; this time, he had to raise his blade to fend off her thrust. Then, trying to buy time, he said, "You, it was you who injured my Dreadriders in that battle. And now one of them lies dead at my feet."

"Yes, and now my blades will taste your blood!" she spat and feinted with her left before slashing in with her right. Hakon flung himself in the other direction, but her blade had come close enough to slice open his cloak. His momentum took him another step away, and he stumbled on a second body, one of his guards.

The wet ground made it hard to keep his balance, and Hakon only regained it in time to feel one of his daughter's blades lick his left bicep. An angry curse slipped from his mouth as a trickle of warm, wet liquid started to course down his forearm.

Hakon went on the offensive after he turned his back on the night and had some maneuvering room. He charged her, driving the point of his sword toward her heart, but she anticipated his actions. He tried again, but his daughter danced clear of his blade, letting him rush by.

Slowing his pace, he took well-measured strokes, testing her defenses, each time pushing her backward and into the darkness. He sensed she was letting him gain ground while assessing him. As he pursued her, the light from the torches began to fade in the fog, making it difficult to see clearly. Then, she suddenly drove in on him again. This time, he thought he was ready and blocked her thrust, countering with an overhanded sweep of his sword. It was a move she seemed to have expected, her weapons crossed and prepared to catch his.

His blade locked in the axis of hers, and for a brief moment, they stood there, face to face. Then, the test of strength took hold as Hakon started pushing his daughter backward. He sneered. "Your muscles do not match your skill."

"They don't have to," she retorted, sweeping his sword away and rolling clear of him. Hakon stood a few yards away, his stance prepared for her continued attack, but he made no move toward her. Instead, he stared at his daughter, surveying her momentarily. She was indeed a fierce and cunning warrior.

She fought with passion and some other sense, allowing her to anticipate her opponent's next move. It was no wonder she had beaten his best Dreadriders. It was a skill he often thought he also possessed. Such talents would make a grand Dreadrider. She was better than any of his warriors, maybe even better than himself. Despite his slightly labored breathing, he asked calmly, "Why do you want to kill me?"

"Because you are the scourge of my land, an outlander who would corrupt it."

"But you are a part of my people, a part of me," Hakon countered, his tone deliberately soft, his words drawn out to emphasize them. "That makes you a Norvegr as well."

"I had no say in that, and neither did my mother," she spat back, her lips curled like a dog ready to bite. "I'm nothing more than a *dìolain*, a bastard, your bastard, as you said!"

"Ah, I see!" Hakon exclaimed. "Anger rules your heart."

"You see nothing," she countered, her voice cracking. "Nothing except that which you can use to corrupt this land and take what is not yours. And I am not yours!"

"I still see your anger," Hakon continued to press. "Could it be that others have nurtured this anger for their gain? If it were not for this hate, you could be standing at my side here in Dun Garm, dressed in the finest furs and fed the finest food. Yet someone planted a seed of hate early in your life, which has now flowered. Only the flower is nothing more than a poisonous weed. A weed which will take over your soul."

She said darkly, "You may be right, but that doesn't change what I've become. It might be a poisoned glen, but the taint in the grass would be hard to draw out now."

"We could try to draw the poison out together," her father gently added as he circled her, hoping to quell her fears of the layers of hate in her built by the Druid's *geas*. "Knowing what drives you can help you understand why it drives you."

She had no response, and they just stared at each other. Hakon wondered if he saw any indecision in her eyes. Then, several warriors startled them as they emerged from the night, and one yelled, "My Jarl, there's a fire in the main hall!"

With that, she said, "We will meet again, and you will die!"

Hakon watched his daughter's lithe form slip into the darkness like a ghost, and he could not help admiring her. She was the ultimate warrior, with every muscle fiber committed to her skills. He wanted to pursue her and convince her she was wrong about him, but with the fog, he knew she would be over the ramparts of his dun before he could organize any pursuit.

Still, she would not get far, and he would quickly be on her trail in the morning.

Covered in mud and looking not one bit like the Jarl of Dun Garm, Hakon turned to his warriors and bellowed, "You're all jumping at shadows! Calm down and get the buckets out. Not much is going to burn after yesterday's rain and this mist. Tell those patrolling the walls we are not under attack and that they need to get down here and help with the fire."

"Já, my Jarl," one of the older warriors said, his tone reflecting his chagrin.

"And have you seen Lang?" Hakon asked.

"Já, he's in the rafters of the main hall, trying to put out the fire."

Hakon was pleased that at least his Dreadrider had the presence of mind to try to stop the blaze without panicking. But there was something more vital for him to tend to, and Hakon commanded, "Get yourselves up there and relieve him. I need Lang in my tower to tend to his brother. And make sure someone finds Runa!"

With that, he turned from his men and strode to Lunt's body. With a grunt, he hefted the Dreadrider into his arms and took him into his tower. Lunt's eyes were still open, staring blankly into space as Hakon set his body on the table. He passed a hand over his lids with a sigh to close them. Losing such a favored young warrior left a bitter taste in his mouth. While he had found a daughter whose skills as a warrior matched his own, maybe even exceeded them, she had taken from him one who had become like a son.

Ultimately, if she did not stand with him, he would have to see her dead.

Breanna

Breanna bolted into the misty darkness, heading toward the south between her father's tower and the main hall and then swinging to the east, hoping it would throw off any pursuit. Faint flickers of torchlight came through the fog, but nothing more. She sensed she had passed the völva's hut and was happy to leave it behind.

The meeting with her father had been disturbing. He seemed to want to play different strings to draw her to him, to play into her being a Norvegr and not a Gael. That was not a surprise, as his völva had advised him. Yet their Druids respected the Norvegr's powers enough to warn them to stay clear of Runa. Nonetheless, Hakon's words echoed in her mind; the seeds planted by her mother now flowered into something like a poisonous weed, corrupting her soul.

No! Breanna wanted to shout, but she wasn't sure of herself, of her motivations or emotions. Her father seemed to enjoy having her at his side. With him, she would not have to fight for acceptance; she looked more Norvegr than Gael. She would be his exalted one.

If it were not for the Tuatha gods, who had directed her to their magic, she wasn't sure if she could go through with her quest. Yet those same gods seemed to think Hakon would bring hordes of his white-haired outlanders to Erin, which meant the future of all Erin lay in her hands.

How could she reconcile this? Her land and people needed her as a Gael, not a Norvegr. Then, there was a whisper in her mind.

"My Hero, know you have been chosen by me, your Heart. Have faith in me, as I have faith in you. There is no love in your father's heart, only his drive for power and control.

"We have a bond forged by the Tuatha gods. They gave me the power to choose Erin's Hero. I have only done so five times before you, as no more were worthy until you."

Then Breanna remembered her time with Danu and the strange, heart-shaped ruby that proclaimed her *"Mine!"*

"Yes, that was my proclamation, my Hero. Fight for us! I will be with you soon!"

Then the ramparts loomed up before her sooner than she expected, startling her out of her communication with her Heart, and she adjusted her stride slightly to take on the wall at nearly a dead run. She wasn't sure how, but she scrambled up the rocky incline without slipping and sliding like the night before. At the top, she ran into Eoin's familiar arms; they must both have had the same idea about their escape path. She could barely make out her Chief's face in the faint torchlight.

Finally, Eoin asked, "Are you all right? What took you? And why are you covered in mud?"

"I had an encounter with the Jarl of this fine place," Breanna answered, her breathing ragged. "Unfortunately, he still is in command, so we must get out of here—now."

Braoin asked, "You fought with the Dreadlord?"

"Aye, my brother," Breanna answered. "Slippery son of a bitch, for sure. Almost had him."

Eoin hesitated, saying, "But he thinks you're—"

She put a finger on his lips to quell the question, so instead, he asked, "Did you bring anyone from Dun Arrogh with you?"

"No, I came alone," Breanna replied.

Eoin looked around, peering into the dark and fog as if it would reveal something he had not seen before, and said, "Then I think someone followed you, for it sounded as if the dun's warriors were under attack and someone caused a fire."

"Fergal!" Breanna growled. "If he brought any of those children we call the Red Branch with him, I'll pound him into the ground! I commanded that he look after them, not drag them to Dun Garm to face a slaughter."

Eoin said urgently, "Let's go find out. We need to know if there are others to protect."

With that, the two men used their swords and muscles to cleave a narrow path through the pickets lining the rampart, and the trio quickly made their way down the far side.

While they had escaped from Dun Garm, Breanna still faced the question of what to do next in her quest to kill the Dreadlord, to kill her father. Given *Lann Dàn* had failed to aid her, visiting the Dark Goddess as Danu had commanded appeared to be the only recourse. It was a thought that made her shiver. Badb Catha, the Mórrigan, ruled over war, death, and all things dark and unseen.

Yet she had no choice—the Goddess of War and Knowledge was critical to her success!

Her Heart said, *"My Hero, you are mine and not alone!"*

Epilogue

Lang climbed from the rafters of the main hall with a bucket and two arrows clenched in his hand. Covered in soot and with the wound in his arm by Hakon's bastard now throbbing once more, Lang had still managed to save nearly all the thatch, and the fire was out. He looked up to assure himself that they had found every flaming arrow. They could have lost the entire hall had it not just rained.

He gave the Gael arrows he had retrieved to a warrior waiting below, commanding, "Make sure the dogs pick up the scent from these. That should ensure we catch those who did this in the morning."

"Já," the man said and stuffed them into his belt.

Another warrior charged into the hall, crying, "Lang, the Dreadlord wants you!"

"Why?" Lang countered as the hair on the back of his neck stood on end.

"It's about your brother," came the reply. "He's been—"

But Lang was already out the door and charging toward Hakon's tower; he didn't hear anything else they said. He didn't need to because he knew Lunt was dead, knew that the Dreadlord's bastard had sent him to Valhalla. Now that he tried to reach for his brother's presence, that part of himself that always knew what Lunt was thinking, the link was gone. His brother, his twin, was not there to be felt. He wasn't sure how he knew, only that he did. Splashing across the muddy yard, he spat, "By Thor's hammer, I'll kill that Valkyrie to finish this battle!"

Lunt's body lay atop the table in Hakon's tower when Lang stormed through the door. Hakon said, "Lang, I've—"

"I know, my brother is dead," Lang interrupted him gruffly as he strode to Lunt's side and jerked to a halt. With a face he knew had to be distorted with pain and rage, Lang could have sworn his twin was sleeping had he not known otherwise. But the red stain on his stomach and the slash across his throat made his death irrefutable. Lang let his grief enfold him, wrapping his arms around the limp form. He clung to Lunt's body for a long moment. How was he going to live without him? They had always protected each other's backs, and now he was alone.

 **Hakon**

"She did it, didn't she? Your bastard killed him."

"Já," Hakon said sadly, not knowing what else to say.

"Then, as Odin is my witness, I shall send her to Valhalla after him!"

Hakon could only groan, for this affair had not ended as he had hoped. And now was certainly not the time to tell Lang that he could not kill his daughter, nor could he say that he wanted his daughter to fight at their side. How he would convince both of them to do what he wanted was not a question Hakon could answer just then—something for the morning to deal with.

Tired, sore, and nicked up, he turned away to give Lang time for his grief.

 **Danu**

The Mother Goddess of Erin sat beside the white pillar on which the Stone of Destiny rested. She shuddered to think what could have gone wrong with their plans had the Dreadlord prevailed in his brief battle with *Croí Dàn's* chosen hero. Then, with the images of Lia Dàn slowly fading away, she sat back and reached out with her mind to Dagda, Lugh, and Badb Catha, calling out, "Please attend me."

Badb Catha was the first to appear in Danu's Hall of Visions, dressed in a long black flowing gown that trailed on the floor behind her, sensual and sultry as always. Giving Danu a slight bow, she said, "Sister-mine, since you called me here suddenly to this room, the matter must be related to a vision from *Lia Dàn*."

"Not a vision, a battle in the Gael's realm," Danu replied. They were such opposites. She was light compared to Badb's darkness; she embodied compassion, whereas her sister required revenge. She used reason to counter her sister's wrath. "Let's wait on Dagda and Lugh."

Dagda was next to arrive, his massive frame imposing as always, as was his smile. He was generally a cheerful god, yet he could decide who lived or died with the enormous magical mace and his healing cauldron. The latter, *Lorg Mór,* sat casually on his shoulder. Lowering his club to the floor, he asked, "My ladies, I assume you have some updates on Erin's Hero?"

Before she could answer, the Sun God flashed into the room, dressed in a white tunic and kilt that Danu often favored. He said, "No need to wait. I am here, at your service, as always."

Danu nodded thanks for their quick response, saying, "We have a problem. *Cróí Dàn's* Hero has stirred the hornet's nest."

Lugh sighed. "Breanna Ban Morna went to Dun Garm. It could be nothing else. Damn that girl. She was to seek Badb Catha straight away, as you commanded her! How bad is it?"

"Aye, she did not listen and went to Dun Garm as you suspected she would," the Mother Goddess replied. "She foolishly aimed to rescue her Chief from the Dreadlord's clutches. While she accomplished her goal, the Dreadlord will be furious that she killed two guards and one of his favored Dreadriders, and now they and their völva have also discovered Breanna has Tuatha magic to wield against them."

Dagda held up one of his massive hands for silence. "She faced him with magical weapons, assuming they would help her?"

"Yes, she did battle with *Lann Dàn*, thinking they would help against mortals," Badb Catha injected. "What a fool—I know Beatha told her the lore behind the Blades of Destiny, that their magic supports warriors when battling magic—but that is water under the bridge. So, what do we do now?"

Dagda said, "Hmm, we have a lass. I need to train her."

"Not yet," Danu countered. "Lugh, you have the military mind."

"Well," said Lugh, "Hakon will have to wait until tomorrow evening to burn the dead Dreadrider's body and send him on to their gods in Valhalla, but then he will have nearly all of his Dreadriders and the rest of his best warriors on the trail of *Cróí Dàn's* Hero and her fellow Gaels. Without horses, they will likely have, at best, three days before Hakon finds them."

"Our Heart needs to be sent to her soon," Danu suggested. "We must watch for a moment when they can best meld in action when Breanna requires courage and bravery. That will make their bond stronger."

Badb Catha sighed and reached for the ring on Breanna's finger with her mind. As its creator, they were linked, and she passed her imperative to the distant piece of fickle magic. When she finished, she nodded, saying, "*Maorgairme* will watch for such a moment and reach out to *Croí Dàn* to let her know it's time."

"Thank you, sister-mine," Danu said with a relieved smile.

Badb shrugged as if it were nothing. "There is another problem. The Dreadlord's völva, that *baobh* called Runa, actively uses her magic to support him. She helped Hakon summon the Formorian god, Tethra, and she will also lead the Dreadlord to Erin's Hero. We need to create diversions to lead them astray."

"Like what?" Lugh questioned.

Badb Catha let a wicked smile slip. "I'll use my precious crows, the ones she sacrifices when she uses her *Asgardian* magic to cast her Blood Runes to seek the *sight*. Use them to misdirect the *baobh*."

Then she closed her eyes and commanded her legion of crows across the land to report any contact with the völva named Runa; as she opened them, she said, "My crows will watch for her."

Danu offered, "One good piece of news is that Erin's Hero has met one of her half-brothers, who also has a *geas* upon him, one of justice instead of destruction, and he has joined her cause. He will help balance her fire."

Dagda added, "That is good. If they can make it to Dun Uisneach, she has another half-brother who could aid her, one protected by that dun's Chieftain and Chieftess."

Then Danu stiffened, momentarily sensing the Heart of Destiny before she came to life.

Ċroí Dàn pulsed like a beating heart against the Mother Goddess's chest, demanding, *"Since I have claimed her as mine, you must send me to Breanna Ban Morna! Now!"*

Danu groused to her fellow gods, "By the sun and the moon, these sentient magical constructs need a lesson in manners!"

Badb Catha privately told her niece, *"Soon, my little Heart, you will claim your Hero. And she will claim you."*

Here ends *Lann Dàn* – Blades of Destiny
Dàn Cycle One

This epic tale of the Gaels continues in:
Lia Dàn – Stone of Destiny
Dàn Cycle Two
And

Ċroí Dàn – Heart of Destiny
Dàn Cycle Three

**For those interested in a sneak peek of
Stone of Destiny, turn the page!**

Acknowledgments

I want to thank Marty, Chris, Cindy, and Kimberly for their contributions to developing the original storyline many years ago, as well as all of my early readers who provided valuable input on what was a rough draft at the time. Marty, Chris, and Cindy are still with me, giving feedback on any new Editions of Dàn Cycle One, Two, and Three. Dàn Cycle Four and Five are underway.

While the First Edition *of Dàn Cycle One and Two* improved over the original work, I required additional editorial input for this Revised Edition. I am delighted to thank Holly Atkinson, who owns/runs Evil Eye Editing (www.evileyeediting.com). For authors who do not believe they need a content editor, think again! Holly and her team have been fantastic!

A big thank you goes to Nadiia Kolpak, a talented illustrative artist from Ukraine, for producing my book covers and the website artwork; she also created the print and eBook layouts. I found Nadiia on Upwork.

As the Tuatha Gods spread my musical talents to other, more worthy humans, I want to recognize Claire Odlum and

Emy Smith for evolving our jointly created lyrics and composi-
tions of the songs in the Dàn Cycle Novels and on the website
(www.destinycycle.com, via YouTube links). I found Claire and
Emy on the Airgigs website. I even gave them the honorary title
of *Dàn Cycle* Bards!

GUIDE TO THE GAELIC LANGUAGE

While this novel is set in fifth-century Ireland, I primarily use modern Gaelic for certain words rather than earlier or older forms of Irish. Yet, even with this, there are Irish and Scottish Gaelic variations to consider. Because certain vowels and consonants in Gaelic have no equivalent in English, it can be a complex language to read. A Gaelic-English dictionary or an online source helps translate between the two languages.

Below is a summary of some differences, which can assist with the pronunciation of these words. I have included phonations in parentheses to aid in sounding out names on the Central Characters & Places and Glossary pages. For those less inclined to make such an effort, sound out the word as you like. How it sounds to you will not insult the Tuatha Gods! I can't say the same for native Gaelic speakers, though.

Vowels & Vowel Combinations: Individual Gaelic vowel sounds are as follows: *a* is typically pronounced *ah*, as in father; *á* or *à* takes on a longer sound, as in Dàn taking on the sound dawn (note: the author chose Scottish Gaelic spelling of Destiny over the Irish Gaelic spelling, as cinniúint is too lengthy); *ae* takes on the sound *i*, as in high; when words end in *e*, it is always sounded out, as in fairie; *i* rarely takes on the sound *eye* and instead is usually an *ee* or *ih* sound, as in feel.

Some vowel combinations take on different sounds from English to Gaelic; *aoi* takes on a long *e*, as in peel; *ao* takes on *ay*, as in pay; *au* takes on the sound *ow*, as in pow. Accents such as ˋand ´ lengthen the sound of a letter.

Consonants: As with vowels, a few Gaelic consonants also take on different sounds from English; *c* always takes on a *k* sound, as in Celtic being pronounced Keltic; *ch* and *kh* are guttural, as in ache; *g* sounds are hard; *h* is not strictly a letter, but rather it's a function to aspirate or lengthen a consonant, and thus *lh* would take on the sound full.

I hope you have some fun with Gaelic!

Central Characters
& Places & Terms

Aife (ee-fa) – Mate of the former Dun Arrogh Chief Cairbre, a Princess of the Blood from Dál nAraidi, and Eoin's mother.

Aos Dána (Ays Daw-ah) – Led by All-Father, wise ones of the Celts known as Druids; comprised of four sects, each wielding Tuatha powers such as the *sight* and *void*, with others controlling the five Elements.

Ard-Rí (Ard-ree) – The High King of Ireland, the Chieftain to whom all Clan Chiefs swear allegiance.

Bards – History keepers, storytellers, and master musicians of the *Aos Dána*.

Bean-Sidhe (Banshee) – *Sidhe* women who are young and beautiful and wail or keen over the dead or those soon to be so; often referred to as harbingers of death; another name for similar fairies is *Sìthiche* (Shee-uh-khe), who can be both benevolent and malevolent; note the Irish and Scottish Gaels spell the word for fairies differently, with it being *Sidhe* and *Sith*, respectively.

Badb Catha (Bahv Kah-ha) – Goddess of Death and Knowledge, commonly called Goddess of War, and the Mórrigan, often taking the form of a battle crow on the earthly plane.

Beatha (Bay-uh) – A Fire Elemental Druid Seeress, called a Fáidh, near Dun Arrogh, one of the *Aos Dána*.

Bradaigh (Brad-ee) – Bastard son of Hakon Skadi and a Gaelic warrior who joins Breanna's Band.

Braoin (Breen) – Bastard son of Hakon Skadi and a Gaelic warrior who joins Breanna's Band.

Breanna Ban Morna (Bree-an-na Bawn Mor-na) – A Red Branch warrior from Dun Arrogh who is of Clan Dálaigh (Daw-lee) and the daughter of Morna and Nevan, with her actual father being Hakon Skadi; the Heart of Destiny chooses her to be Erin's Hero.

Brede – Dreadrider of Garm and the oldest of Hakon Skadi's warriors; he is also one of the Norvegr leaders known as Dreadriders.

Breitheamh (Breh-huv) – Judicial sect of the *Aos Dána* that acts as judges, lawmakers, interpreters, and negotiators.

Cairbre – Former Chief of Dun Arrogh, mated with Aife and Eoin's father; killed by Hakon Skadi soon after the Norvegrs arrived.

Celts (Kelts) – People who once occupied a significant part of Europe and the northern Isles, with those hailing from southwest France and northeast Spain, specifically those from Galicia, being considered the ancestors of the Gaels in Erin.

Cilla Ban Calla – Daughter of Calla, Dun Arrogh's cook.

Claimh Solais (Kly-vuh Soh-lish) – One of the Four Treasures or *Jewels* brought to Erin by Dagda and Danu and wielded initially by the Sun God, Lugh, and he gifted it to Nuada of the Silver Hand, one-time King of the Tuatha; once unsheathed, no enemy could resist the Sword of Light or escape from its path.

Ćroí Dàn (Kree Dawn) – Created by the Mother Goddess, Danu, and known as the Heart of Destiny, *Ćroí Dàn* is a heart-shaped ruby pendant that endows heroes of the land to rise above their mortal beings, become true defenders of Erin, and rally clan warriors to their cause.

Cycle of Time – The Stone of Destiny's magical bridge through time, allowing those with the *sight* to see the many possible timelines of Erin and the world. Also, the Druidic yearly cycle of Winter Solstice, Imbolc, Spring Equinox, Beltane, Summer Solstice, Lammas, Autumn Equinox, and Samhain.

Cuilcagh Mountains (Kwil-cah) – Northwest of Dun Arrogh.

Dagda (Dahg-duh) – All-Father of the Tuatha pantheon, Dagda is the God of Life, Death, and Fertility over the land and its people; he is also the first Druid and a master of all things magical, often considered wise, witty, and wily. Dagda typically resides on the Tuatha island of Murias.

Dál Riata (Dawl Ree-uh-tuh) – An area claimed by Gaelic Clans that became known as Scotti territory in ancient times of the many Celtic tribes of Albion; it once comprised the northeastern part of Ulaida in Erin and the Northwestern part of what is now Scotland, then known as Argyll.

Danu (Dah-noo) – Mother, Earth, and Moon Goddess of Erin, also known as the Triple Goddess and the Silver Huntress, when she takes her wolf form; she is co-creator with the Dagda of the entirety of the *Tuatha Dé Danann* pantheon.

Druid (Drew-id) – *Aos Dána* are Dagda's masters of law, music, foreseeing, healing, and Tuatha magic, such as the *sight*, *void*, and *Cycle of Time*. Some, known as Elementals, can also manipulate the elements of Air, Earth, Water, and Fire.

Dun (Doon) – Earth mounds and pickets that usually surround a settlement of several clans for defensive purposes; duns or ringforts typically consisted of the main hall and several small conical-shaped huts serving as living quarters.

Dun Arrogh (Doon Ah-row) – A moderate-sized ringfort where Clans Mórdha and Dálaigh splinters settled.

Dun Garm – The Dreadlord of Garm's massive ringfort near Loch Ree.

Dun Uisneach (Doon Ish-nach) – A substantial Gaelic ringfort located in southwest Mide along the High King's Road, also known as *Slíghe Mor* (Slee-geh More). Chief Faolán and Chieftess Falyn in southwest Mide oversee it.

Dun Tara – The seat of the High Kings of ancient Ireland, located in eastern Mide.

Eoin Mac Cairbre (Owen Mak Car-bree) – Dun Arrogh and Red Branch Chief of Clan Mórdha, cousin of Fergal, and a Prince of the Blood from Ulaida.

Erin (Eh-rin) - Four primary provinces or kingdoms comprised what the Gaelic called old Ireland. Connachta (Kon-akh-ta) is in the northwest; Mummu (Moo-moo), later called Munster, is in the southwest; Ulaida (Ul-ay-duh) is in the northeast; and Laigin (Lay-gin) is in the southeast. Royal Mide (Roy-uhl My-de) was carved out of the original provinces by the first-century High King Túathal Techtmar, and led the land from Tara. Unfortunately, this last kingdom did not survive as a province on its own after the heroic period of the fifth century passed; High Kings would not reemerge for four to five centuries.

Falias (Fah-lee-us) - One of four fairie islands where the Tuatha resided with Danu and Lugh; often called *Tír na nÓg* (Teer-na-nug) by the Gaels.

Fáidh (Faw-ee) – The prophetic sect of the *Aos Dána,* typically called Seers or ovates.

Fergal Mac Conall (Fur-gul Mak Koh-nawl) – Dun Arrogh Red Branch warrior of Clan Conall, a subordinate clan to Clan Mórdha (Mur-dha) and cousin of Eoin Mac Cairbre.

fianna (fee-un-nuh) – Initially, freeborn Fir Bolg warriors – and after a time, interbred Gaels – formed into the first army by Fionn MacCumhaill and served the High Kings in Tara; Fionn formed the *fianna* into *fians* (fi-anns), or bands of nine, who eventually served local Chieftains and kings when the first reign of the High Kings ended.

Fir Bolg (Feer Bulg) – The original people of Erin who were subjugated first by Fomorians and then by the Tuatha.

Fomorians (Foh-mawr-ee-uhn) – A race that settled in Erin after the fall of Atlantis; subsequently defeated by the Tuatha.

Fragarach (Frea-gar-thach) – A sword, also called Answerer, brought from the otherworld by Lugh, the Celtic God of the Sun; known to be able to pierce any armor, and later gifted to the Celtic God of the Sea, Manannán Mac Lir.

Gaelic (Gay luhk)– A people who came to Erin after the Tuatha, arriving from a part of the Celtic empire known as Galicia, also called Gaels.

Hakon Skadi (Hah-kon Skah-de) – Dreadlord of Garm, son of a Norvegr Jarl, and killer of his father; Norvegrs later became known as Norsemen or Vikings.

Erin | Éire (ay-rah) – The Emerald Isle, also known as Ireland.

Kyras (Ky-rass) – Dun Arrogh Smith of Clan Dálaigh, brother of Nevan, mate to Lissa, Toal's father, and Breanna's uncle.

Lang – Dreadrider of Garm, brother of Lunt; killed by Breanna.

Lann Dàn (Lanna Dawn) – Blades of Destiny, created by Badb Catha, the Goddess of War; they were a pair of long diamond-bladed weapons with oak hafts imbued with the power to battle invaders wielding magic.

Laoch (Lay-ukh) – The nearly forgotten name for the Warrior
Druid Sect, once referred to as Laoch Draíochta (Dree-ukh-
tah), or Warriors of Magic.

Lia Dàn (Lee-ah Dawn) – Stone of Destiny, a round crystal brought
to Erin by the Mother Goddess Danu. It enables those holding
it to see both the past and possible future timelines via the
Cycle of Time.

Lissa – Mate of Kyras, Toal's mother, of Clan Dálaigh.

Lugh (Loo) – Sun God and wielder of Tuatha's magical *Jewels*
and other items of the *Tuatha Dé Danann*, sometimes seen
as a great white stag in his animal or familiar form known
as Cernunnos.

Lunt – Dreadrider of Garm, brother of Lang; killed by Breanna.

Maorgairme (May-or-gair-mee) – An amulet ring created by the
Dark Goddess to aid the bearer with fickle magic and summon
the Tuatha Gods in great need.

Mórrigan (Mohr-ree-gan) – The name of the Goddess of War, Fate,
and Knowledge, also known as Badb Catha or the Dark Goddess, when she takes her crow form.

Morna Ban Cahir (Mor-na Bawyn Kah-hee) – Mate to Nevan,
mother of Orla, Ronat, and Breanna of Clan Dálaigh.

Nevan (Nev-an)– Warrior mate to Morna, brother of Kyras, and
a member of Clan Dálaigh; by Hakon Skadi soon after the
Norvegrs arrived.

Niall Noígíallach (Nye-al Nee-Gal-ach) – The High King in
fifth-century Ireland, also known as the *Ard-Rì*; the ancestor
of the Uí Néill dynasties, which governed significant parts of
the Emerald Isle for many centuries; his son, Lóegaire Mac
Néill, would follow him as the next High King.

Ogham (Oh-am) – Typically only used by the *Aos Dána*, it is the
written language of the Celts.

Ollamh (O-lam) – Healer sect of the *Aos Dána*.

Runa – Norvegr Völva (Vurl-va) or Seeress of Dun Garm, whom the Gaels called a *baobh*, a fury, a *cailleach*; to the Norvegrs, she is their *seið-kona*.

River Shannon – Divides the Kingdoms of Connachta, Mummu, Laigin, and Mide.

Rune Stones – Black stones used by *Asgardian* magic wielders like Runa, etched with symbols to help divine the future.

Sidhe (shee) – What the Gaelic people call fairie or Tuatha mounds and living places; also spelled as *Sìth* (shee) in the northeast part of Ireland and the western coast of Scotland, in the region once known as Dál Riata.

Sight – A common name for the vision state of the *Aos Dána* used to touch the *Cycle of Time* to see a past or possible future.

Tir na nÓg (Teer-Na-Nug) – Alternate name for the Tuatha realm of Falias.

Toal Mac Kyras (Toe-al Mak Ky-rass) – Dun Arrogh Red Branch warrior of Clan Dálaigh, cousin of Breanna.

Tuatha Dé Danann (Too-ah-ha Day Dah-nahn) – Magical beings who came to Erin after the fall of Atlantis, some known as *Sidhe or Sìth*, often mistaken as faerie or fae, which originated in the 1500s. In Destiny Cycle, the author used the spelling fairies to depict these Tuatha beings.

Tuatha Dé Danann Islands – Falais (Fall-eece); Findias (Findee-us); Gorias (Gore-us); and Murias (Mord-us)

Urghabháil an neamhní (ur-guh-vawl un nyow-nee) – Means to "seize the *void*." This state allows some of the warrior class who have reached mastery level to access the magic of the Faerie realm, similar to the *sight* typically used by other Tuatha *Aos Dána* sects to access Erin's *Cycle of Time* through *Lia Dàn*, the Stone of Destiny.

Ulicia (You-lee-see-ah) – An Earth Elemental Druid and Healer, known as an Ollamh in Gaelic, and one of the *Aos Dána* assigned to Dun Arrogh.

MYTHOLOGY & LEGENDS

The *Dàn Cycle* series, you now know, revolves around Gaelic and Celtic mythology, especially that of the Irish. Their myths, legends, and lore have been interpreted in many ways over the centuries. For authors in such a genre, we pick which thread lines to present among those posited by many historians. For those who follow Fae fantasy themes (which I also love), those myths emerged over a thousand years after the Tuatha legends envisioned here. Thus, I attempt to create a setting as close to semi-historical as possible to build this world.

As for the characters, I based some on historical figures and others on fictitious characters. The same goes for titles like Erin's Hero. I draw the names of the gods in this series from well-known myths and legends associated with the Tuatha, and some have multiple formal names that require capitalization.

Speaking of capitalizing words referencing gods, I use the following conventions: Tuatha gods, gods of Asgard, Asgardian gods, or any general god. The names with proper titles are: Tuatha God All-Father, just All-Father, Sun God (with or without a name like Lugh), Mother Goddess, Dark Goddess, Goddess of War, One God, Goddess of Language, God of History, etc.

Additionally, Gaelic words for Druids and their English counterparts are capitalized, thus Bard (*Filídh*), Healer (*Ollamh*), Seer/Seeress (*Fáidh*), and Lawgiver (*Breitheamh*). Similarly, the Druidic Elements powers are Air (*Aer*), Water (*Uisce*), Earth (*Talamh*), Fire (*Tine*), and Aether (*Eitear*).

About Gael Druids & Sigils

In the *Dàn Cycle* series, the first Druid was the Tuatha God All-Father. In the days when the Gaels first came to Erin from the coastal region of the Spanish region once known as Galicia, Dagda created five sects. He passed his magic to them once the *Tuatha Dé Danann* and the Gaels forged the Great Agreement, where they both would halt their battles in exchange for the Gaels paying homage to the Tuatha Gods. In turn, the Tuatha ceded the land of Erin to the Gaels, with some Tuatha remaining in the underhalls of Erin that Danu, All-Father, Badb, and Lugh had created. Others chose to retreat to their magical island realms. Dagda's Druids were the skilled guides who ensured the Gaels remembered the myths and legends of the Tuatha and continued their worship of the adopted gods.

Dagda's five Druidic Sects are Lawgivers, Healers, Seers, Bards, and Warriors, where he passed specific knowledge to each sect, along with how to seize the *void* and the *sight* when they needed to connect the realm of Erin with the Tuatha realms. Using the high council of each Druidic sect, All-Father also passed on the secrets of manipulating the five Elements: Air, Water, Earth, Fire, and Aether (the energy of life). You can find details on each of these sects below.

Fáidh: Seers used their *sight* to touch the *Cycle of Time*, seeking to understand possible future timelines and listen to the voices of their Tuatha gods. Seers and Seeresses often would have an affinity for the Water and Aether Elements and wore green and red robes.

Filídh: As history keepers, storytellers, and master musicians, a Bard used the *void* to retrieve the mass of words that comprised the entirety of the Gaelic people's experience; none could recall that much knowledge without it. They wore yellow and green robes and tended to be Air Elementals, which helped them cast their voice.

Ollamh: Healers could seize the *void* to draw on the deep understanding of healing and pull power from the Tuatha realm to mend the sick and wounded. They wore green and red robes, typically commanding Aether and Earth or Water Elements to heal.

Laoch: Warriors focused on ensuring their Gaels had the expertise to protect their people. The most proficient of these warriors bore the title *Laoch Draíochta*, Warrior of Magic. They could seize the *void* in battle and typically wield one of two Elements, such as Earth and Water or Air and Fire. Their strategy and blade-work skills made them Battle Masters, with the most senior among them commanding all the physical Elements.

Sigils of Power: Using the Druidic (rune-based) language of Ogham, Druids create sigils as amplifiers of intent and typically incorporate one or more of the five Elements. They would etch them in wood, metal, or stone. Applying woad on one's skin (called woading) could also have been used by a Druid to leverage such sigils. The sigil below represents the five Elements in Runic Ogham.

About James

I grew up on a small lake in the upper Midwest of the USA, exploring my natural surroundings, which featured miles of trails and waterways branching out from my family's home on the lake. I could travel across my lake, slip into a tributary creek or river, and go up or down it for hours with my small boat and its little outboard motor. My trusted dog sometimes joined me, standing at the prow like a warrior sentinel. At other times, he would rather sleep in the comfort of his home.

He was often fickle like that, sometimes deciding he needed a "Canadian Walkabout" in the neighborhoods around the lake and getting into trouble. Our family has a long line of Quebecers, and women in our line used a euphemism to describe men who roamed the land in search of *adventure*. Anyway, I remember the little rascal fondly.

Like many during my youth, I experimented with some forbidden things, which quickly grew old. Esoteric matters caught my attention for a time, and I found a young lady with similar thoughts on reincarnation and karma. As I pursued college and tried my hand at fine arts, I discovered my left hand was not so good at the *fine* part. I got married and entered the technology sector to make a living. Then, I switched my major from Fine Arts to English with a focus on Creative Writing.

After a failed first attempt at writing a set of great fantasy novels, work, raising a family, and life took over my time. Writing faded as a priority. Yet it resurfaced years later with this Gaelic adventure set in Celtic Ireland, which started as a dream - literally. We traveled across the pond to see that land, and its people captured my heart and imagination.

Being a quarter Scottish of Clan Ferguson, the Gaels became my people; their history, legends, and mythologies became mine. The Celts of Europe, especially Galicia, where the Gaels originated, became mine. The Druids and their Gods became mine, as did the injustices inflicted on my people, which became a vision.

What if the Gaels of Ireland could change the history of the world by changing the Isle of Erin's timeline? And Britain's, starting with Rome's first-century invasion?

It would take a Hero and the Tuatha Gods who backed her to make that happen.

Welcome to *Dàn Cycle,* or in English, Destiny Cycle.

I hope you enjoyed reading this adventure as much as I did while writing it.

It is where Gaels Rule!
www.destinycycle.com

Interested in joining my Fan Club?

Go to - www.destinycycle.com/about-james
Interested in a sneak peek of Stone of Destiny?
Turn the page!

Lia Dàn - Stone of Destiny: Preview

Destroyer Persued

Toal

Toal Mac Kyras listened intently to the Norvegr warriors on the wall above him. From their panicked tones, they seemed convinced that the High King in Tara had sent a dun full of warriors to attack their walls. The fire in the main hall's roof appeared to fuel the confusion. That made Toal smile. He looked up through the fog, trying to see anything on the rampart; the torchlights were barely visible. Not even enough to show them the ground at their feet.

He asked with more than a hint of concern, "Fergal, between the dark and the fog, how are we going to find Eoin and Bre once they escape?"

Eoin's cousin looked around as if surprised and cursed, "*Tá olann ina hintinn agam!*"

"We all have wool for brains sometimes," Toal chided.

"And those who do, more often than not, end up dead when facing the likes of the Dreadlord," Fergal growled. He paused and added, "If I were Eoin or Breanna and heard those on the wall yelling about the fire, I'd not come here, and I'd not head for the gates. Not closed and barred as they are."

"Too many warriors about?"

"Correct," Fergal answered. "That leaves us with the south and east sides. Let's go back and see what we find. And stick close. I don't want to lose track of you in this murky soup."

"Aye," Toal agreed, shuddering. His imagination ran wild with fairies and demons lurking in the mist as Fergal turned and headed into the darkness. He kept close to the older warrior. If the sun had been out to cast a shadow, he would not have seen his own.

Careful not to make any noise, the pair moved slowly southward along the rampart's base. As the pair passed the southwest corner of the fort, Toal paused, cocking his head to listen. It was quiet, save for the now muffled yelling from the Dreadlord's warriors about a fire in the main hall. Fergal tugged on Toal's arm, leading him toward the southwest corner of the massive fort.

Torches also burned atop this wall all along the rampart, but they still could see little else. When Toal could hear nothing above him, vise-like indecision gripped him. He whispered, "Should we retreat and slip back into the trees or wait it out? If the sun rises and the fog lifts, they could see us. What good will it do if they capture us as well?"

Fergal countered, "But if Breanna manages to free Eoin, we'd leave them when they needed us most."

"Okay then. Let's keep going east along this south side. My arrows came from the west, so more warriors should search there first. That means Bre and Eoin should likely come over somewhere on the eastern rampart."

Fergal grinned, nodding in approval. He took Toal by the arm again and led him to the southeast corner. This time, they went even slower as they headed north along the base of the rampart, hoping to discover something they had missed on their last pass.

When Toal heard voices ahead, he was sure from the accents that they had to belong to Breanna and Eoin. Then, the sound of timbers breaking made him all the more convinced. Fergal seemed to sense the same thing and picked up the pace.

Suddenly, Eoin came stumbling down the steeply pitched dirt and stone wall of Dun Garm, nearly skewering his cousin. The pair went down amid curses and grunts.

Breanna was more graceful as she came to a skittering stop at their feet, her grim expression illuminated by the faint glow of *Lann Dàn* and *Maorgairme*. A white-haired lad followed her. She hissed at Fergal in a quiet but tight voice, "I put you in charge of the Red Branch to keep them safe, not to drag them into the Dreadlord's stronghold to get hacked apart!"

"I didn't drag anyone to Dun Garm except for Toal, who came of his own volition."

Breanna turned to him as if she had just noticed his presence, saying, "And what do you think you're doing here?"

"Trying to help free our Chief," Toal spat as his back stiffened; he was glad his voice didn't crack as it was wont to do of late. "That fire Hakon's warriors are preoccupied with right now just happens to be my doing."

Eoin helped Fergal stand. "Now is not the time to argue about who should and shouldn't have done what. Fergal and Toal meet Braoin—he's with us. Let's get away from this place. Fergal, do you have your chariot?"

"Aye," Fergal said tartly, glaring at Breanna. His gaze returned to Eoin, and he added less tightly, "We left it in the trees northeast of here. The horses should be rested by now and could carry us all."

"Good, then let's get moving," Eoin commanded and started hobbling north along the base of the rampart.

"Wait," Breanna demanded in a stiff, low voice. "The Dreadlord will surely catch us if we return to Dun Arrogh, and with five in it, that chariot won't carry us swiftly enough to go anywhere else. And with how you two are still limping, it'd take us a span or more to get to that creaking old bucket. Once Hakon's hounds have our scent, we'll be done for if we don't have at least a half day's lead on them."

"Then what do you propose?" Fergal suspiciously demanded.

"You and Toal take the chariot," Breanna offered. "It will carry you two faster than the five of us. My sister lives deep enough into Mide that her mate's clan will protect you. I doubt the Dreadlord would risk an attack with the *Ard-Rí* so close at hand in Dun Tara."

"It's a two-day ride at best to Orla's," Eoin commented. "Fergal and Toal would have to move swiftly."

"Or the Dreadlord would catch us," Fergal added, his tone almost accusatory. "I say let Toal take the chariot. He handled it most of the way here anyway and would make better time without me."

"Then, which way would you four go?" Toal asked.

"We certainly need to throw the Dreadlord off our trail," Eoin interjected as he looked over his shoulder at Dun Garm's rampart. "East and south, I'd say, toward Dun Uisneach. Then, once we've outwitted their pursuit, we'll keep going that way. If I remember correctly, my Champion has a goddess to visit."

"I don't like sending Toal off alone," Breanna countered. "You dragged him here, Fergal. You should see that he gets back safely. He's just a boy, after all."

At first, Toal thought his cousin was overly obvious about wanting to be rid of Fergal, but then her words sank in. She had tried to goad Fergal into taking care of him. What did he have to do to prove himself? Had he not helped her find *Lann Dàn* and face Tethra's demons? Weren't his arrows the ones that had helped divert the Dreadlord's warriors so she could free Eoin? His blood boiled at being called a boy. Toal snapped, "I'm old enough to look after myself. Fergal's right—he'd slow me down. I'll lead Hakon's dogs away from your trail, get to Orla's, and find someone to get word to Dun Arrogh that you are all safe."

"Safe, but on the run," Eoin corrected. "Now, we've wasted too much time. Run, Toal. Get to the chariot and yourself to safety."

Breanna nodded stiffly, saying, "Aye, go safely and quickly then, my cousin."

Toal quickly hugged Breanna and bolted into the dark.

Hurriedly groping his way through the dark, misty night, he only knew the grassy plain had ended because his face met up with the gnarled bark of an old black oak. At least he was no longer out in the open where the Dreadlord's men could easily see him once the sun came up. Cold, tired, and dazed from smacking into the tree, he sank to his knees and touched his scraped forehead. His fingers came away a little sticky with blood.

He shrugged his pack off to find a cloth to tie around his head. Exhausted from not getting much sleep the last few days, he could not resist stealing a moment and closed his eyes, slumping against the oak tree. He only needed those few seconds to recover from his dizziness. But before his head cleared, he succumbed, and sleep swept him away.

The dreams that came to Toal were dark and filled with scenes of Dreadriders riding down his friends, their blades hacking off arms and heads. They were gruesome images, images from which he could not wake. Then Tethra's demons surrounded him, the black, misshapen forms pulling him apart limb from limb.

Hakon

A span after sunrise, Hakon watched Alrik and Brede lead the last of his warriors through the gates of Dun Garm. He had sent his wolfhounds, Hati and Skoll, along with the rest of their pack, to follow his most senior Dreadriders. Few remained to man the walls, with most out hunting the Destroyer and her friends. Lang would also be after them if it were not for Runa's potion. She had somehow managed to get the grieving Dreadrider to drink her concoction, and he now slept in his hut.

Lunt's body would be given to their gods in the evening once his servants finished preparing the pyre. But for Hakon, the day held a sour taste. He had lost one of his best warriors, a warrior he had grown more fond of than any who had followed him to this land. Yet he had also found a daughter who was every bit as skilled as Lunt, maybe more so.

Now that he had seen her in battle, Hakon had convinced himself that his best course was to lure his Destroyer into joining him as an ally. But dealing with a woman as an equal was not something he had ever needed to do. Convincing his offspring that he was not the monster she believed would be the challenge of his life. And if he could not win her over, she would have to die.

Hakon had not told Runa about his plan to subvert his daughter to his cause, for she had been busy tending to Lang.

And he understood his völva had been none too pleased with being thumped on the head. As he approached her hut, he tried to frame his argument in his mind.

Runa responded to his knock on her door, though the scowl on her face made it plain she was not happy to see him. "My Jarl, what can I do for you?"

"A little talk, if you will," Hakon said as he stepped into her hut.

Runa did not look up as she turned toward her table and took a seat. "About your daughter. I'm surprised you took so long. That I was wrong about your bastard's sex is obvious, something I regret nearly as much as you. Maybe the other two are just Tuatha decoys to trick my magic."

"Possibly." Hakon shrugged. "We lost Braoin last night, as he appears to have escaped in the night's mayhem."

Runa rubbed her head. "I'll need to cast my Runes again to see if those two remain important in our dance with the Tuatha gods. Yet with fairie magic in her hands, your daughter is undoubtedly the Destroyer. What my black beauties previously foretold us has not been changed by our discovery that he is, in reality, she."

"Aye, and Lunt's death is proof of her skill as a warrior," Hakon said, deciding to take an indirect approach. "And I nearly met the same fate. We were both surprised to see each other, which probably saved my life. Runa, what drives her to seek my death?"

"Even she does not know," the witch replied, eyeing him critically as she poured them tea. "It is the nature of her *geas* to seek your end. Few of us truly know what drives us, and in your daughter's case, she was manipulated over the years by forces beyond the *Cycle's* normal turnings."

"So diverting her from this *geas* would be a challenge?"

"Diverting her?" Runa questioned, pausing before taking a sip of tea, her eyes never leaving his, her expression doubtful.

"After seeing her in battle, I would like to try to win her support," Hakon finally confirmed as he looked into his cup, unwilling to hold her gaze. "A warrior with such skills could be a great asset."

"And a great danger."

Hakon ignored those words as he sipped absently at his tea. Then he asked abruptly, "Can this *geas* cast upon her be broken? Is your magic strong enough to destroy its hold on her?"

Runa frowned. "It may be possible, but I'd need her to be here to try and break the spell. And in case you have forgotten, your daughter is being hunted by more than your warriors. You enlisted the Fomorian god, Tethra, to kill her, and the Tuatha gods provided magical weapons and came to her aid in the demon battle. So between those two factors, getting her back to Dun Garm alive may be more challenging than breaking her *geas*."

"I'll leave that part to you if you leave the rest to me," he said. Runa frowned again but managed a slight nod. Hakon could see the doubt in her eyes and sensed she had more words of caution. Knowing he would have to prod her, he demanded, "Is there something else?"

"You made a pact with Tethra," Runa said quietly. "A pact to kill the Destroyer."

"That I did, but since he didn't live up to his end of the bargain, there's no reason I should hold up my end," he responded as he rose. "I've lost one of my best Dreadriders because of his failure."

"I doubt the Fomorian god will see it that way, especially given the price he has paid thus far for the privilege of helping you. He wants to see your bastard dead now more than before. It's no longer simply because the Tuatha gods are helping her. She's killed scores of his demons, and stopping him from carrying out your original pact will be harder than you think."

"Leave Tethra to me."

"You play with powers far greater than you realize," Runa advised.

Toal

Screaming, Toal bolted awake. He wasn't sure how long he had slept; all he knew was that the sun had risen, and the fog from the night before was gone. Sighing, he got his feet beneath him and retied the cloth around his forehead. It took a moment for the events of the night before to churn through his mind.

Toal rubbed his eyes, then looked through the trees to find the sun, hoping it would tell him how long past sunrise it was. With the clouds and fog gone, sunlight filtered brightly through the branches.

"Danu, save me," he whispered when he realized the sun was clearly above the horizon. Panicked, he picked up his bow and turned north, dodging his way through the tree line as he ran. His body ached, especially his legs, but there was no time to be concerned about minor pains. It was likely that Hakon's warriors were out searching for them already, and Toal had wasted at least a span of the slim lead he was supposed to have.

He found the chariot as he and Fergal had left it, with the hill ponies still tethered to his makeshift picket. Toal quickly hitched them to the cart, and moments later, he was heading north. The narrow path through the forest was bumpy and dangerous, but he dared not take the more accessible plains. Not yet, anyway, not until he was well out of sight of Dun Garm.

It was not long after he had the chariot rolling that he heard hounds baying in the distance. Knowing they must be from the Dreadlord's stronghold, Toal picked up his pace, urging the horses to go faster.

The chariot bucked and rocked like a boat in a storm, and Toal could do little more than hang on. He heard the hounds again and was sure they were closer this time. If they had picked up his scent, he needed speed and not the cover of the woods. Seeing an opening to his left, Toal pulled the reins over, and the chariot burst through the light brush and onto the open plains.

With another snap of his reins, the horses were soon in a full gallop. He found the going easy enough to hold on with only one hand as a cold wind pulled tears from his eyes. The ground flashed by as he chanced a glance back toward Dun Garm. While he could hardly see the massive fort, the dozen or so warriors charging along the forest's edge were unmistakable. The wind drew their white hair back as they urged their mounts after him. A half dozen giant wolfhounds bounded with the Norvegr riders, each easily keeping pace with their masters.

Toal muttered a curse he had heard his father use when he hit his hand with a hammer, then flicked the reins at Fergal's hill ponies again. They surged forward, but gaining ground on his pursuers was not enough, especially with their faster warhorses. He needed something to divert them and spied his bow and the quiver of arrows tied to the railing. When he lunged for his weapon, the chariot lurched over a rock. Toal nearly flew out the back. Only the reins kept him from hitting the ground.

Grabbing at the rail, he clawed slowly toward the front with his bow. Another look at Hakon's warriors told him they were gaining, and he urged his horses to find more speed. They flew on, dragging the cart wildly behind them. Toal managed to get his bow restrung and nocked an arrow. Aiming was another matter. The rocking motion made it seem impossible to hit the riders behind him.

The first arrow flew wide off its mark, and the second nearly took down one of the hounds as the arrow landed right in front of it. The dog tripped and tumbled to the ground, flipping over several times, but he rose and took off after those who had passed him by. He knew killing their dogs would not save him, so he adjusted his aim higher at the riders behind him. This time, he put his arrow into the shoulder of one of his pursuers. The man spun off his mount and crashed to the ground. It brought the others to a halt for a moment. Then the Dreadrider leading them had all hurtling forward again, digging their heels into their horses' flanks.

The white-haired warriors pulled their small, round shields off their saddles as Toal let another arrow fly. His aim was good, but the warrior he had chosen got his leather buckler up in time. Toal tried several more shots, each with the same result. With his quiver half-empty, he groaned at the thought of aiming at the horses but knew there was no other way to slow them down. He turned and fired again. His arrow buried itself in the lead mount's chest, and the rider was pitched over its head as it went down.

The Dreadrider behind the downed warrior quickly changed tactics and veered into the woods, where hitting them would be more challenging. His warriors followed suit, soon weaving their way through the trees. Toal muttered another curse and drove his horses on. Hoping to draw them out, he pulled the reins to the right and headed east, farther out onto the plain. The grass-covered ground continued to flash by as Toal glanced around to see if there were other options. With his pursuers hidden by the woods, he had no choice but to keep going in the same direction, as he had regained some ground on Hakon's riders.

As the chariot drew away from the tree line, the white-haired warriors swerved to the outer limits of the forest. Toal didn't bother wasting his arrows, for his short bow now did not have enough range. Movement to his right caught his eye as he turned to concentrate on getting the most out of his slighter horses. A second band of the Dreadlord's men was closing on him from the far side of the plain, eating up the ground between them. Their warhorses were fresher than his homegrown hill ponies, who were starting to flag.

Deciding to unseat as many warriors as possible, Toal readied his bow again. Within moments, he began notching and releasing again, unseating two more of the Dreadlord's men before they got their bucklers unstrapped. Onward they came, as did the other band of riders behind him. The ones closer to the trees had pulled away from the woodlands, and now both groups were nearly on top of him.

Then, with his quiver down to two arrows, Toal drew back on the reins and pulled his chariot to a stop. Hakon's warriors swarmed around him with their blades drawn and murder in their eyes, and Toal recognized the two Dreadriders from the time when they had come to Dun Arrogh, burned down Breanna's hut, and took Eoin hostage. Both barked orders to their respective charges to stand down.

The one who seemed to be the younger took control of Toal's horses. The other dismounted and stepped onto the chariot, towering over a stiff-lipped Toal. It took all the will he could muster not to flinch; then his resolve grew firmer. If he could face Tethra's demons and survive, staring down a Dreadrider was certainly within him.

Still, he couldn't suppress a groan as the gnarly warrior snatched up his bow and snapped it over his knee.

The Dreadrider growled darkly, "If the Dreadlord didn't want you alive, I'd skewer you right here, boy or no. Those were good men you took down! Kvasir, ride back and tell Runa she's needed. We've wounded men to tend to. And Jotun, you ride with this whelp back to Dun Garm. And be careful that he has no more tricks up his sleeves for us. Like using this little sword."

As the Dreadrider took his sword and stepped down to mount his horse, Toal stood dejectedly. Then, the warrior Jotun joined him, and he was sure he had failed Breanna's band in drawing them off far enough. Hopefully, the dogs did not have his cousin's scent. As to his fate, they'd either kill him or take him hostage. Neither option was good, and if it were the latter, he wondered whether or not he could keep Breanna's secrets and mislead the Dreadlord.

***Lia Dàn* – Stone of Destiny is available now!**
Get your copy today!

Available at Amazon, Apple, Barnes & Noble,
Google, IngramSpark, & Others

Formats: eBook, Paperback, and Audiobook

And do not miss **"Bards of Destiny"** on Spotify, Apple,
YouTube Music, and other streamers for paired music!

Sign up for my Fan Club at
www.destinycycle.com/about-james
to get updates!

www.ingramcontent.com/pod-product-compliance
Lightning Source LLC
Chambersburg PA
CBHW021134310726
48971CB00002B/327